FLOW DOWN LIKE SILVER

Hypatia of Alexandria

a Novel

Books by Ki Longfellow

China Blues*
Chasing Women*
Stinkfoot, a Comic Opera (with Vivian Stanshall)
The Secret Magdalene

*as Pamela Longfellow

FLOW DOWN LIKE SILVER
Hypatia of Alexandria

a Novel

Ki Longfellow

Eio Books

This is a work of fiction. Though based on the known facts of the life of Hypatia of Alexandria, the events and characters inscribed herein spring from the author's imagination.

Published in the United States by

Eio Books
1550 Tiburon Boulevard
Suite B-9
Belvedere, California, 94920 U.S.A.

www.eiobooks.com

Library of Congress Cataloging-in-Publication Data

Longfellow, Ki.
Flow Down Like Silver : Hypatia of Alexandria, a novel / Ki Longfellow.
p. cm.
Includes bibliographical references.
ISBN 978-0-9759255-9-1
1. Hypatia, d. 415--Fiction. 2. Women mathematicians--Egypt--Fiction. 3. Women philosophers--Egypt--Fiction. 4. Alexandria (Egypt)--Fiction. I. Title. II. Title: Hypatia of Alexandria.
PS3562.O499F56 2009
813'.54--dc22 2009032330

Cover designed by Sydney Longfellow
Book designed by Shane Roberts
Cover image: Roman Egypt panel painting
Map by Ki Longfellow

10 9 8 7 6 5 4 3 2 1

First Paperback Edition

TO HYPATIA

She alone survives, immutable, eternal;
Death can scatter the trembling universes
But Beauty still dazzles with her fire,
And all is reborn in her,
And the worlds are still prostrate beneath her white feet!
—Leconte de Lisle

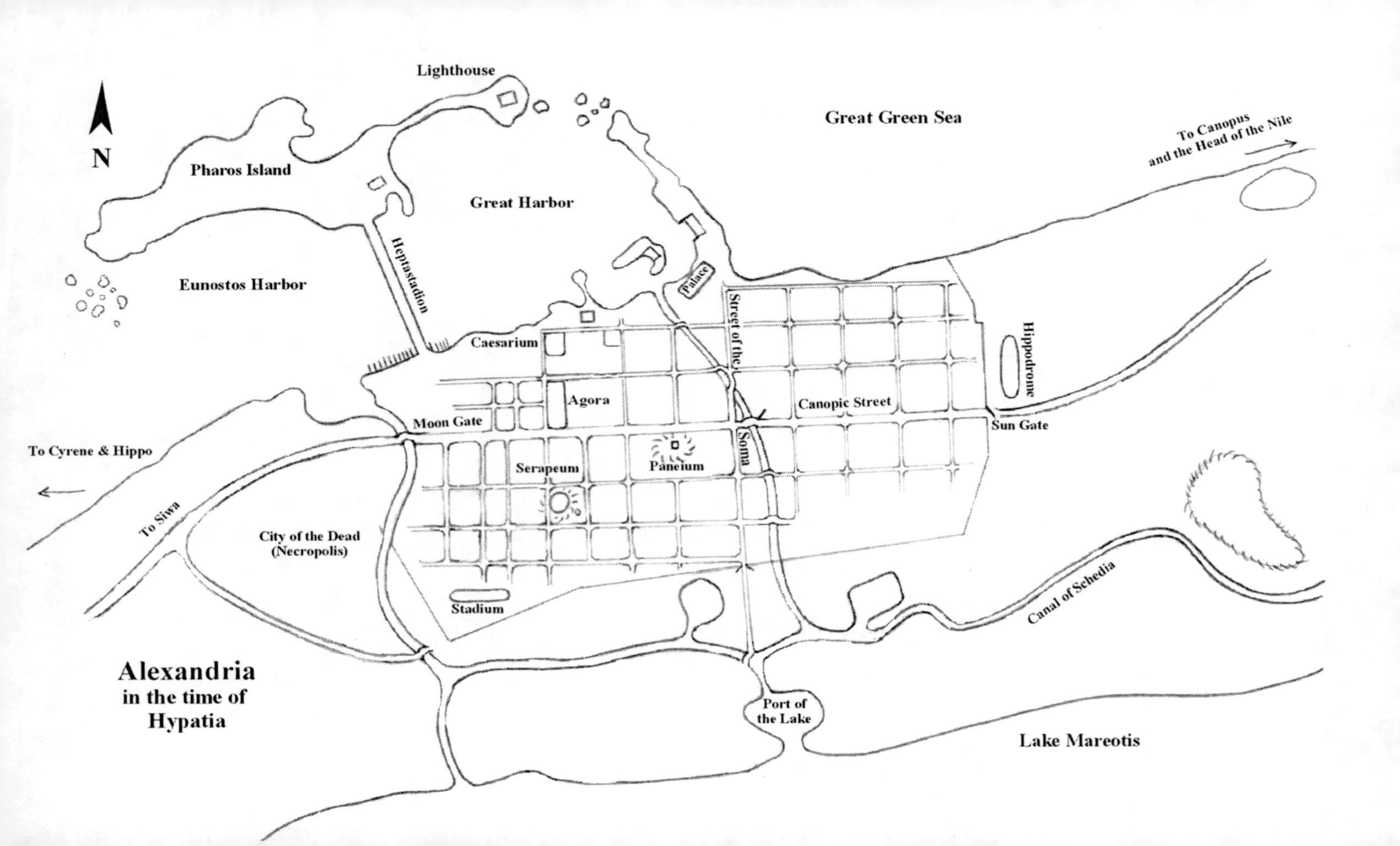
Alexandria
in the time of
Hypatia
N
Lighthouse
Pharos Island
Great Harbor
Great Green Sea
To Canopus
and the Head of the Nile
Eunostos Harbor
Heptastadion
Palace
Caesarium
Street of the
Soma
Hippodrome
Agora
Canopic Street
Moon Gate
Sun Gate
To Cyrene & Hippo
Serapeum
Paneium
To Siwa
City of the Dead
(Necropolis)
Stadium
Canal of Schedia
Port of
the Lake
Lake Mareotis

BOOK ONE

"A time will come when it will seem that the Egyptians in the piety of their hearts have honored their gods in vain. The gods, on leaving the earth, will return to heaven; they will abandon Egypt. That holy earth, land of sanctuaries and temples, will be completely covered with coffins and corpses. O Egypt, Egypt! Nothing will remain of your religion but fables, and later, your children will not even believe them!"—Hermes Trismegistus

PAPER SHIPS

The City of Alexandria, Egypt
Summer, 391

Hypatia

The books will burn!

I, Hypatia of Alexandria, to whom the Library is as life's blood, urge my horses faster. Avenger of Wrongs, Sekhmet, warrior goddess, defend us!

Jaws sore with shouting, hearts as dark as smoke, hands bright with blood, Christians rage through my city—pushed by their bishop beyond tolerance, beyond reason, beyond even madness. From the mouth of the serpent of chaos, tongues of flame lick through the Temple of Serapis seeking the last books of the once and still Great Library of Alexandria.

This day I sailed the *Irisi* far out onto the dragon green back of the sea. This day I drove past the Roman camp on the road to Canopus. If on this day I had chosen instead to study in the Serapeum, I should be there now rather than tearing along the Canopic Way, my horses scattering guilty and innocent alike. At the top of the hill, I leap from my chariot, leaving the lathered grays that have pulled it to stay or to go, it matters not. Fighting my way up one hundred and eight steps to the vast platform on which stands the Serapeum—a thing as wondrous as Pharos, beacon to the Savior Gods—my hair is tangled with salted wind, my tunic stained with ink. This too matters not. What matters are the books.

Every man who reads, who studies, who cares for learning, weeps as they gather armfuls of books, as many as each can carry. There are a hundred men, two hundred. Women are here, priestesses with heaps of scrolls tucked in their mantles. And there amid pandemonium is Father, the greatest mathematician in all of Egypt, whose life of sweet reason knows only this soaring dome of painted clouds, these vast golden halls and silvered porticoes. All sweetness fled, Theon of Alexandria carries the work of the school of Pythagoras piled high in a household basket, clutching as well a few volumes of the *Arithmatica* of Diophantus. And there stands Lais on a floor of pale green alabaster, my sister, more precious than the beating of my own heart. She, too, has a basket. Hers is filled with poems for Lais is a poet. And there is my younger sister, Jone, small and fierce as she pushes her way through a melee of book savers and book burners. I quickly kiss Lais, just as quickly say, "Jone is too young, there is too much danger here."

Lais smiles to calm me. "As a lover of books, is she not old enough to save them?"

"But not old enough to die for them."

"She will not leave if we do not leave."

"Then you must leave. I would not have my sisters hurt."

"And you, younger than me?"

I laugh though I do not feel like laughing. "And what could hurt me?"

Father pulls at my arm, his eyes reddened with smoke and with tears. "Daughter! I cannot carry them all. Find the rest."

He means the rest of Diophantus, the mathematician.

I turn and there is Didymus the Blind led by a student, both Christians and both laden with the work of the Christian philosopher Origen, a task far greater than that of Father's for Origen was a prolific man. And there is the poet Palladas. All seventy of his bitter years pull at his mouth, his eyes, even his ears. Palladas has brought not only baskets but a donkey to bear them. At sight of me, he sinks to his creaking knees. "Dearest! I don't understand. Why do they do this?"

I touch his uplifted brow. "Who understands the needs of a tyrant but a tyrant?"

"But he leaves us nothing!" By "he," Palladas means Emperor Theodosius, Christian and tyrant. "He forbids us our temples. Our celebrations are now his. Isis is named Mary, Holy Virgin. His church steals the ancient deities of Egypt, of Persia, of Greece, of Sumer! It silences the search for meaning, claiming all questions are answered. They're all mad!"

The astronomer Pappas, rushing by with an armful of celestial charts, stops. "By the moon, get up you old fool! Bishop Theophilus is said to be outside. Would you have the wretched man see you on your knees? Greetings, Hypatia. Some day, eh?"

Pappas is off before I can answer. This would be my answer. From Rome to Constantinople to Alexandria, men of the new faith ask: what use literature, mathematics, science, philosophy, music...when He is coming again? I am Hypatia and I teach philosophy, mathematics, science, music. I teach as well poetry and alchemy. Of what use am I?

In the largest hall near to the statue of Serapis, stands the philosopher Olympius. Under the god's blue arms stretching themselves from wall to wall, the floating blue body glittering with silver and sapphire, topaz, hematite and emerald and on the huge blue head a basket of golden grain, Olympius wraps himself in his philosopher's mantle. Gripping the silver shod feet of the gentle Serapis, blue feet that do not touch the green floor, Olympius shouts out for the sacrifice of self in defense of the sacred knowledge of Alexandria.

Olympius is tall and beautiful and so passionate in his love of the mysteries, others think him *pleres tou theou*: filled with the bliss of God. Those who hear him, obey. Philosophers barricade the temple halls, grammarians hasten to gather and pile up whatever might block the temple doors. At the arched main entrance to the domed main hall stands father's fat friend Ammonius, a priest of Thoth. Ammonius holds a pike in one plump hand, a curved knife in the other. At a second arched entrance stands another of father's friends, Helladius, a priest of Ammon, the god who begat the great Alexander himself. Built as the stump of a tree, Helladius carries a Roman sword, its blade already dripping with blood.

As I pass, he salutes me.

Not all heeding the call of Olympius are scholars and not all are "pagans," a word Christians call us intending insult. Some who save books are themselves Christians of the intellectual order of Novatians, crying out against what is done in the name of their savior Jesus Christ. Some, aligned with no god, no sect, no belief, possessing nothing more than the love of Alexandria, stand beside Christian and scholar to defend learning with their lives.

At the barricades, those like my family and myself, come to save books, are allowed in and out. Those who have come to destroy books, to topple statues, or to steal whatever of worth they can find, are also allowed in. Once in, they are either quickly killed or pushed into one or another of the large round "chambers of meditation." I have no idea what will happen to these, but it cannot be good.

Charged by Father with finding the rest of the works of the mathematician Diophantus, I hesitate. Books are like ships carrying worlds within their holds. These are my paper ships. And all need saving. Like any "pagan," I know the smell of burning books. But what of the philosopher Plotinus and his *Enneads*? The mathematics of Diophantus can be reconstructed—already much of his work is stored beneath my skull—but the sublimity of Plotinus? Who could think such thoughts again?

Dodging past gilded pillars, I race down wide stone steps that take me deep under the clamorous temple. There, one passageway leads to others, a confusion of ornamented tunnel after tunnel cut through the limestone on which the temple mound stands—though neither I nor the fire are fooled. It too has found its way here, and more quickly, for here are the books, the parchment and papyrus, the precious flammable paper.

Turning into a sloping corridor, I am brought to a sudden stop by three monks, each hidden deep in the black of their robes. One stands in my way. His skin is the color of bone, the hair of his beard as thin as one aged, yet he is not old. Nor is he young. There is something eternal about him, as anger and fear and hatred are eternal. By a flaw of birth his mouth twists, pulled down hard at one corner so that he seems to leer, though I know he does not leer.

I know him not, but I find he knows me. Hissing my name as he would a demon's, he reaches out as I pull back. "Peter!" calls one of his own, "come away!" There is worry here, for they are only three and the Serapeum is full of those to whom *these* three are the demons.

Peter does not come away. He has gripped my wrist. "Satan, not God, made the female Hypatia."

"Satan is no more than the fear in your heart."

Peter twists now, hard enough to cause pain. "As I live, you will know that Satan lives and is your maker."

"As I live, your life is nothing but envy and ignorance."

Though his friends are made anxious, glancing about, sure that at any moment if not demons, then pagans, will appear to avenge the daughter of Satan, Peter pulls me closer. "All you teach is sin. In Hell, you will know fear itself, pure as fire."

Groping for release from this twisted man, my hand finds a pot in a niche. No more than unglazed clay, it is all I have and I smash it against the wall so that I hold one shard, shaped as a knife, sharp as a knife.

Men approach—Christians or pagans? Whichever, Peter and his monks flee down another passage, and I run on, passing scribes grappling with butchers, unlettered priests knifing scholars, toothless women digging ancient Egyptian cartouches from walls with their bare blooded hands even as those I know as Father's own students beat them to death with clubs. And here is Claudian, another poet, bent double from the books he has piled in a makeshift sheet over his back. Turning into a passageway filled with fallen statuary and the Christians who hammer them into rubble, I turn again along another where two who have rescued a bronze vase use it to smash out the brains of the man who would steal it.

Here is the place I seek. By the quill of Seshat! To reach it I need risk a mass of burning books. In the hall of playwrights: among them Aeschylus, Sophocles, Euripides, the flames burn brightest and hottest, and from here they will continue, only growing stronger and hotter, until all is lost. And there stands an Egyptian youth, filling a large leather satchel with scrolls. He is unknown to me, but the books he saves I know and love well: the *Oracle of the Potter,* the *Dream of Nectaneb,* Virgil's *Aeneid,* the *Argonauts* of Apollonius of Rhodes.

The young lover of romance is too near the flames. Like imps, cinders glow in the black curls of his hair. He pays them no mind, but makes his selections, carefully placing each in his satchel. Beyond him are the nine books of Plotinus. Therefore, it is beyond him I need to reach. If I wait much longer, the fire will block my way in. If the youth goes no faster, they will block his way out. As it is, the smoke makes it hard to breathe. It pains my throat. Soon, it will sear my lungs.

But I must reach Plotinus, and so I run, passing the Egyptian who seems hardly to notice. I pass also a section of assorted fragments rescued from other fires in other times.

And there, in a large niche of dry white limestone, is the work of my philosopher. But how to carry it? Like Father and his carrying away of Diophantus, no basket could contain all. I have no basket. Judging from the look of the youth, older and larger and stronger, I won't be snatching away his satchel. As a Greek, called "sage" by the city of her birth, as well, it seems, Daughter of Satan, I might demand it, but at such a moment even an Egyptian could dispatch me to the Underworld.

Others came prepared: Father and Lais with baskets, the priests and priestesses use mantles, Claudian found a sheet, Palladas brought an entire donkey. The youth wears only a breech cloth, but owns a satchel. All I have is my linen tunic, and under that, nothing at all. The youth is a handsome fellow, tall and straight and finely made, a few small scars on his hands, a larger longer scar on his upper arm. And so? I tear my dress from my body, quickly rip it in half, and of the halves make a sling. I tumble Plotinus into the sling, heft it over my shoulder, then turn to run back through the flames.

For the love of Thoth—what now? The youth is on fire; his hair a small torch, his clothing smokes. Yet all it does is make him move faster.

Is the life's work of Plotinus more important than the short brutal life of a reviled Egyptian who saves romances? Of course it is. Plotinus is vastly more important. Even so—Lais would not forgive me my choice. Already I face Father with Plotinus rather than Diophantus.

Dumping the precious books from my sling, I run back to beat at the youth, and when his flames are extinguished, I push him away from the passage and out into a tunnel still dark and still cool. He never lets go of his satchel. Foolish man-boy. And yet, who is the more foolish? Lying where I have thrown them are the *Enneads,* just beginning to curl in the heat. To reach them now, I must run again through the flames when both the flames and I grow hotter. I run again, scooping Plotinus into my sling, its edges singed from beating at the youth, and I run back.

Is it Serapis who saves me? Or Isis? Or Plotinus himself who wishes to live, even if only as Word? Whoever or whatever, I come out as I went in, the tracks of my tears running like the branching Nile through the soot on my face, my hair standing up here, lying down there, my fingers inked from long labor over mathematical formulas, but no more and no worse than this—save I wear only ash.

The youth has not moved. He remains where I left him, his

fair face, clean of beard, is untouched, but the hair on the right side of his head is crisped to the scalp. I do not gasp. Not at the sight of what must pain him beyond my knowledge of pain, and not at his sight of my naked body. I do no more than gaze at him as he gazes at me.

"My name is Minkah," he says, his Egyptian that of the streets. "I owe you my life."

"And I am sure I will find a good use for it, but now we must leave here. We must save our books."

Helladius, priest of Ammon, guides me out through a side entrance under one of the temple's many arches, this one not yet besieged by those who heed the priests of their gentle Christ.

My gray horses have gone.

Wearing nothing but my heated skin, which Helladius feigns not to notice, I run down from the hill on which stands the temple, racing for home through the unhappy streets of my unhappy city hauling, like Claudian the poet, Plotinus in the sling on my back.

I am followed every step of the way by the Egyptian who carries his works of romance. And though there is pooled blood on the granite of the streets and more blood splashed up the sides of walls, even to a fearsome height on the Pillar of Diocletian, no one dares touch Hypatia of Alexandria or the Egyptian youth who follows her.

Cyril, nephew of Bishop Theophilus of Alexandria

Crammed between Uncle Theophilus and my mother Theophania, I try out this name and that: Cyril, Archdeacon of Alexandria, Cyril, Bishop of Alexandria. This, of course, I do in my head while Mother and Uncle enjoy the attack on the Serapeum from our light-bodied wagon, one drawn by four fleet horses that can leap away at a word—mobs, after all, can turn on anyone, even those who incited them. I look at my uncle when I think this. As Alexandria's bishop, Theophilus fills the poor and the ignorant with tales of eternal torment in unimaginable hells. He promises God's love by doing His Will. It is, of course, my Uncle's will—but I think God will be pleased.

We three are cloaked, our wagon hidden. "Those we fight, Uncle, are they demons?"

"Not all, boy, some merely need correction."

I am not as my mother's brother, afraid of his own mobs. If these were mine, I should stand for all to see they were mine.

Mother is ever eager to see harm done to any, although not to her brother...for his power is the source of her own. And I do hope she would have no harm done to me. But as I am not entirely sure, I keep a close eye out. I, Cyril, would see only those destroyed that God would see destroyed. Demons are clever. The trick is to become more clever than they. Now that I am fourteen, I think I might be the equal of demons.

A woman runs by, her mouth a black hole of shrieks, her hair a torch straight up from her head, her clothing aflame, her face, her arms, her legs crackling like a roasted goose. Is she Christian or pagan? Mother does not care, but I do. If the woman is Christian, demons must pay for her torment.

Uncle taps our driver's shoulder. "We've seen enough."

He lies. We leave because his mob comes too close for his comfort. Our driver whips the horses away.

Poor old Mother. How furious she must be to miss the rest of the burning, the screaming, the terror.

There are two truths I hide in my heart. One. I am superior to both. Two. Neither can live forever.

ISLAND IN THE STORMY SEA

Hypatia

Oh, my city, my city.

I have not cried this day, not within the burning Serapeum, not when I ran home through the streets past vile sights, vile sounds, vile deeds committed by both Christian and pagan alike, not even when I found Father would not speak, nor would he rage, nor would he remain with those who defend the temple, but had instead thrown the books he had saved across the floor, and himself across his bed.

I turned away from a father who would not be seen in this way.

Alexandria is not Rome, a cesspool of Herculean struggles to dominate by right of the sword. It is not Athens, once lit with minds like suns, though nothing more now than a handful of Greeks amid a handful of stones. It is not Constantinople, newly hewn from the ancient Greek city of Byzantion, where struts an emperor who would force all men to believe as he believes...*if* he believes—one can never be sure what truly furnishes the mind or the heart. It is not even Egyptian, set many miles away from the River Nile which is and has ever been Egypt's soul.

It is *Alexandria*! A city like no other city, however old that city might be and however famed...and it lies, as said Dio

Chrysostom, "*—at the conjuncture of the whole world.*" I think it possible no city to come will be as Alexandria is now.

Seven centuries past, the great Alexander stood here, feet planted firm on a spit of hot white limestone between the Great Green Sea and a sweet water lake fed by the distant Nile. In his hands he held the Persian Darius' golden casket, and in the casket the work of Homer, a man he thought a god. Rising before him shimmered the island he had dreamed of. "*As Alexander was sleeping,*" wrote Plutarch, "*he saw a remarkable vision...an island in the stormy sea off Egypt...they call it Pharos.*" Could the dreamer of Macedonia know this city would be his greatest, that it would feed the world? Could he imagine his young body, embalmed in honey and encased in beaten gold, would lie in a rock crystal vault and that his friend from youth, his mentor, his most valorous general, the Greek Ptolemy, would become again Pharaoh, founding a dynasty that lasted until the seventh and greatest of the Cleopatras?

In Alexander's city which is my city, I am accustomed to walk among scholars from Britannia, to nod at Buddhist monks and Indian Brahmins, to laugh with women from Cathay, debate men from Palestine, even, on occasion, hear men of the north—whose eyes are like holes in their heads through which flows the blue sky—speak of medicine or metallurgy or war. All the knowledge in the world is gathered here. Here there are schools that teach all one might know, and here are found all the plays, the poems, the works of philosophy and astrology, the geography, the cosmology, the mechanics, the mathematics, alchemy which is the *art* of separating and joining together: the precious ideas, the secrets, the mysteries!

But now? Alexandria becomes food for the flames of brutal ignorance.

I have left Ife, once maid to my mother but now housekeeper, to tend to the scorched Egyptian with spears of aloe. I have left Plotinus scattered over my workroom floor much as Father left Pythagoras and Diophantus. I have not washed but covered my ashy nakedness with an old tunic of linen, and then I have gone looking for Lais so that I might finally weep...for Lais loves our city as much as I.

My sister is where I thought she would be, sitting in her room on the wide ledge of her second story window looking out over the Royal Quarter. The poets and playwrights she has rescued are stacked neatly in a book bucket, save one, and that one she holds. It is the poet Telesilla who once, when all the males of Argos were killed by the King of Sparta, chopped off her hair, dressed as a warrior and led the women of Argos against him. Because of Telesilla, Herodotus predicted the female would conquer the male.

The body of Lais is warm and it breathes, but the whole of my sister is not here.

I sit myself beside her, awaiting her return.

Socrates could remain unmoving for hours, unspeaking, eyes open yet unseeing, or if seeing, not seeing what all else saw, as his ears were unhearing, his skin unfeeling, his tongue untasting. Plato called what came over Socrates "the Rapt." I would not know what to call what comes over Lais. At such times I have carefully watched and wondered. I think she leaves us, that she does this at will, that some inner part enters what the Egyptians call the *Dazzling Darkness*. I do not know if her body continues to see or to hear or to feel what I see and hear. I do not know if when I speak she understands what I say. This only I know: I cannot remember a time when my older sister did not go where I could not go, and return as if washed in the shine of the moon.

It frustrates and shames me. At times it humbles and angers me. I have told her so. She tells me her gift could be mine, indeed it already is if I would only allow it. I have tried to allow it with all my might. For this, I have achieved nothing but headaches.

Below us, rioting continues in the streets. All around I hear the shouts and the screams of those who cannot take comfort in a sister's bliss. South of the wide Canopic Way, another fire of many fires burns a third of the way up Strabo's pinecone of a mountain, on the top of which sits the Paneium. Is the path that spirals round the manmade mountain filled with the feet of Christians hurrying up to burn the Temple of Pan? Or is it a signal from defender to defender? I become frenzied. If I were Telesilla, I would cut my hair and go there directly. If I were Telesilla, I would carry a sword and a shield so I too might defend with my life those who defend the books. But up from our streets come not merely hideous sounds, but hideous smells. I am afraid. I am only Hypatia and I am afraid. What, besides our precious books, burns?

Is Father also afraid? I push away this biting thought, cleave closer to Lais, holding tight about her waist. Even as she is enraptured, some part of her remembers me, holding me as I hold her. Lais is all to me: sister, brother, teacher, mother, but Lais walks in unearthly gardens I cannot imagine, and I wait outside beside an earthly gate I cannot open nor can I climb.

In her room, lit by only one lamp, Lais quivers in my arms, and I know she returns. I have waited for this and am quick with my questions. "How can you see this, sister, how can you hear this, how can you know what burns, and not feel your own heart burning?"

My demands are as they would be, for I am yet young and the assumptions of youth are cruel. Her answer is as it would be, for this is Lais. "What was so, will be so again, Miw." She calls me "Miw" which means cat, just as she calls our little sister Jone "Panya" which means mouse. I watch as she rises, as she lights candles, one by one. "What seems lost, is never lost. Though it appears not, life is as the Goddess Ma'at, harmonious." And here she turns and I see the fire in the streets reflected in her eyes. "As my Miw forgets nothing, remember now that birth and death are as a play watched over by the sisters Uadjet and Nekhebet. To live is to act a play, a clever ever-changing never-ending play, and no actor is ever other than hero..."

"Hero?" My voice is as an ill-played flute. "But the Christians of Bishop Theophilus mean to burn the work of minds so much greater than their own."

"So it seems. But each is hero to himself. In life's play no theme is neglected. To us, for now it seems tragic—"

"But it *is* tragic, Lais! The books! The books are burning!"

"And to those who burn them, life seems triumphant. Who is to say which play is the truer? Ours or theirs? All are true."

"We are the truth. We are the lovers of wisdom."

"And the others?"

"They are the haters, the ones who fear."

"Do they? Or do they merely fear we will hurt what they love?"

"But what do they love? How do blood and pain and horror and burning come from love?"

"What they love is not this life, Miw, but the one that follows. If you were they: poor, ignorant, suffering, without privilege of any earthly kind, might you too not listen to this new faith which promises so much after death?"

As ever, my sister astounds me. Not Father and not Father's friends who are all Alexandria's greatest living scholars speak as she does. Lais is no scholar. She seldom reads other than poetry. She attends no lectures save, on occasion, mine. She is an authority on nothing others count as reasoned or logical or organized into one system or another. They would not see her thoughts as worthy or even as sane. My sister is *theodidactos*; God-taught. Lais writes poems and only I am their reader. I take them in as I take in breath, and by so doing, I realize I know nothing. In their reading, I am reminded over and over that Lais knows something I do not know and do not know *how* to know.

Gazing out over a proud Alexandria whose face is red with fire and whose ears are filled with screams, I press my head against hers. If I press hard enough, I too might understand... although the "understanding" of Lais often seems cruel to those who cannot understand—a truth I daily feel.

Is it because my head rests against hers that I remember the words of the Jewish rebel Akiba ben Joseph, who lived far away and long ago? "The paper burns, but the words fly away."

Until this moment I had not noticed the tablet that rests in my sister's lap. Leaning over, I read:

I am the Luxurious One
Losing all to gain All.
I am She, alone, who wanders in Darkness.
The deeper I fall, the closer come I to Light.

Lais frowns at her words. "I have not finished this..."

My sister, who cannot or will not speak ill of any, does not or will not speak well of herself. But I can. "Beauty is never finished."

As reward, Lais kisses my mouth.

My shutters are closed not for the noise—though the noise is as great today as it was yesterday—but for the smell. I cannot bear the stench of burning.

The siege of the Serapeum goes on. The killing there and in the streets is as great as it was. Do I act as if it is no more than any other day? Do I return to my work on the *Elements* of Euclid? The papers cover my desk. The tools I use are scattered nearby. At the far end of this same desk sit the laboratory apparatus' invented by the Alexandrian alchemist, Maria the Jewess. Near these, open and inviting, is a book inspired by Maria and by her student, a certain Cleopatra. All copies of the *Cheirokmeta* were to be destroyed by order of the

Emperor Diocletian—but no emperor has ever destroyed all he believes he destroys.

I am ravished by the secret art. There is an alchemy of the material which fascinates in its turning of one physical thing into another. And there is a truer alchemy that is not material at all but a transformation of the spirit, the reunion of the self with the Absolute by seeking states of consciousness that transcends the material. In the Great Work, all is symbol. The seven planetary metals are the seven gates one must open to transmute the body into spirit. More than three thousand years ago words were written on a Sumerian tablet: "The first gate he passed her out of, he restored to her the covering cloak of her body. At the second gate, he restored to her the bracelets of her hands and feet. At the third, he restored to her the binding girdle of her waist. At the fourth, he restored to her the ornaments of her breast. At the fifth, he restored to her the necklace of her neck. At the sixth, he restored to her the earrings of her ears. And at the seventh gate he passed her out of, he restored to her the great crown of her head."

Each gate is a threshold, each a test. And each gate passed through awakens the soul.

As a daughter of Hermes, Thrice Great, he who produced the books of the *Hermetica,* alchemy absorbs me, its meaning is inexhaustible. I am not entirely a fool. I know Lais is as I am, a construction of flesh and of blood, of sinew and bone, that there are parts to her not perfect. But her slightest flaw is as perfection in someone else. She is a manifestation of the purest spirit, a "great miracle." Lais and the work of Hermes Trismegistus have of late been all to me. I have hoped to undergo the fourfold way of the *Emerald Tablet*: become *Materia Prima*, know formless chaos and a time of darkness, dying to myself so that I might be reborn...not as Lais, for Lais is Lais—but as Hypatia, transformed. Thus, my long alchemical nights. Until, that is, the attack on the Serapeum. All that I labored over before the riot is precisely as it was when I left it, my bone ash vessel, my heating element. Yet nothing is as it was when I left it.

I cannot work. I cannot think. I have bathed, but without notice. I have dressed, but without care. I have eaten, but without pleasure. I have made a place for my rescued books, but without order. The wet of the city's heat is still weeks away, yet my skin is slick with sweat as I pace from desk to bed to door to desk.

Already three have made their way to our house in the

Royal District. The first was a student of Father's sent by his fellows, all wishing to know when and where he shall teach them next. Noting that books from the Serapeum are strewn on the floor and that his great teacher hides under his bedding, this one will return to his friends without answer. Next was a local scribe who took refuge in the kitchen, sending out the bravest of our kitchen servants to announce that he wished to collect on his bill, no doubt expecting to be first in a long line. And last was Didymus the Blind come to see how Father fares in his woe.

I too would see Father, so walk with Didymus who walks as ever with a student assigned to guide him through his day.

Didymus, in his eighth decade, senses immediately that he fares much better than Father in his sixth. Though blind, he misses nothing, not that Father lies abed while his friends and fellows continue to risk their lives for the temple or that he covers most of his head. Nor does he miss the presence of someone new at Father's side. When last I saw him, Minkah the burnt Egyptian to whom I am savior, sat on a stool in the courtyard, a plaster of aloe slathered on his head. Now, I am surprised to learn, he is allowed a room near our stables. Somehow, this one has charmed my father.

Didymus would send for a physician but by exposing an arm, Father waves that away. Didymus would send a musician. At that, Father groans. "The son of the woman Sosipatra, diviner of magical secrets, foretold the fall of the Temple. We are doomed, old friend."

"Even so, we must act."

"Act? And how shall I act? I gave my life to my students. I gave my life to those I would study and write commentary on. The only true home I have ever known is gone, its beauty defiled, its wisdom carried away by flames, its sanctity defiled by vilest ignorance. I was head of the greatest library on earth. And now? There is no library. And who am I if no one reads me or hears me? No, Didymus. I cannot act. All I can do is hold to this bed and these walls. Will they take these too?"

"In that case," says Didymus, "I will send an astrologer.'

This makes Father lift his head.

Didymus, having sent for one called Beato of Sais, does not wait for him. The pagan Egyptian astrologer, like the pagan Greek mathematician, is friend to Didymus the Blind, but Didymus is a Christian, and a wise Christian in the city of Theophilus. It would not be wise to be discovered in the same house as an astrologer.

At word an astrologer comes, Jone sneaks by me, half hiding behind a tapestry, gift to our father from his friends. There she sits and pretends to read Euhemerus' *Sacred History*. Trailed by Paniwi, Lais is also attracted by an astrologer. Paniwi is Lais' cat, a wild brown thing with darker brown ears and tail. Paniwi bites and growls and brings dead offerings to Lais, scarcely bothering with anything as trivial as a mouse. Paniwi captures rats. She waylays snakes. She leaps, her long thin body twisting in air, for birds. Twice Lais found a huge red spiky lizard lovingly arranged on her pillow. Once she discovered a half-grown vulture. All this is why the cat is named Paniwi, "the bringer."

Minkah, his head and ear bandaged, pale green stalks of aloe poking out either side, stands behind Father. He looks ridiculous. But as Lais smiles on him, and Father keeps him near, I say nothing.

I cannot sit, nor can I simply stand, but must do as I have done since waking: pace—and with me paces Paniwi.

"Sit down," says Father. I sit. Paniwi jumps into the lap of Lais.

Beato of Sais is even more ancient than Didymus. He arrives with a Gothic slave, one strong enough to carry a large wooden box, and before anyone can speak, holds up one tremulous hand. "In the city of Sais, under the Temple of Naith, there are secret halls and in these halls are kept records of Egypt nine thousand years old. I have seen these things and so know my art to be older than Egypt. Older, even, than those who built the temples of Anatolia before Jericho knew its first stone." As he speaks, he has crept closer to Father who has lowered his bedding. Father's nose is smeared with soot. As for his eyes, they are as big as the eyes of Paniwi hunting in the dark. "You!" Father and the half-hidden Jone jump, but Beato is addressing his slave. "Lay out what is needed." The slave, one of those northern creatures covered in hair as an ape is covered in hair, immediately opens the box. I slowly stand, slowly sidle closer to them, the better to see for myself the tools of a true astrologer. As an astronomer, astrology is well known to me, but I have never practiced the art...though I mean to. Father loves divination. He has written a book on Hermes Trismegistus and I have memorized every word of it.

Beato stares at Father as Father stares at him. Beato is tapping a curved yellow nail on a curved yellow tooth. Lais strokes Paniwi who purrs loud enough to wake one of the many things she has killed. I struggle to resist rummaging through

Beato's wooden box. Especially as in the box is a second box already opened and in this second box resides a mechanism I have only read of. A thing of shining brass gears and pointers and cogs and wheels and balls that describe the movements of the golden sun and the silver moon and the five wanderers and in this way locates their zodiacal positions at any given time. Described by Archimedes, first devised by Poseidonius of Rhodes, now in rare variations possessed only by the rich—Beato of Sais must be a very successful astrologer.

Beato is saying something to Father, no doubt asking him questions so that he might adjust his machine and construct a view of the heavens on the day and time of Father's birth in the year 335, when suddenly I hear my name. I look up to find that while I have been studying Beato's machine, Beato has been studying me.

I move away from his wonderful machine, prepared to assist if I can.

His white beard, crusted with spittle, is orange around his mouth. To me, not to Father, he says, "I have no need of a date for you."

"But...you have come for my father, not me."

"Theon's course is set and he knows it as well as I do. I waste my time here. But you! By the star that fell from the sky at your birth, you have life yet to choose."

I glance at Father, who shrugs, saying, "But such a small star and only one, not a night-sun, or a javelin of evil omen, or a horned star, or a torch or a horse star or one that threw off sparks..."

Beato cuts across father as a comet across the sky. "No fire that falls from heaven is small. None that comes alone is less than sacred. And this one came with a sound of singing. A great destiny awaits her, a great destiny. It is hers, yet it is not hers, for she as Hypatia shall not see it. All she will know is blood and fire. But before this, she will be greater than any man."

I must be making a face as he speaks, as who would not make a face hearing such words, for he quickly turns back to me, adding, "You need not accept your destiny. The stars hint, they do not command. As one called 'sage' what say you?"

What say I? I have no idea. In this moment, I notice Jone. What do I see in her strange little eyes? A feeling: sorrow or a slight or perhaps nothing more than some small digestive pain. In her own way, Jone is as much a mystery to me as is Lais. But where there is a joy to Lais I cannot attain, there is a sorrow to Jone I cannot fathom. I say, "I am no sage. I do not claim such wisdom nor would I want to foretell the future. What great destiny?"

"One that will engrave your name on the pillars that hold up the sky, that will write it over and over in the patterns made by waves, one that will encode it in the veins of those to come for a thousand years, even more. But the cost will be high. How much would you pay for such a destiny?"

Now I find something to say, a thing I truly mean. "I would pay nothing, for I have no desire to know my name will live in this way."

"You!" Beato of Sais again shouts at his slave. "Close the box. I am done here."

And Beato is gone, but not before a glance at Jone, a second glance at the Egyptian, and a third at Lais. At sight of Jone he frowns, at sight of Minkah he seems puzzled, but at the sight of Lais, he sighs. "Child, I offer my pity." There is one more glance for me and a sigh deeper than his sigh for Lais. And then we are alone, my sisters and my father and I—along with the scorched lover of fanciful tales, the youth who has not only followed me home, but seems intent on staying.

Suddenly Father cries out. There are no words, only the one cry.

"Father!" says Lais, immediately on her feet. "What is it?"

Waving his arms so that his bedding falls away, he wails, "What have I done? What have I said? What fate awaits my children as it waited for their mother? Damara, poor Damara!" And with that he has snatched once more at his bedding, this time throwing it not only over his face but over his head.

Lais is rounding his bed, coming towards me, and as she does, she commands, "Jone. Fetch a bowl of hot water. And a root of valerian. A large root. Minkah! Bring your sleeping mat. Father should not be alone."

Minkah is off on the instant. As is Jone.

And now it is me to whom Lais speaks, but quietly so that Father does not hear. "He has spoken her name aloud, Miw."

What Lais means is that on the day of our mother's death, a deaf mute was found in the garden. He asked nothing of us. He ate nothing. He did nothing. At the end of three days and three nights, he was gone. Father declared it an omen that Mother would have us remember her only with silence. As for the three days and three nights, Father quoted Nicomachus of Gerasa who declared the triad the form of completion.

"Father forgets himself. He is ill but we shall make him

better."

Lais nods. "And the astrologer?"

Here, too, I know what she means. She asks what I think of Beato of Sais with all his sighing, as well as what he calls my "destiny."

"Did you see what was in his box?"

If my sister is not diverted, she pretends to be.

AIR, WATER, EARTH, FIRE

Hypatia

How to explain Lais? Beauty is not enough, for many are beautiful. Graceful, yes, but grace can be found in others. The sweetness of her voice enchants, and the tenderness of her concern for all who meet her is felt by the hardest heart. But no, it is not that which can be seen or heard of Lais that matters, though what can be seen and heard is lovely beyond anything written of the seventh Cleopatra or of Nefertiti, even of Helen held captive by love in Troy. It is that which resides within Lais that cannot be held or touched or, by most, if any, understood.

My sister is made of air. She is a poet of pure ecstasy. To read what she writes shames me for all my gifts.

Father, who thinks me sage as do his students, knows nothing of the mysteries if he does not know Lais. And he, like they, do not. None mention her trances; all are embarrassed by them. As for me, I long to learn where she goes, for if not "here," where then *is* she? I think if I desire anything, I desire this: to know what Lais knows.

Sitting at table this evening, there are only my sisters and me and Paniwi. There is also Jone's book for Jone has ever a book no matter the circumstance. Throughout the past few days she reads *The Golden Ass* of Lucius Apuleius Platonicus.

Four days and four nights have passed and still the streets cry out with rage and with pain. Those who attack, attack from faith, not from "knowing." They know nothing, as Socrates could have proved to them, but have faith what they do not know is so. This faith in the proclamation of others is so strong, as is the faith of those who defend, that both sides would die for what they do not know they do not know. It is piteous. It is pathetic. It is distressing beyond the work of Palladas which is full of bitterness and gall.

The Serapeum has not yet fallen, but is besieged on all sides. By order of Bishop Theophilus, what happens here, happens as well in Canopus, a city sited a day's ride away at the marshy mouth of the Canopic Nile—their temples also burn.

As good as his word, Father will not leave his room. Beato of Sais said that Father knew his course. If so, his course is no course at all. He lies in his bed. And there, he has informed us, he will stay until the Council of the Ogdoad appears before him so that Set, who is the god of disorder, can explain why such as the Christian Emperor Theodosius through his agent the Christian Bishop Theophilus is allowed to bring so much sorrow to Alexandria.

Father's calling out to the gods of Egypt might once have amused. When he was yet young, his god was Thales of Miletus and the god of Thales was water. Water underlay all, not divinity. But Thales saw only what he was looking at. What he was not looking at was invisible to him—which explains how he could be walking in the desert at night, counting the stars, and fall directly into an open well. In time, Father came to concern himself with Platonic form. Woven through and through his work is the seven crystalline heavens and each is a heaven of mathematical precision proving the divine in all. Water has been replaced by heavenly ether.

But Father's demand to see the gods of Egypt does not amuse, and it does not amuse us because it does not amuse Father. He is more than serious, he is adamant. Lais and I peek hourly in at him. Where is the father we knew? Where the man who spoke before eager crowds, who enthralled students come from everywhere to hear him, who stood higher than any in the halls of learning, who came home each night to preside at table and laugh...so much that even Jone might smile.

He has, at least, allowed the Egyptian to undress him, to wrestle him into a sleeping robe, and then to be covered. As soon as the covers touched his chin, he pulled them over his head. To speak with him, we must raise a corner and whisper. He seldom answers. He must also have allowed Minkah to shelve his rescued books for they no longer litter the floor.

Lais picks at her food, feeding most to Paniwi. I merely stare at mine. Reading, Jone has eaten two sweet buns and a bowl of soup.

And how shall I describe Jone?

She cannot sail. She is made ill by the sea. She cannot swim. She sinks like a slab of cement. She will not ride. Horses frighten her. She refuses to walk or to climb in the heat or the rain or the wind. In truth, if she need not, she barely moves a muscle. If she has friend at all, it is the African Ife, first among servants in the House of Theon, a house she runs calmly and precisely. Jone reads. She will sit for hours, rooted deep in the earth like a tree, devouring whatever she finds, preferring the epic poets and the novelists, and in the midst of the text, will stop and think about what she reads until one assumes her asleep, an assumption often correct. She has no taste for mathematics but even these texts she samples. Other than reading and eating and sleeping, Jone does nothing unless forced to do so.

Lais once said: "I have too much imagination, Jone too little."

At this, I asked, as would anyone, "And I?"

"Just enough."

I pondered her answer for days. I ponder it still.

Father is tall. Lais is tall. Even I am tall. But Jone is short and soft and round. Our mother, who was neither short nor tall, was not round. Or was she? I have one memory and one memory only. At two, I clutch at Lais, who is four and clutches me. Ife holds us both as we watch our mother die. Even then, Lais was Lais. All throughout, she whispered in my ear, slow sweet sounds to keep me from rushing away, to keep me from climbing into our mother's bed. Her room reeked of blood, as hot and as thick and as red as the shrieks of her agony. On the third and last day, by the light of guttering candles, Jone was cut from our mother's lifeless body.

Her shrieks have receded from my mind, her size and her shape and her voice, but I shall never forget the sight and the smell of my mother's dying.

Though Father has never said so, he would *never* say so, to lose his wife for Jone was so terrible a blow, even now he finds it hard to look long at his last child.

Does Jone know this is the cause of her father's disregard? Perhaps. Perhaps not. We are born who we are. What we birth ourselves into can touch us and turn us but it cannot make us what we are not.

And who am I?

If Father had had a son, just one son, instead of three very different daughters, it would be this son he spent his life trying to make "perfect." But fate delivered him—me. This, it is true, discouraged him, but it did not stop him. Founded on the ideal forms of Plato—*all "above" is perfect; all "below" a copy*—Alexandria's great mathematician insisted on rendering one of us ideal.

Lais would not do. She was already perfect with a perfection he did not understand and could not train. Jone was no choice at all for numbers bored her, languages other than Greek did not interest her, and she refused to do other than read what she and she alone chose to read.

This left him only me. I would know all the sciences from mathematics to astronomy, would speak in a dozen tongues, write as Sappho, orate until men wept with the beauty of my thoughts. I would be a philosopher, a lover of wisdom for its own sake, a historian who would know that nothing ever changes, but instead follows a simple repeating pattern of human need or greed. Father decreed also that my body would be as well tended as my mind. He saw me as Zenobia, Queen of Syria. A century before I was born, Zenobia led the men of Syria and Palestine and Anatolia into the Black Lands, and when Rome would seize Egypt back, she had its prefect beheaded for such impertinence. The woman could walk for days, even if she must scramble up one side of a perilous mountain and down the other. She could ride hot-blooded horses without bridle or bit, using only pressure of knee and hand, or by a soft voice close to a soft ear, knowing them intimately by caring intimately for them.

Father would have me do more. I would row and I would sail, sensing my way by the winds, by the currents and by the stars.

There would be no one like the person he and the best tutors in the world would make of me. Or such was his plan, for Father hated the material and emotional chaos of this world and longed for the pure, immortal, and unchangeable world of the ideal form. Like Plato, he believed that harmony of shape would reveal the sublime.

But a mind is not clay, and though Father was, *is*—even in

bed hiding his head—a master mathematician and a master astronomer, he was not a master potter. A mind cannot be formed into whatever shape a man might choose. A mind has a mind of its own. Certainly mine does. My mind seems often too small for all it contains. There are times it seems too large. And when I ride or sail or stare at the stars or wander in infinite number I become afraid of who, or what, I am...as if I were a wild thing, a mistake.

Damara should have lived. She should have given him his son.

Lais, who would normally leave the table as quickly as I—for we each are fond of solitude and even more fond of our work—does not leave. Instead, she scratches Paniwi's arched back, and speaks. "What if Father remains, as he swears he will, in bed?"

I know immediately what she means. She means that with the loss of the Serapeum, so too is Father's position as Head of the Library lost. Lost as well is his public funding. If he does not form his own school or join others like himself to teach privately—and how shall that happen from bed?—who then will pay the servants and our taxes and the upkeep of our garden and the hundred and one other expenses that keep us in our fine house in the Royal Quarter? Only a few streets away, under the Ptolemaic walls, the once rich Bruchion District is in ruins. This is the doing of the Emperor Aurelian. That Zenobia should capture Egypt so enraged him, he destroyed every park, every building, the whole of the royal docks, even the tomb of Alexander, and no one, not for the whole of a hundred years has rebuilt it. But here on the Street of Gardens between the Street of the Soma and the deep water canal cut from the Port of the Lake to the Royal Harbor, sits the house that has been ours for close on two hundred years. We cannot lose it now, not while Father lives.

Chin propped in my hands, I watch Ife offer Jone a third sweet bun. So much older, yet as small as Jone, Ife openly favors Father's youngest child, a thing which delights my heart. But it is Ife who makes me ask: who will keep us fed? From outside comes the sound of stable lads bedding down our horses for the night. These sounds should comfort, but who will pay them? Who will buy grain for the horses? And what of the scribes we hire? Who will copy our books?

Lais lifts one perfect hand, opening its soft white palm; how empty it is, how languid, how useless for practical effort. The sight of her tender palm puts seal to my fate. If destiny I have, it is to care for Lais. "Could I sell my poems? Would anyone buy?" For pity, I could open my veins.

Though Lais is first to speak of such things, I have already considered them. As well as having become "perfect," among us I am also the most practical. Not for a moment do I imagine, as Father cleaves close to his bed waiting for the gods to explain themselves, such thoughts have entered his head. "If Father does not get up, I shall take over all of his classes."

At this, Jone, slowly chewing, actually raises her head from her book. "You? But you are barely twenty and one. Who would listen to you?"

"Ah, Panya, at seventeen, Cleopatra ruled Egypt and Origen was head of the Catechetical school Didymus heads now. At sixteen, Alexander was regent of Macedonia, and by scarcely twenty-three king of Egypt. Didymus teaches that his Jesus argued with scholars when he was but twelve. They will listen. And they will pay to listen."

I sound convincing. Had I not already from time to time taken Father's place at lectures when he was ill or otherwise occupied, and published three mathematical commentaries which have been taken seriously as well as a book about the geology of Theophrastus? Alexandria calls me "sage." Surely all this puffery counts for something?

Lais lowers her hand and smiles. Lais, smiling, can cause the heart to swoon. Jone lowers her head to finish her bun and her book. They are content. Hypatia will pay the bills if Father refuses to rise again.

If only I could smile with such ease. The fact remains that I am female. I have taught males to great effect. But would these same males be taught by me if they must pay?

From behind the walls of our house, I watch Alexandria driven to her knees.

Emperor Theodosius, tiring of Alexandria's "unrest," has ordered Alexandria's Prefect to have Alexandria's Military Commander step between Christian and heretic. Imperial troops immediately surrounded the Serapeum, demanding all defenders leave or be crucified. The "pagans" left and the Christians flooded in. These have torn the temple to pieces.

The battle is over. Old women scrub blood from the streets.

Bodies are fished from the canals. We have lost.

And just as the gods have kept their silence, Father has kept to his bed. He will have nothing further to do with human passions, concluding that the human state is unjust, immoral, and unworthy. It is also insane. If, says he, he must live in one room to escape it, then he shall live in one room. One room can be, he hopes, controlled by the shutting of a door and the barring of a window.

What this means is that no money comes into our house, but a great deal flows out.

He no longer covers his head, but as for the rest of him, all that stays firmly under his bedding. For a week or so, he even taught from this bed, surrounded by a small class of uncomfortable students as he lectured on the geometry of Euclid or the astronomy of Ptolemy or the harmonics of Nicomachus of Gerasa. But he has stopped even this.

Minkah, his scalp tended to daily by Ife, is become his body servant and in return Father teaches him to speak and to read in Latin. He teaches him of stars and of numbers and of divination. In this, and in many other ways, they delight in each other. Father has seldom delighted in anyone but Didymus, and often Lais and sometimes even me, so that, I suppose, explains a stray Egyptian in our house.

This, as I feared, leaves only Hypatia. I must do as I said I would do. Teach and be paid to teach.

Who would allow me this? How should I start? And then I remember—*who* would allow me this? Who else? Our family's good friend, Didymus the Blind. His school, the Christian Didascalia, takes pagan students hoping they might convert them, but they do not take pagan teachers who might convert back not only pagan but Christian.

But there is this. Didymus knows everyone and everyone knows him. Didymus will help me find work, for Didymus who we love, loves us.

Here, in the Christian district, all appears well with the world. The wide street that runs before the Christian school of Didymus, the narrow streets that pass either side, the public park behind, the Christians of Alexandria pushing their way here and there, the noise they make, the smell, the summer's heat, all remains. Nothing seems changed but me. I am as ever barefoot, yet I am not the wild child who roamed the streets, coming from a lesson or going to, dodging through legs, knocking cabbage from stalls and pots from walls. I am head of my family now.

Sitting in a white cup of a chair at the top of pink marble steps, Didymus awaits me in the great doorway to his school, founded, or so the Christians say, by Mark the Evangelist who they also say wrote the first gospel of Jesus. Old when I was a child, Didymus is so much older now. Bent then, he bends more. But the old man can make people laugh. He can make them cry. With his tales, he can cause them to sigh with longing or to shiver with fear.

All love Didymus who has never sought to force his beliefs on any, especially not on Theon of Alexandria and his motherless brood of daughters. In this he shows great wisdom. Had he done so, the rest of his days would have been spent in the buzz of argument. We should have driven him mad.

To me, that he lost his sight at the age of four has given him greater sight.

"Hypatia!" His voice carries no farther than the pillars either side of the door as I take the stairs two at a time. "Go in," I call, "go in and wait. I shall find you."

"Not without thread. Inside is as the Labyrinth of Minos."

Somewhere deep inside the school Origen wrestled from Mystery sects when Diocletian was emperor and doing his best to remove Christians from physical existence—how reversed the world now!—I sit with Didymus, confessing my problem. He laughs, and I see if teeth he has, they could number no more than three. I find myself thinking of triads and triangles and trinities.

"It is perfection! My dear friend has finally solved his own dilemma."

"What dilemma is that?"

"What to do with three daughters. Ordinarily a man with three daughters, but no wife, would remarry. But Theon loves only numbers and divination and Damara. So what to do with three girls? Is it not a father's responsibility to see his daughters wed and off his hands?"

"But we none of us wish to marry."

"Then you see his dilemma."

"And you see mine?"

"I do. Normally you should all be out in the streets in no

time."

"But that cannot happen."

"And it will not. You are Hypatia. Much is expected of you."

This clenches my jaw. "Perhaps too much."

"I imagine it feels that way, but when have you ever failed your father? Have you not even surpassed him in all things?" I would not answer that, and Didymus knows I would not. "You will teach. You will be greater than any. You will not falter nor will you fail. As said Heraclitus of Ephesus: 'Character is Destiny.' To fail is not in you."

I am surprised when I weep. I weep so suddenly and so deeply and for so long we are both of us shocked. Didymus listens to me cry. He makes no soft sounds to soothe me. He does not touch me. He waits. But crying, I see that I am afraid. I am so afraid. How does he know I shall not fail? With the best will, any can fail. Any can fall. To see my sisters in the street, my father, our faithful Ife, even that Egyptian person...to lose our home, our books, our horses, I could not bear it. But who am I to stop it?

Now I no longer weep, I sob. And still Didymus waits.

And when I am done and sit sniffling and wiping my snotty nose, he says this, "You cannot teach here, of course, but you can teach. And I know the very place."

In an instant, my back is once more straight, my face wiped with the hem of my tunic. "Where!"

"It can be done with the penning of a single letter. He thinks to hire another, but he shall hire you. Oh, I had forgot! If this does not cause Theon to leap from that wretched bed, nothing will. Tell him we have counted the books. Some are lost, this is true, but most are not. Those who did not flee the siege secretly removed almost all." My cheeks, already pink with tears, redden. We both know Father was one of those who fled. "All we need do now is—"

I am out of my chair to kiss his knot of a nose, to pull his scant beard.

He finishes. "—decide what else we need do."

Driving my grays home, I am reminded how small the world that is mine, how rare. I am reminded too how rare is Didymus the Blind. Of all who call themselves Christian, is it only Didymus who hears the true voice of their Christ?

I stand between a new and violent faith that would remove all but its own beliefs from the world, and an old and violent faith with many faces, but all blooded with sacrifice. Passing through the Street of the Glassblowers, I am witness to a sight that is seen not by the week or by the day, but by the hour. Naked save for a leather pouch to cradle his scrotum and penis, a man holds a knife to the throat of a calf. His chest like a bowl, yet with a belly in which a full term baby could fit, he is calling out to a god, demanding that god accept the blood of this poor trembling creature in payment for something he desires.

Between these forces of ignorance, where is there room for the graceful Bast and the loving Hathor?

Who hears the voice of Lais?

SILENCE

Minkah the Egyptian

I am called Minkah, but who has named me this, I do not know. I say I was born in the city of Alexandria, that it was here I first entered this realm of pain and of sorrow, but I would not swear this is true. And no more than where, do I know when. This only I know: I am a true Egyptian. Was I not born poor? Have I not been, for most of my wretched life, homeless? If any I could call by name, were they not toothless or lacking an arm or a leg or in some other way afflicted? If work I could find, was it not menial and when I held out my hand for pay, was I not beaten?

Yet what is so on one day may not be so on another. Egyptian I am and Egyptian I remain. Yet for eight years and more I am as well *Parabalanoi,* one of the Christian brotherhood. I am fed and I am clothed and I am sheltered, but I took no holy orders and swore no solemn vows. No need even to be a *cūlus* of a Christian—a good thing, for if god I have, it is Horus the Elder, god of suffering and poverty—but I am protected in all that I do by a Christian bishop who has use for me and my kind. The people are told we are merciful, that we bury the dead and care for the sick—and we do. But in truth we do much more for the bishop himself, and none of it merciful. The people are not fooled. As *Parabalanoi*, I inspire fear in all. As for those who once drove me from their door, or shielded their daughters from the sight and the smell of me, they do so no longer. They cringe and they tremble. Now, if I demanded it, they would thrust their women at me, even those yet babes. *Take her*, they would plead, *take her—and leave us alone.* Buttholes, the lot of them.

In Egypt, an Egyptian is less than a camel for a camel spits at those who would ride him and hit him and load him down with great burdens. As *Parabalanoi*, I am become at least a camel.

By my own effort I have taught myself to read. By my reading I have learned to speak as my betters speak—a handy skill. I am strong in body and quick in thought. What is shown me once, I learn. I suffer no illness, though I do now bear wounds, one from fire and one from the sword. As close as my shadow, scorn followed me into this world.

And then there is this, as satisfying as status: Egyptians, brought low, are no longer alone in their shame and their anger. Hellenists, Jews, Gnostics, Greeks, philosophers, scientists, poets, mathematicians, historians, astronomers, each suffers a new force in Egypt, a force that seems darker by far than any come before. Ironic, is it not, that that same force affords me my new place in the world? If I were free enough for choice, I might care who offers me coin. I am not free enough.

Our Bishop is a cunning man. He has destroyed the statue of Serapis, the one made to float by lodestones. With no image to worship, there will soon be no god. Men are forgetful. A god dies when he is forgotten, even Serapis who sets souls free. And then he destroyed the Serapeum. It was ground into dust which blew away on the wind and was no more.

In Memphis, once a city of Pharaoh, the Iseum is also sacked and those that are spared, merely await their turn. Emperor Theodosius, by notice nailed to doors, affects to soothe the defenders of the old traditions. He swears none need fear him or his Christians, assures us with messenger after messenger that all might return to what had been—but even the simple are not simple enough to believe such dung.

And yet, like the Nile in the season of Ahket, these difficult times have brought me riches on the crest of the flood. I have work and respect, and though I have paid with fiery pain, I sleep under the roof of the famous Theon of Alexandria in the Royal District, a roof that covers also the heads of his three sleeping daughters. One touches my heart with her goodness and beauty. The other touches my heart and my body. I must be careful here. She is not for me, or I for her. The third, a sad thing by comparison to her sisters, but not without spine. I am given such looks as would turn me to stone if the last were named Medusa.

To remain, I become indispensable to Theon of Alexandria. Called first among mathematicians and astronomers, I call him last among men. Look at him now, curled up and buried in bed! If choice were mine, I'd drag him out by the hair of his beard only to kick his ass all the way to a lecture hall.

Lucky for Theon, I seem alone in my disgust.

Men make their way to his house. Some come alone, more often they come by twos and by threes. But however they arrive, they come by cover of night, and when they come, they gather in his draped and darkened room. Tonight, there are nine in the house of Theon, mathematician, astronomer, and coward. Not one could run more than ten steps without bending over to cough. All are, to me, old. Half sweat like slaves in the sun.

As usual, only his head shows above the bedclothes. As usual, he does not speak but listens. No matter that he does this, all who arrive, friends and scholars alike, believe he will regain himself. I, who have never seen him other than he is now, do not believe this. A man with balls would not shrivel in bed. A man without balls seldom grows them.

Tonight his guests talk of constructing defenses. Standing behind the man all assume is my "master," I learn as I listen for it is these men, old, breathless, and sweating, who defended the Serapeum.

The room is a hubbub of voices. Though the violence has passed, asks one, who knows when it will erupt again? Should they do nothing but wait, asks another, for emperor or bishop or some other tyrant to attack what is left them and see that destroyed as well? Should they disappear as this or that one has done? Or do as the poet Claudian did, flee to Rome so he might sing himself into favor? "Curse Claudian!" they cry.

Curse Claudian? Gifted with wealth, able to read and to write, yet still he would sing to a tyrant? I say: cut his fucking throat.

The poet Palladas, whose skin hangs on his bones as clothes on a line, whines that without public funds he goes hungry. But if he should leave, where can he go? He knows no other city. No other city knows him. "Why leave?" snorts Ammonius, the priest of Thoth who killed three who would spoil the Serapeum—with breasts that droop as the god Hapi's, his deeds are hard to imagine. "Are there still not freedoms in Alexander's city found nowhere else? And has this not been so for more than seven hundred years?" Behind Theon's locked door, these freedoms will, he boldly proclaims, remain true for another seven hundred years.

I do not laugh. I am skilled at not laughing.

Finally, ask all, what is to become of the books? Each has what he took away during the siege of the Serapeum. Even I have books which remain in the satchel in a corner of the room given me, a room smelling of the great beasts living in larger rooms than I across a courtyard of yellow brick.

I endure the same drivel each time they gather: one or another complains that the Great Library is scattered all over the city from the Gate of the Moon to the Necrotic Gate, hidden away in chests, in storage rooms, under beds, in stables, in the homes of people who do not know they are there, even in certain tombs in the City of the Dead. Once catalogued and stored by system, they are no longer, and none are protected by other than the secrecy of those who hide them. Emperor Theodosius may think them destroyed, bishops from Rome to Constantinople may cherish the idea they are gone forever, but they are not. They exist. By their bravery, old men like these, and women—I shall never forget my first sight of Hypatia, or the splendor of her naked body—had a week to remove every book that did not burn. After his first and only haul, brave Theon was not among them.

Here they go again, talking each over each. Impossible to hear what any single man says, but easy to understand what all mean. What to do? What to do? The books must not remain in this place and that place. So much could happen to them, a loss here and a loss there. In no time some will be taken from the city, says a Jew named Meletus, others will be claimed as the property of this one or that one, for, given the chance, all men are thieves.

Well, that's true enough. All may be thieves, but not all here are fools. There will be books that are sold, books that are bartered, books that "disappear." If nothing is done, and done soon, the books might as well have burned.

From one moment to the next, I am enraged. If anger I feel tending to Theon, it is nothing to this. It floods my head. It causes my scalp to throb with pain. It fills my lungs. Theon hides in his bed, but these hide in an endless desert of words. Without thought, I shout, "Buttfuck them all! What is Alexandria without her library!"

In the sudden and lengthy silence, only one voice finally sounds. "Indeed," sighs the wry Pappas, an astronomer who seems Theon's mentor, "...and what are scholars without books?"

I need not hide for my outburst, nor explain my crudity, for now follows complete chaos. All are thrown into frustrated indecision. There must be a new library. How can there be a new library? Empty a building! Use that! And which building would allow this? Build a new one! Where? Somewhere out of the city. A secret place hidden in the eastern marshes. How will those who seek it, find it? Somewhere in the city, but not marked as such. But how to hide this from an emperor who exults in the burning of our books? Theodosius will find them...and try again.

It is Helladius, priest of Ammon, barrel in chest, barrel in body, barrel in voice, who is finally loudest of all. "It falls to each man here to ensure that never happens. How, Theon, shall we do this?" As usual, Theon does not answer, though he does look attentive. This seems to answer for him. Helladius bellows on. "If we experience further threat, we must prepare for further threat. If they would burn more temples, what can we do? We are scholars, magistrates, priests. They are mindless fanatics protected by the *Parabalanoi.*" Here he spits. "Ignorant thugs! May Ammon cast them into the lowest hells of Amenta! May He stuff their mouths with the Stone of Sut!" I would flinch, but as with laughter, I know the art of a straight face. "We have learned by all this and learned grievously. Using violence against violence saved the books, but did not save the temple. As well, violence reduced us to the brutish level of a slavering Goth." All heads nod. They remember his blooded sword. "The new library must be as secret as the books we hide in it. And that is not all we must hide. Our thoughts must be muted, our ideas spoken in whispers. The threat has not passed. That *bishop* awaits us like a lion in the tall grass."

Theon groans at this. They all groan.

The man Pappas stands forth, his voice as a bell. "The greatest minds have lived in this city. The greatest talents have added word upon word, thought upon thought, to its store of knowledge. And all of it, *all* of it, was lately available to any who sought it. How can we bear to lose this? How can any bear to lose it?"

"Surely, it has not come to that?" This is said by the occultist Paulus of Alexandria. His own home lost to fire, yet his goods were removed the day before to the house of his

Christian mother-in-law. Paulus interests me. Is he gifted with sight...or a spy? If spy, then for whom? Not for Theophilus or I should know it. "Theodosius shows charity. He declares we are allowed our beliefs."

"Are you a fool?" snaps Pappas, who I begin to admire. "If we are allowed our beliefs, where are our temples?"

And now, from a chair far from all these talkers, rises up Hypatia. All throughout, as I have stood listening to this one and that, and to all at once, so too has she. At sight of her as at speech from me, once again the silence is immediate. She is stared at. To run through fire for books, to stride naked, her nose in the air, past men maddened with blood...this is one to be feared.

"You talk of a new library," says the daughter of Theon, "you say the new library will not be as the old, it will be secret. But how secret can it be? Scholars will seek it, will speak of it. How then can it be hidden? No more than one foolish mouth, and it will be gone before the waning moon." All is now a rustle of togas, a scratching of beards. As an Egyptian, I grow no beard, but if I did, I would scratch it. Beard scratching is a way to avoid other than beard scratching. "Shall we give them a new library to sack and to burn?" Heads are shaking, nooooo. "Nor can we trust them to one man's house, no matter how large the house or worthy the man."

"What, then," asks a now sober Helladius, "shall we do?"

"We will do as the Jews once did." By name a Greek, Meletus is the one Jew here, and head of the Jewish Schul of Alexandria. Though all other stares are blank, the stare of Meletus threatens. But as Meletus is older than Palladas, older even than Didymus, and has not a single hair on his head but hair enough for a cleaning broom over both eyes, Hypatia pays him no heed. "When Rome threatened the books of the Jews, what did they do? They gathered them from everywhere, took them out into their deserts of arid heat, sealed them in great jars, and hid them in caves. The books exist, though three hundred years have come and gone. This is true, is it not Meletus?"

Clearly, Meletus does not want to answer, but must. "Yes, it is true."

The others stare at the bald Jew as they stared at Hypatia.

"Is this not Egypt?" says this woman of a girl, "and are we not surrounded by deserts, greater than any in Judea? And do we not have caves, and are they not dry and hot?" Yes, they all nod, yes, there are caves in the desert and they are hot.

Pappas holds up a hand. "But what of grave robbers, more numerous than lice?"

"Robbers seek gold, not books, and what they seek is near the Nile, not here." Pappas concedes her point: Alexandria has no pyramids, no valleys of kings and queens. "We will gather the books, each from where it is hidden. We will find the right and proper caves. When these are discovered, there will be drawn three maps that if found or stolen will make no sense to its finder. Each map will be seemingly different yet in meaning the same, and three men will hold in trust these differing maps. You must decide who these three men are. As for the devising of symbol, who better than my father: Alexandria's most fiendish geometer?" Even Theon listens with open mouth. *Yes, yes, yes.* I see them begin to calculate, already wondering which of them would be map-holders.

Pappas has paid close attention, so now asks the obvious question. "And where shall we keep the books before they are hidden in desert caves?"

The answer to this is as ready on Hypatia's tongue as all else she has said. "They will be taken to the one place no Christian would think to look."

"And that is?"

"Only those in this room will know, swear on it."

They all swear, even me, and of them, I hope none betrays what they swear to; this while looking at Paulus and thinking of myself.

"The place is obvious. Where else than in the Didascalia, the confusing, complex, and enormous Christian school of Didymus the Blind?"

Ahhhh, they all sigh. Bold. Ingenious. Risky. For the space of a breath, they pause, then fall to discussing which of them should be the three to hold the maps. Only I am left to gaze upon Theon's second daughter. Not one man here questions her judgment. Yet no man gapes in wonder at wisdom standing before them. I am in danger here; my heart is threatened as well as my loins. I scold myself. Step lightly, Egyptian, speak with care. No sword has proved more dangerous than this.

I banish the woman with thoughts of the man. Bishop Theophilus is my true master. What I hear in this house, should I not tell him?

No doubt. But not now. Yet if not now, when? The answer is simple. When it suits me.

Hypatia's plan to remove the books from private hands and to hide them in a Christian school began that day. I watched them moved through the streets in bullock carts, in bundles on backs as if they were kindling or laundry, even secreted one by one under mantles. My own I carried openly. What Christian would take offense at, or even notice, the work of Theophilus, for each of my books was disguised as one of his.

It was good to see Lais laugh at my joke, irritating to wonder if Hypatia even noticed.

Danger traveled with every book. What if someone tripped and fell and Aristotle be exposed in the street? What if thieves, believing they had found treasure, found Livy instead? What if something should startle an ass, and it go braying off on its own scattering Homer's Margites, what if, what if?—but there was also exhilaration.

It took a month or more, but in the end the books are hidden with Didymus. I enjoyed myself immensely.

As for who would keep a map once it was drawn, my "Master" Theon was chosen first of the three. Meletus, second. I thought neither choice surprising. As it can be done in bed, Theon will devise the maps. Meletus has knowledge of such things, yet has not shared his knowledge—what better recommendation? I should have wagered on Pappas as third choice. Instead they chose Didymus. This means the Great Library is in the hands of a craven mathematician, a reluctant Jew, and a Christian. If any die before the library is restored, their copy will follow on down a list carefully determined. Theon's will go to Hypatia.

I too have a task. Not Theon, but Hypatia, assigns it. I do not ask why she chooses me, who does not know me, but the answer must reside with Theon who trusts me. I, who have never ridden, who have been no closer to a horse than to be trampled when in the way, or sharing a courtyard, am to ride out into the desert where few ever think to venture, and with me rides Hypatia. Whenever she does not lecture to the rich and ambitious, we are to search for a place that no one can find.

I am given a day to learn the art of riding. This is my doing for I have said I learn easily, and when it comes to things of the body, easier still. Hypatia takes me at my word. She and I alone have come out into the desert where I cannot hurt myself or the horse, and here I must prove myself. My beauty rides a fine red mare named Desher. I ride a creature as splendid as Lais. Ia'eh is as Desher, a hot-blooded horse of the high cold deserts, faraway and strange to imagine. Where Desher is the color of blood, Ia'eh is as white as a harbor gull with an eye as black as kohl. Astride her, I must know her, anticipate her, follow her as if I was part of her. Three or more times, I would fall, but I will not. Hypatia watches, a mere girl who can do more than I, who knows more than I, is a high-born Greek watching a low-born Egyptian, and I will not fall. I will ride Ia'eh as I would Hypatia. Not that I shall ever ride Hypatia, but men live by dreaming and I am a dreamer.

When we return, I am handed Xenophon's Hippike and the work of Simonides. "Read these," says my haughty darling, "So you may know the horse in all its ways." And with that she leaves me, who ache in all my parts. It is not only Ia'eh who causes this.

Use and knowledge of the horse elevates my status. My mind is elevated by chance. As I tend to him, Theon chatters away. And because I know what Hypatia does not know—her safety rests on the will of Bishop Theophilus—I accompany Hypatia to her lectures and I listen. From time to time, I wonder: if it should be Minkah who is ordered to endanger that safety, what then? Piss on it. Worry never pays. But by Horus, I have fallen into a vat of honey.

When I ride with Hypatia, we do not go south. Due south lies Lake Mareotis and beyond the lake rise the mountains of Nitria where live the maddest of mad Christian monks. These are harmless solitaries, chilled in caves or exposed on high rocks or starving in ruins, each alone and each dying to meet their god. But there too live those in black robes, gathering like flocks of crows—these are not alone and they are not harmless. They grind their teeth with fanatical "love" of what they call God and hate beyond reason all they consider not God.

We ride as Libyans. No Egyptian fellahin would be seen so far from the chōra where lie their farms, and never on horseback, especially not on the backs of such fine horses as ours. And because even Libyans, should they be seen wandering such remote and trackless places, might be questioned by Roman soldiers or bands of thieves or by the thugs of Theophilus—being myself a thug of Theophilus, I know exactly how such questioning will go—we will say we are traders intent on finding new and better routes to markets. As "questioning" often comes in the form of a swift and silent knife, we ourselves carry knives. I am skilled with knives. Once more Hypatia surprises me. Skillfully sinking a blade deep into a post, she tells me it is wonderful what one can learn from a sailing tutor.

We begin our search in silence, I because I am merely a servant, and she because I am merely a servant. So far we have seen nothing alive other than a distant cheetah standing perfectly still on the top of a ridge and three quick vipers slithering over the sand. This day we go farther, but still avoid the Nitria where the vast bulk of those who delight in suffering lurk. Ia'eh, Lais' filly, is mine as long as I have need of her. Lais herself, though I am told she once rode and rode well, is now more often found in her room writing her poems. Hypatia rides the spirited Desher. As Ia'eh means moon, Desher means no more than her color: red as Ra when he sang the world into existence. We have come many miles southwest of the city and still find our search hot and fruitless as one by one each grouping of caves is rejected for this or that reason.

In this lonely place Hypatia turns in her saddle. "Have you no home, Minkah? Does no one miss you or need you?"

"I have a home and there are those who need me."

I see she is shocked. "For weeks now you live with us, yet abandon your own?"

"Your family needs me. Your father tells me your home is my home."

"Does he now? And your family?"

"Who are they? I have never known."

"But where have you lived? Who has cared for you?"

"I lived in the Temple and the Temple is gone. As for who cared for me, I cared for me."

"But, as only a babe—"

"There was a woman. She took me by night to a garbage pit. There I would live or I would die, that was up to the gods. There was a man who came to the pits, as many do, to take away abandoned children for slaves. Imagine his surprise to find me a male, for most so abandoned are female. In any case, those who come choose only the strongest, so I did not die, but was seized by Jabari the Brave, a worker in wood and metal who had need of an apprentice he need not pay."

"You are a craftsman!"

"I was. Until I ran away to the Temple to escape Jabari, who was not so much brave as brutal. I made myself useful there. I shelved and I sorted and I learned to read."

There comes a strange light in her eye. I do not trust strange lights. "You can devise mechanisms from plans?"

"I can."

"Even if they be complex?"

"Certainly."

Hypatia says nothing more for an hour. I say nothing more for an hour. Banishing mothers and Jabari from my mind, I am remembering what I once read. Long ago, came to this desert a great king and all his men. But up rose a sandstorm as thick as the cough of Set in which all became lost and were never found again. I find I am telling Hypatia this with great enthusiasm. "...and since this is so, I wonder we have not seen their bones."

By the look on her face, I see she has not heard a word. By her speech, she admits it. "Your skill has caused me to think of a device I mean to make, a much improved astrolabe—Father's treatise on these has given me many ideas—as well as a thing that has long plagued my thoughts. As yet, I have no name for it, but when it is made it will allow one to see clearly what lies below water. Bones? What of bones?"

By now I have learned the mind of this one is a strange mind and a surprising mind. And it wanders. I am glad it is not my mind. How burdensome to live so much in the head. I live in my body and feed its desires. I glance at Hypatia, glance away. It seems a fine life to me, and one that gets better by the hour. I think of the sisters. Hypatia is all mind, Lais all spirit, Jone all bodily emotion. "Since the time of Augustus, Romans have banished men to this desert. Earlier, when the Persians conquered Egypt, King Cambyses II and his army of fifty thousand men vanished in a sandstorm and were never seen again. There must be bones everywhere."

"I have heard of this, Minkah. But men are banished to the oasis of Siwa, not here. And King Cambyses was supposedly looking for precisely that oasis in order to destroy the Temple of Ammon by traversing the Great Sand Desert. But surely, that is legend."

"Surely, it is not!"

"It is."

"It is not."

From this point on, she searches for bones as I search for caves. Sandstorms also occupy my thoughts. If one were to suddenly spring up, our bones would mingle with the bones of outcasts and Persians.

"Hypatia! Look!" Ia'eh has suddenly stopped as if she too knew what we look for. I am pointing at an outcrop of dark rock shimmering in the distance. "See how high that place is. When the rains come and flood the desert, the water would never reach here. And see how low it is. What solitary would find it alluring? And how far from any path it is! Should a wanderer lose himself here, he would not seek a way out through this place, but would turn and retrace his steps."

All is heat. It simmers in every direction. It causes the eye to create illusion of palace and temple and great ships of many masts. Hypatia asks, squinting, "It seems perfect. There is no oasis, no water. Are there caves?"

Standing in my stirrups, I shield my eyes with my hand. "Dozens of them."

"We must explore them all."

Glancing at the sun, I frown. "Already it will be dark before we return to the city. We have no time."

"The books cannot stay with Didymus. Neither he nor they are safe. You will search one cave and I another. We shall do this until it is dark. And then we shall sleep here, and begin again at first light."

I know what is so in the house of Theon. Hypatia has a class to teach on the morrow. If the daughter does not teach, the father cannot peaceably lie in his bed. If the father does not lie in his bed, how shall I be of use? "And your students?"

Hypatia shrugs. "They will come. I will not be there. They will wait. I will not appear. They will go home. The following day I will apologize, talk longer, and all will be forgiven."

As used to her wandering mind, I am as used to her fine and easy arrogance. I nod. We will spend the night. Seeing this, she whispers into Desher's ear, and we are away. I follow on Ia'eh, who seems like Pegasus, feathered in white.

I am *Parabalanoi.* I have done harder things than innocently sleep near a woman like this woman far out in the reaches of a wilderness with no man near. But not many.

Three times now, well laden camels have gone out into the night. And each trip I make, those who come with me are at a certain point blindfolded, and each trip I make is taken with different men, most poor, most Egyptians—none are fellow *Parabalanoi.* The caves I first sighted are many. Some reach so far back into the crest of rock, searching them, I could go no farther for loss of light. Some have caves within caves, only reached by crawling through tunnels jagged with sharp and twisted shapes. And some would end in darker holes into which I have peered and these would drop down and down into a deep that if not the Underworld, would certainly do.

If all goes well, and I do not die from the effort, the whole of Alexandria's great library, sealed in jars, will rest in the caves by the birthday of the Persian godman Mithras, though now given as birthday to the Christian godman Jesus. My new "family" grows used to these sorrows. Listening to Lais, I hear whichever godman claims it as his date of birth, it is still the return of the Great God Sun. What matter the new name they give him as he is the same godman? I had never thought of this. The same godman? Of course!

And so it goes. Alexandria believes it has lost its library and grieves. Christians, also believing, rejoice. We few both grieve and rejoice. The library lives, but as both Lais and Hypatia ask: at what cost?

And I, Minkah of the *Parabalanoi*, know the precise location of each cave, each jar, each book. A delicious irony.

BLACK WINGS

Autumn, 391

Hypatia

Seated on a raised chair in a lecture hall granted me in the Caesarium in full view of all, I speak...and as I speak all listen as if I were the sage so many call me.

I lecture on death. I ask them: is it truly possible to steal a life, if, as is written in the Katha Upanishad, the Self is eternal and cannot die? Should this be so, then one who "murders" does no more than transgress against the will of another, whose choice it is to live. At bottom, a murderer offends not against the body, but against the spirit.

Before me, a sea of uplifted faces stretching far to the back of the great hall begun for Mark Anthony by Cleopatra but finished by Octavian Augustus to honor himself, all seeking to hear as I am raised high in my philosopher's cloak before them. Not all are as mesmerized as is a young man from the city of Cyrene, Synesius by name. Not all are pleased. This would include the brother of Synesius, Euoptius who even now scowls at me from the first row of curved benches. There could be no brothers who look less alike. Or who act less alike. Synesius listens as if I were Socrates, Euoptius as if I were Jezebel.

And far from all understand. But no face is a woman's

face for females are not welcome here. All assume a female cannot learn, cannot reason. She is useful, but only in service to men. She causes lust, therefore is lustful. She is weak so must be protected, even from herself. Yet here they sit, scribbling in wax, forming groups to discuss what I have taught that day, following me wherever I go. They preen before me. They strut. Some fall to their knees, expose their breast so that they might expose their heart.

None were born blind; they see I have grown the breasts and belly of a woman. None were born deaf: they hear my woman's voice. So I must wonder: what do they think I am? Do they think me a monster, a chimera, a freak of nature?

There are those, I believe, who do.

I endure it all. They have paid to hear me, and paid me well. Most may lack curiosity and discipline, may never master a thing in this life save drink and dice and the begetting of children on women—even on me if I would allow them—and most are surely fools, but all share one important trait: ambition. None can become prefects or politicians or rise in the new religion without the distinction of a degree. And to receive such a degree from the increasingly famous Hypatia of Alexandria, ah! As for rising in the new religion, many seek a place because as members of the clergy, they are exempt from taxes. How else do the rich stay rich?

But who has hired me to speak; who allows me these past four months to lecture in this huge hall remains the secret of Didymus the Blind. I do not press him for answer.

Musing thus, I have paused so long in my speaking, I must be poked to resume. Who pokes me? Minkah, my gadfly, my irritant, he who sobers me when I grow drunk on myself. He seems also to guard me, but from other than unwelcome suitors, what need? Who am I?

Father's "man" has begun to please me. He pleases all in my family for one or another of his qualities. Minkah is skilled and if he has yet to master a skill, he learns it quickly. He can speak and when he speaks he makes sense. How many can this be said of? Not always of Father or myself, for scholars often do or say such truly foolish things. Even Lais has from time to time uttered nonsense. But what has convinced me is this: both Desher and Ia'eh greet him as quickly as they greet me who have loved them all their lives. Father cannot do without. Ife simpers. Lais seeks his advice. Jone pretends disinterest, but her interest is plain to all. And if I am honest, I am more than pleased. But to say more is to understand more, and I do not understand what it is I feel. This I *do* know. He is Egyptian. As I am a Greek, he can never do more than please me.

In my ear Minkah whispers, "Murder, mistress. You were saying..."

I shake my head to push his away. I do not need to hear what I was saying. I merely lost myself for a moment, and now I am found.

I finish this day's lecture on the nature of Divine Consciousness expressed within the self—which has so far been greeted by nothing more than the soft murmur of interest and the scrapings of stick on wax—by stating with great flourish that the most important concept ever put forth was that matter, *all* matter, with no exceptions from stone to star to starfish to student to sovereign, is as divine as all else in the cosmos, for all flows from Consciousness, the Word that came before the World—and all, in time, will flow back.

And oh! finally—an uproar. Euoptius of Cyrene has turned to face his fellows so he might address as many as possible in loud outrage. His brother, Synesius, makes no noise but stares up in mute dismay. I smile down at him, not sure he hears me say through the din that all this was spoken of by Hindu metaphysicians a thousand years ago. It would not help if he had heard. Many I teach are Christians and to Christians such thoughts are heretical. They tolerate the Greeks, admire the Romans, puzzle over the Persians...but Indians! Outrageous!

Oh foolish Hypatia! Does this clamor mean I shall be contradicted? Does it mean I have gone too far? There have been teachers banished, even stoned, for less. These are the sons of the rich. Without the rich, where should my family be now that I am their sole support?

No matter how they shout or scowl or smash their slates on the floor of the Caesarium, I hold to my seat. This is Alexandria. Freedom of thought and of expression *is* Alexandria. And I am Hypatia of Alexandria.

Behind me, unseen, Minkah has taken hold of my *tribon.* He will pull me back if he has to, force me to safety. But the uproar fades; the shouting is replaced by chatter. They are discussing the idea! Though none will accept it. My Christians think only their Christ divine. My "pagans" think divinity is gained by the few through pain and suffering. My pessimists think nothing is divine but do not say so for that is the most heretical idea of all.

Still, they give it thought. To think wrongly is better than not to think at all...although I may be wrong about this.

Leaving, I am delayed by that one who seems to see me as goddess, little good it does either of us. Synesius of Cyrene, an artless soul, is pushed this way and that by Euoptius, a brother who would have him a bishop. All Synesius desires of life are his horses, his dogs, the hunt, and, I suspect, me. Synesius lacks spine, poor youth; therefore, a bishop he may one day be.

He asks so many questions and so quickly, I hold up my hand for silence. "Synesius! You wear me out. If you wrote me a commentary, one I could read at my leisure?"

It is as if I have kissed him. His large eyes gleam. His small nose quivers. "Write? Of course! I will write you immediately." He is gone on the instant.

Kept so long, I must walk alone by a series of corridors leading away from the Caesarium and out into the stables behind. Minkah has gone on to ensure I am not troubled in the courtyard as I mount my chariot.

Ahead, just before the exit into sunlight, lies the deepest shadows, and from them steps a man in grey. Though I would push by him, I cannot. This one puts his hands on me. Is he an agent of the church and would he, as Minkah hints, wish me harm? His face, hidden by his grey cowl, is unreadable. The voice, when it comes, is also unreadable. "Will you be teaching more of this—"

I know his kind. I finish his question. "Blasphemy?"

But this one surprises me. "Philosophy?"

I have slipped out of his grip, would continue on my way. "I am a teacher. Knowing nothing for sure and thus open to anything, I teach what pleases me."

He has taken hold of me again, this time by the arm. "Is this true? You would listen to any thought?"

"Indeed. So long as it was well expressed."

"Then hear me," he says, shaking the cowl from his head, "I pass through this city on my way to Hippo. But I stopped for the renowned Hypatia. So young! Yet she spoke with words that shone like coins." I should thank him; instead once again I shake loose. He follows me. "I devoured the six sacred books of Mani. I believed what he taught. That there is no omnipotent good power. That all is a battle between good and evil and we are the battleground. Like you, I was a very pagan in my—"

Here, I stop not only myself, but him. "Call me no names. As a mathematician, an astronomer, a philosopher, nothing battles within but me with myself."

He smiles. For the first time I see his face. He is a man reaching his middle years, one with a certain way about him. There is power here. And intelligence. "And to think some now imagine astronomer the same as sorceress...gentle Hypatia—"

"Sir, mistake me not. Gentle describes my sister. It might even describe my father. But it does not describe me."

He smiles again. "In Hippo, though I go to become a priest for Christ, I dream only of the day when gentle will describe me."

"A given name would be more comforting."

"Forgive me! My name is Augustine and I have known women and loved them, but I have never known such a one as you. Barely grown and yet a great mathematician and an influential philosopher and a convincing orator! By you, I know God has once more spoken my name. See me, Hypatia. I, who once reveled in life, am now a man alone: my blessed mother, my beloved son, my lovers, my friends, all gone. That I could persuade you to join me in Hippo! There I could prove Socrates wrong. The height of wisdom is not that one knows nothing, but that one knows what the Savior would have you know. I beg for time to speak with you."

I stop for only a moment for Augustine deserves a moment. He reeks of need and of repression. He longs for what he forbids himself. And yet, he is sincere and intelligent. His proposal, if such it is, does not tempt me. As for his longing, virginal I am and virginal I mean to remain—or at least until I know my own longings—but that which lies back of his eyes repels and upsets me. He seeks assurance. He believes he believes, but his belief is not absolute. He asks for certainty. What is certain?

He holds out his hand. A soft hand, one that has known no toil. In it, he holds a small codex. "I ask that you become my mystical sister, my *soror mystica.* No more than a loving companionship. I would never touch you."

Augustine, on his way to Hippo, is owed at least honesty. "There is touching and there is touching. The touch you speak of, sir, scalds me."

He does not smile nor does he scowl. "I was once as you are now. Please, I beg you, accept this gift. It is only the beginnings of a book I might write, mere notes, but if you would read them?"

I take his slender codex as I step into the sunlight. Minkah, who has been impatiently looking, sees me do this. He sees Augustine who follows. My sweet irritant moves quickly, his hand on the hilt of a knife.

Augustine, who has wit enough not to follow, calls after: "You allow me no time to persuade you?"

"You must be in Hippo, Augustine. Have you eternity to spare?"

In no hurry, I guide my two grays away from the Royal Quarter. By the sun and the sea and the peaceable streets, who would know the darkness that spreads its wings more widely each day?

Wrapping the reins around my right arm as would a racing charioteer, I turn my head so that Minkah will hear me above the clatter of our iron shod wheels. "Do you make a trip tonight?" I mean more books to the caves.

"Yes. And you?" He means will Father and I work on our maps.

"All goes well indeed."

"This is good to know. Although..."

Nothing could prick my curiosity more deeply than hesitation. "Although?"

"Two nights back, I caught sight of one who watched us leave."

"But could they know what you do or where you go?"

"Probably not. But she puzzled me."

"She?"

"Jone."

I laugh, knowing what I know about my little sister and her interest in Minkah. "Jone! Jone has done so little with her life, I am pleased she bothers to watch what others do."

My laughter dies in my mouth. By this rising street and that, I have left behind the storefronts and workshops and come on the site of the Serapeum. It is not there. All that remains is the sphinx to its right and the sphinx to its left and the great pillar of Diocletian on its rock between. Though there is yet the great flat stone of its foundation, this is as swept clean of dirt and debris as Alexandria has been swept clean of its magnificent temple. Oh Seshat, sister of Thoth, what have they done?

Minkah and I ride home in silence as dark as the cave of Plato.

I find Father where I expect to find him—in bed. I expect to tell him of my day and then to return to a book I now read, the *Deipnosophistoe* of Athenaeus, which speaks of women mathematicians that even I, who search for such names, have never heard of. But I do not expect what follows. So soon as he sees me, he sits straight up, shoving away the books and papers and tablets and pens and ink stands and cushions that litter his bedding. He waves his arms. He raises his voice. Who in our house cannot hear him? Who in the house next door cannot hear him? "Daughter! Where have you been? Do you know who awaits you? I could not deny him entrance, but I could, and I *did*, banish him to our shabbiest chamber."

Men are forever demanding to see me. Did I not just meet another? What should cause Father to shout of this one? Content that he has said enough, he says nothing further, instead allowing his chin to sink to his chest, so I must finally ask, "Who is this man?"

"Who?"

"The man you banished to our shabbiest chamber."

"Ah! *Him*, that's who! The destroyer! 'What an ugly beast the ape, and how like us.' Who said that?"

"Marcus Tullius Cicero said that."

"And of all men, who should know better how beastly than Cicero, knowing well the beastly Caesar, Brutus, Pompey, Mark Anthony, Octavian." Father rolls his reddened eyes at me. "And what shall I do without my Hypatia who is my greatest solace? And what shall the beast do with *her*?"

"What on earth are you talking about? Why do you say you must do without me?"

"The thing who demands to see you is a Christian. It has come to destroy you."

A Christian? Mother Goddess Hathor! Two in one day? But destroy me? "And you did not throw him out!"

"How could I? He would not go."

Lately, there are times when Father becomes unbearable. This is one of those times. "My destroyer's name, please."

"Theophilus, the Patriarch of Alexandria."

And now I become, not frightened or outraged, but suffused with curiosity. Theophilus! Aside from the secular prefect Lucius Marius, eyes and ears of the Emperor Theodosius, Theophilus is the most powerful man in Alexandria. For the six years of his rule, I have heard he is ruthless. I have heard he is greedy. I have heard he is cruel. I have seen his terrible deeds, so what is said I do not doubt. But I have also heard he is learned and quick. Of course, I will see him. How often do I speak with one who might challenge me?

I am off and running for my room so that I might remove my philosopher's robe, when I run directly into Jone. And now, instead of Synesius of Cyrene or Augustine passing through to the city of Hippo, or Father in his bed, I am detained by her.

"Do you know who awaits you?"

"Yes."

"Might I come too?"

I am not as surprised as I might be. Jone has begun to stir herself. She has begun, as I have only just said to Minkah, to exhibit curiosity. It is my contention that true intelligence is not Aristotle and his gathering of facts and compiling of lists. Such things are the stuff of mental mechanics meaning ultimately nothing. Intelligence requires first the gift of curiosity. Without curiosity, who would ask questions? Second, intelligence is the ability to synthesize. Facts alone signify little. Neither are they to be trusted. Intelligence is the subtle arrangement of that which might or might not be true, the intuitive selection and the weaving of such selections into a pleasing whole that makes for meaning. Third, intelligence has need of laughter. Without laughter so much that is bitter and dark is allowed into being. That which is bitter and dark may be clever, it may even be cunning, but it is never intelligent. As for wisdom, wisdom is simple. The wise are able to recognize, and to accept, that not only is one never intelligent enough, but that when all is said and done, one knows exactly nothing.

Jone is not stupid. She grows curious. Now if only she might learn laughter.

Already in flight, I flee faster. "I...oh...why not? But be quick, Jone, and be quiet. I would see this one."

THE FIRST GATE

Hypatia

For the first time in months, I am made proud by Father. By "shabbiest chamber," he means a storage room off the pillared atrium.

Father's "beast" looks like any other man. Or rather, like any other rich and powerful man. As the daughter of Theon, never rich but still powerful for being Alexandria's leading mathematician, I have met many such. My life is full of the rich and the powerful. If I know few who have wisdom, I know many who have cunning. This one is cunning. But there is more. There is a cool appraising humor in the shape of his mouth, in the slant of his eye. His skin is bad. Though he is far from old, his face is creased and worn and cratered by pox. Even so, he is a presentable man and smells of cardamom and myrrh.

With Jone walking behind me (such a solemn little thing, so unknowable), and a silent unseen Minkah just beyond the door (unbidden but irrepressible), I have made my entrance. Green is the color of joy and confidence. I wear a long linen chiton dyed as green as malachite. I go without sandals. Philosophers are known by at least two things: their beards and their eccentricities. I can grow no beard nor do I live in a large jar or roll around naked, fornicating in public places.

I have yet to fall down a well while staring up at the stars. Because of this, I am granted my naked feet.

I wear no rings for rings would call attention to the ink, but I do wear a cameo of bloodstone on which is worked the Holy Tetrakys of Pythagoras. My guests will make of this what they will.

Theophilus does not come clothed in his office, but wears what an ordinary person of wealth would wear—save for the necklace of heavy gold and a turquoise ring on his finger. The stone is enormous, its owner larger still. His lack of robe or hat or staff does not diminish him; he fills the small room Father has sent him to.

I have never learned where Theophilus was born, nor do I know the name by which he entered the world (Theophilus is Latin for "god lover," which I suspect he gave himself), but I know the two who have come here with him. The first is named Isidore of Pergamon. Come from a family of wealth to study in Alexandria, he has found favor with Theophilus, enough that he is named archpriest. Not yet thirty, Archpriest Isidore attends my lectures, struggling with geometry, with certain philosophers, but excelling at history and at oratory. Is Father right—am I in danger? Does Isidore attend to serve as the eyes of Theophilus and is he here now to provide witness against me?

I am ashamed to tell it, but as it is true, I must: I am attracted to this one. His face lacks symmetry; even so, it somehow falls into place and is all the more interesting for it. There is an intensity in the eyes and the mouth that compels me to wonder: who is this Isidore? What irony if it should be he who betrays me.

The youth is another matter altogether. He is rounder than Jone and stands even shorter. His flushed face is wider, his full lips as red as liver, his eyes seem slits in leather. Never in one so young have I seen the mark of arrogance so deeply engraved on so unfortunate a face—or the sick containment of fury. He is outraged to be confined to a storeroom, made further rabid by the sight of me. Is this because I am female? Or "pagan"? Or that I teach, and am more often sought out by those who visit this city than his uncle? Each would suffice. Or is it merely because, as he believes himself a superior being, the rest of us sicken him? I think it a mix of all. If not constrained by his uncle, and the constraint is obvious, I believe we would hear a choice and wondrous flow of language. Longer than he can stare at me, I stare at this one whose name is Cyril and is the son of Theophania, the sister of Theophilus, notorious for her cruelty and the helplessness of those chosen to receive it.

As Minkah would say: buttfuck them all. I have not trained in the art of oratory to be taken down so easily by a religious tyrant, an insolent pup, and a spy. I have not fended off each and every advance not to know the rules of defense. Attack first. And quickly.

"My father tells me you mean to destroy me. Is this so?"

Theophilus' mouth opens twice before it makes sound. "Destroy you?"

He recovers rapidly, but I am as rapidly thinking. How did Cleopatra greet Octavian Augustus after the death of Anthony? Was she coy or was she brazen? One thing she was not, even if her inner parts quaked, was less than queenly. I shall act the queen. "You have destroyed so much of mine, it seems only wise to destroy me. Does your faith not wish to remove evidence of all that came before it, especially as all that came before, you now claim as yours? You have stolen dates and names and places and tales of the gods to give them all to your god as if they had never been used before. But you cannot steal me. I will not be silenced. Therefore, God Lover, what shall you do with Hypatia?"

"By God's testes!" exclaims he, looking round for a chair to throw himself in. There is much here, and most of it cast off busts of relatives come before, but chair there is none. "Isidore!"

"Father?"

The priest Isidore, no son of Theophilus, steps forward on the instant. He calls the man "father" for their faith knows no mother. Like dross: mothers, daughters, sisters, lovers, wives, are cast aside, while revering a sleeping maiden named Mary for being entered by "God." Do they forget Zeus? Zeus coupled with any comely maid who caught his eye, willing or unwilling. Yet Christians laugh at Zeus while praising their own seducer. A strange blindness indeed.

"I was not told I should meet an Amazon."

Isidore of Pergamon, the priest who troubles my thoughts, replies, "I knew you would see for yourself."

How disappointing. I am to be flattered before I am felled. If so, I should have hoped for at least wit.

"Embarrass yourselves no further. Why are you here?"

Behind me, I hear Jone give out her second small squeak. Twice now, she is shocked. Once for the word "testes" coupled with the word "God," and now by me. What else would I do?

Hold out my own hands for the binding thereof?

Theophilus, who desires to sit or better recline, but cannot, shifts from foot to foot. His arms bother him. Do they go inside his toga? Outside? Ignoble or no, I take much comfort in this... as does the rude round youth. Does he not love his uncle? Theophilus decides to hold out his hands, his innocent palms revealed. "But you are wrong, daughter of Theon. I hold you in the highest esteem. Neither man nor woman, but something apart. Why else would I suffer your father's ill-will? Why else would I wait on *you* rather than summon you to come to *me*? Why do I show my hand in bringing Isidore, your pupil, so you might know his connection—and why bring family?"

Theophilus has spat out his last word. It appears Theophilus has as little feeling for Cyril as Cyril has for him. Jone has sunk into a corner in this windowless room where shines only one lamp, but I stand in the center, forcing Isidore and his "father" and his father's nephew to take lesser places surrounded by staring stone heads, cast by shadows into hideous shapes. "Work awaits me. You suffer the House of Theon for some reason. If you mean to tell me it, do so."

Theophilus now smiles, a more tender smile than any I saw on the face of Augustine, who must by now, be halfway to Hippo—or so I hope. "I did not summon you for I would not have others know we spoke. I suffered your father because if I had not I should have been asked to leave. I brought Cyril as he expressed an interest in coming." I glance at the interested Cyril, who for the first time has the good grace to lower his impudent eyes. "I brought Isidore to prove he is no spy. He is also, whether you believe it or not, an ardent pupil and much devoted."

I slide my eyes towards this ardent pupil of mine. He makes no face. He does not try to support the words of his father. His lack of trying is subtly done and goes some way towards soothing the shame I feel for my private thoughts. I have said I was virginal and I meant what I said. But as life is as capricious as Paniwi the cat, any state can change.

And now, at last, Theophilus would come to the point. But first he nods at Jone. "She can be trusted?"

"She is my sister."

"Then I must tell you there are plans to have you killed."

Another squeak from Jone, but I am not surprised. Minkah, who hears what is said in the streets as we do not, has warned me of this. Already good with a knife, he goes now to take lessons in the sword and shield and the *pilum*, a throwing spear, from a Roman soldier he trusts. Minkah urges me to wear leather beneath my tunic but I will not. I am, I confess, slightly afraid, but I will not act as if I am.

"I assumed that was *your* plan."

"Your assumption is wrong. Your death would not serve. Rather, it would bring shame on my office. It would bring shame on my beliefs. As you say, and say rightly, I lust for what is yours. God would have your temples. These He has. That which funds your temples will become my funds. I...we, have won. It has taken many long years, but we have gained the souls of men and all your philosophy and all your numbers and all your sacred shapes and your mysteries which are not shared with them, marvelous though you see them, will not win them back. Men suffer and men are afraid. We offer them faith that their suffering will cease. Not on earth, of course. That will never happen. But in the afterlife, there they shall know comfort and peace. What do you offer? Difficult concepts, lofty idealism, secret doctrines, initiations they cannot understand, questions and more questions. We have answered all their questions. All they need do is accept our answers. And if the battle has been bloody, what battle has not? As to battles, which war among men has been more worthy? We fight for the soul. But I would not shed your blood, young woman. Those who think to do so are fools. By the death of Hypatia, whom the people take pride in for her writings and her teachings and her fame, we would lose much of what we have gained."

"I imagine those who think to do so disagree with you?"

"They do. I have listened to much passionate persuasion. I am not persuaded."

"And now?"

"And now I must shed the blood of those who would shed yours. A great pity, but there you are."

"Why do you tell me this?"

Strangely, I have again made him uncomfortable. Not as before, but in some new way, a way I often see in the eyes of men.

His answer comes. "Because I would have you know you are protected. I would have you know I am not some idiot barbarian, a Goth or a Visigoth or a Manichean. I say, who would kill such as you? You are a gift from God. There are Christians who call you Wise. Not one has reported that you seek to dissuade them from their faith. Not one has complained you subvert the Church. All praise your tolerance."

I do not glance at Isidore. It is true I do not attempt to

dissuade any from their faith, but I do try by the use of what I hope is sufficient reason to ease them into something more, something greater. Isidore has not told him this? I ask, "Why then would any among you want me dead?"

Theophilus closes his innocent hands. "No matter which side you take, even God's, there are those who are blind as well as base. We have our share."

"There is more. You are not telling me all."

"That is true. There is more. I allow you to live and to teach because by so doing I appear to be wise and tolerant."

"You want something in return."

"Also true. You will continue to appear wise and tolerant. Your pagans will be calmed. Calm pagans make for, if not calm, calmer Christians. I shall no longer incite my own for I have gained what it was I sought. Your temple is destroyed, your Museum closed, your books are lost. In time, Alexandria will be entirely Christian and this shall be by my doing. I may not be tolerant. I may not even be wise. But I am patient. The bloodshed will cease. There will be built, eventually, a Church of the Blessed Theophilus."

I see that Cyril would laugh. That he does not shows wise restraint. "You require only that I continue teaching just as I have been? But surely by this, you ask nothing of me."

"I am pleased you think so. Your salary and your hall which was mine to give, remains yours."

And with that, the Bishop of Alexandria turns with admirable grace, shooing along his graceless nephew, intent on leaving our house. As for me, I know now to whom Didymus spoke. I should have guessed. No one else but the Roman Prefect held such power; Theophilus holds more.

No doubt sent by Father to see if I still live, my sister Lais enters this shabby room. Behind her follows on Minkah, who knows I still live else he would have entered long since to ensure it.

The sight of Lais produces upon Isidore and on Theophilus, even on Cyril, precisely the effect it produces on all who see her. Awe.

As they leave, I doubt Lais notices either their going or their awe. But I notice Jone's little face. Her round eyes are rounder still and fixed on Isidore.

When all three are gone from our house and Jone is back to her books—or perhaps she now dreams new dreams, those that slow the mind but quicken the body, my poor poor Jone—Lais turns anxious eyes on mine. It is not the male who troubles

Lais. I can think of no male who has ever troubled Lais. Yet rare concern turns her brown eyes black. “Was it the books, Hypatia? Have they found the books, or suspect them? Does rumor reach them?”

I bless these moments when Lais is as human as I. Returning concern with concern, I take her hand. “No, Lais. They do not threaten the books. They threaten me.”

Lais does not find this laughable. Her eyes grow blacker.

I return to find Father dozing over his papers. I stare long at his face. Asleep, it is the face of a great man.

Leaning to kiss his forehead, behind which lives a great mind, I see he has made a mistake working alone on a problem suggested by the great Diophantus. He will never arrive at the correct answer if he continues like this. If Father were awake, I would not correct him for that would cause him shame. As he is asleep, I erase his error and the two that naturally but unfortunately follow, replacing them with the right notations.

He who was once Theon of Alexandria will never know.

And now I am sought by Jone who comes to tell me I have one more visitor before I might work on my portion of the maps. With boundless irritation, I follow her.

By the hock of Apis, it is Isidore.

I shoo away Jone who would witness yet another visitation. I cared not if she stared at Theophilus, but I care a great deal that she does not stare at Isidore.

Jone has not banished Isidore to a small storage room, but left him in the atrium where now he stands, near to the pool open to the sky where Lais keeps fish: Chromis shaped as a vulva, Abdju as silver as rain, and around which are the four sides to this section of our house.

He is first to speak. His speech is rushed. “I am come seeking a moment alone.”

“Yes?”

“I would say that though I love Theophilus who has done much for me, I am not Theophilus.” His intention is not entirely clear. Does he mean he is no bully as is his “father”? Does he mean he disagrees with what is done in the name of his faith? I am confused. “I mean, that I would not have you or your family harmed.”

“And Theophilus would?”

“He is like Athanasius of Alexandria; he would do what he felt he need do to protect the Church.”

Athanasius?" This one is telling me that Bishop Theophilus is as a bishop who came before, dead now for as long as I have lived? Oh, Bes, protector of families, save the world from such as Athanasius of Alexandria! Though revered by hundreds, thousands shudder at his name. Athanasius tortured all who disagreed with him, killed in great numbers Christians as well as "heretics," wrote heroic tales of himself that were lies from beginning to end. It is said that Athanasius founded the dread *Parabalanoi.* "Do you say that Theophilus would hurt my family?"

"I say he would not. Not now. Perhaps not ever. But it might not always be in his interest to choose to stand between you and those who love you not."

I spread my hands in honest surprise. "I am merely a woman, a teacher. I cannot harm your faith nor stop it from creeping like vines ever deeper into the heart and mind of man. I haven't the power. But did I have such power, I would censure no man's beliefs."

Isidore would reach for my hand, but restrains himself. "You are Hypatia of Alexandria. Hypatia is spoken of in the court of the Emperor Theodosius. He has become interested in you. It is too late to curb that interest."

"What are you telling me, Isidore?"

"That you must speak as if anyone listened, anyone at all."

I think of Cyril, who envies his uncle. I think of Cyril's mother Theophania who is said to keep virgins, both male and female, in order to watch them deflowered in the most unspeakable ways. I think of the men robed in black who gather each day behind those who come to my lessons, unmoving, unspeaking, hearing only their own dark thoughts. "By anyone," I ask, "does this also mean you?"

But he is gone without answer.

Looking up through the opening in the roof of our atrium, there is the small wanderer, Venus, who is also Inanna of the Sumerians. At sight of Inanna, I shiver. The Goddess of Love was stripped of her garments one by one as she passed through the seven gates into the lower world of the kingdom of Kigal, so that when she stood before the Great Lady under the Earth, her own sister Erishkigal, Inanna was naked.

Immediately, Erishkigal, who hated her, had her killed and hung on a hook—and when she died, the world above died with her. Yet she rose in three days and the world was born again.

There is more, and like unto tales told of Jesus, but I have had enough of this day. As for this night, I choose not to see it, so retire to my room and my maps. Instead I find Augustine's notes for his intended book on my table. I had forgotten Augustine. I read the first page and the second. I am fascinated. He confesses to much that is base yet aspires to that which is sublime. That he hopes to find this sublimity in what is now a chaotic, divisive, and violent "faith" intensifies my interest. I read until I am forced to sleep.

If thought of Isidore intrudes, each thought is shut in a store room and sealed with the rosette of Inanna, Goddess of fertility.

Fertility of body is not my path. My path is fertility of the mind.

I dream this night of caves. I have had this dream many times, although it is never the same dream. In some the caves are vast, in others so small I would need curl into a ball to fit. All are dark and cold and distorted into shapes I could not draw and can barely comprehend.

I wander through my dreaming caves searching. I think I am looking for Lais who cries. I think I am looking for Jone who cries. I look for a child who cries.

No matter how many caves I find, there is always another cave. No matter how many tunnels I climb, there is always another, higher, cave. No matter how deep I go, there is always a lower, deeper, cave. And no one is ever here and I sob in my dream.

This night, I dream I find not Lais or Jone but Minkah. By looks alone he seems not to be, but I know it is he. He stands before a wall of dark green rock. The rock is smooth and unblemished and he would write on it. But no words form under his brush, instead comes forth strange inky insects which flap strange inky wings as they seek to gain height, but instead must crawl. By their numerous feet, these leave behind slight black tracks over the green of the wall, and each track makes some sort of ultimate sense, but I cannot understand the sense they make.

Minkah the Egyptian writes and writes and writes until the cave is filled with tracks and the whir of wings.

WHITE WINGS

Winter, 391

Hypatia

For months Augustine has sent letters, at least one a day, often two—including, in its entirety: *On Free Choice of the Will*—and each a closely reasoned, densely worded, discourse on what concerns him most: evil. Not merely the idea of evil, but its manifestation. Therefore why choose to read this day's letter before all others? Because it is suspiciously short. No letter from Augustine is ever short. Moments later I run for Lais.

"He means to visit!"

"Who means to visit?"

"Augustine!"

Lais, looking up from her own letter, smiles. "The priest in Hippo who admires you so?"

"The one who writes me so. More than Synesius!"

"But you welcome his letters."

"Letters are not the man. And I cannot say no, please, I am busy—which I am. I cannot plead that I have lectures to give, commentaries to write, books to read, hours I must devote to Father, there is a device I design, and this week alone I meet with three who have come from Rome just to see me."

"Write him back. Tell him he cannot come."

"I cannot!"
"Why not?"
"Because he is already here!"

My life has become Augustine. What I do, he does. What he says, I hear...for if any can talk, it is this man. But he cannot sit still. Nor can his face remain at rest. It changes as his thought changes—and his eyes! Augustine's eyes are as beautiful as a pond deep in the rushes. His robes carelessly worn, his sandals mended and mended again, his hair a cloud of black turning white, he must be out and about. He does not ride. Chariots are a horror. So we walk. By now, there could be no place in Alexandria he has not seen. Born here, raised here, by walking its streets, I have now been where I have never been. If before my city delighted me, now it astounds me. I know wide straight streets and sea air. I know scented rooms, pools of golden fish, and cloth of finest linen. I know flights of words and of numbers. I consider the stars and dream of distant worlds. But others know crooked streets as narrow as hallways, rags stiff with filth, rats underfoot, the scat of pigeons and hawks as a thick and irksome rain, and altars to countless gods each demanding sacrifice of blood or of purse—and the noise! The importuning that we buy some questionable thing! The hands that reach out, the spit as we pass—by the formless mud of Nu, I had no idea!

As for Augustine, raised in a dusty backwater along the coast of North Africa, knowing only Rome and Milan, and now the undistinguished Hippo Regius, he shivers with joy. He would be a teacher, he would instill his passion in others; in Hippo, he has, so far, taught his students nothing. But he bursts with ideas on teaching. He tells me there are three types of students. The first has been taught well, the second has not been taught at all, and the third has been badly taught but does not know it. A teacher must adapt to each of these, and the most difficult type is the last, for this student believes he understands when he does not. Augustine also believes a teacher must allow his students to speak, even to encourage their questions.

In this, I find much to ponder. I see I have not been much of a teacher. Listening, I hope to become a great deal better. As for evil, he asks *why* is the world so fraught with danger? *Why* do so many, even those who enjoy comfort, also suffer pain and sorrow? *How* does a man bear to know that all he does, even if good, comes in the end to nothing but dust and emptiness?

Looking up from all this, I find we are in the Jewish Quarter. A maze of streets, large and small, some of the houses are as old as Alexandria itself. From the beginning, this place is home to our Jews.

"Come, friend," I say, "Let me show where once lived a great man."

It is not far, the small house I seek, the one with a small blue door through which once passed the philosopher Philo Judaeus of Alexandria, but to stand before it seems for Augustine a shrine. "Philo lived here?"

"He did."

"You have read his De Presidentia? *'God is continually ordering matter by his thought...there never was a time he did not create, for the Words have been with him from the beginning.'* Sublime!"

"Tell me then, Augustine, if you believe as did Philo, that matter is ordered by God's thought, would that not mean evil exists in the thoughts of God?"

For this I receive only a startled eye. "Why," he asks, "is this house not marked in any way?"

"That it remains and is tended, marks it."

I think Augustine torn between body and soul. And I, torn between mind and soul, almost understand him. In the belief that body hinders the soul, he denies the body, and so is tormented. In torment, he finds his "evil," and tries to escape it by defining and redefining it. His self-set task becomes an obsession. For me, evil has begun to blur. This, I think, the doing of Lais. For all I call evil, she calls experience. For all I lament, she calls adventure. Beyond generous, beyond accepting, her generous accepting infuriates by stealing away my righteousness. Angered by this or saddened by that, I do as any—find voice in righteousness. Yet truly, righteousness is not a gift but a curse. To believe one is right is to believe another wrong. If the other is wrong, then one has the right to "correct" him. Correction comes in many guises, and most I would call "evil."

Because he would see the great lighthouse and because he would see where Pompey Magnus, seeking asylum from the last of the Ptolemies, was cut down as an ill-fated gift to Caesar, we walk across the Heptastadion. Alexander's causeway, seven times the length of a Greek stadium, links the Island of Pharos with Alexandria on which sits the village of Pharos.

Augustine takes it all in at a glance, saying, "The pirates of Pharos are much like the burgers of Hippo: uneducated, filthy, smelly, and loud."

"Do the people of Hippo steal? Do they stare and talk behind quick hands?"

"Of course."

"Then I should no more wish to see Hippo than I would wish to remain here."

Where before I received a startled eye, now I receive one stern. "Who do you teach, Hypatia? Would you not say that the need of these exceeds all others?"

"No."

"No?"

"The needs of my family come before all."

"These *are* your family."

"There are those who are worthy and those who are not. All of nature teaches us this."

I have displeased him. Augustine turns his idealistic face away. Would he have me lie and call all men and all women equal? I do not speak of status or wealth or comeliness. I speak of intelligence. Few can reason. Fewer reason well. Genius is as rare as a mermaid. I have never seen a mermaid and every genius I have ever known, I know from books. "The shadows lengthen, Augustine. My family awaits me."

At the southern end of the Heptastadion, within sight of the Alexandrian docks lying to the right and to the left, we are stopped by the raising of the platform to allow a grain ship bound for Rome to pass through from the Royal Harbor into the Eunostos Harbor, and here we come on a most terrible sight.

A small crowd, one gathered only by happenstance, is also stopped on their way into the city.

A man is being beaten with cudgels. Already he is down to his knees, his hands covering his head, blood streaming down from both head and hands. Who beats him? Three! And each a fearsome thing with teeth bared as a dog's teeth. A fourth, huge as a bear, stands between us and the blooded man. Behind us, the people watch, terrified, huddled together as a flock of goats before lions. They would help, but how? They would not help. I have no knife, but should I have, I would be no match for the bear of a man. I can think of none who would be a match. Augustine has no knife or cudgel. He has no stick or stone. But he walks forward shouting, "Stop this! You will kill him!"

Not one pays the slightest mind. The poor thing, a merchant by the look of him, is now flat on the ground where they can kick him as well as hit him. But Augustine has caught the attention of the bear of a brute. It walks forward as a bear would walk, to pick up my friend as easily as it would pick up a child, only to throw him down on the stones. I make no sound save a moan deep in my throat. Augustine is back up as fast as he can speak. "I insist! Stop in the name of Christ!"

Near me, a woman clutches a babe. What she says, she says to herself, but I hear. "They *do* this in the name of Christ."

I turn to her. "What do you mean?" She would say no more, but I ask again, "What do you mean?"

If she whispered before, now it's only a breathing: "*Parabalanoi.*"

Oh, I see. I understand. The brotherhood. I have heard them called angels. We are told they bury the dead, tend to the ill, care for the widow. We are told they are a select and loving order of Christians who do the good work of the Bishop of Alexandria. But twice as often, I have heard them called thugs. I have heard them called demons. If I were ill or widowed or dead, I might bless them. But I am alive and I do not bless them. These are the men who killed so many at the Serapeum, these and the monks of the Nitrian mountains.

"But what has he done?"

"He follows the teaching of Arius."

By Discordia, but how Christians bicker—worse than astronomers. They hold councils denying this and claiming that. And now they publically punish one who thinks as the priest Arius of Alexandria taught: that the Son is not equal to the Father? I cry out as the bear reaches once again for my Christian friend, "Come away, Augustine! Come away!"

"How can I leave," he replies, "knowing God must weep. You run, Hypatia, but I will not."

And with these words from Augustine, the eyes of the bear find mine.

The man who is beaten lies still, the three who have beaten him, turn away. And when they turn they turn as the bear turns, towards Augustine and towards me.

"Hypatia?" says one of the three, not large and not small, but covered in blood not his own, and my name in his mouth is as dirt. He spits it out. "Is this the woman who thinks to teach men?"

Those who have cowered and watched move away from me, and away from my talkative friend. The path is clear now. The drawbridge down, the ship on its way to the sea, and the woman with her babe flees across towards the docks of Alexandria. If

I had a babe in arms, I should be running with her. But I do not have a babe and my friend neither moves nor speaks, but stands where he stands, facing these "angels." If Augustine does not leave, I cannot leave. But what it is I *can* do, I have yet to determine, save pushing him off the causeway into the harbor in the hopes though he does not ride, he swims. This is a good idea, a fine idea. I am a strong swimmer. We could be gone on the instant. And as the three start towards me, I start towards Augustine with a mind to shoving as hard as I can.

"Felix Zoilus!" shouts he who has asked in a kind of furious wonder if I teach men, "Stop her!"

But the bear called Felix Zoilus will not stop me. Father's tutors have done their work. If I must, I can be as an acrobat, tumbling towards Augustine, and if I must, kick him into the sea, following on as a maid from Minos using the horns of a charging bull to somersault over its back. I prepare my leap, up on my toes, my thighs tensed, my balance perfect—but I am suddenly grabbed by the edge of my tunic and pulled...and this is not done by Felix Zoilus or by any of the three who have begun to move towards me. A voice sounds in my ear. "Run, Hypatia. Follow the woman and run."

Minkah!

"But Augustine...?"

"Trust me, beloved. Augustine is safe. Now, run!"

And instead of my shoving Augustine, I am shoved by Minkah, and I run as I am told, but as I run I look back to see Minkah standing before the three as well as before the bear of a man and none seem inclined to harm him. He has taken Augustine's arm, is pulling him away, and Augustine allows this.

Great Ammut! How brave our Egyptian. Where once I saved Minkah, now he saves me.

Knowing Minkah will guide my friend to his lodging, I race home on bare and flying feet.

But he has called me "beloved." In such times, any can make a mistake. He must have been thinking of Lais.

I do not tell Lais of my day on the causeway. I do not tell Father. Augustine, packing to return by ship to Hippo, does not mention it. As for Minkah, we say not a word to each other. It is as if it never happened...even the stable lad I sent to see if the man lived, and to help him if so, found no one there.

Accepting water from the jug held by a servant, Lais turns her face to me, a face I judge all beauty by. "From this place, Miw, I see all that gives my heart its greatest joy. To have you with me completes the world."

"Sister! I love none better than you. If it would please you, we shall sit here forever."

Lais laughs. Her laughter never stings or shrinks my heart but is as the music of the lute lifting my spirit.

We recline, my sister and I, on divans in a garden we grow on our roof and from this garden the blue harbors deepen before us and beyond Pharos glimmers the green and shifting sea. Behind us the gold of the city shivers in the sun.

We have done exactly nothing for an hour save speak now and again of horses and books. Because of this, what Lais says next unsettles me.

"What do you make of Minkah?"

"Our Egyptian?"

"The very one."

"What should I make of him? He is Father's man. That he serves Father is all I require."

"Is it?"

"Indeed! What else?"

"Nothing else. I suppose."

"Lais! What do you mean by this? Minkah is a servant."

"Is he?"

"Do I discourse with Socrates? A question for every question?"

"Socrates was, of all men, wisest."

"And you are, of all women, wise as well. Was he also cunning?"

"Who?"

"Socrates!"

"I am not cunning."

"Exactly what I would have said a moment ago."

Lais shifts on her divan, reaching for a fig. Full of grace, yet I note her hesitate, though it is gone in an instant. Even so, I wait to see it again for anything that troubles Lais, troubles me. But it is gone. It was nothing. Lais pops her fig in her mouth. "Do you not think Minkah an interesting man?"

"That he can fashion what I design, this I find interesting.

That he follows me wherever I go, this I find interesting. I have asked him why and he answers: to protect me. I tell him I need no protection. I say I have walked these streets alone as a child. I drive them now alone as an adult. I have never needed a watchdog before. I need none now. Lais! Why on earth do you speak of Minkah?"

"I find him an interesting man."

"You find all of interest."

"Yes, to a degree. But some I find more interesting than others." And here her sloe-eyes are so full of impish humor I can do nothing but flush and turn away.

We are silent again. Lais has sunk her barb. I think of Minkah. An interesting man? An Egyptian, a servant, a creature of the streets, a lover of tall tales and epic adventure. One who called me beloved...but could not have meant me. Could I speak to Minkah as I speak to Augustine? To Father? Even to Synesius? Of course not. I now reach for my own fig but miss my aim, knocking Lais' cup to the tiles. Before I can retrieve it, she has already bent over to do so. Comes a hiss of pain through her teeth.

"Lais! What ails you?"

The one I love most in all the world retrieves her spilled cup, sets it back on the table. "Nothing that will not pass, Miw. Hopping down from Ia'eh, I twisted a muscle in my hip."

"You rode without me?"

"Who has time to ride whenever she pleases and who does not? All that is mine I owe to you."

"I would give you all seven times over."

"I know. But tell me true, is there not something else you see in our Egyptian?"

"Lais! Stop!"

BOOK TWO

"O my Mother Nut, Stretch your wings over me; let me become like the imperishable stars, like the indefatigable stars. O Great Being who is in the world of the dead, At whose feet is Eternity, In whose hand is the Always, Come to me. O great divine beloved Soul, Who is in the mysterious Abyss Come to me."—Egyptian inscription

THE CROAKING OF RAVENS

One year later
Winter, 392

Minkah the Egyptian

I, Minkah, am become Theon's right hand, his left hand, his two skinny legs, and often his sodden head. I empty the pot he pisses in. I sponge his backside. I bring his meals and his drink so I might all the more empty his pot and wash his ass.

I know now the meaning of Theon's name: "to rush." Being alone when I learned this, I barked with laughter.

In any case, I do all I do for the sake of Lais and for the sake of Hypatia. I also do this because now that I have insinuated myself into their home, it is understood that I shall remain here. Theophilus has at long last learned of the meetings in Theon's bedroom. It was inevitable that he would.

Today as many as a dozen crowd round my "masters" bed, all eager to hear the news from Rome. I doubt Theon remembers Rome, much less has news of it. But the more I hear, the more I understand why these men are so interesting to Theophilus.

Pappas stands before Theon, his back to the room, so that only Theon and I might see his face. Pappas is silently urging his old friend to speak out, even to sit up, for sitting would be at least something. The rest still hope the old rag will act the pivot around which all circles. Pappas catches my eye and I his. We say each to each: Theon is not what he was nor will he be. Daily he retreats farther into his bed as a snail into its shell. By eye alone, I promise Pappas I will do all I can to hide this. By eye alone, he thanks me.

Turning back, Pappas speaks as if it were Theon speaking. "Valentinian is dead in Vienne!"

"Ah!" say all with varying degrees of delight.

"Made co-regent at seventeen by Theodosius, now that he is twenty, he hangs himself...or has been hung. Whichever, Valentinian is no more."

Helladius, as much a stump as ever, fingers a curl of cheese left in Theon's bowl. Has he the nerve to eat it? "Either way," he yells, deciding against the theft of cheese, "how exciting for Rome! Romans are lovers of blood, the more blood the better. If it were to rain blood on Rome, full half would fill the streets holding buckets to catch it."

"Well said," laughs Pappas, "and what will you say when I tell you more? Fierce Arbogast, Valentinian's Frankish general, has—without consulting Emperor Theodosius—elevated Valentinian's secretary, one Eugenius, to the Purple?"

Helladius is too astonished to say anything. As for the rest, they gawk.

As if delivering a lecture, Pappas now strolls about the room. "You can imagine the poor soul is terrified, having been only a secretary the day before. But Arbogast reminds him that he, Arbogast, commands the whole of the Western army." Clever Pappas turns himself into a fatherly Arbogast babying the frightened scribbler. "Calm yourself, little Eugenius. Good Arbogast is here while the bad Theodosius is many hard miles away in Constantinople and confused. Will he accept what is done and hope for the best? Will he march on Rome? The distance is hard and it is long and the men who defend you are well-fed and seasoned. Better yet, they march nowhere but rest right here." Pappas drops his Frankish voice. "Friends, I save the best for last."

One turns to the other who turns to another. There is better news than this? What is it? What can it be?

"Eugenius the Terrified has reopened the temples for pagan worship."

Theon has raised his head. Even his eyes focus. "Why?"

Pappas whirls round at the sound of his voice. "Because Eugenius, the new Emperor of the West, who claimed as do thousands to be Christian so they keep their skin, is at heart a pagan."

Those gathered round the bed of Theon rub their hands, or thump each other's back.

"Eugenius relights the eternal fire in the Roman Forum, reforms the Vestal Virgins, and has ordered the Altar of Victory, stolen by Octavian Augustus from the Greeks, put back in the Curia of the Senate."

Now all in Theon's room hug each other, weeping.

Pappas holds up a hand and when all finally notice, each snivels to a stop. "This news will spread faster than fire throughout Egypt, mother and father of Life itself. But never forget that for now we are governed by Theodosius in Constantinople and not by Eugenius in Rome."

Helladius sneers. "But Arbogast is the stronger. Theodosius the Tyrant: emperor, destroyer, slanderer, heart-breaker, is weakened, as are all who take their power from him."

"That may well be, Helladius, but until all this is settled, we must take care. Who can say what the gods will wish on us?"

The face of my dear friend, the Bishop of Alexandria, rises before me. He knows no more than these what any god wishes, even his own. So just in case, the fucker of goats bars his door and sets his guards. I think of the Christians who everywhere surround us, of the black monks gathered in the deserts, of the "thugs" who do the bidding of this bishop. I look from dreaming face to dreaming face. What they dream of is as likely as Jews admitting they had never set foot in Egypt, never been slaves, never fled through a Yahweh-parted sea. It is as likely as Egypt once again ruled by Egyptians. How many emperors have come and gone, each dying by the hand of another who would be emperor? How many have been emperor in one place while another claimed the title in some other place, so setting their soldiers and their gods each against each? How many barbarians will ride out from their unimaginable wastelands to uphold this emperor or that emperor so they too might cloak themselves in the Purple? How long before all the Purple is barbaric?

I have a task of my own this day so I shoo them out. "Come again," I say, "Anytime." By now, all I say is taken as my master's wishes. They are gone in minutes.

Where do I look first? A man like Theon, easily broken, a father who does not support his family, cannot defend the books. Those who surround him seem not to see this, but I do. If not for me, the father would expect Lais, made of air, to wait on his every need. If not for me, Jone, made of wood, would see, buried in his own interests, her father forgets she lives. As for my darling, who I guard by stealth now as I did last week and last month and last year, by her labors she carries her father as if she were a cup and he precious water in the dry times. In truth, Hypatia carries us all. Because of this, I do what I intend no one to notice. I pay for what Theon most whines for: pens, ink, paper, books, the salary of a scribe who is here only when Hypatia lectures. She will never know her father not only fattens on her, he fattens on me...odd choice of words, these, as Theon does not fatten at all, but shrinks by the day. I move his legs daily so that if he must, he might still have use of them. Humming as he sums, he pays me no mind. Nor to Hypatia, other than her use in his work. I resist twisting his toes. I resist many things.

I will never abandon this house, even should he take against me. But when I must leave for an hour or a day, called by the oath of Brotherhood, I pretend I take lessons in defense. I need no lessons. By might of arms, I am able to defend them all. There are other ways as well to be gone from the house, less ostentatious ways, for just as Theophilus keeps watch over Theon, I keep watch over Theophilus.

I have two problems. The first I can solve. The second I cannot. The first is that Theon holds one of three maps. Meletus holds another. Didymus another. If Meletus or Didymus were to be discovered, either would die before surrendering their copy. Would Theon? The answer is a simple no. Therefore he cannot hold a map.

The second is Lais. Though she would have no one know, Lais is ill.

Hypatia

Five years before my birth, a monstrous wave rose up like the Sea Goddess Scylla, swallowing all that was finest of Alexandria.

The Emperor Theodosius is as Scylla.

This day, Pappas informs us that Theodosius has forbidden, on pain of death, all worship but Christian worship in what empire remains to him.

Alexandria, my beloved city, remains to him.

I sit alone on royal walls, broken by earthquake and wave, these last few tumbles of stone all that is left of the great Palace of the Ptolemies. Behind me the Bruchion district once stretched out under its shadow, before me the two harbors still carry ships both great and small, and Pharos with its eye of fire still stands.

Gazing up at an eternity of wheeling light, at mystery beyond mystery beyond all mysteries, I know myself to be as mortal as Cleopatra, as easily swept away as her palace, as small as Pharos placed next to the sun. My world is slowly dying as an alien world is born all around me, one that comes as Jone came, in pain and blood and the death of the mother. And yet, the stars fill me with something akin to the rapture of Lais, pure in itself, containing no part that longs for some other, for here time itself stops, space knows no end, and death is a thing so inconsequential that to fear it seems more than foolish, it seems wasteful of life.

Is this what inhabits my sister who need not look at the stars? If so, even with starry awe, my heart is yet troubled. My city bleeds, Father fails—and I am as doubtful of self as ever, even as my lectures attract scholars come from everywhere.

I have written of all this to Augustine. He writes back, asking: and what shall complaint accomplish? I am chastened.

The dream of the caves in which I wander comes nightly now. Minkah has never again appeared. But each night I find myself lost there and each night I search for a child. So odd, so terribly odd as I know I will never give life to another. Will Jone? Will Lais? Lais does not live as a woman, nor yet does she live as a man. Lais is Lais.

Unless Jone should marry, three daughters are the last of the line of Theon of Alexandria, a father who poured into an unworthy daughter all he would have given a much more suitable son.

It is cold and I shiver as I ride Desher home. I have work to do, letters to answer, a book lies open on my table that I would read. But my thoughts turn to Minkah. I find my thoughts turn often to Minkah. He has become my father's son, but how should I complain of that? Without our Egyptian and his teaching thereof, Father might all the sooner have faded away. No one did more to save the books than he. No one concerns themselves more with my safety. For all this and more, Lais and Jone and I would welcome him at table. But if Father will not come, and he does not, Minkah refuses. I am sorry for this.

Minkah has the wit to make us laugh. Once we all laughed. Laughter is our greatest loss.

Home again in my own room by my own window, I begin anew the letter that came this day from Augustine, but now, quieter than the mouse Lais names her, Jone appears. And then, oddest of all odd things, she who seldom speaks, speaks to me. "Father does not love me."

I am cast into a cave of sorrow. Jone is right. Father does not love her. But this is not to be said, not by me, not by anyone. I had even hoped it would not be known, but Ife knows and it's why she makes it her business to soothe Damara's lost babe. I, who can speak of anything at any time, am silenced and my silence is complete.

My clever little sister hears me. "So you know it is true. He loves you. He loves Lais. He loved Mother. But he does not love me. He thinks it was I who killed her."

I manage a startled, "No!"

Sudden as a snake, Jone's head swivels on her neck. "You will not lie to me! Not you!"

This from Jone, so quiet, so still, so passive? In humbled return, I say, "I will not lie."

"Then you know he thinks this."

"I do."

Jone does not cry. I have never seen her cry. But she has closed her eyes and sits now, and if she does not weep, it is only from strength of will. "I am not loved, not even by you."

I would gather her up in my arms; I would croon to her as I have seen Ife croon. But Jone does not allow me this. All I have left are words. "You are right. It is not my place to speak for others. But as for me, I have always loved you. Though I do not know you, though you keep yourself hidden, I love you with all my heart."

Jone does not melt at my true words. Instead, she stares deep into my eyes. If I do not lie, if I love her as I say I do, can she trust me? Jone has need to speak.

"Tell me what you have come to say, Jone. I promise I will not repeat it or judge it."

A moment more, a looking round to make sure we are unobserved, a flick of her tongue across her lips: "I have been reading." If I say, "Of course," she will sense the irony. If she senses irony, my serious little sister will walk away, and that will be that. I am silent. "And I have spoken to some who convince me. I have decided to convert."

As she says nothing further, I must ask, though I fear I

already know, "Convert to what?"

"I would be Christian." It is hard, but I do not react. "Do you know *why* I would be Christian?" I cannot imagine. Our family is high-born, literate, and Greek. Father and I are in love with reason. Lais is love itself. I shake my head: no, I have no idea. Jone waits to give me her answer. If she times it for effect, her timing is perfect as is her almost whisper. "Because the Christian Father forgives."

I count the moments so that my timing equals hers. I absorb what has been said to me. I decide. "In that case, little one, we must find you a school."

At this, Jone's face changes as lightning changes the dark. She, who seldom touches any, throws her arms around my neck, and cries, "I could not ask, but you guess! Clever Hypatia." And with that our "Panya" leaves as swiftly as she came.

I cannot return to my letter. Any awe that was mine has fled. It is not fear or concern that Jone turns Christian that grips me. It is *why* she turns Christian. If I were to tell Father, would it matter? He cannot love what he cannot love. And Jone, by this night's conversation, is no fool. He cannot now pretend to love what he cannot love.

Tomorrow I shall enroll her in the Didascalia, the Catechetical School of Alexandria.

How useful Didymus is to my family. May he live forever.

And how difficult life these last two years. But surely, as Heraclitus wrote, it will turn and turn again.

The first month of 393

Students curve round me as a cat's tail curves round a seated cat. Half the Caesarium is filled.

I have managed no more than a moment concerning the incommensurate dimension of lines forming the sides and diagonals of the square, saying these represent an imponderable mystery leading us to the precipice of the infinite, beyond which all certainty is lost for here the thinking mind loses all comprehension and stands before the mystery of the All, when of a sudden, there comes a strange heat and then a great silence—and then, a tipping of the dais toward the sea. I am thrown first to one side of my chair, then to the other. The floor before me sinks. And then, with a tremendous jolt, all is thrown down by Eris, Goddess of chaos. What has stood upright, falls, what has lain flat, rises, what has kept silent, roars. A crack opens in the tiled and painted ceiling high above, dropping gorgeous chunks of deadly debris down upon us. In seconds, the air chokes us with dust.

All know what happens here. All shout or flee or cower under stepped benches, one pushes at that which he cannot remove, another crawls dazed and bleeding towards nothing. Four surround the one who is trapped, failing to lift away the stone.

I have never endured an earthquake of size, never felt other than feeble tremors. That which caused the wave that took the palace took also the lives of thousands. It took the city of Cyrene. What will this one take?

Leaping from my chair, I would not be elsewhere, not if it would square the circle or renew the reading of Sappho.

Running out through the swaying pillars of the lecture hall and into the swaying Street of the Great Harbor, Synesius of Cyrene is right behind me, his brother Euoptius right behind him. But Minkah runs before us.

We four come to an abrupt and shocking halt. Everywhere, the tops or the sides or the carved concrete moldings of the buildings are gone. Octavian's two stolen obelisks shift on their bases so that, in looking, my own head shifts. Will they fall? Will the salted green waters pour in yet again, flooding the harbors and the canals, swallowing in one huge gulp the city itself?

No matter if they are Christian or if they are not Christian, my students scatter.

I do not run. I turn where I stand, surveying what has come of this shaking. Minkah turns with me, as does Synesius and his brother. For a time even Euoptius is open-mouthed before the gods, for not only is he shocked, he is stunned by a piece of fallen gilt. Near the palace of Hadrian, there are *insulae* of many stories where are housed the masses, each *insulae* five and six, even seven, stories tall, and in some floor after floor can be seen, sagging now without support, and what was inside falls outside: beds, tables, dishes, baskets, lamps, terra cotta pots, cradles, even the poor cradled babes themselves. The staircases, steep narrow things onto which people cling, lean out and away, as do sewage pipes. Of these, many are broken. And beneath these, the side streets are close to impassable from all that has fallen upon them. Everywhere there are the dead and the wounded. Everywhere there is panic and lamentation. Downed horses scream, oxen bellow, all the birds have flown. Everywhere there are those who clamber over unutterable destruction in an attempt to gather their goods or rescue their kin. All smells of human waste. All is the color of dust and blood. The sun at noon is pale and gives no heat. Everyone calls out for their god. The din is incredible.

Minkah would go where I would go. But I beseech him to take the horses; he must see to Father and to my sisters. As for me, I seek the worst damage. I would find the deepest widest fissures.

Augustine and his thoughts of evil rise up in me. If we are good, say many, the gods are good. If we do evil, the gods exact their toll. How then do the good die in earthquakes and the bad earn kingdoms by grievous murder? Why does the earth shake in some places and never in others? Good men and bad reside everywhere. Proud Eratosthenes, he who first named the search for such answers "geology," asked these same questions when he was not measuring the earth. The sober Aristotle also asked. Augustine asks now. But none know the answer. I ask: could the shaking become so tremendous it would split the world in two?

There is a second, larger, stronger, jolt and the street I run on moves under my feet like a woven mat pulled along the floor. I would fall to my knees, even land flat on my face, were it not for the strong arm that stops me. It is not Minkah. Minkah is away as I bid him. It is not Synesius nor is it Euoptius. Last I saw either, Synesius, unharmed, led his brother away, Euoptius bleeding from his great nose.

Spitting dust and grit from my mouth, I look up at my savior. Isidore of Pergamon pulls me aright, the priest who remains the favorite of Bishop Theophilus but has not remained my student. Beside him stands Cyril, nephew of Theophilus, grown taller as well as wider. If he has also grown in arrogance, it does not show now. Cyril trembles. His eyes, round as his round face, dart from side to side. His mouth, once a disturbing red, is now a dry white. His skin is whiter than his mouth. I imagine a privy would be most welcome to young Cyril.

We three stand near an *insulae* that shifts on its base like the obelisks of rose red granite. Cladding falls from its walls in small chunks and large. If it goes past its center of balance, all beneath will be crushed flat—and *we* are beneath. I gather my *tribon* around me, a *tribon* yet white as the sail of our boat, the *Irisi*, and run. Isidore and Cyril run with me. But I do not run to safety. I have never intended safety.

Isidore calls out, "Where are you going?"

"Wherever the earth has opened widest."

"Why!"

"To say I have seen it."

I am as fleet as the fierce Atalanta who would not marry, but Isidore is equally fleet. I look back only once. Cyril cannot run. Before half a block, the wheezing fearful boy is left far behind and where he goes after he is lost to sight I could not guess.

Behind us, the building topples and the screaming trebles—and now the fires start. Small fires begun by cooking stoves grow larger. Large fires flare into flames that swallow all that attracts them.

We come on a crack in the granite of a side street running south from the Canopic Way big enough to dwarf a racing chariot and all four of its horses. Behind us, from the offices and markets and great lecture halls of the sprawling Agora, the city's constant heart, come shrieks and shouts and the thud of fallen statues, but I kneel on the edge of a precipice of an infinite void, looking down at the bowels of the world. Isidore kneels with me.

"Is this your hell, Isidore?"

"Nothing is as hellish as your polyhedrons."

Isidore, who I have neither seen nor heard since the night we spoke in my atrium, has wit? In the midst of terror and sorrow, I forget myself. I would laugh. But before I can do so, Isidore speaks, "So many are hurt. So many are frightened. I am *Parabalanoi.* I am needed."

Parabalanoi! By Nisaba, Goddess of death, Isidore of the steep sided city of Pergamon is a brute for bishops? More shocked by this than the shaking of the earth, I watch him leave me and I think: not all in the Bishop's brotherhood are brutes. Some must be who they say they are. I catch myself out. I am searching for a way to find this man "good." I would find him good because I find him...interesting.

The House of Theon still stands. The horses have calmed in their marble stalls. Ife has seen that our servants are safe. Nothing burns, nothing has sunk and nothing risen. Yet something is wrong.

I find these gathered in Father's room: Lais, Jone, Minkah, Ife. Father is under his covers. What could be more normal? And yet? As no other speaks first, I must. "Is all well? Is anyone hurt?"

At this, the top of Father's thinning skull slowly emerges as would a desert owl from its burrow. He turns his large face on its thin neck to stare at me, his movements uncertain, his faded eyes crossed. So like those cast into the streets, there to live under bridges or in reeds by the lake or even in sewers. I am made ill to see it.

"Daughter!" he shouts, "Did you forget my intestines?"

I glance at Lais. That one glance is all I need. Already weakened in body by a life lived in bed, much sunken in spirit by the attack on what he holds to be certain: that perfection is possible, that Plato "saw" the form of heaven, that Euclid could describe divinity, that Mind was truer and finer than matter, Father's mind is lost.

I have forgotten what I would say, forgotten that my *tribon* is now the color of brick, that my skin and hair are matted with the dust of cement, forgotten that I looked into the earth itself—how elemental the world beneath!—and think now only of Father. And of myself. In truth, I think only of myself.

For close on two years I alone have held our lives in my hands, assuring myself that the day would come when Father would rise from this accursed bed to take up life again. The thought has even excited me. We should *both* teach. We should *both* earn salaries. His pride would return. With more money, we could hire more scribes, one solely to copy the poems of Lais. I have arranged to send our little mouse to Didymus. If she would be a Christian, where better? Yet how do I find the money I need to pay for such a school? Unless Theon of Alexandria stands again, teaches again, I must carry these burdens myself. To do so, I need more money.

But here, before me, is truth. Father will not stand again. He will not teach again. There is only me...and who am I? I am not strong enough, not wise enough. I recoil at the sacrifice. What of *my* work? What of *my* dreams? If he becomes ill? If I must pay a doctor as well as a school?

"Father!" In my voice is enough enthusiasm to wake an *opion* user. "I have seen into the bowels of the earth."

Our burrowing owl blinks at me. "Bowels! Where is my crow?"

How long does each of us stare at Father before we hear a dreadful thud, followed by the crash of a bowl on the floor?

Lais has fainted dead away. Ife has dropped her bowl in surprise and horror.

Before I can reach her, Minkah has. He lifts Lais from

where she has fallen. Jone steps, deliberately or not, between the sight of this and Father, who might not notice regardless. We none of us speak, but instead stare into the eyes of the other, horrified.

The last voice is Father's. "A crow, Paulus. It has to be a very *big* crow."

Mere moments later, Lais awakens. Looking about at our white faces, our terrified eyes, she smiles. "Father and his organs. The earth and its shaking. I could bear no more."

I laugh. Minkah laughs. Ife does not laugh, but allows herself a smile. And Father has covered his head.

Minkah the Egyptian

Theon has not lost what's left of his mind. My "master" is drugged. As I bring all he eats and all he drinks, what could be easier than slipping something into whatever I serve him? This day of shaking is perfect. They will blame the day. I chose mandrake and an opium extract. That he raves before he sleeps caused me alarm, but I was never afraid of exposure. Not familiar with my mind, how could he, or they, know my intentions?

When Lais is safe in her room and Jone in hers, when I am certain Hypatia retreats to her bewildering work spread out in bewildering profusion over her table of green stone, I return to the room of Theon. As I knew he would be, he sleeps as a babe. To wake him would take the earth to shake again, which is possible, but I have accounted for that. What was fed him would take the collapse of his house to undo.

Now where would Theon, who stirs but little, hide his copy of the map that could, to the right eye, divulge the location of the hidden library? I try the obvious first: secreted among his collection of scrolls. Not there. I look through his chests. Nothing. When first I attached myself to this man, I tidied his room. Clutter disturbs me. It confuses my eye and therefore my mind. But having made order of what was disorderly, could there be a locker, a loose board, a drapery behind which is—nothing. Could this man who lives in a bed have actually hidden the map entrusted to him *outside* his room? Unthinkable. He rarely sets foot outside his room.

Think, Minkah, trained by *Parabalanoi*. Who is Theon? How does he live? Where would his mind go when pondering the great task of hiding his map? Aha! His map is under his feather mattress. I roll him over so that one more push would send his drugged body tumbling to the floor. I lift his mattress, and there it is. If he were awake to feel it, I would stab a pin in his foot, then deny he felt pain. I have done it before. Enough denial by me, and even he is unsure, especially as he is no longer supple enough to view the tops, much less the bottoms, of his feet. What an ass. Still, if I take his map, will he miss it? About as much as he misses Jone. Living so close to this father of three, I'm certain he's forgotten it.

It is the work of a moment to remove the map, tuck it away in my clothing, and roll the drugged fool back to the center of his bed. Now it is I, Minkah the trusted servant, who must hide this map. Before drugging Theon, I had already thought of the perfect place. It will not be found, not so long as I have care of it.

How content I would be if I did not know that Lais grows worse. By the day her cheeks grow paler, her body weaker, she cannot breathe with ease. All this she hides, but I have seen her pain when she thinks herself alone. What sickens her, I cannot tell. If only she would tell me, tell Hypatia, tell *anyone*... on that day I would find the finest doctor in all the world. I would pay all I have to secure him.

LAIS

Spring, 393

Hypatia

In Father's house it is the time of *Un*, the Egyptian hare born with open eyes. *Un*, also a measurer of time, brings a new year and new life.

Christians have taken this as well. Throughout the Roman world, they celebrate their Christ's rising from the dead. The name they call it, *Easter*, derives from Astarte, Goddess of the Moon. Astarte measures time. Didymus tells me he knows this. He knows too that the rising of his "son of god" is the return of the true sun. Yet his school teaches none of it. Our friend has explained that as most men are simple, the simple are taught only simple things. In this, Didymus, lover of Christ, is as all mystery teachers come before him. There is what is taught to the masses: the outward exoteric, and what is taught the select few: the hidden esoteric.

Lais has trembled often, fainted twice more. She cannot catch her breath. At times she cannot sit for pain. All of this she would have no one see, but I see. And, as I find, so does Minkah.

And still our physician discovers nothing wrong. Daniel of Gaza is not Agnodice of Athens who dressed as a man in order to follow her then forbidden calling, yet he is skilled enough. Minkah and I, when we meet, can speak of nothing else. If there is nothing wrong, what then is wrong? What causes her fainting? Why do her hands shake? Why the rasp in her throat? Lais has always been somehow removed from the world of strife and of suffering. Such things do not touch her.

Therefore, if not a change in the world, what has changed within her?

I have kept talk of Lais from Father, who seems to grow stronger as she grows weaker, not that he will rise from his bed. He has said nothing to frighten or concern us since his babble of dismembered crows. He has not again spoken of our mother, Damara. He seems content in his room. Minkah brings him all that he needs, and removes all that he does not need. I visit for an hour each day as he now writes a new book he calls *On Signs and the Examination of Birds and the Croaking of Ravens.*

When Father finishes his new book, a work he asks no help with, thank Seshat, he desires we begin a commentary on the *Mathematical Treatise* of Claudius Ptolemy. So long as he sees no ill omens—how could he when all he sees are the four walls of his room?—I am much encouraged.

As for Jone, she thrives in the school of Didymus. I see her seldom now, as she is either there, or secluded in her room with Ife, reading aloud the so far simple texts her teachers set before her. Passing by, I have heard her voice filled with wonder, I have heard it filled with joyful tears, and I have heard Ife read with her. May the gods bless Ife with eternal life.

Didymus assures me Jone will progress. He does not say she shall become one of the select few.

In the middle of the night I awaken to weeping. Slipping out of bed, lamp in hand, I follow the mournful sound. Nothing from Father who sleeps with one pale bony foot exposed. Jone slumbers clutching a schoolbook in one hand, a nibbled fig in the other. The book is one of Didymus's own, Treatise on the Holy Spirit. I find no servant awake and lamenting. Frightened, I run along the hall, both hall and I as pale as the moon.

It is Lais. But Lais does not cry. How could it be she who cries?

Lais is on her feet in the dark. I light her candles one after the other until her sleeping chamber is ablaze. I light the triple oil lamps that hang in every corner. She paces her room in the light as she'd paced it in the dark, wearing nothing but a fine white sleeping tunic. The white of her sleeping tunic and the white of her skin give off such light as do strange enchanted creatures I have seen pulled from the sea by moonlight. But it is not reflected light. The lamp and candlelight do not do this. The moon does not do this. It is the brightness within her.

"Lais," I whisper, "why do you weep?"

"From pain, sister. I weep from the pain."

Lais has answered me. Not only answered me, but said something I have never heard from such a sister. Lais does not complain.

"My poor lamb! Tell me. Where is your pain?"

Lais touches her lower back. "Here." She touches her side above her left hip. "Here." She clutches her belly. "Everywhere. How shaming I can no longer keep silent."

"How long, Lais, how long has this been so?"

She does not shake her head. To move her head seems more than she can bear. "Two years. More."

Two years! *Before* the decree of Emperor Theodosius that allowed Theophilus to burn the temples. *Before* Father's world was set upon and before I need become the father. Before all this, the world of Lais was already threatened. And we neither of us knew, Father and I, too concerned with gnawing our own wounds like wild dogs in a snare.

I kiss her forehead. I kiss her cheek. "Leave, Lais. Go where it is you can go."

Her answer comes only as breath inhaled. "I cannot."

"Cannot? But why?"

"I am bound to my body by pain." Lais begins to rock and I rock with her, back and forth, back and forth, until she cries out, "Oh, Miw! Is this what others endure? While I knew bliss, they knew pain? I am not worthy. I am not worthy."

"Hush, sister, hush. None is so worthy as you."

I do not leave Lais the rest of the night. Sometime towards the dawning of the holy sun, she falls into a troubled sleep, broken by a catch in her throat, as if she would at any moment stop breathing. Even asleep she feels pain, and even asleep she tries not to show her pain. As I lie beside her, I tenderly kiss her brow. For all her pain, it is not hot. There is no fever, no delirium. Daniel has seen her daily. Daily, he smiles and tells us it will pass.

But it will not pass. Two years? Something is terribly wrong.

As she trembles in her sleep, I offer Persephone, Goddess of death and resurrection, my life if it would please her more than the life of Lais.

Persephone, daughter of Demeter, does not choose me.

Like Father, Lais no longer leaves her room. Unlike Father,

she cannot. Lais would fall if she stood. Her breath comes less easily by the day. She will not eat yet her belly grows rounder. For days, it seems she retreats into something that is not trance, but a sleepy languor. I cannot follow, but I can hope that there she finds peace. If not me or Minkah, Ife is with her.

As Lais is, the city I knew is dying. Even as it has quickly repaired itself from the great shaking of the earth, yet it dies just the same. A new belief, one that will tolerate no discussion or dissension, grows in Alexandria, silencing all, just as something grows in Lais, silencing my beloved sister. I can barely speak of this, even to myself, but the power to write left Lais a month ago, and now the power of speech leaves her. Daniel no longer says there is nothing wrong. He says there is a growth within her, lurking behind a wall of flesh, spreading as a fungus spreads—in the dark.

He could open her belly as cook would gut a fish. Such things have been done for thousands of years. But cutting rarely achieves more than a few days more of life. And a much quicker death.

Minkah would find a new doctor, a more daring doctor. I ask him to search one out, and to do it quickly. No matter the cost, I will pay it. He protests, saying he will pay. If laughter I had left, I would not laugh but smile. I tenderly kiss his cheek. I thank him for his offer, but both he and I know he cannot afford a physician's wages. Nor can I, not unless I were to take Jone from her school, and this I will not do. But there are those who will lend the money. There are those who know I will repay them, with interest, any interest.

Minkah, who loves my sister as I love my sister, who cares for my father as I care for my father, who treats Jone as an equal so that my poor little sister would do much for him, is now my greatest confidante, greater than Augustine.

There is only one other. Isidore of Pergamon.

When I do not teach or work with Father or sit with Lais or listen to Jone enthuse over lessons or cope with my correspondence that becomes a deluge—if only I had an amanuensis!—I ride with Isidore the priest.

I am half alive. I am half dead. If I die with Lais, I live with Isidore the Christian.

Since the day of the earthquake, we have come across each other, if not by the effort of one, then by the effort of the other. What do we speak of, this lover of a Jesus as written by the Christian philosopher Origen, a priest who walks with the dread *Parabalanoi*...and Hypatia the "pagan" who loves—oh, but I love so much and so much of it fades as a mirage fades without heat. Father grows, not younger, but less responsible. He shoulders nothing, notices nothing but that which is in front of his nose. By this, he is more now my son than my father. Jone grows every day stranger, more distant, seems bursting with some inner seed. But the plant thereof? How will it grow and what fruit shall it bear?

And Lais, and Lais...how shall I live without Lais?

With Minkah I speak of all this, leaving out nothing. With Minkah, I am a Hypatia of the broken heart. With Isidore, as in my letters to Augustine, I speak only of what is rapturous. My thoughts, the thoughts of great minds come before, of great minds yet to come. In this, I do not censure myself. What can I lose by my tongue? My life? And what is that? If Lais should pass through the world for so brief a time, what then remains? Nothing of beauty, nothing of love. So much is dead that while alive was seen by none. So much is dead, that once trumpeted is now forgotten. So much is yet to come to whom my time will be as if it had never been. Who will miss Hypatia?

If Isidore censures himself, I do not care. If I am to lose all I value, I will not lose as well my right to speak. By this, I would lose myself. But even to Isidore, I do not mention the books. There are days when we come within miles of them, hiding in their caves, curled in their jars, lost in their inky thoughts.

I begin to love this man in a way I have never known love, but I do not mention the books. And by this I know I have not found love for to truly love is to truly trust.

Home from another public lecture, and Ife is suddenly at me. Her flat dark face a moving play of feeling, she is barely articulate. "Come. You must come. She can't...where is Minkah?"

I am already moving. I know what Ife cannot say. She speaks of Lais. Lais cannot what? Breathe? See? Move? And where is Minkah?

"Fetch Olinda. Now!"

Olinda of Clarus is become our physician. New to Alexandria, she comes with praise from Rome to Athens. Olinda is here because only in Egypt is she allowed to study the human body.

She can cut it open, pull out what is inside, strip muscle from bone. Egyptians have cut into bodies since Egypt began.

A small woman with a small face starred with small intelligent eyes, she presses a small hand against the large belly of Lais only to tell us what Daniel of Gaza told us: what troubles Lais resides inside her body, that to cut could kill her, probably *would* kill her, but not to cut will also kill her. I have asked, "Then, shall you try?" Olinda has answered, "I will try if it must come to that, but first there are other methods I would attempt."

For a month now, it has seemed our new physician succeeds. But so soon as I open the door of my sister's room, I know that this success is no success at all.

Lais lies in her bed. But she does not sleep, nor does she lie in stupor. Both my sister and her bed shake violently. It is as if another earthquake, one so personal it seeks only Lais, has seized her. As I stand rooted to the floor, her back suddenly arches, so high it seems she stands as the Goddess Nut, balanced only on the heels of her rigid feet and the top of her rigid head. Her neck is stretched so far it seems it might snap, her jaw clenched so tight I fear for her bone. Her arms are flung out from her body, her hands clenched, her nails dug so deep in her palms, she bleeds.

I would scream. I would shout out her name. But Minkah is all at once beside me, pushing me away from Lais. He has taken hold of her, meaning to try and force her spine to straighten. But it does not straighten. What possesses her is strong enough to hold up both Minkah and Lais.

It is now that I scream.

Not until all seems over does Father arrive. Weak now, trembling, he leans on Jone. Jone, who knows his heart, endures supporting a father who has never supported her. All for love of Lais, the servants cluster near the door, only parting for Olinda to pass through.

Although Lais appears to rest, it is not over but merely progressed as it will. No one of us moves, nor makes a sound as Olinda gently opens my sister's eyes. Both are rolled up in their sockets. What should be white is red. She runs her hands over the body of my poor sweet lamb, her neck, her breast, her wrists. We wait, each of us lost in our own pain, our own helpless horror, until at last, Olinda turns not to Father, but to me. "The masses grow faster. Fluid fills her. I must open her belly."

Our father suddenly and quietly cries, his tears dropping

one by one onto the shoulder of his youngest child. He speaks. "Is there nothing else?"

Olinda, washing the sweat from my sister's face—asleep now, or unconscious—looks up. "I have seen wonders in my time, cures where there should be no cure, recovery from certain death without treatment, operations which should have killed."

"I would do anything," I say, "see anyone, go anywhere. Where do I find wonder?"

"In Siwa."

Father turns to me, his eyes drained of Theon. "You must go immediately. You must come back immediately. You must save your sister."

The oasis of Siwa is so distant and so difficult to reach, it would take the whole of two nights and one day to go and return—and this, only if Desher and I do not stop but keep up a brutally fast and constant pace. If this would not kill me, it would surely kill Desher though she is as yet young.

It is late Spring. The days are hot. In the desert they are hotter still.

I will do it in two days and three nights. One day only will I give myself at the temple. If possible, less. But not one hour more.

My sister sleeps. Sleeping, she looks as she has always looked, as if no more perfect thing lived. I beg Olinda to ensure Lais does not die before I return. Olinda, a truth-teller, replies that Lais will live as long as she will live. She has been given a potion, but that does not mean a healthy sleep. It means that rather than dying quickly, she dies slowly.

I am a mathematician, a philosopher, an astronomer. The people believe what they are told. I believe nothing, consider everything. All I have ever seen, all I have ever thought, each magical shape and numinous number has told me that life is governed by something. Born into this world for the joy of it or merely as adventure, no matter how brief or how brutal, the greatest minds have believed divinity underlies all.

I do not speak of some separate being, some singular masculinity that judges us, and is sometimes pleased and sometimes angered. How like a demanding father this, and how like cringing children we are made by such fearful imaginings. Nor do I speak of an ultimate plan in which we, like pieces on a gaming board, have no say. But I *do* speak of intention, by which I mean each man's unique and perfect destiny, crafted from his own proud, self-directed, divinity. We each of us intend the way of our life, no matter it seems cursed or blessed. It is neither. It is the Self experiencing the self.

Divinity resides in All, Desher no less than myself, the scorpion on a stone no less than Desher, the stone no less than the scorpion. But had I never read the philosopher Iamblichus, never absorbed Plotinus, never found my mind moved by the "Idea of ideas" of Philo Judaeus, never mastered Euclid, if Pythagoras and the wife of Pythagoras and Hermes Trismegistus did not flow through my veins like blood, my sister could have shown me this.

And so it follows that the divine Desher and I go in hope of hearing Lais intends to live by riding to the Temple of Ammon in the oasis of Siwa where the Libyan people live, where they have lived forever, and where no Christian has yet to set foot.

Minkah would go with us, but cannot. Who is there to entrust my sister to other than Minkah and Ife? I will leave at first light. I will allow myself two hours of rest, an hour to prepare what I would take, and the rest I will spend with Lais.

Paniwi lies along the length of her mistress. She does not purr nor does she sleep. She has grown thin. I had not noticed how thin, or how ragged her fur. She does not hiss at me. By this, I know Paniwi grieves as I grieve.

As did Lais while Damara died, I now do. I lean close and whisper into the perfect ear of my perfect sister. "When I return, you will write a poem about Desher and me. Next year, when I am twenty-four and you an old woman of twenty-six, we shall read this poem and laugh. We shall read it once a year, and each time we shall laugh all the more. There will be made copies for every person of worth in the world and they will read your words and slap their learned foreheads for not being as wise as you. But I shall make one more copy and that copy I will place in its own jar which I will take to the caves, and there it will remain until it is one day found in some unimaginable future. And the finder will read your poems and will know that once there lived a being of such beauty and such wisdom she will weep she can never know her."

I hold my sister's hand. It is warm with life, yet as motionless as death.

"But she *can* know you, Lais, by your words she will know you."

Minkah the Egyptian

I wait without rest outside the door of one disguised in body as a woman, but is as Hypatia says: a being of light so bright we are blind to her. When Hypatia is gone to Siwa, Theon must do without Minkah the Egyptian for I shall tend Lais as if she were mine, which she is not; as if I were hers, which I am.

There will come no other time she is in need and I not here, even if I must risk my skin. As for my oath to the brotherhood, pah! Theophilus can keep his money. What I am paid should buy him the skull of the martyred Apostle Mark and even the rope he was dragged to his death with…that is, if there ever was a Mark and he ever showed up in Alexandria, which I fucking doubt.

I have done my self-appointed task. Theon's map is safe and will not be found. I watch the old infant carefully, withering away under his covers, suckling at his wine. Each day he forgets more. By now the map is a chimera. I have paid Olinda her fee, swearing all other fees will be met. Olinda promises to tell Hypatia she requires no fee, not for one such as Lais. If Theophilus could do as his Christ is said to have done, I would compel him to call Lais back from the Underworld. But Theophilus holds no power other than fear. That he himself fears is the source of the *Parabalanoi.*

Does the man Hypatia rides with, wretched Isidore, creature of a guileful bishop, tell my darling who he is? I think not. But then, do I?

Listening outside the door, I sense that with one more step, Lais will fall into the *Duat*. Or fly. It does not matter which. Either way, she will be gone from this place—and that I could not abide.

THE SECOND GATE

Hypatia

Even Alexander knew doubt. Seeking Siwa and the shrine of Zeus Ammon, he crossed these same fine sands, this same hard clay, the same red mud that clings to Desher's hooves. He would find the People of the Oasis whom Homer called the "Lotus Eaters."

From the back of my red mare all I see are low lying ridges shimmying in the heat and a white sky above a white land. Staring at Desher's bright red mane and her bright red ears, I imagine red mud on the immortal hooves of the white-starred black Bucephalus. I imagine the bones of five hundred Persians scattered by jackals like the clay shards of a shattered pot. I do not allow myself to imagine Lais.

Alexander sought Siwa to be proclaimed a god by the oracle...for if god he was, and not a mere Macedonian youth dressed as a general, how easy to conquer a people—especially the people of Egypt.

Alexander was given what he came for. Olinda of Clarus said only that I might find solace there. Father, who seeks divination by mathematics, urged me on though he'd seen no sign. Even so, I would crawl to Siwa. I would ride Desher to the head of the Nile, sail the *Irisi*, my one small boat with its one small sail, out through the Pillars of Hercules, following the sun down into the sea if by so doing I could catch in a silvered net my sister's life and bring it home.

I ride again as a nomadic Libyan, dressed in a Libyan *haik*. I could be man or woman, young or old, rich or poor—who could tell? As well, it protects against the sun which weighs down as a paper-press weighs on papyrus. For Desher, I carry water as the water here, when found, is brackish. There are times when what seems a desert, seems more a shallow sea. There are times when the waters flee until there is nothing left but vast brown ponds slowly turning from thickening puddles to thick red mud. It is this mud we move through now.

I carry two knives. Both are close to hand.

Father would have me perfect? I might ride any horse for any distance. Should my horse fail, I can walk, even run as an Ethiop. My tutors were as varied as that which they taught. One, instructing me in ropes and sails and winds and currents, instructed me also in the use of knives far beyond cutting line or gutting fish. Another, teaching me to climb mountains, taught me what I might eat and what I might drink and how I might keep warm or keep cool under conditions that would normally kill. And one taught me the strange art of the weak man besting the strong. In this, the secret is to use the strength of the stronger, larger, man against him.

So though I ride alone, and am a woman, I am not as unsafe as I might seem. I do not fear my fellow man—I fear the heat. Like the long legged long-tailed cat-dog of the desert, from which was taken the ancient *udjat* of Egypt, I smear kohl across my top lids and my bottom lids, then down from the corners of each eye along the sides of my nose ending at the edges of my lips. I do the same for Desher. By this we see farther and the sun does not blind us. I eat only dates and only when I must. I rest Desher when I come on a grove of acacias, which are all there is of green growing things, if cheetahs are not resting there before us. If gazelles, we shoo them away. If jerboas, we watch them pop in and out of their burrows, squeaking with delight to see others of their kind, and so to hop madly together about the acacia grove.

But now, as the sun slides behind a high dune of sand as white as salt, Desher and I allow ourselves some few hours of sleep under more acacias. Sponging water over her mouth and her nostrils, exchanging breath for breath, kneeling to clean her hooves of caked mud, I find myself thinking of the sun and of time. She and I have only so much time to do what we do...

yet what is time? Philosophers have discussed it until they believe it has substance. They know time as *that which is, that which was,* and *that which will be.* But time, having no existence in itself, can only be measured by the mechanics of nature. By the sands in a sandglass, the phases of the moon, by the rising and the sinking of the sun, by the life left in Lais, we count duration. But only by reference to these, and not by any absolute called "time," do we measure our past, count our days, and estimate our future in the ever present Now.

Something is suddenly here, which Desher knows before me. Raising her head and her tail, she snorts down her nose, as I spin in place, a cloth not a knife in my hand. Far above, sits Isidore the archpriest astride some great blowing stallion, both hard used and both encrusted with mud so that he and his horse are not the coppery red of Desher but the dull red of duller mud huts. I am too alarmed for civility.

"You followed me?"

"In a manner of speaking."

"You followed me or you did not follow me."

"I learned of your intentions and they became my intentions."

"Why?"

"You should not ride alone."

"I am not unaware and I am not unprepared."

"Even you cannot be entirely prepared for what is overwhelming."

I study his face, one which has grown dear to me, yet not truly known. "You mean the monks of Nitria who do not love pagans? Or mathematicians? Or women? Who howl at the thought of three in one?"

"I do."

"These were those who would have me killed?"

"They would."

"But Theophilus has put a stop to that."

"Even Theophilus cannot stop a disease. And with things as they are in Rome, many talk against him now."

"Oh, Isidore. What a teaching you espouse."

"It is not the teacher or the teaching. It's those taught. My faith attracts many an unstable heart. Too many."

"But how should they know I am here?"

"I know."

"But no doubt you asked and you were trusted."

"Your house is not as you see it, Hypatia. One or two are not who you think they are."

"What do you mean? Who do you speak of?"

But he would say no more.

By now, Desher and I are somewhere marked by no rock or rise or baked and brittle mud. Even in this place with Isidore, hot and sore and tired, I am relentless. I cannot and would not stop my mind from its babble. And yet, how seductive to fall into sand and sky and sun and there dream as Lais once dreamed—but I am only what I am, a thing of the mind that feels itself separate from sand and sky and sun, questioning constantly all it sees and all it hears. I believe nothing, not even what my senses assure me is so, for fear that by holding to one belief I lose the possibility of another. I am one who pokes and prods the gods, questing for meaning. When I stare up at the stars, I count them and while counting, wonder: are they as the sun? Around them, are there earths? Do creatures who think and who feel look down, harboring such thoughts as mine?

And then there is this: those who desire absolute certainties are prepared to believe anything. I travel with a man who has, of all possibilities, chosen one belief and one belief only, and he has done so on faith alone. This, to me, is more than curious; it is foolish...though I would never say so, not exactly.

"Isidore," I ask in a tone as light as the breath I have breathed into Desher and she into me, "was your faith taught you by your mother and your father, or did you come to it by some other means?"

My priest has been nodding as he rides. This awakens him. "It came to me as food comes to a man who starves and in order to partake of it, I left the home of my parents for they would not eat."

"Ah. And how did it come? Was there a sign?"

"Bishop Theophilus fed me the truth and though he does not partake himself, I know in his belly the truth safely lives."

"But tell me, Isidore, how is it you know this truth to be true?"

"Because the Christ decrees it so."

"And when he lived, he wrote his truths for all to read?"

"No. Jesus spoke, he did not write."

"Then those who heard him, *they* wrote, and what they wrote were the words of Jesus?"

"Yes."

"I have read all these testaments, and in each of them the words and the actions of your Christ varies. Which, of them all, are the exact deeds he accomplished and which the exact words he spoke?"

"All of them."

"All? So at one moment he could say he brought peace to the world and in another he brought only a sword? And in yet another moment, he might proclaim love for all, even the least of us, and in another he would consign a worthless servant to eternal torment?"

Isidore's face turns hard. I knew this might happen. It often happens when I ask questions. I go too far and have offended his reason for his reason cannot answer. And because of this, he questions mine, by saying, "You do not understand."

"I understand your gospels were not written by men who knew your savior. I understand that as the years widen between his life and theirs, those who write of him change him word by word. Help me understand your faith in this. Help me understand why you can follow what seems a conflicted man whose life and teaching vary from gospel to gospel, and yet is called loving, while you can be also *Parabalanoi.*"

I am punished by hours of silence. But by Ananke, goddess of fate, I ask because it is my nature to ask. If what I ask cannot be answered, it is then my nature to trouble myself seeking for answer. I will not apologize. I have asked my questions only to hear his answers. That he does not answer is answer enough. Yet, I am sorry. As we ride, I glance over from time to time. Seen only in profile, he is fair.

The land begins to rise. Sand becomes less and rock becomes more. And life surrounds us. Foxes slink by, hares scatter, I see what seems a white brown-necked goat, yet is not a goat. On its head are two sharp horns as long, or longer, than my arm. They spring up and back, ending in a fearsome tip, though the "goat" is as fearsome as...a goat. I have seen these horns before. They hang on the walls of men who kill them only for sport.

Towards evening, as if standing on the tallest step of a flight of tall stairs, we gaze out over the rim of a sunken oasis—finally: Siwa, "The Land of the Palms," *Sekht-am.* Seen through the heated air, *Sekht-am* seems to jump or shift suddenly sideways, or merely to sit and quiver. It is enormous, many miles long and many miles wide, and within it, stands a small mountain. Alexandria's mountain made to site the Temple to Pan is a perfect cone; this mountain is oblique. With no seeming pattern or sense, its off-center flanks are dotted with homes of mud and shops of mud each held together with palm tree trunks. Near the top of the mountain is a fortress, ruined now, and round the base of the mountain are the palms that give this place its name and the houses their strength, and up from the palms rise everywhere huge rocks like the heads of gods, like the forked tails of sea monsters, like pyramids, like giraffes, like Pharos, like fists. One rock is tallest of all, and on that rock surely sits the Temple of the Oracle.

Down on the oasis floor we come to a small lake of clear water caused by a spring bubbling up from under the earth. Desher rejoices by rolling on its reeded banks, stinking of green. Isidore's stallion would rejoice in Desher but by my quick hiss, nothing comes of his expectations—as well it should not. Desher was born, as was Ia'eh, in a cold desert far from this heated place, one high and windblown and harsh. Isidore's horse is thick of neck and of leg; his head coarse and his rump huge. A mating between two such as these would offend Epona, the Goddess of horses. It would offend even the ass of Apuleius.

My feet in cool water, I look up at the Temple of Ammon clinging to its rock as a lizard would cling. Simple in shape, small in size, humble in aspect, it stands some distance from the mountain of mud dwellings, surrounded on all sides by palms and the dusty debris of palms. My history tutor said the oracle existed before Egypt, but about the Temple itself, she confessed she did not know. Too many stories told, too many beliefs to unravel, and each, like Isidore's gospels, a contradiction of the other. Now that I see for myself—ignoring the fluted columns added so much later to make it "Greek"—it is old indeed.

There is a second temple sited in a second grove, not of palms but of date and olive trees. This one, attaching itself to the first by a precarious causeway two thousand years ago, is covered with graffiti.

Andromeda came to the Temple of Siwa only to be cast into the sea where sea serpents found and ate her. Hercules once came to make sure of his chances before fighting Bursiris. Perseus came before he took the head of Medusa. The Spartan Lysander came twice. Who would come twice if he were disappointed the first time? Here as well came Hannibal. Pindar wrote of this strange and lonely place. Hidden inside the temple is said to be the only copy of his poem.

Is it any wonder Alexander sought it out, or that Olinda offered it as hope?

Since Isidore has yet to speak to me, I say nothing of this, content that my heart quickens. This is what I have come for. If by coming here, my sister's life is saved, the journey which has lost me precious time at her side is worth every moment it lasts. Light fades from the day. Shadows grow and stretch. There is only now, and tomorrow, and then I rush back to Lais. If she means to die, she will not die without me.

Leaving our horses tied so one cannot reach the other, we make the long climb up narrow stone stairs and the whole way I cough out palm dust. The top is flat and on it the Lotus Eaters have built their mud houses, abutting them against the sides of the temple. Above the door of the temple is carved the face of Medusa, worshipped by the women of Libya as a serpent goddess. And this we also find: the temple door is shut and barred.

Banging on the door produces nothing but noise and an indulgent smile from Isidore. Nothing in Alexandria is as old as this temple. It was ancient when Alexander stood here. Did he too bang on the door?

No time to waste, I must get in. There are no windows. I think to circle the building. There is no circling the building. The sides facing north and west are merely extensions of the sheer rock rising up from the palms far below. To follow the wall south from the columned front door takes me to another wall that extends to the southern edge of the rock.

So here we are, come all this way, and other than a few poor feathered Libyans peering from the doors of their homes of mud brick and rock salt, there is no one to greet me, to allow me near the oracle, not even to collect the "donation" which of course I brought, as much as might be required.

"Someone will come in the morning," says Isidore, who has spoken only when he must since becoming silent. "So unless you mean to batter down the door, or somehow slip through the openings high in the wall, you must be content to wait this night."

He is right. I cannot batter down the door. I look up. By Thoth! Far above are two narrow openings over the door. Could I scale the sheer wall, slip through the slits? I calculate the possibility. The rope Desher carries is too short. But were it not, though I am slender, the slits are more slender still.

"Come," says Isidore, "There must be a caravansary. We will eat and we will rest. At first light, we will return to the temple. If there is still no one to allow us entrance, *then* we will break down the door. In one way or another, you shall see your oracle."

Isidore speaks to me! How glad my heart. And how sad. I do not wish to care. I have only so much left to give now that

I give all to Lais.

It is the men of Siwa who wear woven cords around their heads and through them place long thin feathers. It is the men who curl their beards and simper as they hide behind doors. But it is both men and women who are varied in race. Long banished here are Romans, Greeks, Persians, even sky-eyed men of the north. The women of whatever race are bold, and strangely lovely. Though I am without stature here, and Isidore's robes and cross mean nothing, all at the inn greet us with smiles and bows as deep as would be granted Alexander. They tell us the guardian of the Temple of Zeus Ammon lives on the far side of the oblique mountain. She shall be summoned this night.

The room we are then offered is communal, there is no other kind. Dozens sleep on pallets scattered over the floor. Isidore and I cannot stay in such a room for all who spend the night are male. So yet again, we make our beds under a grouping together of palms.

Isidore might be asleep. He might not. I am awake and sorely tired of our silence. One who believes is like a lover; he would hear nothing ill of his beloved. Isidore is such a lover whose beloved is Christ. "Isidore," I whisper, "I have a thoughtless tongue. Forgive me."

He is awake. I hear him turn on his mat to face me as I continue flat on my back. I hear him say, "I forgive you. The brotherhood is not what you think."

"It is not?"

"It is much maligned."

The brotherhood *is* what I think it; all know this. But Isidore is archpriest, and shielded by Theophilus. He would know only that part that does good in the world. Did he not rush away to help the suffering on the day of the shaking of the earth? Again my reasoning soothes me.

In an oasis far from where Lais lies dying, I would solace myself by speaking of stars, of the nature of man, of the mind, of the Divine Proportion described by Pythagoras. Is it not, I would say to Isidore, a beautiful symmetry that a line divided according to Euclid's mean and extreme ratio will prove the larger segment to be in the same proportion to the smaller segment as the line itself is to the larger segment? And should one fold the smaller segment onto the larger segment: two more segments with this same ratio will appear, and so on and so on forever! Adding word to word, I would rush on. To look on the human face or to hold a human hand, to lay one's head as a bride on another and listen to the beat of their heart, to gaze at the wings of a moth or the petals of the lotus, to behold the shape of a shell or be transported by the flow of musical notes—if God has spoken, surely this is that language. In short, I would hide in a tangle of words. But Isidore has so moved his divinely proportioned hand that it now touches mine. I do not move. He lifts my hand to his lips. I allow this. He kisses my palm. This also I allow. And within me something stirs. It is not mind. It is not heart. It is the heat of the body, and it speaks to me the way hunger speaks and its speaking grows louder until it becomes a drum in my ears. Isidore touches now more than my hand. He has raised himself from his side so that he leans over me, pushing the folds of my *haik* away from my shoulders. And still I allow this. In truth, I raise my body towards his, my mouth towards his, my sex towards his. And when I feel his naked mouth on mine and his sex through cloth on mine, I understand what I feel. I understand what it means. Reason no longer controls what I do. It is feeling that compels this allowing. I feel more than I have ever felt, save grief as my mother died so that Jone might live, or horror as Lais arced over her bed as the Goddess Nut arcs over the earth.

Isidore's smell is as pepper, his beard tastes of salt, but I allow him even this. What more shall I allow? All that I believe of myself is fading and all I did not know of myself becomes blindingly bright. How long before what I allow goes so far that I cannot disallow it? I *want* what comes. I want it. But who is the "I" that wants this thing that animals do, that is done from the highest to the lowest? Where is the "I" that does not want this, that has never wanted this, that knows what will come of it?

Isidore lies atop me now, his length against my length, and his clothing has come away as has mine. We glisten in the heat we make. My skin slides over his—and I will give myself to him. Isidore's mouth is as near my ear as mine was near to the ear of Lais. "As I have vowed celibacy," he whispers, "my vows have proved easy. With you, I deny them all. This is the true reason I followed."

Can I say the same to him?

He raises himself on his arms, arms that are twisted with muscle. He looks down at me, at my face, my neck, my breasts, my belly, the maiden sex his own strength pushes against, and with a groan he pulls me over on top of him so that I now lie looking down at his face. He is beautiful. Even the strong smell of his sweat is beautiful as is the blank need in his eyes. I desire what he would do to me. I desire what I would do to him. But the answer is no, I cannot say the same to him. And there is this: I do not trust what he says. I do not trust what he does. He wants nothing more of me than his stallion wants of Desher.

"Stop, Isidore."

But he does not stop, rather he raises his face to my neck and I feel his teeth just as I feel the tip of his member begin to slip inside my body.

"Stop!"

The teeth and his phallus dig deeper. The slightest push, and my maidenhead is gone.

"As you are my friend, you will stop."

But he will not.

The knife that is as hard as he, as long as he, the one I've slipped under my mat is in my hand. It rests now against his throat. "I will kill you, Isidore, I swear this. If you take from me what I would not willingly give, I will take your life from you."

"You lie to me as you lie to yourself. You are not unwilling, merely afraid. And you will not kill me."

With a quick movement of his arm, a movement I would be prepared for if not for the tumult of my senses, Isidore twists away my knife, and with one mighty grip of his arms, he flips me over and under him, and then he is fully inside me. I gasp with pain. I gasp with a feeling that is not as I expect it to be. I am filled with what is not me, is not welcome, is not pleasurable. As he has nipped me with his teeth, I sink mine in his shoulder so he might pull away in pain, but he does not—not until he goes rigid with some strange sensation, a sensation I do not share, not until he shouts out in private ecstasy and I am suddenly on my feet staring down at him, my sex wet and dripping with what is him, not me, and I know that although he is one who can listen for hours as I speak, he is also nothing more than a man who wants what a man wants. I see now why he is *Parabalanoi.* It is in him, this taking away.

Staring up at me, he smiles. Staring down at him, I say, "Is this yet another teaching of your Christ, one I have not read?"

His smile does not fade; it drops as rock from a high place. He rolls away from me. His heart may not be, but his body is warm and sated.

I do not return to my mat, but to the small lake where I wash myself, and wash myself. I scrub until I would scream with pain. And then I return to sit up against a palm, and there I remain awake. I no longer follow the tracks in the starry night. My mind is dark. It is chaos. I am Socrates. I know nothing.

When we awake, Isidore and I are again silent. But this silence is as the lowermost tomb in the City of the Dead. Yet we rise and we dress and we mount our horses so that side by side we ride to the foot of the rock on which stands the Temple of the Oracle.

A woman awaits us. She is not old. She is not young. She is not interesting. Her hand is out for my "donation" before ever a thing is said and in it I place more than is needed, for I see her eyes widen at the sight of the coin I bring. For this she unlocks the temple door and walks inside. She does not wait for me, but merely assumes I will follow. Thankfully, Isidore does not.

Inside is as simple as outside: a stone courtyard, a small first hall, a smaller second hall, and then the stone sanctuary, smallest of all. In the sanctuary there is nothing more than a short wide pillar seated on the sanded stone floor. The top of the pillar is shaped as a pine cone. The pine cone is an *omphalos*, said to allow direct communication with the gods. Not well fashioned yet the pillar and the pine cone are most certainly old. The stone they are made from is black, not as obsidian is black, but as sacred black stones are black, stones that have fallen from the sky.

There the woman who holds the keys to the Temple of the Oracle turns and faces me. We stand, she and I, in the small cold sanctuary of timeless stone whose only light comes from the two slits high in the wall. The walls to either side are inscribed with the aged markings of kings. I pay them no heed. The night has entirely changed me. I feel somehow less, somehow more. I have grown older in one night. I am not defiled as the Jews or the Christians would have me. I am not spoiled for my life as a woman, for I do not have a life as a woman. If I had lost an arm, would I not be still Hypatia? When I grow old, will I not be still Hypatia? I *am* what I *am*, mortal among mortals, and nothing defiles save what I might do to myself. My body is mine, and with it I shall do as I wish. That which I did not wish for does not defile me. It defiles Isidore.

I do not ask if this woman speaks for the oracle. I do not wait for a sign. I make no obeisance. I stand upright before the cone smoothed with age, and the woman smoothed with oil, and I say, "Oracle, I ask for my sister's life."

How long do I wait for an answer? I could not say. Nothing moves. Nothing sounds. There is nothing but the walls and the *omphalos* and the woman who looks like any woman of Siwa. Yet, it seems something gathers around my head, something without form, yet has weight and has heat. It becomes oppressive...until I might shake my head to release it, until I might weaken and stride from this place. I half turn, and by this I see how changed the eyes of the woman. They seem covered by another lid. They seem not to look outward but inward. They seem as the eyes of Lais when last I saw them.

What she says now is said in a voice I must strain to hear. "Lais does not die. She Lives."

There has been no light without source, no rites without understanding, no sound other than six simple words. But I did *not* tell the woman my sister's name.

My heart, which has risen and set, rises again. Lais lives!

DARK LIGHT DARK

Hypatia

The ride back is quick and silent. Isidore does not attempt to explain nor does he plead for forgiveness, nor does he, in defense, reject me. If he is ashamed or angry or penitent or even triumphant, I cannot tell. He rides at my side, rests when I rest, gives his horse, as I do Desher, most of his water.

I grieve for our friendship.

I am a woman now...or so all would say. I was forced to this and I was not forced. I wanted it to be and I did not want it. In return for my ambivalence, we did as Isidore wanted. By his beliefs, he has committed a sin. By mine, I have done no more than experience a thing I was not yet ready to experience. Would I experience it again? It awakens the flesh, it heats the blood. If done in trust, it bonds the body of one to the body of another. In this act certain mystics find a path to revelation. My answer is yes, I will "become a woman" again—but not with Isidore of Pergamon. He has forced his will on mine. I am more than angered, I feel lessened. I would *not* be less.

I fret to be away from him.

In the few hours Isidore and I truly sleep, my knives are near. He speaks only at the death of a sand viper found coiled near my sleeping feet. Flicking it up with a stick, he stands on its writhing body as he cuts off its head.

As I break camp, he guts my snake, slipping the soft roll of brown mottled skin into a leather bag hung over his saddle. Seeing that I watch, he says, "This snake will remind me of our voyage to Siwa."

I say nothing in return, for if I did I would say I would not be reminded of his part in our voyage to Siwa.

A few miles out from Alexandria, he quietly turns his horse south so that he might enter the city by the gate near Rhakotis. I will pass through the Gate of the Moon in the wall north of Rhakotis. Either way, we must both pass over the Draco River which is in truth the last of the tremendous Canal of Schedia which twice empties into Lake Mareotis as it flows west from the Canopic Nile, and on which ships make their way from the Nile to the lake or to the sea and back again. In our last moment, we make no farewells, merely urge our horses where we would go, but when I think it timely, I ask Desher to pause so that I might gaze upon the last of him. I find Isidore has done the same.

I am mortified.

Desher senses home. Though she has traveled far and she has traveled hard, she eagerly nickers and quickens her pace—and there stands our house, just as we left it. No sign of mourning hangs near the great door on the Street of the Gardens. The stable boy who comes for Desher does not weep as we clatter into the stable yard. Isidore is forgotten on the instant.

I stride through the atrium towards the courtyard around which are the rooms for women. I pass the kitchen where all seems as it should save it is empty, past the dining hall, also empty. No matter. Father is in bed surrounded by paper. Ife is at market. Those she orders about in her soft and patient way are at chores. Jone is in school. And Minkah? Where else should he be but tending to Lais? No matter that Father is forever sending Minkah here and there for more ink, more pens, more paper, more of the sweets he favors, Minkah is with Lais.

Alone in the atrium, I consider the silence. My heart slows as each odd thing is explained. Then speeds up again. I must know for myself that her spirit remains in her body.

I will not run to her room. I run to her room.

The door is closed, but is that not as it should be? The door of one who is ill is kept closed. Who would shame them?

But just as I reach out my hand to clasp the bronze of her handle, the door is suddenly slammed outward, and rushes by me a kitchen servant with a bowl in her hands. Hot water? Vomit? A poultice made by Olinda?

"Oh," is all I am spared for greeting, and the girl is off—and I am in through the door as fast as she comes out.

All look up who are in my sister's room where few have ever come. I notice first Minkah. Then Jone, who is not at the school of Didymus the Blind but is seated against the wall, her mouth soundlessly moving as a knotted string moves through her fingers. Didymus himself sits on a pillowed bench, his arm linked with that of the astronomer Pappas, both their faces far from the faces I am used to. And there is the occultist Paulus of Alexandria, and there Meletus the Jew and Palladas the poet, and there my own student Synesius of Cyrene who I am most surprised to see. Wonder of wonders, among this great group is Theon of Alexandria reclining on a divan. Two years in bed have made sticks of his legs.

Paniwi crouches on the windowsill where Lais so often sits without speaking, without moving, sometimes it seems without breathing. "The Bringer" glares as wildly at all this as do I.

Olinda of Clarus leans over the bed I cannot see, and at her elbow a short, bent, red bearded male offers her a tray.

As I look at them, all look at me, even, for a moment, Olinda. I have ridden for days in the desert. I have not bathed nor have I changed out of my Libyan *haik*. The riding shoes I have unhappily worn were tossed away as I crossed our threshold. My feet would shame a worker in the City of the Dead. I smell of horse and of Isidore. I do not wait for explanation, just as Olinda does not wait to give one, but returns to her task as I stride across the cold tiles so I might see my sister.

Linen covers the unclothed body of Lais from her feet to the edge of her pubis, more linen covers her breasts and shoulders, but her head and arms and belly are bared to all. Minkah keeps her left arm steady at the shoulder, my doting student Synesius does the same on her right...why Synesius? Ife crouches at her feet, holding them still. Though small, Ife is strong. On a tripod sits a bowl, in the bowl coals so hot they glow, and in the glowing coals, three bars of metal. Olinda's bent assistant holds open a book filled with diagrams called *On Pernicious Growth in the Body*. I know this book. It is by Galen of Pergamon, once physician to Marcus Aurelius.

I move no closer but stare at Lais, whose suffering face is everywhere pale, save for the deep purple moons that cradle her eyes. She is piteously thin, yet her stomach is as distended as a woman far gone with child. If she is awake, I cannot tell. If she knows I am here, I cannot tell. Her hair, no longer thick, no longer shining, splays out over her pillow. Her lips are chapped raw. Even as this, she is mysterious with beauty.

"Why is she held so strongly?" I quietly ask of Didymus, though the sound of my beating heart must surely be heard by all. "Is she not drugged?"

"Even so. No chance is taken."

"But I have been to the—"

"Shush!" This great sibilance comes not from Didymus or from Olinda but from Father. "Unless you are needed, for the love of Zeno, be quiet."

My mouth is shut on the instant. It is then I spend the worst hours of my life, more terrible even than the dying of Damara or the long destruction of the Serapeum.

With the heel of her hand, Olinda presses down on my sister's belly as a bread-maker kneads bread. With each push, there is a moan. But at one strong push, even drugged, there comes from the mouth of Lais a shriek of pain, and from the mouth of Synesius a round sound of horror. Minkah holds to his place though the color of his cheek fades from the brown of the Nile at flood to the pale brown of a winter wren's wing. Without a word, Olinda nods at her assistant who, without a word, hands her a scalpel. I would hide my eyes, turn away, leave this place, but as I did not leave my mother, I will not leave my sister. And this I note: Father does not blink an eye, but remains silent and still, as well as grim. As for Jone, more lives behind her eyes than I can fathom, but for now I pay it no heed.

With one deft movement Olinda slices through the skin and muscle of my sister's rounded belly. Immediately the little man presses one of the hot bars against the cut to staunch the bleeding, and the hiss this makes chills my bone. I find myself flailing inside my own skull. As well as blood, there flows clear fluid, as water in its color and consistency; the bedding of Lais is soaked.

The large thick flap of bleeding skin is laid down over my sister's hidden pubis, exposing the precious organs beneath, then, handed a flat knife curved at the end, Olinda gently pushes at the colon so that she might see the liver. She does the same with the stomach, sadly shrunken now yet still as a pear in shape. There is a small strange bulb of growth near the liver. I watch, I hear, I smell, I am near to fainting. As my tears fall, I am ashamed to say that my gorge rises.

"If this is all, my cutting is not in vain." So saying, Olinda lifts the stomach up from where it rests.

It is then we see what more lives in the beautiful body of

Lais.

It is like a bare baby bird dead in its cracked open egg, like the mass of jellied meat in a forced open oyster, like a suppurating sore that has eaten its way through the skin of the mouth. It is the size of a scream. There is not one among us who does not draw breath and draw back at the sight. But there is one among us who rushes from the room. Throughout Jone had become increasingly ashen. I do not blame her if she hangs her head over the privy.

"What is it?" whispers Father, too shocked to speak louder.

Olinda does not answer, busy with a small metal pick she has taken from the burning coals, but her assistant whispers back, "Some would say it is an egg laid by a devil."

"No demon, you idiot, would dare lay its egg in my daughter. Therefore, what do the rational say?"

Olinda now replies, ever so carefully burning and cutting away the monstrous thing that has been killing the eldest daughter of Theon of Alexandria. "It is an aberrant growth of the stomach. But why? You will not find a physician who knows. I need perfect quiet and perfect stillness now. If I cut any but the putrid mass, she will die."

There is perfect silence and perfect stillness. Even from Paniwi, who has never ceased glaring down with her huge orange eyes.

And then the thing is lifted away from where it has been secretly growing, a thing that could never be made of that which is Lais, but lived as a stranger, and is now thrown as an unwanted babe into a bowl on the floor. At speed, the little man throws a cloth over the bowl, and also at speed, Olinda takes a needle curved as a thorn, threads it with gut, and deftly sews the skin of my sister's belly together again. The thing is done.

Synesius, now released, rushes away as Jone rushed away. Not knowing I was gone to Siwa, he had come merely to ask me yet another question, only to find his young strength needed for Lais.

His goodbye is given quickly and from behind his hand.

Father is back in his bed, Jone back in her school. Our

Egyptian once again tends Father. Ife would be lost without him. And so should I.

I go back to my teaching and my studies, and as I have had greater and greater need of doing, I have hired an amanuensis. Rinat comes to me through Meletus, taught by him in his schul for rabbinical Jews. A daughter of the daughter of one of his friends, she is younger than Jone and is in all things her opposite: quick, slender, open-hearted, dainty in her habits. Rinat is a treasure.

Lais lies attended by Olinda. Minkah is there every moment he can be.

I live in a workroom of books, devices for measuring the positions and movements of the stars, my geometer's tools, my alchemical apparatus, my counting board. My workroom is reached through a door over which sits a bust of Thoth, god of knowledge and inventor of number. Thoth is a trickster, which is as it should be: numbers are sly. Near him stands an altar to his sister Seshat, Goddess of archives and writing. I write on a table made of stone as green as emeralds, Damara's table, or make drawings of the device Minkah will create when Lais is not so needful of him. But no more than an hour passes that I do not run to Lais to smile at her, to see her smile at me.

As the oracle of the oasis foretold, Lais lives.

On this day at dawn, I allow myself to leave our house for other than lectures. On the back of the fast moving Desher, I pass over the Draco Bridge and under the Moon Gate, then away from the City of the Dead along a road that will not take us out into the desert but along the edge of the lapping sea. I am not filled with death or the hiding of books, not even of the mathematics I must teach this afternoon in the public gardens—as it was Father's, it is my duty to give free lectures; without a library or secular schools, the poor cannot hope to learn even their letters—I am filled instead with what Father spoke of last night over Chaturanga, an Indian game of war. Tapping his finger on the back of his piece, a war elephant, and eying the piece that stood in its way, my piece, no more than a foot soldier, but a dangerous foot soldier, Father had noted that Aristotle had implied not only an actual infinity but a potential infinity.

Lost to all but the rhythmic pounding of Desher's hooves and the whoofs of air forced from Desher's lungs, I think: potential infinity? Infinity there *is*, or infinity there is *not*. If it is, it is actual. If not, how is it potential? I ask as Parmenides of Elea asked: "What would cause it to be when it was not?" And then, what is meant by infinity? Though number itself is inherently a limitation, there is no limit to the number of numbers. Can number therefore describe infinity? Euclid would laugh at such a question. He would say that infinity is not a numeric conclusion we never reach. But I would say: like number, the infinite has no limits of any kind, not of size or shape or duration.

A thought suddenly strikes me, one so fundamentally obvious, I bring Desher out of a full gallop into a dead stop, sending up a spray of sand.

If there is infinity, then all we know must be infinite which would include time and space. Being infinite, neither would have ever begun nor would they ever end. And by this, the world simply *is*. Without a first creation, what need for a first creator? What need to placate or fear that which does not exist?

Desher's wet red neck mapped with pulsing veins, her huge red nostrils flared wide to gulp air, I sit on my mare in quiet wonder, oblivious to all else. Even Plotinus believed in some sort of generation by virtue of the contemplation of what he called "a prior," by which he meant that which was before, or outside, reality. But what if there is no "before," no "prior," no "cause," no "inside," no "outside," no "end"? What if there is only the now and the experience of now, without beginning, without end, existing only in Mind forever and forever?

A voice, close and deep and intimate, says, "How fortunate I am this day."

Spun away on the instant from infinite Mind, I come back to the world of turn and turn again. And there before me, mounted on a roach-maned high-tailed beauty dressed in golden blankets with a bridle and reins woven through with gold, sits Theophilus, Alexandria's Christian Bishop. If Scythians still swept out of the North bringing terror to all, how they would applaud him. As Isidore did not, Theophilus rides what Persians name *wind foot*, a mare. Stallions stop too often, piss where they stop, are given to hubris and sexual excitement and betraying their presence. But mares are subtle. This one has dropped her ears, at the same time pointing them backwards towards Theophilus. She tells me what she thinks of him. He is cruel to her. She is afraid of him.

I look beyond Theophilus. Glance at the cliffs above him. Off towards the endless sands. He seems as alone as I, yet he has brought his god with him, a huge cross of gold set with precious stones, each one as big as a coin. On his gold cross hangs a silver man, the nails in his silver hands small red rubies, the nails in his silver feet a larger red stone. I am made churlish to see Theophilus. I am made churlish to see that he wears around his neck a man tortured by rubies and silver. I ride to be alone. I ride to celebrate that I *can* ride, that Lais is not left at home alone and dying.

I say: "Do not detain me, sir, I have work to do." And with that, I chirrup to Desher, who leaps instantly forward. Behind I hear the voice of Theophilus, "If you leave, you force me to once again visit your home, for we have business, you and I."

If any demon I know, it is *this* demon: curiosity. In the year and a half since we spoke in a storage room, Theophilus has kept his word. I am not dead by the hand of some Galilean, as the "pagan" Emperor Julian called his kind. And I have kept mine. I have taught, both privately and publicly. My word was easy to keep, just as I said it would be. Therefore—what business have I with our grand Patriarch?

I am vexed that I would know. But I tap Desher's glossy red shoulder, wheeling her back towards the blinding arms of the rising sun.

Theophilus is not Greek nor is he Roman nor yet Egyptian. His hair, curled on both head and beard, are like the cliffs that arise from the sand, not golden, not yellow, but the brown of dirt baked hard in the sun. His eyes are not the blue of the sky or the sea. They are the mottled green of small lizards, those who live hidden away in the walls, only to come out at darkest night to call with loud rusty voices.

"You will not visit my home. My sister only now recovers."

"I have heard this."

It does not soothe, hearing I am known by this man. But people talk. Events unfold. In action, character becomes clear. I have lived through all the terror he has brought to my city. No doubt I shall live through more. And if I am talked of, so too, is he. Theophilus is ambitious far beyond the word ambition. He would build churches with anyone's money save his own—but he does not do so to honor the "only begotten son" of his pieced together god who hangs even now around his neck. The churches are monuments to himself. This is not surprising. Few men of ability truly believe what they profess to believe, not even the Emperor Constantine who publicly converted to Christianity, but whose last breath honored the name of *Sol Invictus* through which emanated the radiation of the Cosmic Mind.

My hand ready on Desher's reins, I wait to hear what he means to say. But I will not ask.

Theophilus does not dally with me. "Isidore is changed. He is harmed in some way." Isidore? I did not expect this as our subject. "Where once I could trust him in all ways, that trust seems threatened."

How odd that he and I should feel as one about Isidore. "What has this to do with me?"

"When you went to Siwa, did he not go with you?"

"Did Isidore tell you this?"

"Isidore tells me nothing. He does not need to. Many eyes and many ears and many mouths are mine. Isidore is not the priest he was. He seems distracted."

"Again, what is this to me?"

"I have plans for my priest. I need him pure."

I am again under palms on a mat in the sand. Pure? Why do men obsess so over the body and its simple harmless functions, shared by all? Augustine believes the body corrupt, even Empedocles spoke of falling into body. Everywhere the fashion is duality: body and soul are opposed. I do not agree with Augustine or Empedocles. I cannot follow fashion. I am as pure as I think myself to be. If I am impure in the eyes of others, especially this poxed "patriarch," I care not a fig or a date or a shattered pot. If God, as this one claims, created the world and all that is in the world, how then can anything made by His Hand be impure?

It seems Father's Beast sees all this in my face. He grows larger. "You know who I am. You know what I can do."

"I do. My father grows daily more ill from your abundant skills."

Does this make him smile inside? I think it does, and so thinking, wish I had not given him the pleasure.

"Then you know that only by my word are you allowed to teach."

I too smile inside. The word of Theophilus is only as strong as the word of Theodosius, Emperor of the East. Eugenius, zealous pagan, ex-secretary, and Emperor of the West, grows stronger, as does his pagan general, Arbogast. And the Western Empire itself? Almost to a man, it desires the return of its gods. What happens there could happen here, for surely Arbogast casts longing eyes on Egypt and its vast supply of grain. Should he prevail, what then could this beast "allow"?

Sitting straight on the back of my noble horse, hoping to appear as noble as she, I say, "Why do you menace me?"

Theophilus too sits upright, maneuvering his mare with his heels so that she arches her glossy brown neck and snorts down her wet black nostrils, causing the golden bells on her bridle and reins to jangle and clang. This is to show me my place. Desher has no bells. She has no tassels or breast collar, no bridle studded with gems. "Only this, schoolteacher. If Isidore appears at your lectures, if he stops you as you would ride by, if he comes to your home, you will not speak to him."

"And if he speaks to me?"

"You will not listen."

"And if I do?"

"Then you will be required to cease your teaching."

I sit for a moment, stunned. It is not that I would see Isidore, for I would not. It is that I am told who I might speak to and who I might not speak to. I would, if I were standing, slap his face. Not by worth but by position, has he power over me. To Kur and its crevasse of dust with his power! And yet, if I cannot teach, how do I care for my family? Physicians, schooling, servants, horses, books, paper, sweets, the services of Rinat…all these are costly. He has left me no choice.

"I will not see him. Nor will he see me."

This time his smile exposes itself on his face. His smile seizes at my stomach, squeezes it like a rag. Once again, I speak to Desher, and am gone. Unlike my mistake with Isidore, I do not look back. I do not know if Theophilus watches me go, or if he does not. Desher and I do not stop until we have galloped a mile on the sand at the edge of the sea. And *then* I look back. If Theophilus remains where he was, I cannot see him.

BLOOD BROTHERS

Minkah the Egyptian

If Theon turns my spleen, Theophilus cracks my bones.

This day I planned to surprise Hypatia with the completion of her wondrous device. As yet unnamed by either of us, it allows its user to view life to a certain depth in the sea without need of getting wet or holding one's breath. I am as proud of it as if it were entirely mine. To test our device, Hypatia has taught me to sail her small boat with its single mast, but the *Irisi* does not love me as much as does Ia'eh. There is an instinct to it, an understanding of hull and sail and wave and wind, and the patterns thereof, that Hypatia possesses and I do not. But as I have yet to run her aground or tack into a grain barge or sail over a rock, I am trusted to sail alone in the Royal Harbor. All morning, I had hung over the bow of the *Irisi*, rocking in the wake of large boats and small, peering down at fish and shells and sea plants and a wealth of miraculous creatures I had no name for, never dreaming such a world dared exist, all the while exclaiming over what I saw though none could hear my voice but me.

I come home to a waiting monk. A mallet, a ladle, one of his bishop's relics, anything to thump him with: but I am called and I must go.

Fortunately, Synesius has wheedled Hypatia into reading some paper of his and if I know Synesius he will not leave until they are both exhausted. It is good to know Synesius, as well as Hypatia, is home with Lais.

A foot through the door of the house of Theophilus, and I am instantly alert. Here sits or stands my "brothers," but only the fiercest. Some quietly talk each to each, some sit alone and are silent, one lies flat out on a pink marble bench, snoring. As big as the warrior Ajax though twice as brainless, if he should sleep throughout the proceedings—whatever they might be—then he will sleep. There are those who would regret waking Felix Zoilus—if they survived their error.

Looking round, I am pricked by distaste. I say I do what I do for the money. Why else join such as these? But I have lied. I am *Parabalanoi* for the shame.

As a witless youth, it remains true I was enraged by abuse and outraged by want, but deeper than either, burned a red core of shame. To stand taller, I longed to rend and to tear, even to kill. I was easy to find. We are everywhere. Approached by the *Parabalanoi*, chosen and trained, what triumph! Through violence, directed and shared, what *cunnus* of a mother dared throw me away, what *merda* in a marketplace dared beat me? It was I who could throw away, I who could beat a back. To provoke fear, to cause others horror or shame, by the jaw of Petbe, god of vengeance, what a wild and willing joy this was! But to cut down, to see blood rush from veins, life fade from eyes, this brought a pleasure so fierce a shout would rise in my throat and I would cry out, elated. In time, even my own kind feared me. Some here now would draw back at my approach. Not Felix, of course. But there is none as Felix.

And yet I read books. But only in secret. I once thought them a weakness.

That was the Minkah then. Who is Minkah now? In this house, I am *Parabalanoi*, a "soldier" for Theophilus. To be blunt, I am a murderous bully with a taste for tales of heroes and sacrifice.

And when I am not here? An interesting question.

Athanasius of Alexandria, who was bishop before the bishop before Theophilus, or perhaps the bishop before that—who counts their ruinous living and dying?—may have created us, and he may not have. Whichever, through us he indulged in a terrible orgy of blood for the love of his god. No fool, he paid his thugs well. Bishop Theophilus is also no fool. Though I have caused no terror nor killed to order for months, and even with the expense of Theon and Olinda, I have hidden away a tidy sum. Now and again, land occurs to me, fine clothes, my own horse to match Ia'eh and Desher. Women too, cross my mind, and women I have had from time to time. But as for love,

I love none but Hypatia, and Hypatia would scorn such love. I could not bear to see that scorn, so do all I must to ensure I do not. I am Minkah the Egyptian. I tend to her father. I watch over Lais. I listen as if interested to Jone and Ife who both now speak as one, and that one sounds as a voice from the only book they read. I am Minkah the Egyptian who is there to protect Hypatia when she goes farther than a foot from her door. I am reminded of Felix Zoilus who snores louder than ever. Tricky business the day I stopped Felix from snapping Augustine's neck on the Heptastadion. And then to snap Hypatia's. Asking Augustine to move away for a moment, I quietly explained to my "brothers" that should they harm either, they would answer to Theophilus. Even Felix stepped back.

Who is Minkah? He has no idea.

Nearby swaggers a man who once entered a house with me. In that house, by order of Theophilus, we killed all we could find, two brothers, the wife of one, and her children: a girl of three and a girl of five. My companion then wrung the neck of a small spotted dog he found whining near the dead children.

All the good I can say of Minkah the Egyptian is that he did not kill a spotted dog, nor did he kill a child or a woman.

In his own good time, our host arrives. Behind him walks Cyril, the privileged nephew, and behind Cyril, walks Isidore, the favored priest from a favored home in Pergamon. I have seen enough of Isidore, so attend to Cyril. How old is this ugly pup? Fifteen, sixteen? However young or old, however fat, he acts the prince. But then, when it comes to princes—I think in particular of Arcadius and Honorius, the feeble spawn of our tremendous emperor, Theodosius—a man need not be much.

Theophilus arrives quoting. "If thine eye be single, thy whole body shall be full of light. But if thine eye be evil, thy whole body shall be full of darkness. Therefore, if the light that is in thee be darkness, how great is that darkness!" He pauses. He stares about him. Felix snores on. The rest have come to their feet. This includes me. "The apostle Matthew said this, and if he were here now, he would say it again: *How great is that darkness*! Has there been any greater!"

Who other than me knows what our great paymaster is maundering on about? By their faces, none. He means that Eugenius has been officially, and with great pomp, crowned Emperor of the West. For Theophilus and his church, what could this mean but disaster? Priests of the old religions are everywhere flocking back to their western temples, the people flocking back to their pagan priests.

To express other than righteous horror would mean fighting my way out of this house, and even I would get no farther than the original Caesar on the Ides of March.

No doubt Theophilus and Isidore were up half the night examining their "book." Though we would do as we are ordered to do, they would cause us to do it with a religious passion.

Theophilus, noting all the blank looks, tells us what he wants and why he wants it. We are to bring terror and woe to certain men of influence, those that Alexandria still heeds. There will be no killing or burning or raping or pillage. We will begin with acts meant only to warn, to tell them that what occurs in the Kingdom of the West will not occur in the Kingdom of the East. If this does not work—we will do more, a great deal more.

The brotherhood growls as one. They curse as they shake their fists. No matter if the cause is just or unjust, they will do as their master wills because those who will not—and who will not?—will find terror and woe turned back on themselves and those they care for, assuming they care for anyone. The woman and child killer has a wife and children of his own. His children have dogs.

We are to begin our work for God immediately. Ordered to line up before Isidore for orders, I mutter over and over: *only Theon, I will kill only Theon.* But when my turn comes, I am told by Cyril to step aside. In an instant I could snap his spine. He knows it. I know he knows it. We both know I resist the urge. Besides, Theophilus will see me privately.

In a far corner where no one can hear, I salute him as a Roman soldier of the rank and file would salute Caesar. "Sir!"

Theophilus is not amused. "You are well known to me, Minkah the Egyptian. I have followed your exploits closely." Not good news. Which exploits? "And know therefore you reside in the House of Theon, the mathematician."

He and I have already acknowledged this, and have come to a tacit understanding that I remain in the House of Theon, mathematician. But I will play his game. "I do."

"If Theon is terrorized, the meetings in his house will stop. I would not have them stop."

I see the flaw here. Shall I point it out? If Theon is *not* terrorized, his terrorized fellows might conclude he is guilty of complicity to save his own hide. *I* would certainly think this. Already he's shown how weak his spine. There is another flaw. If Theon's fellows are persecuted, they might stop meeting from fear alone. I open my mouth to speak, but am silenced by Cyril. One moment he is not there, the next moment he is. A sneaky boy, and quiet for his heft. I could not have done better myself.

"My uncle would not have you speak."

In that case, I will not. Theophilus can spot his difficulties for himself. As for Cyril, I would remove his head on the spot, but as I prize my own head above his, again I resist...though I do stare until it is he who must lower his bulging impudent eyes.

Theophilus continues as if Cyril were not here at all. Cyril, who is very much here, might be thought by his face to be as calm as a dozing cat, but he is not. The tips of both ears are as red as a pomegranate.

"Therefore, no one will be sent to see Theon."

Not glancing at Cyril—after all, he is not here—I say, "And his daughter, the one who teaches?"

"I gave her my word. She keeps hers. No one will touch Hypatia nor cause her to cease her lectures."

Cyril is furious. But whether at his uncle for being shamed before me, or for sparing Theon and Hypatia, I could not say. I understand now who is the more dangerous: not Theophilus, but his nephew Cyril. Fortunately for all, he is yet a boy and has no power here.

"If neither Theon nor Hypatia are included, what then would you have of me?"

"I have work meant for you alone as you alone of the brotherhood are unsuspected. As soon as all is arranged, I will send for—"

"Cyril!"

The room comes to a halt, all turning as one towards the source of this unnerving shriek. Theophania, whom all fear, arrives triumphant. The mother of Cyril is beautiful in a way that Lais is not. If her hair is red or yellow or brown or black, who could say? It is ever one or the other of these. Her nose is as finely made as a hunting dog's, her neck like a white ibis, her eye paint as striking as ancient paintings on tombs, her form as curved as an amphorae. How she birthed such as Cyril has long been a source of inspired, though thoroughly brutish, talk. She is enveloped in so fine a linen the hard nipples of her breasts can be clearly seen, as can her pubis: black, not red or yellow or brown. And this is the sister of a bishop? Every man here lowers his eyes, not so they would not see, but so they would not be caught looking. I do not lower my eyes. If she would display, I would admire. Not for nothing do I relish my reputation.

Straight through a pack of the wolfish brotherhood, she rushes towards Cyril, and once there, pinches his fat arm with her slender fingers.

"Ouch!"

"You have been through my things! I *know* it was you. You will come, and you will come *now* to give me back what you stole from me."

All wait to hear what the boy stole, but all wait in vain for Cyril is gone from here before Theophania can pinch him again, or say more to his mortal shame.

Left on her own, his mother pretends to suddenly note where she is. How prettily she blushes, how charmingly she spins on her slippered heel, how gracefully she floats away. And how murderously furious the face of Theophilus, her brother.

I am entirely amused. Especially as he has forgotten to tell me what it is he plans I do since I am "unsuspected."

Jone, youngest daughter of Theon of Alexandria

"Daughter! Attend!"

Mortifying! Father now calls on me, the one he scarce thinks of from one year to the next. I am Jone. I am she who killed the mother. I am nothing in this house, until I am...and only because Minkah is gone, faithful Minkah.

I hate Father. I do. I hate him. He does not call for Lais, oh no! How can poor helpless Lais be expected to fetch him this and fetch him that? Lais is so terribly ill. And if she were not so ill, she should still not be intruded upon for Lais has her poems which I am not allowed to see and her trances which I *do* see and think them nothing but a sickness caused by that which grew in her stomach. As for Hypatia, never! Hypatia works *with* him, not *for* him. Hypatia is much too grand to bring him fruit or wine or to find a brush or a seal or some other thing he has dropped and cannot get out of his own bed to find. Besides, she has a student in her workroom, one who pays. He could send for the Jewess, the one who scribbles for Hypatia, but does he? Not once. Is she not paid? Of course! A servant! Hypatia should hire another servant. Ife can't do everything. And I will not. I have my own work to do, important work. I have texts to read and to comment on for school.

What does he call for now? God, give me patience. You ask me to honor my father and my mother. I have no mother. And what father I have does not honor me. But I will obey. I will obey the command of the Father who is in Heaven by tending to the man who is called my father on earth.

For the fifth time this day, I open Father's door. "What?"

Father is in bed. What a surprise. He peers at me. Is he trying to remember my name? "See here?" He's waving a large sheet of paper covered with his messes. From what I can see, it's a triangle in a circle in a triangle in some other shape he has a name for, although I do not. "I want you to fetch the twine off the shelf...I think Minkah keeps it on a shelf. Then I would like you to stand over there, as far from me as you can." Oh, I can do that. "Wait. First you take one end of the twine." I take one end of the twine. "Then walk there, no, no, not *there*, there."

I move from one place to the other, and no place I choose will do. There is twine looped around the back of a chair, strung up between one image of some pagan idol and another pagan idol. We are making what seems a spider's web. I will scream. I will scream down this house. Help me Father, for I have sinned.

"For the sake of Thoth, girl, will you stand still!"

"Thoth!" I scream so hard I hurt my throat. "*Thoth*! I do nothing for the sake of demons." And with that I am away from his room which smells like sour wine and sweat and sick and bad teeth and something male I cannot even imagine. He calls, "Stop!" but I do not stop. He calls again, "Come back, you! Come back!"

I will not come back. Not once this day has he called me by name.

Minkah the Egyptian

For three days, my "master" has trembled under his covers. The attacks against the houses of the pagan poet Palladas, of the pagan priest Helladius, of the astronomer Pappas, of the occultist Paulus—if Paulus is a spy, this is wise on the part of Theophilus—of Meletus the Jew, terrify him. Even the Christian Didymus the Blind is "warned."

Having come to his senses through no effort of mine, Theophilus attacks as well the House of Theon. The dung thrown against our walls could feed a field.

What Theophilus would have his spy, Minkah, do, isn't much. I need not dirty my hands with dung. I am to report on what is said and done by these men in response. Emboldened by the rise of the Emperor Eugenius, yet strongly discouraged by the *Parabalanoi*, will Alexandria's "pagans" attempt a return to the old ways? I could tell Theophilus without spying: some will, but most will not. My "brothers" do what they do well... and should a man have the stones to stand up, few remain standing against harm done to their child or a child of their child.

Compared with much I have done, this is nothing. How is it, then, that violence towards a man means less to me than deceit? Overt violence takes a kind of courage. Spying on the unsuspecting requires nothing more than low cunning. For how long now have I been anything other than deceitful? Who here knows I am in the pay of Theophilus? I pretend to care for Theon when I do not. I act the humble Egyptian when I am not.

Grooming Ia'eh, my nerves sing. That I had someone to speak to, but by only a single word—*Parabalanoi*—I should be driven from the company of Hypatia, of Lais, of learning, all I have learned to love.

Ears pricked forward, Ia'eh nibbles my shoulder. Each morning, after I have exercised Ia'eh and groomed her, she expects a date. I rest my head on her neck, inhale her warm scent, a joy beyond price.

"In time," I croon to the white mare of Lais, "you will run again with beauty on your back. But for now, you must content yourself with me."

As I say this, I make my decision. By what comes of it, I will learn who Minkah is.

Lais is alone. She who has endured so much does not lie in her bed as does Theon who had managed to endure little by his avoidance of whatever he might avoid. Lais sits on a couch by her window and on her knees is her writing tablet.

Turning her face, I am yet again stunned by her beauty. I have read the Greeks. They say that beauty never palls, never ceases to have its effect. There is something in man that reacts to beauty as it reacts to nothing else.

If I had not spent my life learning control of my senses, I should fall on my knees before her. Not as I would humble myself before Hypatia, but as I would revere an unworldly thing: a Dryad found in the forest, an Oread from the mountains, Oceanids in waters of salt or Naiads in sweet. There is a scent of magic to Lais.

"Minkah! What a pleasure to see you. Sit. Visit with me. My friends are afraid to come, fearing I will be weakened. But they are wrong. I would be strengthened."

Lais has lifted her pen from her paper, has set aside her tablet. I wish it would not, but my heart sinks to know she means to do nothing more than hear me. She knows I have come to speak with her. What else does she know? I am here now and I will follow the destiny my decision has driven me to.

"I am not what I seem."

"I know."

"I am *Parabalanoi*."

"I know."

"But I did not enter your house sent by the brotherhood."

"I know."

Her answers, not immediately heard by me, locked as I am in the words I have been saying, come through. "You know?"

"Yes, Minkah. I know."

"How do you know?"

And now she laughs. Her laughter is not meant to hurt or to threaten, but comes from her delight in what we say and how we say it. "Oh, Minkah, I know because I have watched you. I know because you tell me in so many ways. No poor Egyptian would act as you have acted in this house. I know also because my poems tell me."

I cannot respond to this last. I do not understand it. "Does Hypatia know?"

"I think not."

"Will you tell her?"

"It is not for me to do so. If she would learn, it must be by your telling her as you tell me."

"Does anyone else know?"

"I think not. In this house, what you pretend to be you *are*. What you are in this house, you become outside this house. But you have come to speak with me. What would you say?"

I am dumbstruck. She speaks to the center of things. "It is not the house, Lais. It is you, it is Hypatia, who have changed me."

"Ah, but it *is* the house for a house is those who live within it. Father has changed you as well. Though you love him not,

Theon loves you."

She knows this too. I am seen by Lais. I squirm in my skin. It is terrifying to be seen. I clench my fists until I am pained. "Yet I remain *Parabalanoi.* I remain sworn to an oath."

"Yes."

"Theophilus orders me to report on the friends of your father who do not know what you know."

"Oh, my friend! What shall you do?"

"I don't know. Knowing nowhere else, I come for your advice."

"What are you moved to do?"

"If I do not spy, I will be killed."

"And if you do?"

"I will be shamed."

"Which hurts more?"

"Deceit."

Lais' laughter causes my laughter. Laughing, I say, "Yet deceit seems the only answer. But if I deceive, it shall be Minkah the Egyptian who chooses *who* to deceive."

"And who shall you choose?"

"Theophilus."

Lais laughs again. I will dream of her laughter. I will remember it when most needed. She holds out her writing tablet. "Would you honor me by reading what I write this day?"

I tremble as I take the tablet she offers. With no word crossed out, no sign of hesitation, I read what is written.

I ask for nothing.
In return I give All.
There is no earning my Love.
No work needed, no effort
Save to listen to what is already heard,
To see what is already seen.
To know what is already known.
Do I seem to ask too little?
Would you give although I ask not?
Then this you can give me and I will accept.
I will take your heart.
You will find it waiting for you
When you return.

THE THIRD GATE

Autumn, 393

Hypatia

Lais floats through our rooms again. She sits in the sun of our gardens. Her incision heals. Flesh softens her bones. She swears she feels no pain. All praise Olinda.

Even Jone knows pleasure. Because we show interest in her reading—at the moment *The True Word* by Celsus—making no criticism of a Christian teacher, a glimmer of joy lightens our little sister's serious face. Our reward is this: we are informed that from now on she will read nothing "pagan." This means she will not be reading anything her own family writes. But as she never has, what loss is this?

Minkah goes about singing some song of the Egyptian streets. I would beg him to stop if I were not so near song myself. Paniwi drops huge rats at the feet of Lais. Both rat and Paniwi look much the worse for wear, though Paniwi is clearly the winner.

I lecture and so many come, so many travel great distances, so many pay. If any truly hear me, I could not say. I teach that Mind creates the illusion of matter. I teach that matter does not "exist," not as we think it does. The Galileans swear that matter is made of lesser stuff into which we have fallen. Flawed by our fall, we are trapped in a world of opposing principals—good and evil, life and death, love and hate, light and dark, liars and truth-tellers, flesh and the spirit—until we are saved. But this is Persian dualism as taught by Zarathushtra "revealed" to him by his Wise Lord, Ahura Mazda.

The faithful are not told that once another thing was taught of their Christ, a teaching I myself have found only remnants of. The books of those who knew him, or who understood him, claim his life was lived as a spiritual myth, that by it he sought to show the divinity of all. I have searched for these books in vain. If not destroyed, the new teaching has hidden the old teaching as well as the Library is hid.

And yet times soften. It seems as it was before the loss of our temples although ours are not regained for this is Alexandria and Theodosius remains Emperor of the East and so rules Egypt. But Eugenius is Emperor of the West. Pagans there: of Italy, of Gaul, of Spain, of Britain, of North Africa once more openly show themselves. Mystery traditions accept initiates and those who would join number in the thousands.

Before this too passes, I work all the hours I can to make use of it.

New thoughts furnish my head. As if servants had tossed out all that is old, and brought in all that is new, I keep Rinat busy enough for a room of her own in which she might sleep. There is so much to say. I cannot reach the heavens—what do I know of the stars? The number of primes is infinite—is there a pattern? And if there is a pattern, has it meaning? I cannot answer. This is all I am sure of: I know that I AM, for I cannot truly assert that I AM NOT.

Perhaps Rinat works to capture unworthy thoughts. But they are my thoughts, and I am filled to bursting with them.

Hope, found in Siwa, is like a hungry lion. It rises to its feet.

Lais and I recline in our bath. Rose petals and sponges float on the oiled water. Paniwi, not one for steam, follows even into the bathhouse, though she must sit on a high tiled ledge where she constantly cleans her fur. As for me, I lie back basking in my sister's life. I revel in the scent of her, the fine fair hair on her slender arms, the elegant line of her forehead as it flows down to the elegant line of her nose, the small scar on her chin where once she fell from the back of Ia'eh. As for the scar on her belly, even this I find beautiful. Made by Olinda, it has saved my sister's life.

She has heard of my trip to Siwa, all but that which occurred under the palms. That Isidore was there, she knows, but asks me nothing. I am nothing like as discreet. I probe. When she was not with us, where did she go? During the time her belly was open, what did she feel? Now that she has returned to this world, does it please her?

I make my sister laugh. “Hypatia, Hypatia. No one asks so many questions, and none so quickly so that the person asked cannot keep up, and yet more come. In my bath, I will answer only one. Which shall it be?”

“The first one.”

“Of course, the most difficult—but as I have promised, I reply. I left the cave of my body, sister. I left what I thought home. I left Egypt. And while gone, I had no idea of time or loss. All was bliss.”

“What do you mean by ‘I’?”

“I mean that within me which perceives. I saw, I heard, I had thoughts and emotions. But of body or bodily sensation, there was none.”

“What do you mean by bliss?”

“What would you mean by bliss?”

“I have no idea. I have never known bliss. But where did this *I* of yours go?”

“‘Where’ means nothing. Where is a thing of *this* world. The I of me, which perceives without need of body, was not in this world.”

“Then some other world?”

“If it was, it was not made as this world is made.”

“Were there gods?”

“Gods? If by gods, you mean others without body or concern for the world left behind, then yes, there were ‘gods.’”

“Were you happy?”

“Oh yes.”

“You were happier there?”

“I would have been, if not for your being here.”

“You play with me.”

Lais takes up my hand. She kisses my wet and oily palm. “What else is there but play, beloved?”

If I thought Father might rise, I am mistaken. He no longer lives in bed because he despairs; he lives in bed because it suits him. He is warm and he is comfortable. He is coddled and he is safe. Or so it must seem to him. All he might desire is brought him. All those he might wish to speak with, visit. If he has, even once, considered what his choice might mean to me, he does not show it, nor does he seem in the slightest abashed that his daughter earns what is needed to assure him he has a bed, not to mention a room to wall it with and a roof to cover it over. In truth, our father has gone from despair to a kind of childlike contentment.

The way here has been difficult, often it angered me, but I have come finally to accept what must be borne. Has he not raised three females without a wife? Did he not climb to the height of such fame as comes to mathematicians? If there were no Emperor Constantine, no Emperor Theodosius, no Bishop Theophilus, Theon of Alexandria would be teaching still. There is also this: if all had not happened as it did, what should I be? I have been restless, curious, an irritant to those who wish peace and quiet. These "qualities" have found a home in teaching.

There is one thing only that rankles. The younger my father becomes, the older must I become.

He has finished his work on the bleating of sheep and the croaking of ravens and whatever else. Today, we begin work on his commentary on the *Mathematical Treatise* of Claudius Ptolemy. To this end, I have spent hours in the garden on our roof creating an *Astronomical Canon*...for though Ptolemy's catalog of stars is impressive, still, Claudius Ptolemy the synthesizer, was wrong in a great number of his conclusions which I must somehow prove to Alexandria's leading mathematician—though his reputation fades. Minkah is forbidden to tell Father what is said of him outside our house; with all he endures, to hear himself replaced—by me!—might further unbalance what is already tilted.

This evening I arrive filled with hope that Father will agree the sun lies at the center of our system, not the earth.

"First," admonishes Father, "Aristotle does not agree."

"True, but—"

"And second, Archimedes does not agree."

"True, but—"

"And third, Theon of Alexandria does not agree."

"Father. Christians once again teach that the world is flat and the universe shaped like a tabernacle."

Father snorts down his nose which causes the hairs that grow there to quiver. "Even a simpleton, when shown, can see a ship sail away over a horizon, disappearing little by little. And when the ship returns, it appears little by little."

"Yet—flat we remain to many."

Father is still quick. He knows what I would say. "I await the day you personally disprove Aristotle. Until then, Claudius Ptolemy is correct."

"But the pure unfounded invention of what he calls "epicycles," so tortuous and so unnecessary if one would merely accept the obvious—"

"Claudius Ptolemy wrote the *Tetrabiblos*. Has anyone been clearer on the subject of astrology? His astronomy is equally clear."

"It is, demonstrably, a mess."

"Do I smell boiled milk? I am starving."

I leave Father to his hot milk, and the intolerable Aristotle to his self-serving argument that the "female is the male deformed," and that "semen is the seat of the soul." It was while reading Aristotle that I first knew anger towards the male. Did he not whine whenever his superior masculine eyes caught sight of women at market? How terrible it is to be woman...but only because of men.

Winter, 393

Minkah the Egyptian

Lais begs Hypatia to take her to the races. Hypatia begs me.

I shake my head. "What if she becomes over-excited? What if she is yet too weak?"

Hypatia argues for Lais. "But Minkah, Alexios is arrived back from his triumphs in Constantinople. He races this day. There is no charioteer my sister dotes on more than Alexios. He will leave again. What if he does not return?"

I pretend to weaken. "Perhaps if we asked Olinda?"

"Olinda visits a patient in Pelusium. And Lais has been so long at home. Her cheeks glow with health, her body is plump, her stomach flat. She would not walk, Minkah, I would never have her walk. Nor will she ride Ia'eh. I will hire a curtained litter, the most expensive, one with heaped pillows and the strongest bearers. Nor, as we did as children, will she remain all day, not even half the day. We shall see only the race of her hero. Surely there is no harm? At the first sign she tires, she shall come home."

I hold up my hand for silence. "If Lais would go, then she will go."

"Thank you!"

If Hypatia cannot see what has just happened, I can. Theon was not asked. Hypatia is mistress here. She need ask no one. Yet I was asked. If Minkah the Egyptian had said no, Lais would not attend the races this day.

When all is arranged, we go east from the Royal Quarter along the Canopic Way, four times wider than any street in the city, extending from its western walls to its eastern walls. Sharing sweet dates and wine, we pass the Jewish quarter, the countless hostels that cater to travelers, then out through the tremendous Sun Gate of the once Emperor Antonius Pius—that improbable thing, a good king—and there, before us, rises up the great Hippodrome.

From the gates to the private boxes, all move aside for Lais and Hypatia. Rome's Prefect, Lucius Marius, whose wife bulges with child, sits two boxes away. Both nod in greeting. Alexandria's magistrates, its generals and ambassadors, the wealthiest of its merchants, smile. There recline or pose or leap from level to level Hypatia's students, among them Synesius. Each of these calls out. Below us carouse a gaggle of philosophers who, upon sight of Hypatia, bow, and upon sight of Lais, bask.

And there is Theophilus and there the priest he loves: elusive Isidore—forbidden Hypatia, thank the gods. And there, Cyril, piglet to Theophilus' boar, his hunger for power hidden in a hunger for food. And there sprawls the darkest of the *Parabalanoi*, Peter the Reader, his mouth twisted down and to the side. I pretend I know them not as they pretend they do not know me.

Hypatia has brought along the fur of an animal to wrap around Lais, pillows for her comfort, a shawl of silk to cover her head. As Hypatia fusses over Lais, I jump to my feet. Below the chariots appear, throwing up dust and color, and how we all roar! Four horses each to a chariot, each horse so similar they might be the same horse: matched blacks, grays, reds, whites, blood bays, browns. My money is on the blood bays. The bays are driven by Nabil, an Egyptian.

Alexios drives the team of blacks. As lowborn as I, he is twenty and six and richer than Cicero. Planted in his chariot with the reins of all four of his horses wrapped round his muscled arm, his muscled back straining to hold them, his muscled legs perfectly balanced, he ignores the crowd which does not ignore him. "Alexios! Alexios! Alexios!"

Fucking catamite...and if he is not, I'll eat my sandal.

Below us, men ready the staggered spring-loaded gates at the angled end of the oval track. Drivers steady their horses, all of whom would race away on the instant if allowed.

Lais leans towards Hypatia, and I half turn to hear her; if she is faint or in pain, I would know this. Though she whispers, her words are clear. "There is none I love better than you... always remember."

Hypatia kisses her sister's palm. "And none I love better than you."

Suddenly, up from the track comes the shouting of those who maneuver the gates, the shouting of those who hold the chariots, the shouting of those who will drive them. Hypatia and I are drawn away by the muttering of horses deep in their throats, the calls of the charioteers, each goading each, the creak of leather stretched to breaking, the turning of the wheels and the complaining of the wooden gates.

Lucius Marius drops a cloth to signal the start. Alexios and his blacks are first away—and as Hypatia thrusts herself up, so too do I. The chariots rub wheels, throwing sparks high in the air, the hooves of the horses strike the ground as metalworkers strike anvils, over and over, and five times round the *spina* each charioteer does his utter best, or utter worst, to tip his opponents, tangle their traces, send them crashing into the walls...any trick they might play to win the day. Coming fast, the bays crowd the blacks.

"Smash him, Nabil! Show him your ass!"

The whites careen off a wall as all disappear yet again behind the *spina* with its lengthy top a clutter of marble gods and bronze dolphins obstructing the view only to reappear a moment later in their rush back. Before they do, the crowd holds its breath. The crashes come at the turns round the two ends of the *spina*, the deaths occur. But there is no crash, no death. There is only Alexios, and his blacks. Piss and shit! Though blood flows from the nostrils of one, though another has a long slash on a pastern, he whips them home to such a shout from the crowd as would deafen, if I were not also shouting as Hypatia is shouting. She cries, "Alexios wins, Lais! He wins!"

But Lais does not look at the track nor does she look at the horses, nor does she look at the triumphant Alexios. Her chin is slumped into the curve of her chest and her arms hang straight from her shoulders so that her hands rest on their backs on the stone and her fingers curl up like the fingers of the dead. Hypatia's shawl has fallen over her face.

Hypatia

My sister, my heart, died this day. The Sun God returns as she leaves us.

In the skies over Alexandria, a great white star has appeared suddenly in the constellation of the Scorpion, brighter than the red star Antares. I, an astronomer, cannot be bothered to look. Emperor Theodosius has ordered, for the first time in a thousand years, an end to the "pagan" games of Olympia. I, called pagan, cannot summon concern. In Hippo, where Augustine struggles with evil, the Galileans have declared which of their many "gospels" is true to the number of four, and have rejected all others, which number in the hundreds. What means this to me, Hypatia, who knows no truth?

Dark deadens the world outside our windows. It is darker still in my heart. From the moment I last heard her speak of love for me, she has never spoken again. She has never opened her eyes. She did not move as Minkah tenderly placed her in her litter for the run home, he and I sick with terror every step of the way, nor when we lay her limp on her bed.

At first sight of her, Olinda of Clarus gently placed her finger in the center of my sister's forehead, saying, "All that remains is for her body to follow her spirit."

I convulsed with shock and with sorrow.

I know the precise moment Lais left this world for another, for in that moment Paniwi turned her wild yellow eyes on me, gave out a great yowl, then leapt from the bed of her mistress and straight out the window. The leap was perfect...no sound of her leaping or of her landing.

Jone who does not read, has not even a book to hold, tries to warm me with her own small body. Jone is not warm, but the warmth of her intention would warm me if I could know warmth—for I have heard the words of Olinda and know them to be true words. Though her body is only now gone, Lais left this world as she sat by my side in the Hippodrome.

Paniwi knows what I know. I have killed my sister. As Athena by accident killed Pallas, the sister she loved more than herself, so too I have killed my sister who I loved more than myself. This is what is also true: truth is not to be found at the Oracle of Siwa.

I am not Athena who then called herself Pallas Athena to confess to her darkness within. I will not, as did Athena in memoriam, sculpt with my own hands a huge statue of Lais. I am not worthy of the heroics of a goddess, though I am as equally dark as she. It is I who am at fault and I who must attone for my fault.

The boat in which we learned to sail was named by Lais *Irisi*—"fashioned by Isis." The *Irisi* lives hidden away in the Royal Harbor near what is left of Mark Anthony's Timonium, the temple he had constructed after his defeat at Actium so he might dedicate it to another like himself, the bitter and abandoned Timon of Athens.

That Father will fall faster and farther does not touch me. That Jone will—and how shall Jone react? I cannot answer. I do not care to try and answer. If any feeling is left me, it is sorrow for Minkah. How he must rue the day he made my family his.

Alexandria is alive. The Great Harbor washes her thighs of white marble as she stretches herself against the curved shore. But I am not alive as I set my course. No moon sails the sky. Only by the lights from countless apartments high and low, do I know the tiny island of Antirrhodos slides by on my left.

A sail is a wing, a boat is a bird. Caught in the wind, we go with the wind.

The short tunic I wear is dark with dirt and salt sea spray and the sweat of my body. I have no food. I have water, for there is ever a gallon or more stored in the small compartment under the *Irisi's* foredeck.

I have lost my sense of time. How long since sailing away through the dark and treacherous mouth of the Great Harbor, allowing Spirit to feel the way through rock and shoal? It is full winter, the season of storms when even the great ships of grain are lost to the wild Green Sea. Small boats like the *Irisi* seldom last against the might of wind and wave.

The skies have been the grey of stone, the seas a series of small waves running like leaves before the wind. There is as yet no challenge to my little boat who rides them as I would ride Desher. Somewhere, a great leaping of dolphins curved up out of the waters only to enter again as sleek as silver and silk. These strange creatures of perfect grace and wild with joy have been the last to come near, and if that was one day past, or two, I could not say.

With only sky above and sea below, I head neither east toward the city of Canopus lost in its maze of reeds, nor west toward the city of Synesius, the ruined Cyrene. I will not see Augustine's Hippo, nor do I hope to cross the whole of the open waters to Rome where I have never been nor have I ever longed to be. I might find some fabled island of Greece. I might not. I have no astrolabe. It sits unfinished by Minkah on my mother's emerald green table. Yet I know I sail straight for the belly of the sea. The sun rises. The sun sets. Moving above the clouds as a woman moves behind curtains of soft white linen. By night, if it is clear, I would know my position by the stars, but the nights are not clear. The only true choice I make is not to sail south where Alexandria continues whether I am there to teach or I am not.

I seldom move from the stern. If I am becalmed, I will make a canopy of my sail and drift. If I meet with a storm, I will use all my skill to ride it. But if I cannot, then I cannot. The skin of my left hand is rubbed red from the sheet line. I leave blood on the *Irisi's* white trapezoid sail. The skin of my right arm is bruised by the steering oar. The skin of my body blackens as the skin of my mouth splits like fissures in rock. By these signs of the body, I know time has passed, more than it seems since running from the room of Lais.

Sometimes I sleep seated and leaning against the oar. Sometimes I do not sleep. Sometimes, a rat who has found a home in the *Irisi*, curls under my bench to keep company with me. It is as thick as the hilt of a sword and its fur the color of a blade. Once I found a roach in my hair. I am bitten by fleas. But if hunger is theirs, all are welcome to whatever use they can make of me. If hunger was mine, it is long since silent. I allow myself small sips of water. In this way I have water to last a few days. When I sleep, I lash down the oar and shorten the sail. When I am awake, I sail, sometimes by day, sometimes by night. On the one clear night, I raised my weary eyes to the stars. I imagined them holes through which shine the souls of the hidden palace of *Tuat*. I imagined them each a sun as our sun around which some other earth circles. I imagined them the eyes of gods or of demons. I felt stared at. I shut my own eyes and still I saw them.

If I survive what I now do, it will not be by my own choosing. Not that I choose to die. Nor do I choose to live. I do no choosing at all.

On the first night, responding to *Irisi's* billowed white sail, my mind still questioned: was there a time when the world was not? If it was not and then it was, something can appear from nothing. If so, how? If not, then all is actually *nothing*, and what we experience as "world" is in truth a magical dream. But do I *know* this? I know what many great minds have been taught, for they have taught me. But who has taught them? How far back does it go, this teaching?

On the second night, I thought only of home. Did Father gnaw at his pillow? Has he yet to notice my absence? Minkah must be half mad with the death of Lais—has he found time in his madness for me? And Jone, Lais' well loved "mouse." Who does she seek solace with?

I have determined to remain still in both body and mind and to accept what swims towards me. For something comes, of that I am certain.

It is day again. I have fallen asleep as I do more and more, and as I sleep, tormented by dreams of snakes with scales of fire and trees uprooting from soil to walk the earth and of winged insects writing nonsense on walls, the rat I share my boat with has curled itself around my feet. We are both the warmer for it.

From one instant to the next, I come awake, slapped in the face by a cold hand of water. The sky, pale blue when last I saw it, is a curved metal mirror, and a gelid wind has come up that snaps first here and then there. I know what I see, what I hear, what I smell. A storm comes, a great storm. Stupor flees as a cur flees a stone. I am fully alert to my danger. Weakened by lack of food and water, I have strength enough to grasp the sheet line, causing the *Irisi* to wear on the wind.

The cold deepens by the moment, the wind strengthens, the waves grow farther apart, and each rises higher than the one before. We ship water, the *Irisi* and I, our rigging strained to the utmost.

And now rises a wave to starboard that seems come out of nowhere, and not such a wave as follows one after the other like floods in the Nile or tremors in the earth, but a wave like the tremendous raising up of a great watery head out of the sea, a cobra's flared head...and in the blue-water cobra are caught fish whose scales gleam with blue light, and strange dark shapes that toss and circle and swirl, torn and twisted up from the deep sea floor. Higher and higher rises the cobra with its cowl of living water until it hangs over the *Irisi* before it falls with the heaving of the sea...and this wave will swamp us. Immediately, I slack my line to spill wind. There is nothing to do but head into this wave, hoping the *Irisi* and I might ride up and over it—and we do. But then, behind, comes another wave larger still, and another behind that, and the *Irisi* takes water over her bow as, head-on, she plunges into the next wave and the next. Salt sea water washes over the gunwale and into the *Irisi's* sole, and I, holding fast to the oar, plant my bare feet hard into the wet sole so that I might quickly switch headings and quarter the sea, all in the hope I will ride up the waves. But still I ship water, so much so that I am turned side into wave and at that the *Irisi* lays over, her blooded white sail so close to the shipping sea how shall she right herself?

I call out in the crash of wave on wave and the seeming sound of the *Irisi* breaking asunder, "Spirit! Is this what is mine?"

If there is answer, I cannot hear it for then comes the greatest wave of all, not a cobra but a sphinx of a wave, and it breaks over the mast and over me...and I am on the instant washed overboard. For one long moment I grip the gunwale as a shriveled thing, a blackened thing. I am no thing. Through salted lips that bleed, through a salted throat that sears with pain, I cry out, "Take me. Do not take me. Choose!"

My strength deserts me. I cannot hold on. Falling away from the *Irisi*, I endure what I hope will be my last thought.

Let me be with Lais.

I awake, if I awake, to the dark. If hand I still have, I cannot see it. If body I still have, I do not feel it. If sound there is, I cannot hear it. If there is still something of me that might reach out to touch, I cannot move it. If there is still an I and if that I is called a name I dimly perceive as mine—*Hypatia, Hypatia*—I could not prove it.

I have passed beyond the gate, but as what?

Time passes...or it does not. Without sound or sight or touch or taste or smell, how does one tell?

Even dead, I am full of questions. But if dead, I have brought with me my heart. If I would be comforted in death by lack of feeling, to my horror I am not. If I would be met in death by the bliss of those gone before, to my sorrow I am not. But if I would be obscure, lost, abandoned to a meaningless nothing, this I have gained.

I drift farther and farther into deeper and deeper green. I hear, though what I hear is strange beyond strange. Long low musical sounds, as mournful as a widow at a tomb. High short sounds, as curious as a dog at a door. Clicks like insects in the heavy heat of the day. Enveloped by waving fronds of slick yellow green, I too sway as the fronds sway and my hair is like the sea grass. I do not breathe. I have no sense of breathing. I have no sense of a need to breathe.

I grow quiet within. Fans of sea bubbles rise from somewhere far below. I am without mind and all is Mind. Like a sea snake, delight curls up my spine and all the while, lights like tiny stars, dance in the deep waters. I become full of import. I become transported by meaning. I weep at the bottom of the sea.

I am not sunk in the sea, but lie on the sand that lies by the edge of the waters. What remains of my tunic is yet wet, but not so wet I am recently washed ashore. I have been here for a space of time. The skin of my legs and my arms and my face are as much sand as the beach is sand.

Flat on my back, I turn my head to see only sea and sand that curves away until I can see no farther. I turn my head again and there is the *Irisi* and beyond the *Irisi* the lighthouse, made small by distance. She is keeled over on her side, her mast snapped in two, her sail torn and lying, as I do, curled in the sand. From a hole in her side creeps my rat. It too lives.

The *Irisi* is not lost, but damaged. I can see she will become again what she was. I too am damaged but I will never become again what I was. A thing that has drowned in the sea is a thing claimed by the sea.

By what means I am returned to life I do not recall. But someone or something has chosen. And I can do nothing but accept what has been decided by my taking the *Irisi* out into the sea, alone, in the season of storms.

I turn my head away from our little boat and begin to count the grains of numinous sand.

I return to a house in deepest mourning. With the loss

of Lais, the house itself seems lost. The servants go about in silence. Even the horses make no sound. All lives, yet nothing is truly alive.

I return to a city in mourning for Lais was beloved of all. I return to my teaching because I must continue to teach or those of my household who so silently mourn will do so in rags.

But in truth "I" do not return at all. Hypatia as she was is gone. The Hypatia who rose from the sea is as yet undiscovered, and until she is found, I play the part of the Hypatia all know. I do this for myself as well as for others. If I did not, who should I be?

If any suspect the struggle and the change, it is Minkah.

During this time of sorrow I do only one thing that flows out from the Hypatia who recently lived. In the farthest reaches of a night soft with the light of a silvered moon curved as Diana's Bow, and timed by the flight of Venus, I light the flame that will heat the rare *aqua animus* in which silver, to my mind more noble than gold, will metamorphose into that which is no longer silver, no longer *aqua animus*, but the transcendent *aqua spiritus*. To fast for three days and then to drink of Spiritual Water under the face of the moon, to call upon Isis, Demeter, Inanna, I hope to shine with a light as lustrous as silver for I too will transmute...and in this state I will cry out to Lais. I would have her hear me. Of more worth, I would hear her.

I awaken to find myself lying in a slant of moonlight. Above me stands Paniwi who, for the second time, leaps from a window. As fast as she, I am up and searching for her in the street below our house. She stops to look back just once before becoming no more than shadow...and then a shadow lost in shadows.

"Lais," I call out, "my life is yours. Live through me."

Later, not knowing why, I cut off my hair.

BOOK THREE

"I am the First and the Last...I am the knowledge of my inquiry, And the finding of those who seek after me, And the command of those who ask of me, and the power of the powers in my knowledge of the angels who have been sent at my word, And of gods in their seasons by my counsel, And the spirits of every man who exists with me, And of women who dwell with me."—
The Thunder, Perfect Mind

NILDJAT MIW

The Return of the Sun, 399

Hypatia of Alexandria

Six years have passed and with them my life. I am now Hypatia of Alexandria, revered throughout the Empire. The books I write, the students I send out, those who travel great distances merely to hear me speak, the praise of Augustine and of Synesius—all this should swell my heart if not my head.

On this day, Jone believes her Christ was born. Minkah calls it "The Return of the Distant One," for on this day Het-Heret, without beginning or end, is coaxed back by the sorrowing land, desolate without her. As a Greek, Father prefers to think the sun returns with Persephone, Light bringer, Life giver. By whatever name, cold turns to warm, dark to light, despair to hope. Yet I remain still at heart. Lais died on this day; it is a perfect day for what Minkah and I will do.

If I have grieved, so too has Minkah. I have lost not only my beloved sister and faithful friend, I have lost inspiration...the one true thing that proved Spirit exists. Minkah has lost love. For more than a year, we did not mention her name. But slowly we spoke, a remembrance, a feeling, and as the years passed and each year we sat at her tomb, it is as if she were with us again. Lais has not died. Not so long as I live and Minkah lives. And each year, I grow closer to our Egyptian, seeing him as the brother Father would have him. There are times when I see him as more, but I shudder away this dishonorable thought. He is my brother. His heart lives with Lais.

We walk, Ia'eh and Minkah, Desher and I, towards the dark ridge of stone where the books lie hidden, awaiting the day they should be found again. I would urge Desher to speed, but cannot, for Lais' poems reside in earthen jars and these reside in leather bindings—if they should be broken in my need to see sooner done what was promised!

When Cleopatra ruled, the books numbered four hundred thousand ...and this, I think, is true. By the time of Theon of Alexandria, an age in which the books were no longer in the Great Library of the Palace of the Ptolemies, which was also no longer, but housed instead in the "daughter" library of the Serapeum, they numbered three hundred and sixty thousand. Those lost to the burning of Bishop Theophilus amounted to a tenth of these. But no matter if full half were lost, that Minkah brought out from Alexandria so many amazed me then; it amazes me still. He not only carried them here, but brought back an account of where each cave was sited, and which jars were placed in which cave.

"There," says Minkah, pointing, "an hour more now, maybe less."

I have waited these six years to bring my sister to the caves. *Sas, sissa, sex, sesh*; no matter the language, six is similar and similarly understood. Only in Greek is it named *Hexad* for Greeks never hiss *sssss*, they exhale *h*.

The Christians say their god made the world in six days. But they do not know why, though their book asks: *Doth not nature itself teach you?* The Nation of the Bee builds its hives by the number six, the fish orders its scales, the tortoise its shell, the insect its legs, the snake its skin. In six is the perfect balanced three: structure, purpose, order. Father taught, as did Nicomachus of Gerasa before him, that six is the number of completion.

I intend all I do for my sister to be *ma'at*, in perfect balance, as was she. "Observe due measure, for right timing is in all things the most important factor." This was said by Hesiod who enjoyed many wonderful thoughts. Therefore, Lais will rest in the Cave of Poets with Enheduanna of Ur, with Sappho, with Pindar, with Simonides of Ceos, with Stesichorus, with Telesilla...the list is wondrously endless.

Minkah's hour has passed. We arrive at the caves.

As he prepares himself, removing his cloak, uncoiling the rope of hemp from Ia'eh's saddle, I ask that I might choose where best to honor her.

"That choice is your right."

Something causes me concern. "You would say more?"

"The cave is deep."

"But you took down much larger jars."

"I am strong, and I had help."

"I am strong, and I have you."

Minkah, who knows me well, does not argue. "What we do, we do for Lais. If we fall, we fall."

"And if we fall?"

"We shall remain with the poets and Lais will sing as we die."

"Where is the harm?"

"There is no harm."

I lay aside my cloak, unpack the large bag Desher has carried as well as she has carried me. Around my waist I tie the rope I too have brought. I tie it also to Minkah's rope.

Minkah is stronger; on his back he will carry my sister's jars secured in a padded satchel and the satchel will be tied to his body so that it does not swing out as he climbs. Our two lanterns apiece are tied to an arrangement of woven reeds, left hidden in a niche of rock for just such a return. These weigh little and fit over our shoulders in a most cunning way. This is also how we carry water.

"How clever these, Minkah."

As he goes first and I follow, the color of his cheek tells me how pleased he is I know he has made them. In moments, the memory of our coming here strips away the years. Once, day after day, books arrived in their hundreds to be placed in twelve chosen caves. Twelve labors of Hercules, twelve disciples of Jesus, twelve ordeals of Gilgamesh, Odysseus sailed twelve ships, Osiris walks with twelve retainers, twelve notes in the chromatic scale...and this only the smallest part of twelves. Twelve numbers the Zodiac.

The cavern we enter is flooded with winter sunlight for half its distance, and I follow with care for this is a cave he alone explored. Far above bats rustle and squeak, on either side the cave stretches out, further in one direction than another, and as the cool of the day becomes cooler here, so too the light of the day grows dimmer and dimmer. Louder than the bats are the crickets, a din on the ears.

Minkah ignores obvious tunnels, avoids as best he can the bat droppings swarming with tiny black beetles. We cover our noses and mouths with thick cloth against the bitter stench, but there is nothing to stop the watering of my eyes. In moments, my leather riding boots—not even I would go barefoot here—are damp with the droppings of unnumbered bats and the yellow grease of crushed beetles.

He stops. "Here, we must light our lantern. One only, for the second lantern will be needed later."

This chills me more than the cooler air, but I make no sign. I will follow where he leads, endure what he endures, so that my sister's poems find the place that awaits them.

Farther into the dark where even bats do not venture, Minkah steps with care round an outcrop of rock half the height of Pharos, then drops to crawl through a tunnel created by fallen rock. When finally we stand again, we are in a low cave full of what seem the carved columns lining the Street of the Soma, but are more as melted tallow in their twists and turns. Minkah points at a small grouping of stones. "These are here to mark the way. Though they seem as random as sand, they are not."

My Egyptian is long called Companion by a group secretly formed, one Synesius pleaded with me to secretly teach, for some, though they call themselves Christian, hunger for the old wisdom. And how bright he is, how much he learns. I may have only one living sister, but I have a twice-brother of idea and of family. Touching his arm near the scar he no longer hides, I say, "They are seven which remains aloof from other numbers. Not only do these mark the way, but declare that as the true shape of a heptagon eludes, neither will the library be found." Minkah stares at me for so long I am made uncomfortable. "Do I err?"

"Theon is right to be filled with pride at fathering such as you, and right to be afraid."

"Afraid?"

"Your mind humbles all others."

I now stare at Minkah until he too is made uncomfortable. "My father fears me?"

"I was wrong to say so. Come. It is only now that we face true danger."

Squeezing through a tight crevice of jagged rock which tears at my clothing, catches at my hair and the flat basket of reeds on my back, we come out onto a narrow ledge, less than that which encircles the lighthouse. Here, shoulder to shoulder, we must face the wall for balance and touch. Behind us, above us, below us, is nothing. If not for our lanterns it would be blacker than black, for black has a sense to it, a shape. This is an immaculate darkness in which the mind could lose its way. Into mine comes an image of the gentle Didymus who lived without light, whose world was heard with the ear, inhaled through the nose, felt with the hand—was it as dark as this? Here, the world of light has never reached. Tricks are played on the senses, time fades, even dimension. To know for certain which is down is to fall.

I press my hands harder against the cold uneven rock. "You came here! You dared this?"

I am smiled at by lantern light. As Minkah grows older, he grows more comely. I wonder now on a spit of a ledge lit only by our two small lanterns whose light is helpless against the power of the dark, does he remain without the company of women? If Lais causes this, she would not be pleased—and she would tell him so. My sister was not of the body, but Minkah is. As am I. Does he deny his as I deny mine? If so, are we fools?

"Not alone. There were others: Synesius, a few Companions, friends of the streets of Rhakotis who dared it with me."

"Then these must know where we have hidden the Library!"

"Each came blindfolded. Each left blindfolded. Even Synesius. None were told what we carried. Do not move. It is time for our ropes. When I call, you will follow me down."

"The first time, how did you know you would find a bottom?"

"I did not know."

What is there to say to that? But Minkah is already gone, slipping over the ledge by his rope, a loop of which is passed round a thick thumb of stone. Mere moments later, he calls...it could not be terribly far to the invisible floor below. I, too, slip over the ledge, held steady by both Minkah's rope and my own, only to find myself swinging in space. "Minkah! Once down, how do we climb up?"

"Do as I showed you, use the rope as a ladder."

And then, I too am down, balancing on broken rocks, clinging to the rope that remains fastened to the ledge high above.

"Light your second lantern, Hypatia. We are here."

I gasp, though not with dismay. I am filled with wonder.

All around are the great sealed jars, and in them, our books, our precious books. There is more. The walls are covered in images: men who are hunters, women who ride strange beasts, animals of every sort, birds, wheels, hands, feet, what seems to be writing. I am struck dumb by the sight, my arm holding up my lantern as close as I can so I might see as much as I can.

Minkah speaks through my awe. "Choose where to place the poems of Lais."

"But who did this? Who painted these things?"

Shrugging, Minkah removes the jars from his basket of reeds. "Who can tell who? Or when? Or even why?" The earthen containers now sit on a flat bit of rock that shines in the light of my lanterns. On each glazed jar is painted a rose of five petals, and under this white rose of innocence and wisdom is written the name of Lais, all done by the finest hand. And where shall they now spend what might be eternity? By that grouping of poets, or that one? There are too many and our time here is measured by the oil in our lanterns. Lais will decide.

The moment I think this, my eyes alight on a small cave within this large cave. There! The three small jars of Lais will rest before a grouping of nine, the number of eternity, making the twelve that is divine balance. Caring not which poet is in which jar, I know only which poet lives in the jars newly placed here, and that is knowing enough.

As we turn away, beginning the difficult climb back up the rope, I speak this last thing to Lais, my voice echoing. "You will be found, sister, for nothing of beauty is ever lost."

Riding out of the desert, Minkah and I follow a path through the catacombs in the City of the Dead towards the gate in the southern wall of Alexandria. Near it flows the River Draco, no river at all, but a sharp turning north from the Schedia Canal. Near the canal and the gate there is a small shrine to Bastet, gentle protector, the cat-headed daughter of Ra, now forced to honor a Roman soldier, Adrian of Nicomedia, so moved by Diocletian's Christian martyrs he too was martyred. This I know because of Jone.

Before leaving our house, Jone quoted her choice of scripture to Father, to me, to Minkah, to Ife who of us all listened with interest, to my much valued Jewess Rinat who though offended still smiled, to the lads in the stables and the women in the kitchen. As in any teaching, there is that which is taught those few who can "hear," and that which is taught the many who cannot "hear." If there comes a time Jone has ears, so far as I know, it has not come yet.

Jone heard no word of farewell from Father. To compensate for what could not be excused, I babbled, treading on her heels as she left, only to see a small gathering of women awaiting her as they stood on a celestial map—Father had retiled the atrium floor with tesserae of colored stones to honor Lais who well loved his stars. And just as our father had no word for Jone, these had no word for me. My sister, our little mouse, now lives in a house for Christian women near the school Didymus once led. All are either widows or virgins. What it is she does each day I do not know, nor how she supports herself, for we see her so seldom and she asks for so little. Though I receive no reply, I dictate one letter a week. In it, I recount all that occurs in the house of her father, sign with both my name and his, and send off a grateful Ife as messenger. Is my use of Father's name an error? To commit an error is the root of the word "sin," a word that lives in the mouth of Jone as a bell lives in a bell tower. If I "sin," it is with all good intent.

Minkah and I pause in our return from the distant caves to water Ia'eh and Desher. As we too need water, we have both dismounted to drink from the well near the shrine of Bastet.

I breathe into Desher's soft nostril; telling her of my love in this way. She breathes into mine. Minkah, speaking to Ia'eh as I speak to Desher, touches my arm as he passes. It horrifies as well as thrills. Long asleep, my body awakens. When there is time, I shall think about this. But not now. Not now.

Near the well—set in the shade of a misty-leaved tamarisk tree, one that grows more in stone than dirt—a sound comes, faint as allusion, yet I know it instantly. It comes from the shrine and does not repeat, yet I am away from the well, making for the door of the stolen shrine. Behind me follows Minkah.

A cat has birthed her kittens in this dark deserted place, but only one of five lives. Colored as grasses in summer, striped as the lake through reeds, this last life wobbles far from its siblings, calling for its mother, bumping its nose on the cold stone walls. That four are dead, that one will not live out the day, means the mother too is dead for no cat would abandon her kits. I sweep up the last alive, hold it in the palm of one hand, coo to it. Its eyes are unopened, its open mouth makes only a squeak. Its ears have yet to unfurl. It is frightened and lost. It starves.

This kitten is mine. It has waited for me in the shrine of Bastet. It knew I would come. I know this as I know my name.

I know it as I know the name of the kitten that will become the cat who called out to me.

The moment Lais died, Paniwi leapt through her window. "The Bringer" belonged to Lais and she left with Lais. With the passing of these six years, I am now called by a cat of my own. Whether male or female, I cannot tell, but to find it when it would die is an omen of great import. The omen suckling the tips of my fingers is Nildjat, meaning "the contemplative cat who peers into the realm of the spirit." It is Miw for the name Lais once called me by.

There is written on a Royal Tomb in Thebes: "*Thou art the Great Cat, the avenger of the Gods, and the judge of words, and the president of the sovereign chiefs and the governor of the holy Circle; thou art indeed...the Great Cat.*"

My great cat will be as a cat and speak for the gods.

Slipping my gift into the soft leather bag that hangs from Desher's saddle, I mount quickly. "Hurry, Minkah. Nildjat Miw must eat."

Spring, 400

If Minkah is away, Father calls on me. Having lived so long in bed, his arms and legs have shriveled. His back has weakened. Olinda, who now comes for an hour once every week, tells me an unfading redness covers those parts of his body touching his bed. If only he would rise again, dress again, walk again—but he will not.

Of Father's sixty-five years, full nine have been spent on his back. He continues to work, but produces nothing of worth for his mind seems as his back. I cannot force him to do what he would not, but I *can* make him move in his bed. The papers I would show him, I place just out of his reach. The new inks I bring him, the books he calls for, the food he would eat, all these are just far enough away so he must sit up to snatch at them. Olinda instructs me, saying even these small movements do much to keep him in health. I would keep him in health. My mother is gone, Lais is gone, Jone is gone. I would not lose my father.

Today I bring him my cat.

"Ah," he says, "what is this?"

We watch her make her way up to what there is to see of him: his grizzled head. Female, Nildjat Miw grows quickly, remains yellow, seems to acquire more stripes with the passing of each day. As for her voice, it is extraordinary. It is loud and it is varied. She talks as she climbs.

"She found me, Father. She called out."

"How fortuitous for you. Listen to her! She is as you were. As a babe, our house knew no silence."

"Surely not!"

"Hah! There was never a babe like you. Lais was born in grace and had no need to speak. Jone," and even now, he cannot hide his distaste, and even now I pretend not see it, "barely spoke a word at any age. Who knew what went through her mind? Who knew if she had one? But you! From birth you expressed yourself unceasingly. Your grasp of words increased as drops of rain increase in storms. By one, you spoke in both Greek and Latin. Six months later you added the Egyptian of our servants. Your mother saw the genius that guides you."

Transfixed not only by what he says, I sit silenced as memory rushes back like water flooding a field. I remember my cradle. I remember my mother's warm breast. I remember that I could think and that my thinking was wordless but full of images, vibrant and filled with import. I remember I caught at the words I heard, hoarded them for the day I would speak. Though I could not form words, I could wordlessly sing, knowing melody before I knew speech. I remember believing all could do this, and as I learned month by month, year by year, that they could not, I remember fear.

Father is tickling the belly of Nildjat Miw. How shameless she is. "Damara saw the spirit which fills you, the single star that fell as you were born. Reaching out for you in your cradle, she saw, hovering near, a being made of clouds."

"You have never said this before."

"Have I not? I thought I had."

Nildjat has reached Father's beard and there she bats at it as she bats at balls of fluff she finds on the floor. Father laughs.

A letter awaits me from Augustine which includes a finish to what he first gave me, his *Confessions*, but so long as Father laughs, I would not leave here.

MINKAH

Autumn, 400

Minkah the Egyptian

Theophilus summons me.

This day was bound to come. I am still *Parabalanoi.*

Pah. I see he has given himself a finer house than the one he'd stolen before it—in Alexandria, it is never wise for the rich to draw notice. Also not good to find it sited three streets away from the House of Hypatia. It sits at the edge of the canal and all day long ships from the Great Harbor seeking the lake, or ships from the lake seeking the harbor, come and go. He can't miss a thing. The floor is tiled with fish. The ceiling is painted with birds. Medusa covers a wall. In the reflecting pool stands a statue of Hestia, Goddess of the hearth.

What excuse was used for *this* theft?

Houses are not all he steals. How long before Hestia is repainted and called "Mary, the mother of God"? But what will he do with Medusa?

I wait in an antechamber. There is a monk robed in brown who stands outside the door. There is a brown-robed monk who stands inside the door. A third monk in brown guards the entrance to the room where Theophilus holds court. In pose, they are as Roman sentries, though they carry no weapons I can see. This does not mean they carry no weapons. One has a face like jackal-headed Anubis, another like the bottom of a pot, the last is as lovely as a cherub. Each is a man of faith, but

I would be loath to disturb them, not all three at once.

Someone else, no doubt also summoned, is with the bishop. I hear now and again a word exchanged, now and again the thump of a fist on a desk, or a wall. Whoever Theophilus is with does not please him, nor is he who visits, best pleased. I cannot hear what they say, but I can easily sense how they feel. Anger, frustration, threat. But who threatens whom? It seems first one, then the other. Suddenly the bishop's door is thrown open, and this is so unexpected, the pot-faced monk drops his knife.

Isidore of Pergamon. I might have guessed. Come from money, well-spoken, well-read, well-liked by some, nicely made in body and face, though no beauty, like me, he is *Parabalanoi*, as brutish as the worst of us. And yet his hands are never bloodied. Many mutter against him. Does he think himself too good for such things? Or is he a coward? I choose coward with a weak stomach. If not for Theophilus, Isidore would long ago been found in an alley, his testicles stuffed in his mouth.

Because we are both *Parabalanoi*, I am given a curt nod of recognition as the angry priest strides past, though his robes of high office are whisked away in case I defile them.

"Minkah!"

Theophilus is recovered. Certainly he seems not to mind that his "favorite" strides from his house. When I come near, he grasps my arm, turning it over to expose the scar that runs from shoulder to elbow.

"I do not forget this was done in defense of me." I demur. It is true, of course. I *did* save his life when a maddened priest of the Goddess Isis would take it. But best not to preen. Preening is the privilege of power. "Enter. Sit down. Wine? Water? Whatever you'd like. You!" He yells at an Egyptian slave who brings me both water and wine. "It's been too long. Tell me what have you been doing?"

"If anyone, you know what I've been doing."

I make him laugh. He snaps his fingers. "The spies I have now. A miserable bunch."

"Indeed."

"Tell me of the house of Theon. All goes well?"

"Well enough."

"The old man grows young again, too young. I hear if he grows any younger, he shall need swaddling and a cradle."

I merely nod at this.

"And Hypatia? She is surely healed of her sister?"

"She will never heal."

"Women. Too weak for this world. And yet this one is not precisely a woman, is she?"

Though he may not intend me to see what he has revealed, I do see. He means she is so much more than he, he can scarcely comprehend the leap from where he sits to where she stands.

"She is a woman."

"Only a woman?"

Does he ask if she is subversive? I must be careful. "Only a woman."

He pretends to think about this. He crooks a finger, heavy with gold, so that his waiting slave pours him wine. "Yet on this day, she is given Alexandria's chair of philosophy and mathematics. Aside from fanatics and fools who wear at me as stone is worn by water, there is none to doubt that in all the world Hypatia of Alexandria is a queen of mathematics, of astronomy, of philosophy, even of theology. There is a celebration. I am surprised we cannot hear its wretched beginnings from where we both sit." He pauses. There is nothing to hear but the breath through his nose. He sounds as a winded horse. "Tonight I attend her banquet though some advise me to make my excuses, saying mathematics is no more than divination and divination the handiwork of a tireless demon. Mark my words, bishops from Jerusalem to Dijon to Thebes to Nisibis will ruin this church we build, though it takes them years." Listening, I can only hope he is right. "Especially that vacillating fool now installed as the Bishop of Constantinople. You have heard of him, called John of Antioch?" At the name, Theophilus stands abruptly, knocking a vase from a table which his slave rushes forward to rescue. "I am the Bishop of Alexandria. It is my right to choose the new bishop of Constantinople—*my* right! Was I allowed this right? No! My choice was ignored." His choice for bishop of Constantinople, the archdeacon Isidore, has just left the room, as ignored in going as Theophilus was in his choosing. "The devil himself dug up the old turnip, virtually dragged him by his string of a beard from Antioch to Constantinople. In the dead of night, this was done. In the *dead* of night so the faithful of Antioch would not know they had lost him. Why should they care! But they *do* care! And this sanctioned by the Emperor Arcadius! How dare he! How dare even a son of Theodosius, may God grant him eternal peace, slight my office!"

"I have heard of John," I say, neglecting to mention I know as well of his 'devil,' the eunuch Eutropius. Before getting himself killed by hubris, Eutropius controlled both the feeble Arcadius and his empress, the ferocious Eudoxia. Eutropius had spies as numerous as the spies of Theophilus...in other words as many as maggots on a carcass. To gain John, his own choice of bishop, Eutropius threatened to expose the avarice of Theophilus. But for this, Isidore the pretty priest from Pergamon would even now be seated as bishop in the city of Constantinople.

Back to lolling about on a couch of fat pillows, Alexandria's Patriarch has spilled wine on the red silk of his pallium, but does not notice. "They say John of Antioch speaks so well he sings, that for this he is called John Chrysostom. Eudoxia adores him." As if biting into a fetid fig, he spits on the carpet, inhales more wine, and dismisses the subject of singing bishops. "What kind of woman is she?"

I do not pretend I believe he means the cunning Eudoxia, Arcadius' lowborn barbarian wife. I know he means the brilliant though naïve Hypatia. "A woman so far beyond the pettiness of politics, she can mean nothing to those who are not."

Only the slight widening of his eyes tells me that Theophilus feels insult. But he is much too clever to worry over trifles. I have answered the question he has asked me: is Hypatia a threat or is she not by her rise to even higher prominence and influence? I have told him she is not. Years ago, by careful wording, I placed in his mind the thought that she was harmless. Years have passed and my words become like daubs on walls. I cannot pretend Hypatia weak or witless or over-rated. But I am as yet free to call her harmless by intent.

Theophilus calls for more wine. I content myself with water. A clear head with this man is more than wise, it is imperative. "Do you know why you are not called to serve me these many years?"

He knows I know. We play some tedious game. "So that I might be your eyes and ears in the house of Theon."

"And you will remain in that house. By you, I know who visits there. I know what is talked of. By you, I know I might know more when and if I need to." Here, he leans forward, expressing by look all the power that is his. "Minkah, if not for your use in another's house, you would have found a high place in mine."

He is sincere. It's chilling. If I had not found a place in the house of Hypatia, for it *is* her house—the spies of Theophilus who also spy on me describe well the state of the father—would I have allowed myself a place in the house of Theophilus?

To put it more clearly: how low would I sink for money? I regret that I *cannot* answer, not if the amount would buy me ease from shame. How much would I do to save myself?

Our hope of a return to the old ways died six years ago. Theodosius, father of two idiots: Arcadius, now Emperor of the East and Honorius, now Emperor of the West, marched his army of Visigoths and Syrians out from Constantinople and on through the Julian Alps as far as the Frigidus River, there to meet with Arbogast and his army of Franks and Gauls. Without hesitation, Theodosius launched his men at the defenders of the pagan usurper and secretary, Eugenius, Emperor of the West.

In one day, Arbogast crushed him. Kneeling in blood, even Theodosius believed he had lost his attempt to wrest back the Empire of the West from heretics and demons.

That night, before the decisive battle none thought he could win, Theodosius spoke privately with his Christian god. "Father!" he must have cried, "save my Empire for if I lose, you lose."

At first light, Theodosius rallied what few troops were left him and attacked again. And lo! a great gale came up and blew in the face of his enemy, and the wind blew so hard it reversed the course of their arrows and blinded their eyes with dirt. By this, the lines of Arbogast broke, fleeing in fear, leaving the field to what all described as an astonished Theodosius.

An hour later the captured Emperor of the West was kneeling before the Emperor of the East, when, suddenly, a soldier leapt forward to strike the horrified head of Eugenius from his horrified body.

Or so Alexandria was told by its bishop. This much was certainly so: Theodosius once again ruled both East and West. Truth is, the steep valley in which all this took place was well chosen. The sudden strong winds that blew up to blind the army of Eugenius were common, and came always from the same direction. Theodosius would know this. His only mistake was to meet up with Arbogast before the winds. But how easy to bedazzle the ignorant with his praying and his "miracle."

Theophilus is, for the moment, quiet. Maybe I will discover why I am summoned. And maybe not. A bishop is as forgetful as the next man. I wait, thinking: the god of Emperor Theodosius gave with one hand, but took back with the other. He took the wife of Theodosius. He took her child. In the city of Milan, four months after his victory over the foes of his faith, he took Theodosius himself by disease.

And yet though Theodosius is dead and his sons are weak, Christians rise again. Raids on the lives and property of Alexandrian Jews and pagans, still confined to the poor, will escalate. Alexandria has more temples to burn, more heresy to stamp out, more false doctrine to quell, more lives need ending.

How far would I go? I might be persuaded to harm Theon of Alexandria. I might even be persuaded by oath and by threat to go so far as to kill the old boil, even do away with a few of his friends. Lucky so many have fled Alexandria.

Would I tell of the books? Would I reveal the maps?

Here my absorbing thoughts—the vile deeds of my fellow man, who I am no better than, never fail to amuse and disgust me—are interrupted by my employer, reanimated. I recline on a couch in the "borrowed" house of the Bishop of Alexandria and I would be wise not to drift off again. He leans too close, saying, "Have you seen, Minkah, have you heard? I build a church on the site of the Serapeum."

"Indeed?"

Again, I have made this man laugh. "So dry, so Egyptian. But then, what do Egyptians, whose gods are animals and endless in number, know of faith?"

"As much as you, I imagine. Without men, there are no gods."

I tempt his quick temper. This fake Pharaoh—increasingly obvious as the costumes of bishops become increasingly ridiculous and freighted with stolen symbol—mistakes the deities of Egypt as separate and simple, never noting they are all One, the elegant play of each aspect of the "dazzling darkness" from which they emanate. And if I myself could not express my beliefs, Hypatia would do so, just as Hypatia helped phrase these thoughts I now think.

Men like Theophilus prey on the weakness of fear. In this moment I could kill him as easily as I would Theon—no more than the quick slash of a blade. But to what gain? I do not fear him; I fear his power. There is a difference. He might die, but his power will not. There will come another to seize it. And after that, another.

Theophilus humors me. "I admire you, Minkah. I admire the risks you take. As for my church, I intend it to honor John the Baptist."

"Good choice. Bound to be popular. But without the head, will there be bones enough to cherish and to grow rich from?"

My fine bishop, rising, stiffens from his toes to his smile.

"As said, I admire you—but then, I've admired many who are now dead. You will keep to your place and when I have need of you, you will come."

He has made himself clear. So too have I. Neither fools the other.

"You, of course, know Isidore."

Finally. We come to the reason I am here. "Yes."

"I would know where he goes, what he does, who he speaks to. He will not steal from me again." Isidore, a thief? I am not surprised. But to steal from his benefactor? "I have need of the money he claims he holds back for the poor. You will keep me informed of Isidore."

"Naturally."

Sent on my way, I smile: things have come to that, have they?

I walk straight into Peter the Reader—proving, if nothing else, a dark cloud hovers over this day.

Here is the man who first saw who I was. Without work, without shelter, without prospects, caught reading a history of Troy—not one that compares to a thing Hypatia might read but certainly one Jone once devoured—it was Peter with a mouth as twisted as his mind who offered me up to the *Parabalanoi.*

Before that day, I was already a thief. Ever since, I am much less. Peter saw I was nothing, that I would never be other than nothing. Buying me drink, he spoke of the good works I would do, the prestige I would garner, the money I would earn. The man knew a perfect dunce when he saw one. He knew rage. He knew how useful the rash and ignorant young. I was pointed as deftly as an arrow at a target for none are so easily goaded to unthinking action as tormented powerless males. And so I swore my oath, like many come before, only later to learn, like many come before, what it was I was sworn to. By this, I learned also the truth of myself. I did not leave when I knew the truth. Instead I discovered how much I would do for pay. Later, I learned even the pleasure of it.

Peter the Reader, dressed head to foot in black, his white misshapen face made whiter by the black of his cowl, is a fanatic of the worst sort. He does what he does not for money or for a pleasure born of revenge, but for what he calls god. If I know his god, and I do not, but if I did, I can't imagine he wishes anything from someone like Peter but distance.

He does not let me pass. "You gladden my heart. How long has it been?"

With Theophilus, a man of ironic humor, I might slip close

to truth. Peter is not ironic. As for humor, it would crack his jaw to smile. I must be as deceitful as he. "I am kept busy, Peter. We each have our part to play."

"I know your part. You play it well."

"Thank you." And with this, I would be away, but he has more to say.

"Better than most, old friend, you must know a time comes when that woman's tongue will stop wagging."

Yet again, Hypatia is threatened. I take a step towards Peter, who takes an awkward step back—I see my reputation holds—when another voice stops me, one that turns my head faster than the crack of a chariot whip.

"Minkah! That I should find you here! I never once thought—"

Piss! Like lion eating hyena eating genet eating rat, there is something each man fears. I hold out my hand. "My dear Jone."

Jone would hold out her own hand, but pulls back with unfeigned modesty. "You've been with the bishop? I have an audience. I've tried for so long to see his eminence, and now, he calls me—so here I am, baffled but eager."

"Indeed."

And I make my escape. But not before noticing that Jone has grown less, by which I mean she has shed fat. With the loss of width in her face, I see a hint of Hypatia there, a hint of Lais. But in the eyes lives neither.

Jone, youngest daughter of Theon of Alexandria

He calls me Jone. He calls me "my dear Jone"!

When I was only a child, I felt myself in love with a priest called Isidore. But what does a child know of love? I am no longer a child.

But that Minkah has the acquaintance of our beloved bishop and that he, so exalted, knows Minkah! That he also knows Peter is a lesser pleasure, yet still a pleasure. I do not like Peter. I know no one who does. But neither I nor anyone else questions his faith.

When did I first pray that Minkah would find God? I have not missed a day since. At night in my bed I imagine him a priest and I his *diakonos*. I would so gladly act his servant! I imagine he becomes a saint and I his patroness. I do not imagine him as husband, yet there are dreams that come...oh, but of those, I cannot speak, not even to myself.

But what am I thinking? Without meaning to, I find my chin has risen, that my eyes widen as if I might brazenly stare around me, that an upward curve threatens my mouth. I rid myself of such posturing. The Patriarch awaits me.

As is right, I am offered no chair. As is right, the bishop does not stand in my presence. I am a woman. He is a man. Is there anything else to say? As is right, a second woman of faith is present for decency, standing near the door with her hands folded and her eyes lowered, and as is right, both she and I are silent. Bishop Theophilus will speak when he is moved to speak. As is right, whatever it is he says, I shall agree to.

He has his back to me. In the bright light of the window, he shines as our Lord must have shone in sun or shade. He speaks before he turns. "As you came in, Jone of The House of Women, did you see a young man, an Egyptian?"

"I did, father."

"You know him, do you not?"

"For many years, father."

"What do you think of him?"

"He is a good man. He honors my father, he protects my sister. I have heard nothing ill of him."

The bishop turns. Would it be blasphemous to say his face causes me fear? I remind myself that many are called to the Lord. Who am I to question who is called and who is not, or that their faces are filled with the marks of pox, that their jowls sag like the jowls of caged apes, that their noses are purple and smell of vats in vineyards?

"Do you see him often?"

"No father."

"Why not?"

"I live now with Christian women. I have so much to do each day: distributing alms to the poor, tending the ill, finding ways into the homes of pagans so I might speak to a woman there who is said to be seeking us—"

"All, of course, worthy. But I wish something more of you."

"Yes, father?"

"You will visit your home again. Once a week will do. You will carefully watch the young man you saw leaving my home. And once a week you will return here and tell me what you have heard and what you have seen."

I do not ask why. It is not my place to ask why. But I think I know. Minkah is being tested for something. Could it be as priest!

"I shall do as you wish, father."

"Of course you will."

BY HER WORDS THEY SHALL KNOW HER

Early Autumn, 401

Hypatia of Alexandria

Jone visits the house again...how slender she is, and taller!

My serious little sister finds her room as it was. As I keep an altar to Psyche, Goddess of the soul, Jone keeps an altar to a man hung from a *tau* cross as Osirus was hung from a tree. Jone's Christ is not made of silver but of wood and seems no more than all other godmen, save for this one thing: he spoke of love for all. There is little of this to be found in the church formed in his name, yet...it interests me.

When she is with us, she eats quietly, reads quietly, is in bed by the setting of the sun and up long before it rises.

But she is here and that is all that matters.

That which I would not say to others, I tell my yellow cat.

"I am no longer young, Miw."

Nildjat Miw opens an eye.

"Thirty years. Imagine. Thirty summers, thirty winters.

And still not a woman."

Miw, a well seasoned female—who could miss the call of her suitors?—opens another eye.

"It is time I learned the art of love-making. To know only the palms of Siwa is to know nothing."

Miw shows an eyetooth. She agrees.

"But where shall I learn this skill? I am not as you, taking any old thing that climbs over my wall."

Nildjat Miw stares at me. I know what she thinks for I think it myself.

"No, I cannot. Though for years he sleeps under my roof and disturbs my rest, he is forbidden me."

Miw sneers.

"You are wrong. I have long since shed the notion he is unworthy of me. If any, I am unworthy of him. But he is my brother and loves me not, Great Cat, and that is that. I shall begin with an older man, one who does not need me and would not brag of his conquest. After that, we shall see—but none who is married and none a student. And never with a priest."

Nildjat Miw produces a noise I think a laugh. One would never guess from their bearing, but cats have a fine sense of humor.

Before taking a lover, I visit the Cyrenian family of the devoted Synesius to buy what is source to their wealth: wild silphion. A lover will take enough of my time, two lovers twice as much. A child would require all of my time. Silphion will prevent conception.

The man I choose first is Hero of Carthage. As he is only a visiting geometer and in all ways suits my needs, I accept his invitation to dine. And so forth. Next I choose the young son of a wealthy merchant. This one is as lovely as an athlete, his skin golden and hairless. And so forth.

Augustine gave up physical love for his god. I, who only now taste this love, find giving pleasure does not lessen, but advances the heart. I am a Greek and a lover of life and of wisdom. My mouth, my sex, opens as mind opens when understanding comes. As for receiving pleasure, ah…if I were Nildjat Miw, I might purr—but only for so long. Physical love is pleasurable, yes, but like Augustine and his god, does not compare to the pleasures of the mind. And then there are complications. The heart is not simple; some bring their heart to my bed. Even so, if I continue as I've begun, I shall become a Nildjat Miw of love-making.

"Miw? Is it wise to take so many men? Is it cruel to choose one over the other?"

I hear her answer as she brushes against me. *Men are like cats. In this way, Hypatia is a cat.*

I return from the bed of yet another man to instantly seek Nildjat Miw. As Lais' room is now mine, this is where I find her, stretched out on the wide white ledge my sister once dreamed on.

"I have horrid news, cat." Seeking solace from both Miw and the Etesian wind in from the northern sea, I climb up beside her. "Theophilus builds a church on the site of the sacred Serapeum."

Nildjat Miw circles in my lap. Miw is nothing like Paniwi. Paniwi lurked. Paniwi leapt. Paniwi caught and she killed and she offered all to Lais. Nildjat Miw is content to listen to my talk of men, to mrrrrrr and growl and yeeeooow in response. The gleam-footed Xanthos carried Achilles on his back and spoke with a human voice. Hesiod's Hawk admonished his dinner, the Nightingale. Miw would be better a poet's hawk or a hero's horse for no cat makes the noises she makes.

"The past is so easily lost, Miw, so quickly forgotten—what of the spirits of water and fire and air and earth that danced in these places? What of the search for meaning?" Miw kneads my belly and I feel her claws though she keeps them sheathed. "I ask Christians: where are your questions? Where are your great doubters, those who lead us all to discovery? I am greeted by pity. They say: how is there doubt when Christ has brought certainty to the world? What have you been eating, Miw? Gah. But Lais would pat my hand, she would smile. She would say, 'Lament not. Nothing is forgotten. This too will pass.' And I would reply, 'Just as the good that follows will also pass.' 'And that,' she would counter, 'is the way of the world. Light follows dark as dark follows light.' 'But why?' I would cry out. 'Why not, beloved? Take joy in the splendid game.'"

Miw jumps from my lap as I stand. I need to wash away Ambrose, my first, but I think not my last, Jew. My skin needs scraping and oiling. With the loss of the Caesarium, I lecture somewhere new. There is less room for my chariot and horses, but it will do. Assigned one of many halls attached to the Agora, from it I can see the Court of Law, a confusing cluster of varied shops, and the street where once a huge hole gaped into which Isidore of Pergamon and I also gaped. My students overflow into the courtyard. One more and I will need to speak in a public park or on a wide white beach. No matter. I will teach until I am made to stop teaching...and when that day comes, I shall not retreat to my bed. In his bed, Father grows old. He grows foolish. Is this what Beato the astrologer saw? I have not met Beato again. I do not know.

Nildjat Miw ever at my feet, I look out over the fine fat faces of the rich, youths from Antioch to Milan to Narbo to Segovia, all honking like geese to attend me. The smell grows worse. Full half are Christian therefore told that bodily cleanliness is sign of a pagan, and to bathe is a monstrous sensuality not suited to faith. By Hygieia, Goddess of health and cleanliness, we shall all sicken here.

Any who can find a copper coin and a seat might attend this lecture. Some have found seats but offer no coin. Yet I am paid. So many are here who know little, if not less. That any learn at all is a gain to the world, and therefore to me. In public I am humorless, knowing it is thought a sign of wisdom. Humor and light-heartedness is reserved for my secret Companions who laugh with wisdom.

Not at the front, but at the back stand a row of monks, each robed in black, each face shadowed by a black hood. Each seems already dead. These are new faces, strange faces, closed faces. Not one is a student of mine. Pausing as if I must think some great thought, I count them: eight. Eight is the octopus. It is the spinner, the spider, the weaver of fate. Eight is transformation—but into what? One of the eight wears no cowl. His face is as white as lime. In it twists his mouth and in it his eyes are curses. Who could forget this man? He is that one called Peter who stood before me in the burning Serapeum and called me the devil's daughter. But he too must be spawned by a demon, for how else did he escape the temple when no other of his kind did?

Before I speak, clad in my philosopher's *tribon*, seated on my philosopher's chair, I lean down so I might speak first to Nildjat Miw. "Shall we die this day? I am not yet ready to die." My yellow cat shivers. Is this an answer? Or a flea?

I have decided to speak of numbers, beginning with 1, the Monad, and ending with 10, the Decad, so that those who listen might understand what Plato meant when he wrote: *Numbers are the highest degree of knowledge. It is knowledge itself.* Tablets appear on laps. The hall settles.

I hold up a finger. "People once counted in this way: one." I hold up two fingers. "Two." I spread my arms to include them all from first row to highest, from right aisle to left aisle, to those who scowl near the door. "Many." There are smiles at such simplicity, which in truth is not simple at all, but a leap of great imagination. "Sumerians counted in this way: man, woman, many." The smiles are now broader and this because the word "woman" is spoken as if such a one deserved counting. "One, which is the cosmic unity *All There Is*, and Two, which is duality sent out from the singularity of One as joyous expression, are the parents of the illusion of Many. As the foundation of number, is this not simple? A thousand years ago, this was written in the *Isha Upanishad* of India. 'Where shall he have grief, how shall he be deluded, who sees everywhere the Oneness'? I tell you, as the master and mystic Lao Tzu would tell you, there is nothing to be gained by complexity but bewildered confusion. There is nothing to be found in an overabundance of information, but intimidation. I have no wish to confuse or intimidate. I myself am confused enough."

There is one who laughs and so loudly I look up, to find looking back—Isidore! The skin of my cheek burns. My mouth dries. Eight monks in black. Eight spiders weaving. Eight years since last I set eyes on the favorite of Bishop Theophilus. On his right sits Synesius long since returned to Cyrene to breed horses and dogs. But if in Alexandria, Synesius is a constant—after all, he is first among Companions. On his left sits the brother of Synesius, the captious Euoptius of Cyrene who is not a Companion. Euoptius strives to blacken my heart by sneering. He fails, for I see only Isidore.

I find I am speaking no longer of number, but of Pythagoras of Samos to whom number was god. I find myself saying, "Pythagoras studied in Egypt for twenty two years, learning all it could teach him. They say he could appear in two places at one time, that urging fishermen to cast their failed net again, it came back silver with fish. A white eagle spoke his name. He healed the sick, made young the old; like the Buddha, he could remember lives he had already lived. And when he taught, he would teach only those who could listen, and by listening, *hear*. But before he taught them, they must endure years of silence."

There is a rustling in the hall, a sighing and a wheezing. I know what is thought without having to hear it. These are the deeds of Jesus. Further, how many here, Christian or not, would consent to such rigors to learn anything, feel anything, know anything? One, would be my answer if asked, and his name is Synesius: but only if he were allowed his dogs and his horses. That Isidore would not consent, hurts some secret place in me.

Lais rises in my mind. My sister needed no "deeds," no master, no proof of "ear." Lais was Spirit—just as she is this moment. If Death holds answers; I am often eager to die. If not, it annihilates...also alluring.

I continue speaking. "A certain Cyron, who loved Pythagoras, could not listen closely enough or become silent enough, so was refused the teaching. Made ill with disappointment, he set fire to the hall in which Pythagoras spoke. All inside were killed, including the teacher he had hoped to please, Pythagoras of Samos." Half entranced with the horror and meaning of my story, I say this final thing, "But how many here have heard of Cyron and how many Pythagoras? Though his body was consumed, his mind lived on. To destroy what one cannot have, or cannot understand, destroys nothing. A man may murder another, temples may fall, flames may take books, and fear force silence, but ideas are eternal."

I fall suddenly awake. By Pallas! Full third of those before me are Christian. Eight are Christian fanatics living in the Mountains of Nitria calling down woe on all who do not believe as they believe. These have murdered men, toppled temples, burned books, and silenced dissent.

I am as much stone as the stone of the chair I sit in. I look out from my eyes but see only in at my racing thoughts. My promise to Theophilus is at long last broken. I shall lose my place. If I lose my place, I lose all. And yet there is no stir, no hum as the disturbing of a hive.

I find I am looking at Isidore, and there see nothing but my friend of the time before Siwa. Synesius, whose brother would have him a bishop, plays with his beard. Euoptius picks at his sleeve.

From one face to another, I gaze out at them. The black monks in back do nothing.

Did they not hear me? Did I not speak? And then I understand. They do not see who they are.

Desher and I gallop out before the sun to wait under the shade of the tamarisk tree near the Temple of Bastet where Nildjat Miw was born. We whirl in place to face the rising of Ra who cradles the golden city in arms of gold.

On this third day, as agreed, Isidore arrives, riding a black mare. His face is as it was, radiant with interest, shadowed with mistrust.

I wonder what it is he sees in mine?

It is old, this tree, and as thick of trunk as it is wide of branch and fine of leaf, yet it does not conceal us. Desher shudders under me. She thrusts her head forward forcing the mare to move back.

Isidore speaks first. "I have thought of you." I will not be made to say I have thought of him. "You have lost your sister. I cannot know your grief, but I can know how you grieved."

"I grieve. It does not lessen." We are silent again. Our horses nicker, Ra warms our backs, flies visit the Shrine of Bastet. I finally speak. "As I was long ago told I could not know you, were you not told you could not know me?"

"Emphatically."

"How then do you come to hear me, and so openly?"

"I grow weary of what I am told."

"By any, or by only one?"

"By only one."

"Are you not afraid of this one?"

I have made Isidore laugh. It is good to see him laugh. It is good to hear laughter. "Of course I am afraid of Theophilus. Who would wish to be punished?"

"And how should you be punished?"

"There are so many ways."

I do not ask the ways. They seem obvious enough. "You write that you would join my Companions."

"I would."

"As a priest, you are forbidden to practice mathematics. As for astrology, is it not called evil itself? I would teach you astronomy, Isidore, mathematics, the philosophical mysteries of those you call pagan. The Companions seek the 'true life,' a merging with the One. If a priest were to credit this, or even to listen, such a priest would be cast out from his church. Why would you join the Companions?"

"I would find any way to see and to hear you."

From too much speech, I lapse into too little.

Isidore fills the silence. "I ask also to learn. Though many surely are, a Christian need not be a fool. I would be a Christian. I would follow Christ. Jesus was not ignorant. Why should I be?" Swishing her black tail, his mare turns under him, so that he must rein her back. "There is another reason, Hypatia." Not sure I would hear this reason, I allow Desher to turn as well, and do not rein her back. "What was done by me against your will and your wishes cannot be forgiven. But I ask for understanding."

I have understood him. I have understood myself. "You are a male. I am a female. We were alone. Though I was an innocent, I was not entirely reluctant. The fault is half mine."

Isidore is made speechless. To render him such brings with it a flush of pleasure. If such pleasure is unworthy, then I am unworthy. I would ride away now. Neither he nor I can remain long before we are seen. As for Companion, that is a matter for all to discuss.

"I am no Cyron, Hypatia. I do not burn books and I do not kill what I cannot have. Your understanding is a gift. I have a gift in return, something you will wonder at."

Blood pushes at my veins. Could he say other that would intrigue me more?

"Tonight, at the sixth hour, come to the church Theophilus builds."

I am shocked. This is the site of the destroyed Serapeum. For Isidore, devils have stepped aside for angels, but for me divinity dies. "You ask that I come alone?"

"Yes."

"Through a tomb of night?"

"Yes."

I have seen a dark no night can equal. I say, "I will come."

Desher, her hide as red as the blade of a sorcerer's knife, is eager to run. I slide my hand up her neck. I whisper in her ear. And we are gone.

"Tell me, yellow cat, if I go and go alone, do I do the wise thing?"

Miw, seated on Damara's table of emerald green near a chart of stars, has not spoken, not even to purr, but her eyes do not leave mine.

"Or does Isidore mean me harm? He once said there were those I knew but did not know. Did he mean himself?"

Still no word from Nildjat Miw. As Miw stares at me, I stare at her.

"You will not answer? Not even to save my life as I saved yours? If not for me, who would feed you? Whose lap would you find to weigh down with your great furred body?"

My yellow cat rises, she yawns, then jumps straight into the air to land with immaculate grace on the ibis head of Thoth. Her action is graceful, it takes her precisely where she would go; she makes no error. Thoth is the logos, the mind of god, the heart and the tongue of Ra. As well as writing, he is speech.

Nildjat Miw has answered.

By the steady drip of my water clock, I must go now if I would go. My cat and I are decided; I shall meet Isidore. But will I accept him, favored priest of Theophilus, into the secret teachings? This, as yet, I do not know.

Minkah the Egyptian

I resign myself to Hypatia's comings and goings as I have resigned myself to so much that cuts at my heart. But that she should leave her house at the darkest hour, sneak away when all but the worst of Alexandria sleeps, means more than her usual adventures—and what that can only mean to Minkah, the Egyptian, is that I must follow.

She takes Desher. To enter the stables without disturbance to any, to walk her horse away without saddle or bridle, this is a skill I have not mastered. Ia'eh snorts at the loss of Desher, tosses her head at me, but she cannot come along for together she and I cannot be silent. Slipping away, I ask Chons, protector of night travelers, to ensure that my rash darling does not go farther than I can run.

Moving quickly, Hypatia leads Desher by no more than a hand entwined in her mane. They take streets Hypatia does not normally take: a side street near a small theater, another small street leading to a fish market, a third that enters into the wide Street of Alexander, this one paved in rosy granite. Here she vaults onto Desher's bare back. Watching from a doorway, I am heartened to see it. Alone and on foot, even as she is armed, she is prey. On Desher, she is free to flee. Hypatia's mare is fast and she is agile. So too is Hypatia. Each will take the other home. I am also disheartened. Will she now move faster than I can follow? The answer is no. Hypatia keeps Desher to a walk.

The sound the mare makes, her hooves on stone, drowns any sound I might make. As they keep to the exact middle of each street, so I keep to the deepest shadows. From time to time we come on a drunk or a thief or a ragged bundle. The latter might be dead. It might be alive. None of these bother a woman on a horse who can outrun them, or an Egyptian whose knife is plainly seen.

We go on in this way until well past the new city walls Theophilus has built. Where does Hypatia go?

Isidore, of course—my good friend and fellow *Parabalanoi*, who met her this day where she and I found Nildjat Miw. Though not there long, they remained long enough.

I bear what I must, but if Isidore is included in those she "entertains"—this I could not bear. The thought he might be what I will never be steals away my soul. I am a lowborn Egyptian, Hypatia a highborn Greek. But Isidore of Pergamon, though born to wealth and elevated by Theophilus to high position, is not worthy of my darling. I clench my jaw and I follow.

Hypatia dismounts in front of what was once the Serapeum. The steps remain. The platform. But now, dimly seen by starlight, what was once one of the greatest temples in the world is a half built church, ugly, as well as enormous beyond need. None could miss it as the work of Theophilus.

As I thought, out from the pillars at the top of the marble steps, steps Isidore, Isis curse him.

He beckons. Bidding Desher remain without reins to bind her, or lad to guard her, Hypatia rapidly mounts the steps.

As soon as they disappear through the doors, I am up the steps after them.

LABYRINTH

Hypatia of Alexandria

Isidore signs me to silence, then turns to enter a building I would never set foot in, bare or sandaled, save for a gift I am promised. If he promises me again what he gave under dry palms in the Oasis of Siwa, my gift to him will be his own death. Strapped to my forearm is the knife I now wear wherever I go.

There is a moon in the depths of this night as thin as a single lash, as dim as dawn sensed through closed eyes. I stare at the hinted moon. All I am left of trust is my trust in Desher and in Nildjat Miw and in Minkah and in the waxing and waning of the moon.

"Hypatia!" Isidore hisses his concern that I tarry. "We should not be seen."

I turn to follow.

Theophilus builds a thing that takes my breath away in horror. A church that is no more in plan than any Roman basilica—a functional civic hall—yet he uses as entry the great silver doors of the Serapeum! Following Isidore, I hurry first through a maw of a forecourt, then down the gullet of a porch, to find myself in a long central corridor under windows tall and arched. No roof covers this carcass. All is lit inside as it was outside, by the stars and by the sly blink of a moon.

A temple stood here that once was mine, but is no longer. Here my father was the pride of Alexandria, but is no longer. Theon of Alexandria is not welcome in this place. Hypatia of Alexandria is not welcome in this place. And where once I knew every silvered hall, every golden statue and white marble staircase, every entry and exit, the width of the widest chamber and the soaring height of the painted dome, now I am entirely lost. My heart doubles its beat, my feet slow their pace. Faced with a second corridor, half the width of the one I travel, I hesitate. It crosses the first at a perfect right angle. Glancing to the left and to the right, this second corridor disappears on either side into blackness. It seems a crucifixion and I the crucified.

Where am I? Where do I go? In the belly of this monster, I know fear. "Isidore!"

"Hush!"

Isidore's black robe and black hood make him impossible to see, but not impossible to hear. He waits at the ending to this cold corridor beside the beginnings of an altar. Unfinished, this altar is where each line of perspective leads. It is the focus of all Theophilus erects here...and his finest insult. I would stamp my feet in fury. I would rend my cloak in sorrow. I would take my knife from its case and carve a star within a circle on the wood that once formed an altar to Isis. *Duat*, the underworld within, must be remembered...even here. More insult surrounds me. The Serapeum's columns are stolen, its carved wooden panels, its shaped masonry, even its roof tiles of bronze shining as Pharos. That I could rip each from its place, grind all to dust.

"Look only at this, Hypatia." Isidore is pointing at the old temple paving. "To house the bones of John the Baptizer, Theophilus demanded a holy sepulcher. Still his favorite, it was I who designed this sepulcher. Come! See what I have found." So saying, he lights a lamp, then kneels to touch a stone here and one there, and by this, a section of the floor rises as the hatch of a ship—but without effort.

Immediately Isidore sets off down wide stone steps into pure darkness, and I follow, lost in both wonder and thought. Isidore has said, "still his favorite"—is he no longer? What has occurred between our bishop and his priest?

Countless stories are told I never hear, each day events unfold among countless people I will never know. A neighbor prospers, wives are beaten, husbands cuckolded, a drunk dies in the street, an emperor falls, all holds interest, some sadden, some elate...but what does any of it matter in the face of the eternal mysteries? Where are we, why are we here, where have we come from and where do we go? And yet, if Isidore is not favored by Theophilus, what is he?

Descending, it is not as it was rushing down and down to save the books, for nowhere was as deep as this. It is not as it was swinging by ropes from a reeking cave of bats and beetles and crickets into a cave deeper still, for no human hand carved out that vast dark place where Minkah and I left the poems of Lais. But these are well defined steps, each fashioned with skill from solid limestone that was not placed here, but was bored into, and this done so long ago the center of each and every stone is worn away by generations of feet.

Who, before us, used them?

Striding about in the village of Rhakotis, a place old, isolated, as well as exceedingly unimportant, Alexander laid out in barley flour where his streets should be, his temples, his palace, his docks, his canals, his public buildings, the quarters that would house the people who would come here. And with voice alone told where the causeway would be, that great joining of Pharos and land which would result in the two greatest harbors on the north coast of Egypt.

Dinocrates of Rhodes designed Alexandria from the scattering of flour. The Greek Pharaoh Ptolemy made Alexandria glorious. Did either know of these steps delving deep under the covering sands? How old are they? Certainly older than Alexandria and older than Rhakotis—no more then than a fishing village and no more now than the Egyptian District—they must first have been carved in the Egypt of Rameses. What I have thought legend is fact. Long before Alexander and long before his city, this place was alive with Egyptian ships and Egyptian secrets.

What Isidore has found has surely been found before... else why build the Serapeum so far from the palace? Why build it in humble Rhakotis? It follows, then, that Ptolemy I Soter has gone before me, and all the Ptolemies come after: Ptolemy II Philadelphius, Ptolemy III Euergetes, and on and on until Cleopatra VII. Pharaohs, emperors, priests of Serapis, the greatest of scholars; only these would have been allowed. My heart, which had slowed in its beating, beats faster again. No dream of loss causes this, but dream of gain. The world below awaits me even if desecrated and robbed. That it exists is excitement enough.

Isidore turns. “Wait here. There are lights to light.” Moving away, his lamp fades. I am left uneasy, silent and still in an utter lack of light. If Isidore means me harm, this is his moment.

There comes a series of faint sounds on the steps behind me. Rats? Spiders? Scorpions? Lizards? Large lizards? I have nothing but the comforting handle of my comforting blade. One moment passes, two, three, a dozen...and then, finally, a lamp is lit, then another, and another, and I find—Seker, god of light, protector of spirits who wander the underworld!—that I have waited in a cave. No, not a cave, a vast round domed room. Every surface is carved in fantastical ways, ancient gods stand in innumerable niches, the walls are painted more brightly than the walls and the columns of the city of Thebes, the dome is made of blue glass. And now I see what Isidore intends as a gift! Herodotus would know what I see just as I know. Deep under the thick platform on which the Serapeum stood, deeper than the chambers that housed the library, is carved out of limestone bedrock a labyrinth of baffling and intricate passages.

Isidore beckons me forward, and quickly returning my knife to its sheath, forward I go. Together we enter the labyrinth. No matter the cost, what could keep me away? Would Lais have hesitated? Lais would have gone forth in awe, imbuing all that she passed through with awe.

Entering the doorway around which leering faces loom, I remember Herodotus facing his own Egyptian labyrinth in the place he called The City of the Crocodiles. *"...from room to room and from court to court, all was an endless wonder to me, as we passed from a courtyard into rooms, from rooms into galleries, from galleries into more rooms and thence into yet more courtyards. The roof of every chamber, courtyard, and gallery is, like the walls, of stone. The walls are covered with carved figures, and each court is exquisitely built of white marble and surrounded by a colonnade."*

Stunned by the sight, touching this strange object and that, I ask, "Who else knows of this, Isidore?"

"Wait. This is not all."

Not all? My heart beats in the tips of my fingers. My mind seems larger than the head that contains it. What more could there be?

For what seems forever, we follow the pattern laid on the floor, framed by the stone walls and roofed by a ceiling of arched stone, and the farther we go, the more I know we circle for a time to the right, and then for a time to the left, and as we circle we draw ever closer to a center. I understand this pattern. If one could see it drawn on paper it would seem looped as a thumbprint. Sound echoes here, the air is wet, the farther we go the more the walls drip with seeping water. Unlike the dry desert caves found by Minkah, this place was dug deep into a spur of ridged rock between the Great Green Sea and Lake Mareotis. Throughout there are canals and small streams. The stone beneath our feet is a mirror of black water.

And then we come on the heart of the thing.

In the exact center of the small space in the middle of the labyrinth stands a great chest on a tall ebony table. The chest is bound in bronze.

Isidore gazes as I gaze. "Open it."

And so I do. No gold glitters, no jewel burns, no bones molder. Instead, I find scrolls, and beneath scrolls, codices. I can scarcely breathe, scarcely reach out to touch with the tip of one trembling finger.

"No one has seen this but me. The steps were found three days ago. So soon as they were, I forbade all to enter until where they led could be searched. I searched alone. And then I came looking for you."

I would thank him. I would touch him. I would dance here in a labyrinth hidden for years. That it exists is not known to my father, nor is it known to my father's friends. If such as these have no knowledge, who was it who did? Whoever and whenever, I behold now the books I have looked for, asked about, sought knowledge of, always failing to find them. These are the books of those who followed a certain Jew they thought a man, not a god. They contain, or so it is secretly said, his teachings, lost now to any called Christian.

"Why, Isidore? Why come to me and not Theophilus? Why show me and not him?"

In answer, he takes up the first scroll. He unrolls it so that its title shows: *Gospel of Mary*. He takes up a codex: *Gospel of Judas*. He then takes up a bundle of scrolls, tied with rotted twine. The twine has recently been broken, recently retied. In his hands, it easily breaks again. Of those that tumble back into the chest, he hands me one. This one I unroll and this one I begin to read. "*These then are the thoughts of Mariamne, daughter of Josephus of the tribe of Benjamin. In the waning of my earthly days, I recount the life of the Daughter of Wisdom, who came in time to be known as the Magdalene.*"

When I look up, Isidore says, "Theophilus would burn these before he would read them." Do I hear less than love in his mouthing the name Theophilus? "And if not Theophilus, a host of others. Whoever placed them here, kept them safe. They are not safe now. This is to become a place of pilgrimage." I am not mistaken, I do hear it. Something has caused a change in Isidore's love for Alexandria's bishop. "When the temple was destroyed, water began seeping in from the great cistern. Already mold begins to grow and whole sections are lost. I cannot keep them and I will not destroy them. You must take them away."

He holds open the satchel he carries, a satchel whose meaning is now clear to me. I do not hesitate. As if it were the day of the Serapeum, once again I gather up books to take them away. But this time I celebrate. They are safe and they are mine.

Minkah the Egyptian

I do not follow Hypatia home. Holding close her papery prize, she rides Desher, hides her knife...safe in a city where more love her than do not love her. I follow the priest, who does not turn north to the stolen house of Theophilus where he has lived in rooms of his own these past ten years, nor towards some other place his faith provides its priests, but turns instead south on narrow streets towards the narrow-necked Port of Lake Mareotis.

As a shadow among shadows behind the purposeful *Parabalanoi*, I know what few know, but all would discover if such things mattered to other than those involved: though once Theophilus loved Isidore as Isidore loved Theophilus, no love flows now. Five years have passed since the Bishop of Alexandria would have made Isidore the Bishop of Constantinople, dragging him up to the height he himself has attained. One year since Theophilus expressed his first doubt about Origen. Ever the politician, the moment the Christian philosopher became officially condemned by the church, Theophilus abandoned him. But Isidore did not abandon his beloved Origen of Alexandria, Egyptian and philosopher. Love between priest and bishop has turned to loathing. If there is one thing Christians cannot abide of each other, it is to disagree over doctrine.

Isidore does not stop at the docks of laden and unladen boats come from over the lake. He does not stop at a shuttered inn or pass through a darkened door, but takes a rutted path at the end of a modest street leading him out to the reeds, thick as bundled straw, tall as a camel's hump. They seem impenetrable, but are not. Growing along the edge of the lake for many miles west and more miles east, as well as in a rank of rustling green two hundred cubits wide from north to south, many a path winds through them, entering a perilous world harboring brigands of many kinds...just as the island of Pharos has long harbored brigands of only one kind: pirates.

I am careful here. Among these reeds are clearings and in the clearings reeded huts and in the huts, men and women one would be wise to avoid by day as well as by night.

The priest knows his way. The path he follows branches here and there, but he ever chooses the one that leads to the left. He walks and I follow behind until he comes on a clearing not large enough for a hut, and here waits a man robed in black from head to foot. I know the robe as well as I know the man. This is not merely a single Origen-loving monk from the Mountains of Nitria who rebels against the Bishop of Alexandria. This is Peter the Reader.

When last I saw him, he stood in the house of Theophilus. He will never do so again. Theophilus, suddenly an enemy of Origen, called a synod to condemn for heresy Peter and his monks for none would deny Origen. He allowed no one a defense. All so condemned live now in caves high in the mountains of the southern desert rather than walk the streets Theophilus walks, or where his *Parabalanoi* walk. Peter once led the brotherhood. But for Peter, my life would be different. I would not have it different. Praise accursed Peter whose monks are men of fierce heart, stout will, and of bloody mindedness unto murder in the name of their god. Of discernment, reason, learning: virtually none are possessed of any. Yet all love Origen. Or not. He is difficult to follow. They believe anyway. Hypatia teaches her Companions that to believe without understanding is common among men of any faith...what is "faith" but belief without proof?

It astounds me. I believe nothing. I do what I do so I might live. Peter does what he does in the belief that none deserve life who deny his faith. Does Isidore hold now with such madness? Has his rift with Theophilus driven him to this? If so, proud Isidore has fallen far.

He and Peter the Reader push their way towards the lake, and when they are swallowed by the night-black reeds, I follow. Waiting at the edge of the lake is a boat of reeds and in this boat Isidore and his Nitrian friend paddle out across the water—to where, I neither know nor care. But this I do know. Theophilus, who once loved Isidore, now loves a priest called Timothy. Timothy is not *Parabalanoi* though he will soon be what Isidore was, Archdeacon of Alexandria.

I have seen all I need for the moment. When I wish it, I will learn more.

Hypatia of Alexandria

My body begs for sleep, but my mind runs as Desher runs—tirelessly. When dawn comes, I have not slept for even an hour.

Isidore calls these books, gifts. I call them miracles. It is as if Lais has walked through my door, as if she holds Paniwi in her arms, as if she sits down beside me to say, "I am here, Miw. What would you have of me?"

Under my hand, given me by the surprising grace of a man with whom I have known both trust and terrible doubt, are copies of Egyptian books I have heard of but never before seen: *The Gospel of Thomas*, the *Gospel of Philip*, *of the Egyptians*, *of Truth*, The *Apocryphon of James*, the *Tripartite Tractate*, a handful of letters from Saul of Tarsus, a few from the poet Valentinus, and more and more. And in them I see how desperate the need for release from the stifling Law of the Jews. And in them I find a turning away from what is called the Dominion of Evil which is the Suffering World and a putting away of the impoverished heart seeking an End Time where the righteous will live and the heretic die. I cannot find the battle between this bishop and that to impose his unquestioned faith on all. What is here is a heroic attempt through myth to proclaim the divine nature in All.

I read the first of the scrolls transcribed by a Seth of Damascus: "*It comes at last, to this—I am changed from water to wine. I who was dead now live. I know my own name. I AM. These then are the thoughts of Mariamne, daughter of Josephus of the tribe of Benjamin. In the waning of my earthly days, I recount the life of the Daughter of Wisdom, who came in time to be known as the Magdalene.*"

And then I read the work of the poet Valentinus.

Once, long ago, Jone sat struggling with two problems Father had given her, both matters of Euclidian geometry. Though Christians revile mathematics, and none was taught at the school of Didymus—who himself was a fair geometer—

Father said he would take her from her place at the Didascalia if she did not learn geometry. This meant she must learn at home and from Father. The first problem required her to divide a given geometrical figure into two or more equal parts. The second asked her to create parts in given ratios.

Jone made marks on her waxen tablet, smoothed them away, made more marks, smoothed those. Then she made no mark at all, but sat staring at her hands. They were limp, her fingers like dead things, plump and white and still. Suddenly, with one violent sweep of her arm, her tablet flew into a wall as spittle flew from her lips. "Hypatia! What do they mean, these numbers! How do these shapes fit my world!"

"Mathematics is a magic box, Panya, a thing of rare and scented wood. It has no lid, no drawer, no latch to unlock. At first glance there seems no opening. Yet if you should turn it this way and that way, if you would curve a line or straighten a curve, or wander in mind where logic seldom goes but instinct never sleeps, the beautiful box will open itself."

"But what is *in* the box?"

"Shells that curl and curve towards the infinite, stars that will burn for eternity, waves flowing over the skin of the sea in patterns of cunning madness. You will find the gods in your geometrical box of magic."

"Gods? I have found God through Jesus. All the rest means *nothing*."

I grieved for Jone.

But now I myself have opened a magic box, a thing of rare and scented wood, and out of it has sprung curled and curving ideas!

The doubt that has plagued me falls away. Not because I understand, but because I have purpose. I shall no longer teach the philosophy of others, but shall formulate anew what it is I know and see and feel. By my efforts, I hope to embrace everything, weave all together, external and internal, into one lucid piece.

I set about my work immediately. Such a task will take the rest of my life.

THE FOURTH GATE

Late summer, 403

Hypatia of Alexandria

Miw is two years older but more than two years bigger. If she grows any larger, it will prove she has lion in her. She is more than lion in her soul.

All through the morning she watched me prepare a paper I present to those called Companions. In her two years of growing, my poor patient Companions have spent the same two years following along as I work my way towards the regaining of Gnosis—personal knowledge of personal divinity.

"To unlearn is harder than learning, Miw. To put away the tools I have mastered to take up those I have not mastered—what a struggle!"

Miw samples the closest papyrus. Too hot to be inside, my yellow cat and I have walked the short distance to the cool canal that flows by the House of Theophilus. Should he look out from an upper window, he might see us...but so? Are we not free cat and free mistress?

"You might think me alone, Miw—but I have consummate guidance. Of all the papers now mine, I value highest those of Seth of Damascus and those of Valentinus of Alexandria. To think that Seth transcribed the words of the Magdalene, beloved of Christ, and that Valentinus, who knew the secret teachings of Paul, was nearly Bishop of Rome. If either had been 'heard,' how changed the message of Christ would be."

Nildjat Miw is asleep. I must haul her home over my shoulder.

This evening, my chosen few gather to hear my still halting synthesis of All That Is. If any sense I err, it will be questioned. If any suspect I stray from my path, I will be guided back. If I cannot be understood, I will be told...and I will try again to be clear, precise, complete.

I am called their "divine guide." I call them my "saints."

With the help of my saints, I struggle towards spiritual vision, not as a single experience but as a steady state of being. In the utter confusion that appears "reality," I am convinced each piece fits the whole, and that the whole is expressed in each piece.

In short, these two years have been both exhausting and exhilarating. I could not speak for my Companions.

I would not have missed the wedding of Synesius of Cyrene for the complete works of Aristotle. My first and most faithful Companion, rich as well as Christian, married the daughter of a humble country historian. Not only does her father immerse himself in the vanished Etruscans, he is not a Christian. Nor is his daughter Catherine. In fact, the entire family is a happy nest of philosophers, writers, teachers and pagans.

Synesius married to avoid serving the church. And I, as an honored wedding guest, was let loose in a private library locked away from all but the most trusted friends. Miles from Alexandria, somewhere on the eastern shore of Lake Mareotis, I devoured it.

Four months later, Catherine, wife to Synesius, birthed a boy child.

Still abed, I scratch Nildjat Miw under her chin. "Synesius named the babe Hypatios. What do you think of that, Miw? More interesting still, what do you think Catherine makes of that?"

Miw stretches her neck in ecstasy.

"Indeed. And now another child roots itself in her womb. Synesius is a busy man. But then, Catherine is an interesting woman. She says little but I have never seen such listening. I would know more of her. And what do you think of Minkah as Companion?"

My yellow cat twitches an ear. I think she approves. Who can truly know with a creature so charged with mystery as a cat?

"I think it splendid. And none grumble. Not even to complain he is Egyptian or that he is poor. But oh! how they complain of Isidore! This one tells me his mind is not swift. That one whispers his understanding far from complete. Another tells me his tongue is tangled. As if I did not know! I would reverse my decision if not for his gift! How do I repay his gift?"

Throwing back a linen sheet, I pad barefoot towards the baths. The Companions will soon be here and I would be ready for them. Behind me, Miw is off to the kitchens seeking her breakfast.

Rubbing warm oil on my legs, scraping it off with a *strigil*, I struggle with indecision—should Isidore remain a Companion? I know what all the others would say, but Didymus, what would he have done?

Two faces remain in my mind as clear as when I last saw them: my sister's and the face of Didymus the Blind. The death of my mother Damara shattered the child I once was. The death of Lais took from me the foolishness of youth. Didymus' death by old age diminished me. It further diminished Father, who had suffered the loss of his wife, the loss of his profession, the loss of his prestige, and the loss of his eldest daughter. Never spoken of, lost too was the hope of a son, exchanged for one more female, that one who took his wife. For me, the absence of this sweetest friend is as great as the continuing loss of the ancient disciplines other than Christian theology—which if truth be known, is our theology, rewritten—for the voice of Didymus was a true voice and it melded with ours, tempering ours, as ours, I fondly believe, tempered his. Without him, few Christians of stature remain who would not raise his hand against Father and me. Save Augustine. Augustine is a true friend. But Augustine is many miles from here.

Close by Damara, Lais lies in the west. Each year Jone and Minkah and I visit their tomb in the City of the Dead. Didymus lies in the east. Each year Jone and Minkah and I walk to his chapel of pink stone near the Garden of Nemesis. Jone wails every step of the way to Didymus. Father, pleading an excess of grief, visits none.

Jone, youngest daughter of Theon of Alexandria

"Come, sister, come listen if you like."

Hypatia invites me to another of her gatherings where all call themselves Companions. Which usually means that unless that wisp of a thing that has married Synesius is present, I am the only female among males, and I *have* listened and I *have* listened and I have watched my sister draw lines and circles and shapes on an overlarge tablet, and I have heard her speak, but if she were speaking in Persian her words could not mean less to me. I do not understand. My father understands, or he used to. Who knows what he understands now? Or, for that matter, cares? Even Lais, who had no interest in such things, understood better than I. As for Hypatia! I would stamp my feet in frenzy. I would shout out from the sheer torture of Hypatia as sister. Who could blame me? All these adore her unto idolatry. They call her *holy.* Who could bear to be as nothing, as less than nothing, compared? And who would not leave, as I have, as soon as they found a place in the world where one could breathe and one could be seen and one could be valued? Anyone would. All the women say so. This too they say: it is not right for a woman to stand over a man. It is not right that a woman's voice be heard before his. And this they say also: that my sister dares such things is proof there are demons involved.

There she is, Hypatia! I must be quick to hide myself before I am seen.

In my father's house, the best place to hide is near the first large door leading from the courtyard off the Street of the Gardens into the atrium. There is a small room nearby, one meant for a guard though my sister keeps no guard. But if there were a guard, he could look out through a narrow slit in the wall and from it espy the whole of the courtyard without being seen himself. From the door leading into this small room, he could peek out also at the atrium and, if careful, not be seen, But as there is no guard, I can sit for hours and see who comes and who goes and for how long they stay and whether they bring something of interest or whether they bring only themselves. All this I remember—did not my teacher, the blessed Didymus the Blind, praise my memory, often and often!—no need to write the names or the days or the times.

Today Hypatia teaches yet again a class she thinks secret. That there is a class has never been secret. Nor are the names of those who attend. Or if a secret, it is not so from me. Of twelve, there are ten I have named to Bishop Theophilus. Synesius of Cyrene, and one of Synesius' dearest friends, Auxentius of Cyrene. Herculianus, a dearer friend. I do know they sit as close as wife to husband. Olympius, a wealthy Syrian landowner who talks of horses and hunting. Hesychius, who sits often with Olympius. Ision, who I admit tells stories of every sort wonderfully well. When Ision speaks, I try not to miss a word. Syrus, spoken of by Synesius as only "our friend" and Alexander, the uncle of Syrus. There is the "most sympathetic" Gaius and Theotecnus whom they call "father." If this means he is a priest, I could not say. What is a secret is what it is these companions are taught. Try as I might, and I *do* try for my bishop would know, I cannot penetrate this larger secret. It is not that I have not heard the teaching, and often. But I have stopped attending. First: because I learn nothing. Second: if demons are involved, by the Holy Spirit, is it right that I risk my own soul? All this I have explained to our Holy Bishop Theophilus and he has forgiven me. All he asks now is that I hide in the little guard room I have told him of, and that I remember who comes and who goes.

Through me, Bishop Theophilus knows who visits my sister. He knows who visits my father, the same old gaggle of soothsayers and astrologists and fools. Bishop Theophilus knows that those who once came for Father, now come more for Hypatia, and that no man of importance who visits or even passes through Alexandria does not call on my sister. He knows she locks herself in her work room and studies something I have yet to discover, though I have promised him I will. And I *will*—I swear on the Blessed Virgin Mary. All I know, he knows—except this. I have not mentioned the name Isidore nor have I mentioned the name Minkah.

I hope this is not a sin, but I imagine my hope is in vain. No matter how I squirm, I cannot forget he asked me clearly to watch and report on Minkah.

I must be still now. My sister's companions arrive.

Minkah the Egyptian

Jone's reason to visit the House of Hypatia is clear as water to me—one spy can spot another. By the coils of Apep, what good company I keep. Two betrayers in one house: the first a sad unwanted child, the second as determined as a robber of graves. We are as mirrors, Jone and I. It is perfection.

What does Jone tell Theophilus? Who attends our meetings? No name would surprise him, not even the name of Isidore, who turns out as much a failure as a Companion as he does a *Parabalanoi*. He cannot be fully either for lack of spine and lack of mind. As for the listing of my name, where else should I be but here...as I too am a spy?

Walking past Jone who thinks herself unseen in her guard's room, Synesius and I share a sigh of indulgence. Jone is ever a source of amusement. In truth, if I could, I would save her from such things.

But as she is already "saved," I would fail before I began.

Hypatia of Alexandria

I pace, waiting for the Companions to seat themselves in the atrium wherever they will, for Synesius to gather pillows for his full-bellied Catherine, who holds a sleeping Hypatios. I wait for Minkah who must tend to some demand of Father's. We all wait as Isidore, late as ever, settles. Nildjat Miw sits on the rim of the pool, talking to fish. Any who understand, hide.

"Tonight," I say when all is still, "I will tell you a story of Sophia. Sophia's tale is ancient, told before the people of India and the people of the Land of Silk, before the Egyptians, before even the Sumerians who are old indeed, and her name is as varied as the people who spoke of her. Like all 'true' stories, Sophia's asks eternal questions which are the questions I ask of you. Who are we? Why are we here? What is here? Why do we suffer? What is death?"

My "saints" make faces, each face wondering if he or she is meant to answer these questions. Before any try, I speak on.

"Before the Beginning of the World there was no thing. The Egyptians called this no thing the Dazzling Darkness. They called it Absolute Mystery. The greatest of all Gnostic teachers and poets, Valentinus, called it *Bythos* , the Deep, teaching that *Bythos* was pure unmanifest Consciousness. But what would a conscious No Thing which is No Where in No Time be conscious *of*? Plato had already taught that the first principle—stemming from this Consciousness—is intellect whose only function can be to think, and the only possible object of thought must be itself. And then, at some unknowable point of no time, Consciousness contemplated itself into a First Idea: it knew itself by becoming both that which is known and that which knows, experience and witness. And from this sprang the Many, meaning the World and all it contains. Valentinus devised the Idea of the Godhead who, by thought alone, manifested itself as both male and female in the form of the Son. From the Son came forth the Aeons, gendered pairs which are the divine powers or natures. Together these made up the *Pleroma*, or the Fullness of Consciousness, and each pair played a role in the emerging world. The last of these pairs was Sophia, which is Greek for Wisdom, and Christ, which is Greek for Savior."

Already Isidore would speak, or otherwise make himself known. But I allow him no room.

"But, said Valentinus, by being sent forth, the Aeons forgot their creator, yet longed to remember, sensing themselves incomplete. On behalf of them all, Sophia carried this burden of longing, setting out on a quest to know God. Believing herself alone, she strayed farther and farther from *Pleroma*, growing fearful and full of anguish. Wandering in sorrow through a world spun of her own pain and her own longing for Source, Sophia lost herself in illusion. And there, her suffering grew so great she cried out, God take me home! And in that moment, her paired Aeon, the Christ, woke her from her suffering dream so that once again she knew her true eternal divinity in Consciousness."

Isidore is now as a child who longs to leave a table. He would speak. He would not speak. He would leave. He would stay. Though the other Companions would not have me see, I cannot miss the rolling of eyes, the sucking of teeth, the shifting in place. Even Minkah, ever composed, loses patience with Isidore.

I open my arms. I smile. "Isidore, what torments you?"

"All this is...I couldn't say. What you say, it is all well and good—but Valentinus? Valentinus is a heretic."

"Is he? Have they made him one now? He was not when he lived. When he lived he was friend to Origen."

Isidore, for a single moment, is speechless. We see he did not know this. But he finds his voice, a voice I increasingly despair of. "I find this talk of Sophia incomprehensible. It makes no sense. A thing which is no thing imagines other things? There must be a reasoning Creator! How could something come from nothing?"

"It did not."

"But you said..."

"Valentinus did not teach the tale of Sophia as true. By it, he wove truths."

"What truths? I have heard nothing true."

"Then do not hear this. All who teach a beginning are wrong. The world had no beginning. And what has no beginning is as a circle and can have no end, therefore all who wait for End Times will wait forever. Plato and Plotinus were wrong. There is no first principle. There is no time, no space, no self, no matter. The world was not thought into being from nothing. It always was and always will be, constantly imagined by *All That Is* and *All That Is* is precisely that: All. Sophia is the self we imagine we are, believing ourselves doomed to wander alone and lost through the world of sorrowing matter. She is soul creating the perception of reality. Christ is Sophia's double and equal, what we sense as duality."

Isidore's breath comes faster and faster as I speak until it is labored. "A female is equal to Christ?"

"Have you not heard me? Christ is Gnosis, who comes if we call. He awakens the dreamer."

"Woman! Are you saying the Christ was neither man nor God?"

Why answer? He would not understand my answer. Turning away, I speak to those who can "hear." "And when he comes, we remember once again that we are eternal and loved and filled with Spirit. Sophia is the soul. Christ is that which enlightens the soul. Christians have denied and hidden Sophia in their *Holy Spirit*, a mysterious concept they do not explain. And by so doing, they have unbalanced the world. Without Sophia, Christ is alone...and is not called. Without Christ, we remain asleep, lost in self-created illusion."

There. I have told them what it is I begin to sense has something of truth about it. When I look again, Isidore is gone. I had not noticed his leaving.

Nildjat Miw remains, the tip of her tongue poking from her closed mouth where it appears now forgotten. One tooth shows, sharp as a thorn. And then, she speaks—a most complex series of sounds. I feel as Isidore; I can only imagine what they might mean. I smile and I scratch her chin. "Indeed," I say, sure that I agree to something profound.

And then the atrium fills with the voices of my Companions.

The debate I have engendered lasts for hours, and when it is over I am limp with thought.

Though I believed him gone, Isidore sits in my workroom. That I do not scream with surprise surprises me. It is late and it is hot. We swim in wet heat.

His back is bent with despair, his face black with anger. I think of Synesius. His whole life seems a lament. Synesius would be bishop or he would not, he would leave what he loves or he would not. Isidore's life seems a tale of ill-use. He would remain, humbled, without access to power. He would find another kind of power. He would have riches. He would not.

I can help neither of them.

He speaks without looking at me. "I am lost in the jaws of a lion."

"Do you ask for advice?"

"As I love you, it is exactly your advice I cannot take. I attend your lectures, Hypatia, I am called Companion. But I remain a priest of Christ, and my faith is strong."

"I love not your faith, but you..."—he would hear the word "love"; he leans forward to savor it, but it sticks in my throat—"...I care for. No matter the price, you must follow your true belief."

Throughout, his eyes are bleak. What smolders within him escapes into flame. "But the price, Hypatia! So high; how can I pay? To curry favor with Rome and with Constantinople, Theophilus abandons Origen." He slaps his thigh with a sound like the short sharp bark of a dog. "Origen! What greater teacher of Christ has walked this earth? Who brought together so much that was disparate, yet so worthy? Philo the Jew, Numenius of Apamea who loved Pythagoras and Plato, your own Valentinus, these and more he bound round with his own godly thoughts. Origen, not Theophilus, gave Christianity what it did not have, but which Hellenists gloried in and even Gnostics achieved: an orderly and self consistent system! To remain with Origen I cannot also remain near Theophilus. But if not a hermit, what choice is left me? Do you know where it is I must go and do you know who is already there?"

He tells me what he has told me before. I answer as I have answered before. I am decided. Isidore must leave the Companions. Though I had hoped we did, we hold nothing for him. I will tell him so kindly, but I will tell him. And I do know where he must go; to the caves of men hardened by rage and made brutal by ignorance, fanatics driven from Alexandria by the hunger of their bishop. This too decides me. I must cause him pain. To cause pain is to feel pain. "As you cannot deny Origen, you will crouch in a cave, own only what you can carry, eat only what can be found there. But you will sleep as a babe for you will be a principled man."

Isidore shakes his head. "All this is so. And because it is so, I cannot sleep. I cannot eat. I cannot think. I ask myself, over and over, in heaven's holy name, how do I do this?"

"Isidore, I have read the gospels, the Bible, the commentaries. The church of Theophilus darkens the light. It takes from the world what was offered it by Jesus and by Origen: that the soul is eternal, existing before the body as it will exist after, that all come and go in this world living each life as an actor takes part in a play, and that no soul suffers an eternal hell. Like ancient masters in the Valley of the Indus, Origen believed even the souls of demons, if demons there are, would return to their Source. Are souls not free, he asked, and will they not, when perfected, restore themselves in *apokatastasis* to the Perfect Mind?"

Isidore comes close, too close. "I knew you, of all, would see through to the truth...and I am asked to deny Origen! If I do not comply, Theophilus will strip me of my priesthood!"

"Then you must leave."

From flame, Isadore is swept yet again into gloom. "But so too do I love my life here."

"You love the role you play, as I love mine. Like Sophia, we are daily fooled by them. Even Origen lost himself in matter."

"Never."

"Thinking to banish desire, did he not make himself a neuter?"

"Lies!"

"But to the senses, what else but matter exists?"

I see what I do. I coerce him to do what I would have him do—leave Alexandria. By his leaving, the Companions are free of him, and I am relieved of honesty.

"You advise that I go to Nitria?"

I do—because it is best for me. But is it best for him? "Your bishop is gone to depose John Chrysostom, the Bishop of Constantinople..."

Isidore's mouth curls up. In it, there is undisguised vanity. "Which John refuses to attend, just as Theophilus refused to attend the synod John called against him."

"Just so. Does it not seem wise to make use of his absence?"

I am watching a small brown spider. Only moments past, she caught a fly and is wrapping it quickly in silver thread. "But if I go to Nitria," Isidore is saying, and only now I notice how sounds his voice—into the midst of worry and hurt has crept an unpleasant hint of petulance—"I will no longer be a Companion."

This could be stopped by a word, cleansed by a final honesty. As a cruel child, I would have spoken it by now. But I have drowned in the sea. I have lost Lais, most beloved of me. The books I treasure are hidden so that even I cannot read them. My time, and the time of all like me, grows short. But none of this stoppers my tongue. Something else, something in Isidore, keeps me quiet.

Quicker than the spider has seized her fly, Isidore seizes hold of my arm. "Have you nothing to say?" His eyes burn with a dark and unhealthy light. It is not the light I saw as we lay together under the palms of an oracle's oasis. It is not the light of desire, not even of lust. There is a possessiveness in it, a kind of thick and reckless fury that comes with being opposed. It is as the face of Theophilus when John was chosen as bishop over Isidore. It is as the faces of men and of women running through the streets with blooded hands and blooded thoughts, or of those in black who stand at the back of my lecture hall. In this moment I know why my heart has left Isidore.

I do not know this man. I do not *want* to know this man. I have taught him, loved him, dreamt of him, longed for him, shared his error, and forgiven him for it. For months I have fallen away, thinking him not worthy of me. I have wronged myself. I can forgive my fickle heart. He is *Parabalanoi*. He has always been *Parabalanoi*.

"I would be Bishop of Constantinople if not for a vile eunuch! And now I am reduced to caves and shitting in holes. You, only a woman, would choose this for me? Do you not know who I *am*?"

"Tell me, Isidore. *Who* are you?"

"Better yet, ask this! Who is the woman so chaste she would kill me before yielding herself...yet now gives herself to all?"

He frightens me; I will not show it. He causes me dread; he will not see it. He has cut into my heart; I will not bleed for him.

"I am who I am."

"Indeed." He is close now, so close I smell the perfume he uses to sweeten his breath. "But who is the Egyptian who lives in your house and eats your food and hears your teaching and goes you know not where."

"What do you mean? What are you saying? I *know* who Minkah is."

"Do you? Do you really know who you found stealing books in your library, who you have made a Companion?"

My frightened heart, once warm and then cool, now turns cold. "There is none I know better. If you would still please me, priest, shun my company as I shall shun yours."

"Ask him, Hypatia, ask this man you know so well who his paymaster is."

Paymaster? What has my brother to do with money? I would ask but Isidore is gone.

Would I have really asked?

THEON

Late Spring, 405

Jone, youngest daughter of Theon of Alexandria

Father is dying. I cannot imagine what could concern me less unless it is his mathematics. I know he dies and why he dies because in each of the years I follow the command of our Holy Bishop Theophilus, I have made sure of all that occurs in my sister's house and that I report it faithfully.

Twice now, I have crept quietly into my father's darkened room. The stench is terrible no matter how Minkah perfumes with myrrh his draperies and cushions or how many flacons filled with sweet oils and jars of unguents he sets about. I leave as soon as I come. Father knows me not. But this is as nothing. When has he ever known me or me him? I would not know him now if I could. He is repulsive. Covered with sores, he raves, he coughs, he whines. Even Olinda stays away. For one thing, as with Lais and her horrid disease of the stomach, the poor woman can do little with Father and his putrid fever. For another, Father is as ridiculous in the face of death as he was in the face of disappointment. Imagine taking to one's bed for fourteen years. And the words he calls his physician! The gestures he makes towards Minkah! Not even at market have I heard or seen things so vile. And he knows not his savior. I would not want to be Father when he is called to judgment.

But all that is by-the-by. Father will die and that will be the end of that, one less sinner in the world. But this I do feel.

Humble before my God, and as great a sinner as all men are, and all women even more so, I make now this confession: I cannot care for Bishop Theophilus no matter how worthy he is of all good regard. After all, God has chosen him to lead a great city, and yet...there it is. Here, in the privacy of my own heart where only Christ can see, I confess also this: I not only cannot care for my city's bishop, he causes me great unease. This is, no doubt, a fault of my own since it could not be a failure of his, and yet...there it is. And as I am confessing, this too I admit: I love Minkah with that same heart that does not love Bishop Theophilus. Love for one and lack of love for the other are both great sins, this I know as I know the color of the three small eggs that each year hatch in the nest outside my cell window, and I will surely pay for these sins in some way that is yet to be revealed to me. But this at least I can claim as mine: neither knows how I feel. It is my sin and only mine. A comfort...and there it is.

I have one more sin, the worst sin of all. I do not know where it is, I could not find it, but I know the library lives. I know Minkah has helped hide it somewhere far into the desert. Minkah could not know how evil his act. He had only just found us, only just come to know Father and Lais and Hypatia. I believe even now he is innocent. His innocence and my guilt cause me to pray far into the night.

I sit this day in the house of the bishop waiting for one of our talks about Hypatia and who visits and how long they stay and if anything was said he should know. It is my sixth or seventh visit since he returned from his travels. He had meant to go all the way across the Great Sea to Constantinople to hold a synod against John Chrysostom who is bishop there, and then go on to some other place for some other purpose. That was two years ago. I am not supposed to know this, but our bishop was not allowed to set foot in the city of the Emperor of the East so was forced to hold his synod against their bishop in some lowlier place. John Chrysostom did not deign to appear, yet Bishop Theophilus condemned him whether he was there or not. I am also not supposed to know that his condemnation bore no weight with the Most Holy Innocent, Bishop of Rome. Because of this, our bishop demanded a second synod against Constantinople's bishop. That too was ill received. Pity our poor Holy Bishop. And then he traveled to somewhere north of Ravenna, and was there set upon by Goths or Visigoths or whichever army of heathens threatens the Empires now...there are so many and they cause so much fear and turmoil, I cannot keep up. They ride into a place, they rape and they pillage, one or another of them calls himself "emperor" until he too is cut down. Those who are left ride away. Another godless sort from some other heathenish place rides against the Empire, and all happens again. In any case, our bishop escaped Ravenna.

Since returning home, his temper has been, in a word, evil. We all of us know he is coming from rooms away by the clanking of his jewelry and the unceasing howl of his voice. He howls, it seems, because even though the Empress of the East, the witch Eudoxia, cast John from her church and her city, she soon called him back. Apparently, she could not deny him, and this because though the rich love him not, the poor love him well, at the same time reviling our bishop for the exile of their bishop. But then, right away Eudoxia cast John Chrysostom out again, not because our bishop wished it, but because he spoke against women and against Eudoxia and the statues she caused to be carved of herself...and why should he not! Every word I hear he has said, is no more than Jesus said, or Paul, or any worthy father of the faith come later, and who is Empress Eudoxia to have gone against all these, or so shamefully have shown herself in gold and stone? I allow myself a small gloat, for when God saw all that she did, He exacted a great price in His just and enormous rage. First He sent a tremendous storm to rage against her city and its people, which destroyed much and killed many, and then, seven days later, He slew her in childbirth, taking also her child. How just is God!

I would think the storm and her death would soothe Bishop Theophilus. Nothing soothes him. He acts the wounded bull. It seems to me, considering the fate of Eudoxia, that our bishop should make his peace with their bishop, wherever the poor man is now. John is not in Constantinople, but where he is, if any know, I am not one of them.

But here is a thing. No matter what I feel or do not feel for Bishop Theophilus, I am eager to make my visits to his house, for there now lives the son of his sister, a young man called Cyril who accompanied our Bishop on his troublesome travels. And while it is true the nephew of our bishop is hasty in thought and so also in action, and his ire when crossed is somewhat excessive, there is something about him...exactly what, I cannot clearly say, though I can try: Cyril is what Theophilus is not. Both are men of faith, yet I suspect the faith of Theophilus could be set aside for any number of reasons, and has been. I know Cyril's could not.

I know also I could never feel for him as I feel for Minkah—

after all, Cyril is shaped like one of my sister's geometric cones, and his face is, well, to be kind, unwholesome in its pallor, and as for his teeth, my goodness!—still, if allowed, I would be his friend on the instant.

There is a sudden great to-do along a corridor and, oh! The door slams open on the antechamber I wait in, and here is Cyril. I would speak to him! But my heart races so, I cannot. He is the nephew of the Bishop of Alexandria. He has been educated to follow on after Theophilus. And who am I?

"You!"

I jump where I sit. But I do not look up and I do not unfold my hands. I cannot use his name. I cannot call him "father" for he is not yet a priest...though why Theophilus neglects to make him one seems odd to me. But there you go. And I cannot call him master for I have no connection. How do I answer? "Sir?"

"Your sister is Hypatia?"

Of course. Hypatia. I should have known. I fester as a boil. "Yes, sir."

"I hear, for a woman, she is brilliant. Some say, too brilliant."

"Yes, sir."

So saying, Cyril looks to his left and to his right. There is a monk at either door. He leans close so only I might hear. "And then there are those far from brilliant. Look at the Synod of the Oak. Uncle used mobs to coerce the bishops who bothered to come. Mobs are like wild beasts. You can't depend on them to be there and if they do come, you can't be sure what they'll say or do. Why, they could turn on you, for God's sake."

At this, the door to the bishop's great chamber opens and as it opens, Cyril's mouth closes, turning instead into a smile full of unpleasant teeth. I do wish he would not smile. From inside, we both hear his uncle call out, "Nephew! Come. We must talk."

I sit, waiting my turn. Though he hides it, Cyril no more loves Theophilus than do I. And he told *me*! We shall be friends.

Hypatia of Alexandria

In constant shadow, for light hurts his eyes, my cat and I find Father asleep.

As once I leaned over to whisper in the ear of Lais, I now whisper in my father's ear. "I have set aside all other work: Euclid, Plotinus, even our work on Zeno of Citium...each neglected for this new thing, this tremendous thing. Oh, that I could speak and you could hear me. Are you not still Theon of Alexandria, and do you not yet have a wondrous mind?"

I weep as I say this. I weep because I cannot remember my father's wondrous mind. Did he once stand upright lecturing before great crowds at the Museum or the Serapeum? Was he tall? Did he hold back his shoulders and hold high his head straight as a mast? All the days of my youth, this was the man who taught me the glory of number, who pointed out the planets in their courses, the stars that fell, who indulged each whim: the lyre and the harp, the mixing of paint and of ink, the making of paper—it was endless what I asked and what he granted.

And now he is an old man dying in an old bed. And if he is not forgotten, it is only because I tell any who ask, and many who do not, that what I have learned I have learned from Theon of Alexandria.

He cannot last. Olinda does what she can, but still the fever rises and with it comes delirium. Fewer and fewer are the hours in which I find my father still lives in the eyes of this dying man. And yet I continue to speak as if he were here. "I study the words of a woman called Mariamne who said the world and all it contains is a dream dreamed by Consciousness, and if that is so, numbers are a part of this beautiful dream, and we are its dreamers. Do you dream now? Have you hidden in dream?" I touch his hand. It is not cold nor yet is it warm. It does not move. "Euclid's smaller and smaller points become eventually nothing. Zeno's footsteps, halving the distance from tree to tree, never arrive. Parmenides said nothing happens. We believed we knew what they meant, but did we, Father?"

Father has opened his eyes. They are milky with sleep, dull with dying.

"Father!" I lean even closer to his ear. "Do you hear me?"

Father turns his face into mine. "How could I not hear you? Are you not shouting? What are you wearing? What is that? I can see straight through it."

It is true. I have adopted, when not lecturing, the fashion of thin silk, so thin the shape of my body might be glimpsed, but only in full sunlight. Here it is as the gloom of Kur, the crevasse of dust.

"Have you wed? Have you birthed a boy?" Sitting back, I am shocked. I do not answer. I cannot answer. He struggles to sit up. How long has he done other than lay flat, save for his head propped up by pillows? I rush to help him. Father struggles, Miw strolls calmly out the door. "What," whines Father, "is a woman if not a portal through which man makes his way into this world?"

Believing he jests, I jest. "A woman is the other half of a man, the more perfect half."

He thrashes his head from side to side. He looks for something in his cell of a shadowed room. "I want my grandson."

"I have no child, neither male nor female."

Father cannot sit up. He is much too weak, so sinks back on his bedding. "As my only daughter—"

"You have another daughter, Father. Jone."

"As my only daughter, you will marry. I order it."

With a cloth kept near, I wipe the spittle from his lips, the crusted muck from his beard. "Why answer to a man, when I am already wedded to truth?"

"You know no man?"

I think of the men I "know." They have been many and varied. Some young, some old, some rich, some poor, some who love me more than I love them...all, to one degree or another, a revelation. "Men are amusing, Father, no more."

"Serious men are not amused to be found amusing."

"No doubt. But too much seriousness shows a lack of good sense. And must I remind my own father of Plato? 'All the pursuits of men are the pursuits of women also.'"

Father now passes wind so foul, Minkah's perfumes are blown away. As I leave, my feet are chilled by the tiles of a room bereft of the sun. Behind me, Father yells, "You will marry Minkah. Where is Minkah?"

Minkah the Egyptian

"Minkah, my son. You will write my will as I dictate it."

Take dictation? I do much for the man, but not this. "Rinat is in the house. Hypatia will send her here. Now, if you wish."

"Rinat? Who is Rinat?"

As I have done for years, I refrain from crushing the idiot's windpipe. I have no wish that he truly die. With time, I have learned pity. A hard lesson, but mastered nonetheless. Theon is weak. It is his nature to be clever, yet foolish; as it is the nature of Hypatia to be more than clever and exceedingly strong. It is my nature to serve and to learn what it is wise to serve and what it is not wise to serve. Few rise above their own nature. Theon is not one of these.

The old man snivels. The heat that boils his blood seems less. He is not delirious nor has he coughed this day. He does not complain his head aches like a tooth. As I have seen Olinda do a hundred times and more, I place my hand on his sweated forehead. He snatches it away. "I want it written now. I want it in your handwriting. It will be done as is right and proper in Latin, the language of law-makers, and when it is done, this Rinat can witness it."

"Women can witness nothing, Theon."

"They cannot?"

Delirious or not, he has at least one toe in some other world. "Only men might do so."

"Fine. Forget Rinat. As witnesses, gather up all the best equipped males you can find. But no Christians. Christians mustn't get their hands on a thing, nothing! You hear me, Minkah? Not even the piss in my pot." I hear him. In this, at least, he is right. Theophilus and his ilk force many to leave to the Church what properly belongs to family and to friends. Everywhere, it becomes scandalous, but everywhere, the dying comply for fear of reprisal which comes in many guises. "And now," says he, "let us begin."

"You do not die."

"I will die."

This is inarguable. "But not now."

"Pah. Begin."

Gathering paper and pen and writing board, I am ready. At the last, what does it cost to please the old boil? Hypatia is safe in her workroom. The house goes about its placid day. The Companions do not meet until this evening. I have nothing to report to Theophilus. And Theon has nothing to leave. A few minutes work at most. Later, to clear the palate, I will ride Ia'eh who needs the exercise as much as I.

Theon is asleep. Relieved, I begin setting all down again. He is not asleep. He is reciting. "I, Theon of Alexandria, leave to my only daughter..." I do not write "only," but do write the name "Hypatia." "...the original copies of books written by me, and all other books in my possession. I leave her also the table of green stone that was brought to this house by my beloved Damara. I wish the necessary sum spent building my tomb in the Necropolis, as good and as fine as any, for I am Theon of Alexandria. There will be carved ivory and painted glass. There will be singing birds. There will be statues of Thoth and of Osiris, there will be Greek gods and goddesses, but there will be nothing Christian! Not a thing, hear me!" He breaks from his narration; I break from my writing so he might rant. "And if a symbol or some other thing that was once ours, is now theirs by theft, do not include it. Think, Minkah! What if in some distant time my tomb is discovered and by these stolen symbols I am mistaken for Christian? Even now, my bones rattle with horror. I should die again! You and Hypatia will ensure this does not happen." I nod. I smile. My pen is poised. "Good. We continue. I will be wrapped in my wall hanging." I look up. Wall hanging? Commissioned by his friends as a gift on his fiftieth birthday, it depicts Alexandria's leading mathematicians and philosophers. Theon occupies the most prominent position among them. I had forgotten it. "Incense is to burn constantly." No small expense, incense. "Copies of my work will be sealed within a box made of red granite and bound with blue copper and this box will be secreted near my body, the exact position of which to be determined by Hypatia. In this box will also be placed a certain map." Again, I lift my pen. Theon has no right to bury his copy of one of three maps that lead to the Great Library. Also, he has no map. When he is well and truly dead, I shall give the map to Hypatia as long ago agreed. "In my burial chamber will be placed near mine the body of Damara, taken from the tomb in which she now lies. There will be also built a second chamber as grand as the first for the body of my much loved Lais, taken as well from the tomb of Damara, and in time this second chamber will contain the body of Hypatia and the body of Minkah the Egyptian." As Hypatia has had all this prepared at her own expense for the past three years, this too I do not write down, although I pretend to. No need to note that Jone will take the place of Minkah. "To defray some of the cost, the tomb of Damara and Lais will be sold. It is a fine tomb and should fetch a fine price. All else that is mine, my house, my goods, my money to whatever sum..." I do not mention he has no money; that all money for years now is Hypatia's money, earned by her in spite of him. "...I leave to my son, Minkah the Egyptian." My hand is off the page on the word "son."

"You cannot leave me your house, Theon. This is Hypatia's house. It is Jone's house."

Where he finds the breath is surprising, but the volume of his voice exceeds my tolerance. "This is my house, *mine*, and I will leave it to whomever I wish! Write what I have said to write!"

I could and would leave now, be done with this foolishness... but if I do not remain to curb the worst, someone else will write it exactly as he speaks it. Bugger. But as I fully intend exhibiting this drivel to Hypatia knowing she and I will rewrite it together—and only then will it be witnessed—I write on.

Speaking has exhausted the man. Speaking loudly has taken away what is left of his voice. Again, he closes his eyes, and again I make a move to sneak away, seeking Hypatia with this *will* of his so we might laugh as we laugh over the poetry of Palladas, making such changes as are fair to his daughters, but comes again that crust of a voice I have heard for fourteen years. "Write further." I reseat myself, pen hovering. Eyes closed, he opens his mouth. "If, by one year from the date of my death, my son Minkah the Egyptian should be married to my daughter, Hypatia..." How many times must I raise my pen? Theon continues. I do not. "...and by two years from the date of my death, got her with child, be it male or female, my house and all it contains reverts to the name of Hypatia of Alexandria."

I would pull his grey beard from his grey face. He has forced his will on Hypatia for years. Even dead, he would continue. He thinks he will soon die? He is closer than he imagines.

"You are not writing!" Theon's eyes have opened. They stare directly into mine. "Write what I have said, and when you have written, show me the page." I write. I show him what I have written. Fortunately, he reads only this last so does not notice all that is missing. "You will now leave my testament on that table, and then you will bring males, two or three, it matters not. I will have this signed and witnessed before supper."

The cunning old *cunnus*. Theon has taught me Latin. Therefore in Latin, I write the word *cacō* at the bottom. Under my breath, I translate: *shit*.

Theon of Alexandria

Standing on the topmost step of the Serapeum, I raise my arms before multitudes—and am deafened by shouts and applause and the high-pitched ululating of women.

"You see, Hypatia! Thousands of years, and could any construct a square of area equal to that of a circle? No, they could not! Antiphon the Sophist, Oenopides and Hippocrates of Chios, Bryson of Heraclea, Hippias of Elis, not even Anaxagoras in his prison cell or Archimedes with his spiral curve or Liu Hsiao in the Imperial House of Han could solve such a problem. Nor could the mighty Aristotle. But I, Theon of Alexandria, have squared the circle!"

Hypatia leans her head on my shoulder, content to place herself behind me. "How, then, did you do it, Father? Tell me. Tell us *all*."

And so I would have, and at length, but for the tremendous crash that brings my head up from a pillow…am I in bed? How odd. Bed is no place for Theon of Alexandria! I run for my window. What sounds? An earthquake? Will it shake my home to rubble?

Comes another great crash, and this one followed by a man shouting. "A pox on your house, demon-maker! A pox on all it contains!"

Again I come awake to find I am still in bed. The bed is cold, its bedding on the floor. And where is Damara?

"Necromancer! Magic worker!"

I know what I hear—the voice of a man unschooled; in short, a fool. Someone who sells me my meat or my flour or my oil, or even one of those who buy night-soil to sell on to farmers in their fields. Should one of these learn I have circled the square, it would fall as music fell on the ear of a squid.

Damara?

Another voice follows the last, and a third crash follows the second, all this come from outside my window. Dolts and *henen-tep*, they throw stones, bricks, pots, at my shutters! How many? Do any bear torches? That is the important question. Stones and shouting can be borne, but fire?

Damara!

"Come out, old man, father of witches!"

And now a woman's screech: "She stands before men! She teaches deviltry! A demon must live in her belly! Father of demons, show yourself!"

Who stands before men?

The pain sweeps through me like a wind of sulfurous dust come in from the desert, dark yellow and full of woe. There is a pain in my legs, my arms, my back, gnawing like the teeth of jackals, like the howling things outside. And yet, their presumption has made them wise. They think to insult, but instead they exalt me—for I *am* a demon. I am *Daemon*. I have heard its voice and it is my voice. I have squared the circle.

THE FIFTH GATE

Hypatia of Alexandria

Ife found Father curled in his bed as a snail in its shell and as dead as a rat in Paniwi's mouth. Her screams as she ran through the house woke us all, even the horses.

By refusing to live, Father began his dying the day the Serapeum fell. I remember the last words of Plotinus: *Raise up the divine within you to the first-born divine.* Father's last years and last words will be as little remembered as dust swept from the floor. But as for his first years and his first words, by these Theon will live.

Sitting at my mother's table, I have read his will. Witnessed and binding, that Jone is disinherited fills me with anger...one more cause for her hatred. And how does her hatred further? It hurts she who hates more than it hurts that which is hated. And yet, there is a shiver of understanding that troubles my spine.

Father has made himself clear. If I do not wed a brother not truly a brother I must leave, for the house is now Minkah's. I ask myself and I ask sincerely: would I wed Minkah? And the answer, so long unheard and so long delayed, is this—yes. Though it is not his wish and though he loved Lais as I now know I love him, still I would marry. And here is the way I might do it without shame and without dishonor, by the will of my dead father. I should be seen to have Minkah as mine so that Jone would not lose her home. There is a truth to this. Jone must not lose her home. But yes, yes, I would marry Minkah.

And then, before I can stop it or soften it, this thought intrudes: Minkah is an Egyptian! How should I, Hypatia, a Greek, marry so far beneath me! Such an unworthy thought, an ugly thought, more shaming than love for a man who loves another.

There is a small clay pot on the table. Without thought, I bring it up, only to smash it down, the shards cutting my hands, my arms. A mind may know a thing, the spirit may embrace it, but the voice that chatters in the head clings ever to shameful beliefs. An Egyptian is less than a Greek? To find I am as men who believe themselves far above women—by the star of Isis, in this moment I am made ill by no one so much as Hypatia. By this, I efface even Father's last cruelty to Jone.

I believe Minkah. I believe he and I would have changed the will if Father had not forced his hand. I believe him because I love him, because over and over he has proved his love for my father, for Jone, for the House of Theon, even of me, though that love is not as the one I now see I bear for him. And I as well believe him because I understand Father, as wily in his way as a money lender. All that is in his will is precisely as he was: thoughtless as well as careful, caring as well as unfeeling, demanding as well as giving, traditional as well as eccentric, and throughout more a child than a man. In the mind of Father, the world was as Plotinus would have it: *"All things are full of signs, and it is a wise man who can learn about one thing from another."* That Minkah's life was saved by me, that he followed me home, that he has never left, that he has become the son Father lost by the loss of Damara, that he has learned all Father could teach him, that he has by his own choice protected me from year to year, that he by his own efforts transported the whole of the precious library into the desert caves, that he is Egyptian and knows not his birth-name or place so could have fallen from the stars: all this formed a pattern that well pleased the ideals of the idealistic Theon of Alexandria. As it now, fully and completely, pleases me.

Later I will grieve. Later I will feel the loss of my father. But now I am filled with anger at so much that he has done and that he has not done. Angry at myself for allowing him his small cruelties, for humoring him in those that were far from small. I am angry he spent so much time dying rather than living. I am angry he is dead.

Minkah and I sit at Damara's green table which is now my green table. He says nothing about the smashed pot or the blood on my hands. Instead, we stare down at Father's words, witnessed by our stable master and by our stable master's assistant. Nildjat Miw does not sit on Father's last wishes. I am not as Miw. I would throw it on the fire. But not for the loss of a house and not for Jone who in her faith has no need of a house. I would burn it because Father harms Minkah. How shall he care for its stables and its gardens and its servants and its repairs, its endless repetitive expense? He must sell the horses, the ornaments, the furniture, let go the servants...and still the expense will go on, and on. To lose the house, any man would find this shaming. Minkah will find it more shameful still. Unless we wed.

Minkah's voice startles Miw into making a sound, easy of interpretation. She is annoyed. "Your father cannot give me what was not his. This is your house, Hypatia. It has long been your house. I will have papers drawn up to that effect. I will sign them immediately."

"It was Father's house, Minkah."

"Without you to lean on, he would have lost it long ago."

"Without me to lean on, he might never have fallen."

"But he did fall. And he did not rise again."

"You think this, Minkah? That my father could not have risen again if he would have?"

"Theon did what was in him to do. He fell. He remained where he had fallen. He allowed others to carry the weight that was his to bear. In response, Hypatia did what was in her to do. She did not fall. Though young and a woman, she carried her family. She carried me. This is her house."

Listening, I love him more. Listening, I see plain yet one more thing I have been blind to. "You did not love my father."

For the space of a moment, Minkah is quiet. I watch as some resolution forms in his eyes. I think what I see is that he will speak truth to me, truth I might wish I had never heard. "No, Hypatia. I did not love Theon. Yet I came to understand him. I forgave him his weaknesses long ago. But I could not love him for them. I could love Lais."

"All loved Lais." My voice is as small as my breathing. There is more. I know he will tell me more. He gathers himself to do so and I cannot stop him, would not stop him. By the passing of Father, more than Father will pass.

"And I love you."

"Of course. As a sister, just as I love you as brother."

"I do not love you as a sister. If I could in all honor, I would do as your father wishes."

"You would marry me?"

"Yes, Hypatia, I would marry you."

I am thrown into tumult. Minkah and I might wed? It would keep me in the house of my birth. It would keep the house for Jone should she ever come home. And to hear that he loves me? I who have heard these words from so many, but who have never truly heard them at all, hear them now and thrill to them now. I would leap from my chair. I would cleave to it. I would turn to Minkah and give him my heart. I would turn away so he does not see how he touches me. And why am I torn between when I have won all? Hypatia, speak truth! Because I would lose my freedom.

This is more than freedom from the whims and needs and demands of a husband, more than his assuming control over my home and wealth—my freedom is that I am seen by the world to be free of a man, but even more, to be seen by women as free. I stand as a woman alone and by standing alone, stand all the taller. And what I can do, they can do.

I would say this, I would tell him I have loved him since the day we stood in the depths of the Serapeum daring fire for the books, I would explain all but the loss of status, but Minkah is already speaking. "I would have you as wife, but I cannot."

"Cannot?"

"I am not who you think I am."

Across the years, Isidore sounds in my ear. *Who is this Minkah the Egyptian who lives in your house and eats your food and hears your teaching and goes you do not know where? Ask him who he is.* As if the earth shook under me, I tremble. "Who do I think you are?"

"You believe I was born poor, and in this you are right. You believe me an Egyptian of the streets, and in this you are right. You believe me a craftsman, and in this you are right. You believe I love not the Christian come among us to destroy what causes them fear and discomfort, and again you are right."

"Then who is it I do not know?"

"You believe I am still poor. You believe I am good and have done good. You believe I would never cause harm. In this you are wrong."

"What do you mean, Minkah? What are you saying?"

"As Isidore was, I am *Parabalanoi.* I do the bidding of Bishop

Theophilus. In your home, for so long as I have lived here, you have harbored a spy, one who has performed his shameful tasks faithfully even though he loves you."

I stare at him. I *stare* at him. Immobilized with horror, yet how fast my thoughts—Theophilus must know of the library! But before I can react to this latest calamity, before I even know *how* to react, comes a great crash outside a door I had not thought to close. The statue of Thoth falls. Nildjat Miw jumps from her place on my table, not away, but towards the door. His knife drawn, Minkah is there a moment after Miw. What they have found is Jone, senseless on the tiles near the god of knowledge.

Jone, youngest daughter of Theon of Alexandria

Which touches me? I scramble to my feet on the instant. I push away the hand that holds mine. Minkah's hand. I would spit on him. I would spit on them all, even the cat, Hypatia's enormous cat, who curls and curls like a snake round my ankles, who leaps when she finds me, who forces her face into my face, talking and talking and saying such odd and terrifying things I long ago learned to shut my ears.

Minkah speaks. "Jone? Do you sicken?" Yes, I would say, *you* sicken me, you who I know now to be a deceiver. But I say nothing. I cannot even look at him,

Hypatia speaks, who is full of demons. "I will send for Olinda. Do you need Olinda?"

Minkah would marry Hypatia? I am ill enough to vomit.

My belly clenches as a fist, my head swims as if I were on the *Irisi*. I hate the *Irisi*. Under it sinks a deepness I swoon to imagine. When I would speak I manage only a dry hacking retch.

There is no female as my sister. There should be no female as my sister. Nor one as Lais. Demons took that one. First they laid their egg beneath the skin of her belly, then they took her mind, and finally they took her body. Sweet Mother of God, how came I to be born here? How came I to be sister to these? I raise my eyes to the eyes of Hypatia. False. False. *False*. If I could see through, what would I see? The deep under *Irisi*? I hold up my hand, palm facing them both. "Get away from me."

I turn and I run from this house. Even for the Holy Bishop, I will never return, never.

That it is now Minkah's, I care not. That Father is finally dead, I care not. That Minkah would marry Hypatia, I will learn to care *not*!

Hypatia of Alexandria

I turn my face from the tragedy that is Jone to the horror that is Minkah.

Our Egyptian is a spy. Father and father's friends, even the Companions, what they have said and what they have done, this is known to the Patriarch Theophilus through the one I called brother, through the one I have loved though I knew it not. The library! Minkah knows every cave, every jar. Could this mean that Theophilus knows every cave, every jar…even that which contains the poems of Lais our "brother" claims to have loved?

"Minkah?" Even on my own ear, my voice falls as the linen pall over the face of my newly dead father. It seems as lifeless as the drone of the prayers of priests to aid in his journey with Anubis.

"Yes?" Minkah's voice is every bit as dead as mine.

"Is the library still there?"

"It is as it was."

"This you swear?"

He would move towards me, but as Jone, I hold up my hand, palm outward. "I have loved you, Minkah. I have placed my trust in you."

"It was not misplaced."

"You can say this, a spy for Theophilus?"

"I can say this."

I cannot listen. I cannot move. I cannot understand even the need for nourishment. I am as destroyed as Jone.

He takes another step forward. "Hypatia!"

As he moves forward, I slide my chair back. "Leave me. I am homeless. I am without father or sister or brother. I am Hypatia and I do not know who I am."

"You are not homeless and though I am not worthy to stay,

I cannot leave. Not yet. You must hear me out."

With all the pure black anger I have never allowed myself to feel or others to see, I turn on him. I, who have denied myself rage, am filled with rage. Lais, who most deserved Life, was murdered by life. Those without reason silence in loud righteousness those with exalted understanding. Jone was not loved as all deserve love and so cannot love. There is no cure for this. It is done. I was taken when I would not be taken, yet still soothed my abuser—a woman's curse, for women, like children, forever accept blame. As for Father...the disgust he has caused me has weighted my belly with bile for years. And now this. This! To find my friend, my brother, my love, betrays me!

I stand so suddenly my chair is thrown back. I rush towards Minkah who does not step back. What I would scream, I would scream in his face. But just as I reach him, I pass him by, seeking to find the only place ever I found peace: the window ledge of Lais.

Nildjat Miw, anticipating, runs before me.

Minkah the Egyptian

Theon's death has been my death. Followed by her cat, her strange unquiet cat, I watch Hypatia leave me. All around there is nothing but silence. In all its forms, death rules this house.

If I walked, I would stagger. If I sat, I would slump. If I remain as I am, standing in the door to Hypatia's room, as made of stone as Thoth or his sister Seshat, I might never move. In all my life I have known what next to do. I do not know now. For years my confession has lived on my tongue. I saw it there as clearly as if I were to take up a pen and write, not a poem or a comment, but a play. I would imagine that it played out one way. I would imagine it played out in another way. Or in yet a third way. At times, Hypatia would laugh at my exposure. At times, she would cry. Most often she would both cry and laugh. Each time I would stand before her: humble, repentant, but charged with love. I knew it would remain my love, not hers, but that was long ago accepted. The point would be my declaration. The point would be my honesty and her forgiveness. In the plays I wrote but did not truly write, no matter how each began, how each clashed and rang with heated words, with rended cloth, with arrows of accusation, in the end, we should understand each other.

I was right. We understand each other. I am to leave this house. And she has left me.

I loved Lais. I love her still. But that love was as Persian *opion*. Lais was made of the stuff of dreams. Hypatia is life. Neither dream nor life are mine. I am Minkah and though I would not, I must be as I was made to be: the stuff of nightmares. There are these few things I can do. I will have Olinda sent for so Hypatia might have medicines if they are needed. I snatch up her father's will where it has lain throughout. I will burn the thing as it is now. Those who were witness to it know me well. They will soon know the last wishes of Theon for I will tell them what it is they have signed. None would desire, any more than I, to see Hypatia disinherited. None would desire Jone to be slighted. All will keep their silence. I shall write another will. This they will hear before signing. Hypatia will keep her house.

I will also do these things. I will retrieve the map that is now hers. And then I will write the play I never wrote. In a letter to Hypatia, I will explain all, hide nothing. It will be left along with the map on her table of green stone, and then I will remove my person from the house of the woman I love.

What I shall do next is not for me to know. I am empty of life. I am empty.

Jone, youngest daughter of Theon of Alexandria

I am no one but Jone and all that I love loves me not. Even a dog longs for love.

I run from my sister's house and into the great park which lies on the far side of the wide Street of Gardens.

Loving Mother of our Savior, hear thou thy servant's cry. Star of the deep and Portal of the sky! Mother of Him who was from nothing made.

Over and over as a wheel rolls under a wagon, I pray: *Sinking I strive and call to thee for aid. Sinking I strive and call to thee for aid. Sinking I strive and call to thee for aid!*...until, lo!

thanks to the Lord, I am blessed with the answer I seek and it stops me as I run. *"And you must daily seek the companionship of the saints, so that you may find support in their words."*

I have reached the small amphitheater within the park. Someone lectures this day. Few listen. I hear nothing but a jumble of words. I see nothing but a small dark man with a large white beard throwing out his arms as people nod or doze or eat what they have brought with them. Oh, that so few listened to Hypatia, that they not overflow her lecture hall. Why do they listen? What do they hear? Do they not sense the demon that sits on her tongue? I turn on my heel and run back towards the street seeking the companionship of saints.

Those I pass stare at me. Before God, I bear myself modestly and I am used to being stared at. My habit is not light nor is it linen; it is woolen, hot and dark under the Alexandrian sun. I cover my head. I lower my eyes. The mark of my faith and my chastity remains uncommon among those come from all over the world, each clad in the dress of their origin, speaking tongues I do not understand, thinking thoughts that blind them to the true God. But those like me grow. Where once the widows and virgins of Christ had only one house, now there are two and talk of a third House of Women in the city of Canopus. We shall be seen one day, and we shall be heard and we shall save *all* though they know not they are lost, nor would they welcome the saving. God asks—and who denies God?

A hand reaches out, filthy, diseased, to grasp at my skirts, but I pull away.

And if they refuse to be saved? Why, then, they shall be cast down forever. Though it seems harsh, it is not...for no soul is sent to Satan before the offer of salvation. The choice is not ours, but theirs. Praise God.

Some step aside for me. Some block my way. One laughs aloud. I do not mind. Those who do not follow Jesus will find Jesus does not follow them. This thought eases my way through the sweating stinking shouting crowd on the Street of Gardens.

I hurry to Bishop Theophilus. I mean to tell him about Minkah. I will say what I was all along expected to say, but did not.

Alma Redemptoris Mater, hear thou thy servant's cry. Come to my aid, come! What I will do is more shaming than standing outside my sister's door, more shaming than hearing the Egyptian I have loved declare he would marry Hypatia, more shaming than having heard Father named me not in his will. I would stop. I would turn away. I would walk back to the house of the women I live with. But I do not. Instead I do not walk, but pick up my heavy skirts and run, directly past the ships that daily fill the canal, through the gateway of the courtyard of Bishop Theophilus without thought for the bald monk who guards the first door or for the monk who guards the second. This monk's left eye is much larger than his right eye; both widen as I pass. The monks know me. They are used to my coming and my going. None stop my progress.

Our bishop is not in his great offices. He is not in his fine garden. He is not in the huge house at all. I run here and there. I cause a small commotion as I search for him, calling out. But no matter where I go, he is not there, and in the end I am saved—by the sweet grace of the Mother of God, I am saved. I, who could not stop myself, have been stopped by a Mother's love.

What joy! I am saved from myself.

Finding I achieved some part of the house I have never before seen, I hold my side from the stitch. *Praise Mary. Praise Jesus. Praise Theophilus for not being discovered at home.* For now, when I speak of Minkah, and I *will* speak of Minkah, it will not be to complain of my own hurt, my own sorrow, my own shame, but because in so doing I shall save him. *Praise God.*

"*Misella landica, nay?* You here again?"

Yet another monk who guards yet another door makes a noise down his long hooked nose. I do not understand his noise. I do not understand Latin. But I understand who it is who has spoken. I turn slowly towards Cyril of Alexandria, my eyes lowered, my hands folded, slowing my breath, slowing the beat of my heart, reining in my wild and shameful needs.

"Yes, sir, I am here."

The Bishop has not given Cyril the position left vacant by Isidore, turned traitor with the monks of the Nitria, those who love Origen. I do not love Origen. Origen once wrote much as my sister speaks now. Instead a man named Timothy is Archdeacon. I imagine Cyril, who is only a lector, a mere reader and not even a priest, knows why. Surely his own uncle will offer him some greater post...although the only greater post I can think of is the throne of Saint Mark upon which Theophilus already sits.

Aside from the snorting monk, only Cyril and I occupy the place I have come to. He grows no better looking as the years pass, though he seems to grow shorter and stouter, but I begin to understand that the outside of a man is not the inside of a man. I learn this lesson as I have learned all my lessons, with great and lasting pain. Cyril walks round and round me, rather as Hypatia walks round a horse before buying, or Lais once turned a scroll before reading. So young and so wise. So imperious. I am silent before his inspection. "How opportune you should come here today." I force myself not to turn with him, but to stand quietly awaiting an explanation. "My uncle visits a certain Augustine of Hippo. Your sister knows this man. They exchange letters."

"Yes," I say, eager to show off my knowledge, "I have copied as many of them as I could, brought them to..."

I am waved into silence.

"And I am left to govern his daily affairs, a task I find myself well suited for." He is behind me now. I cannot see him and when I cannot see him there seems a different quality to his voice. It is harsher. Or louder. There is certainly a hitch in it. It seems the kind of voice half-remedied of defect. I know this, having been forced to attend more than I could stand of Hypatia's classes in oratory. "He has taken with him the best of his servants until his return late in the autumn leaving me with the dregs..." From where I stand I see that the monk whose nose curves towards his mouth does not move so much as a hair. "...which I would rectify. And you, little mule, would, I believe, serve me well. I confess I had not thought of you at all. But now that I do, the choice is perfect."

How grateful I am he stops going round and round. His circling has unsettled my stomach. But how should I serve him? I have so much to do. I pray. I weave. I visit the poor offering salvation. I weave and I pray and I seek out the unwanted children, all girls, so we might raise them up in God. I weave. Actually, most of my time is spent in weaving. Our priests need robes. Our altars need clothes.

"You will now gather what little you own and move into my house. In the morning you begin as my handmaid."

"Me, sir? I have...few skills."

"You are the sister of Hypatia. That is skill enough."

My thoughts turn to chalk on my skin. I will miss the small cell I have come to love. I will not miss weaving. What a terrible changeable disagreeable day.

What is a handmaid? Why do I ask? I do not speak Latin but I know what *opus mulierum* means—woman's work.

BOOK FOUR

"I am the Invisible One within the All...I am immeasurable, ineffable, yet whenever I wish, I shall reveal myself of my own accord. I am the head of the All, I exist before the All, and I am the All, Since I exist in everyone. I am a Voice speaking softly. I exist from the first. I dwell within the Silence... And it is the hidden voice that dwells within me, within the incomprehensible, immeasurable Thought, within the immeasurable Silence."—Trimorphic Protennoia, The Three Forms of the First Thought

10

Aboard the Blue Raven,
a Roman grain ship sailing the Great Sea
Winter, 409

Hypatia of Alexandria

I have lost Lais, mother, father, Jone, Rinat, Ife, my well loved Companions who grieved over my unexplained leaving.

I have lost Minkah.

To Synesius, I said I should return, perhaps in a year, perhaps less. I said I would write him, constantly. But it has been more than a year. Four years have passed and Alexandria is still a week away.

Where have I been? Wherever my cheerless whim took me. And with me came Nildjat Miw and Desher for neither could be left behind. By land and by sea, though no longer young, they went where I went.

Sailing first to Crete, then on to Athens and all the while I was as Io—seduced by Zeus, so forced by Hera to wander pursued by a gadfly. Travel is hard. What seemed a week on a map became a month on the swelling sea or over a mountainous road. I found my books in libraries, in the homes of prominent men, in schools where they were required to be read. I was feted and praised and asked to speak. And so I did speak, but not with passion and not on Valentinus or Seth, or on my own work. If not for Miw, I would have ridden Desher back to her high cold desert and there lost us both in the wind and the sand.

In once glorious Athens, I stood before thousands in the Platonic Academy of Plutarch the Younger and his daughter Asclepigenia. My subject was Euclid, the greatest of geometers. Developing a system for measuring the surface of anything, he began with points and lines. A point, he taught, has no dimension of any kind and a line is nothing more than the shortest distance between two points. "Which," I said, gazing down at the usual rapt faces, "brings us to an interesting problem: without dimension, does something exist? And if a point does not exist, does the line a series of points makes exist? And if neither point nor line exists, what does?"

And so forth and so on. My own voice on my own ear was no more than a distant irritation.

Then came the cities of Neopolis, Pergamum, Ephesus, Tarsus, and more and more...until each was blurred in my mind as the sky is blurred by the horse-driven dust of the ceaseless, countless, barbarians who ride against the empire, both east and west.

For a time, we breathed the fetid air of Rome, a city like its theater: bloody, foolish, and filthy. It is also as its politics: dangerous, complex and personal. It has no library, no central collection for scholars—only the rich owned books which they did not read. We arrived to find it besieged and starving. The poor ate roaches. They ate dung. They gnawed on the corpses of neighbors, for the dead were as numerous as rats. And outside the Aurelian walls, the Visigoths ate and drank and pissed and shouted, taunting Rome's despair.

As I was who I was: of no interest and no threat to the Visigoth king, Alaric allowed me past. Once in, my hosts, kin to Synesius, said the Pope of Rome would have called on the ancient gods to drive away the Visigoths, but as no one could be found who remembered the rites, no god, Christian or "pagan," lifted a spectral hand.

We spent, my cat and horse and I, less than a week in that dreadful place. Any longer, and we should have been eaten.

Meanwhile, far to the north, the Emperor of the West,

Honorius, was building a chicken coop. Invited to a private audience in Ravenna, city of marshes, I declined, pleading ill health, so was sent a sketch of the coop—an astonishing thing. As large as the triple-decked ships on which we sailed, it could have fed and housed the poor of Rhakotis. As Rome suffered, Honorius tended his chickens.

Along with the sketch came a letter suggesting I rest in his country villa. There, a mile from the camp of the Visigoths, I met a delight of a girl I shall ever call friend. Aelia Galla Placidia was half-sister to both Arcadius, Emperor of the East, and Honorius, Emperor of the West.

Deep in a winter's night, Miw in my lap, I unburdened myself to the daughter of the man who would destroy my world. I saw nothing of Theodosius in Galla. I saw only great delicacy as she listened in silence until I had exhausted myself. And then she spoke.

"You love a man of the streets, a man of violence in the pay of your enemy, and he loves you...shall I tell you something? I love a man of violence, one who starves and kills my people, worse, he is already married. He has not said he loves me but I would flee with him at a word. We are the same you and I."

I, in the midst of self-pity and complaint, stopped as if a cliff rose before me. "Who is it you love?"

"Athaulf, brother-in-law to Alaric, King of the Visigoths. I am safe because he keeps me safe. This villa is untouched because he decrees it so. He visits when no one sees. Should I not be ashamed? But love does not know shame."

I am called wise. Before Galla I felt foolish. She loved who she loved and, as I did not, accepted what she loved.

And yet I did not set sail for home, but in shame and confusion traveled on.

The Imperial summons came in the Christian city of Antioch, called by its citizens "Rival to Alexandria," but called by me "Capital of Earthquakes" for under my bare feet the ground rumbled as a stomach grumbled, hungry to be fed. I was called to appear before Theodosius II, Emperor of the East. Theodosius II, nephew of Honorius therefore nephew to Galla, was eight years old. Easy enough to again claim illness—but as the true emperor was Flavius Anthemius, the boy's Praetorian Prefect, and as it was Flavius Anthemius who had commanded me, and as Anthemius was considered by Synesius and Augustine to be a worthy man, I accepted his demand.

The trek west from Antioch in Syria to Constantinople on the land route from Europe to Asia, was long and hard, but my way was paid, a villa was promised, Desher need not walk the whole of the stony spine of Anatolia but could at times, like Nildjat Miw, be carried in a cart bedded with finest straw. The road chosen was seldom troubled: our guard a mere *contubernium.* Of the eight legionaries and two servants, I knew by name only their *Decanus,* who was, of all things, an Ostrogoth. Tall and thin as an obelisk, his hair was as wild as Desher's straw, his skin as pink as Ia'eh's nose, his name Gundisalv.

Only Gundisalv spoke, and then only to grunt. Such speech soothed me as I need not reply.

We climbed up through the Cilician Gates, the high and narrow pass through the Tarsus Mountains, walking on bare rocks and early snow. Beyond that, we were to drop down again to a fertile plain, and from there ferry over the narrow Bosporus, its inlet Keras, and a "Golden Horn" thick with ships and shouting. Gundisalv conveyed all this by gesture and growling.

In all my travels, I had yet to see so desolate a land...the cold was more a chill of the spirit than of the skin, though the skin was cold enough. Huddling into myself, I dreamed of the color of number, trusting Desher to pick her way through the endless grey rocks under an endless grey sky—when, at a crossroads somewhere in Galatia, she suddenly shied, stepping violently sideways, and I, unprepared, slipped from her back. From one moment to the next the world was a rampage of color.

"*Bagaudae*!" shouted Gundisalv, whose first thought was to scoop me up and dump me into the wagon of straw where hid Miw—but immediately I vaulted back onto Desher, knife in my hand. A knife was not useless, but it was far from enough against bandits who'd appeared on all sides, each waving a sword.

We were only eleven. Those who would solve by theft the problem of poverty in a declining Empire, were twice our number. A thing of hair and rags came at Desher with a *gladius* meaning to take her down at the leg with its long narrow blade, but I was over the side of my saddle, swinging close to the ground, and caught the fellow under the ribs with my knife, so it was he, not Desher, who fell, and while falling, I swept up his sword.

Like baboons, each bared its teeth, each screamed as a wild thing. Gundisalv, cutting away at two who would unhorse him, paused only once at the sight of me fighting beside him. We were fewer but also fitter, faster, better trained, and we rode.

It was over in moments. Those who survived us fled faster than they came. And we were left with one dead and one grievously cut. This one we placed in the wagon with Nildjat Miw who surprised me by curling herself against his blooded shoulder.

All shook their heads with wonder that we lived. To live made them merry and we jogged away as soon as they'd buried their man beneath a pile of stones as high as the belly of his horse.

Gundisalv jogged beside me, exposing black teeth in a stretch of a grin. Staring; he shook his head so that his beard became caught in his cloak and he freed it by hacking off some with his knife. For days, he had said nothing. That day? "A woman who fights. I have heard of women who fight. Far to the north on an island there are women painted blue who fight more fiercely than men. But I have never seen this, I have only been told. And there are women far to the east who come out of the mountains of snow and these women no man would want to meet even if he rides with a hundred men, but again this I have only been told. Not once have I seen for myself. But now I see you and I would cry out with the wonder of it. I saw you mount and ride your horse as the best of our riders...and such a horse! I would pay much for her. I saw you fight with knife and with sword and I, who have never seen such a thing, will never forget it. A woman warrior! I, Gundisalv, could die now and I should be happy to do so for I have seen something worth the dying."

We rode down from the ridge on which we had been so exposed and into a defile whose sides were steep rock. *Bagaudae* were foolish to attack us on the ridge for in the defile our horses would have been less able to turn and to kick out and to rear. But when a man is hungry, these things are harder to see.

We were nine with one dead and one wounded. But the men were easy and talked of stopping soon and eating well, for nothing is as good for the belly as a fight well fought.

The second attack came with no screaming, no baring of teeth. There was only a silent rising up from behind rock of men made desperate by need and I saw our first battle had been only a way to take our mettle and a life or two. Having done both, we were now set upon by not twice as many as we, but four times as many. Desher moved again with the grace of youth, and I with the skill learned from observing Minkah who knew the sword as I know my knife.

And we lost one and we lost two, and I slashed at all who came near and more came and more. If they had taken our mettle, they did not take Desher's. If I cut down one, she took another with the flash of a hard hoof. If I leapt from her back and under her belly to hamstring one who would hamstring her, she took the neck of some other between her teeth and shook him until he was senseless.

Gundisalv, hacking at a ragged creature that had hold of his horse's long mane, yelled at one of ours to take care...but too late. Our man was pulled backwards from his horse only to disappear under a dozen of them, each slashing and stabbing at the poor thing. Up on her haunches, Desher whirled in place just as one, bolder than any and naked save for his loincloth, vaulted with admirable grace at Gundisalv, landing on his horse's rump where he balanced on bare feet, and with one hand gripped Gundisalv's hair, pulling his head back so he might with the other cut Gundisalv's throat. But as he raised his sword, I hacked off the hand that held the hair, and both hand and brigand dropped away.

It was this which finally took their heart. Though we had lost half our number, they had lost more than half. It was enough. They were gone as silently as they came.

By those still living, I was lifted high in the air, and they laughed and they whistled...joyous to find life again theirs, especially valorous life. Gundisalv swore with a great clanking of sword against breast-piece that his life was now mine.

Then and there I returned to gloom. Minkah had sworn this.

Constantinople was as a hive of newly swarmed bees. Enormous walls, doubling its size, went up from the Sea of Marmara to the Golden Horn, ordered by Flavius Anthemius... not against Barbarians, but against the hordes of starving brigands plaguing the Empire, east and west. I had met his *bagaudae* and understood his walls.

The promised villa proved pleasant, its stables suitable for noble Desher, and Miw made no complaint, not even when meeting our host, Orestes. Orestes was as handsome as Helios. And so? I had no stomach for love. In one way or another, all I loved was dead. But it was hell to work in the racket of wall building.

No matter which city, letters from my Companions awaited me, letters from Augustine, household letters from Ife, but no one outdid Synesius. In the house of Orestes were not only nine separate letters devoted to the horrors of Constantinople, a city he loathed having been forced to sit in it for three years to gain the ear of Emperor Arcadius, but also his latest book:

Dion, or about His Life. Reading of his hero Dion's adventures, all in defense of a riotous life as opposed to one of self-denial, I found myself painted into its pages. By the wrath of the father of Galla Placidia, was I that imperious, a disdainer of "lesser men"? And yet, *Dion* amused me. In it the ignorant desert monks were "black mantles" while those who opposed them were "white mantles."

In the din that was Constantinople, I seldom went out, but should I, I was dogged by slavish Gundisalv who slept in the stables near Desher.

Came the day I must meet Flavius Anthemius in the Forum Tauri. By meet, I mean speak before. What occurred then, I did not know. Nor care.

For fear of her loss in strange streets, Nildjat Miw was locked away in our borrowed villa, Desher in her stall. The Forum Tauri was a straight drop down from Orestes' hilltop villa to the Sea of Marmora. I walked it, but not alone. Gundisalv walked behind me until we found ourselves on the colonnaded Mese, as wide and busy with lives as the Canopic Way. The Mese, and all streets leading off, was littered with stolen statues, all the quicker to grow this New Rome with its seven hills. The doors, the stone columns, the marble for walls and the tiles on the floors, these were gathered from places not happy to lose them.

I walked content. Even dogged by Gundisalv, an Ostrogoth broad as a wagon, it was good to be known by no one.

I had hoped to be early, but the Forum was already crammed with craning heads. Shown to my seat as if I was tardy, as if I was rude, I took my place, Gundisalv standing behind me, and listened to Atticus, the Bishop of Constantinople. By this I knew immediately I was not there to lecture; I was there to be harangued. On the spot, I knew I would not speak but would leave both Forum and city by nightfall. There was no comfort in this and no discomfort. If I was tested, I would pass it in my way, not theirs.

"By Paul," shouted Atticus, a small-boned man with large lungs, "we are *not* told that Eve suffered *alone* from deception, but that 'Woman' was deceived, meaning *all* women!" Here the man stared directly at me. "What else does the blessed Paul say? 'Let a woman learn in silence.' 'Let no woman raise her voice in church.' The law has placed woman in subjugation to man. 'If women want to learn anything, let them learn from their husbands at home.'"

Ungreeted, made to appear late, seated alone, this was the

creature chosen to berate me? His tone was unvaried, his form sloppy, his vocabulary limited, and as for his content...heard once in a class taught by Father, this one would fly out the door on his ear. Synesius called me high-handed? He did not miss his mark. My heart may have slowed, but my pride lived on.

I rose. I turned my head just so, only enough to catch sight of the child Theodosius II, cross-eyed with boredom. But the eyes of Flavius Anthemius were like sums I must solve. "And if the husband knows nothing?"

"What?" Atticus could not believe I would dare speak while he was speaking.

I strode forward, Gundisalv on my heels. "And if the husband knows nothing, how then shall he teach his wife? If he has nothing to teach, both will live in ignorance."

His small face a knot of smug assumption, Atticus answered, "A husband will know enough."

"Enough what? Who alive knows anything at all?"

Atticus was confused. "In Paul's time—"

"...he did not say what you claim he said, nor did he write the letters you say he wrote. All these were penned by others long after his death. At Paul's side preached his wife, Thecla, more learned than the man I see before me now."

Behind me, I heard a huge intake of breath. Three of Theodosius' four sisters were there: Arcadia, Marina, and Pulcheria. The breather could only be Pulcheria, barely ten, but a Jone, though made of fire, not earth. Atticus proclaimed a woman not divine. He proclaimed her less than human. As a woman, did I endanger myself? Would his god strike me down? I had arrived not caring. I spoke not caring.

His neck stretched from its collar like Honorius' prized rooster, Atticus crowed, "Blasphemy! Lies!"

"It is you who lie, and your lies are intolerant and cruel—even unto evil. Socrates taught the only evil was ignorance."

"You call me evil!"

"I call you ignorant—and to hear the ignorant speak out with authority is a great evil. You touch people's hearts. You reach for their souls. You repeat what you have heard. You question nothing. You expect no one to question you. Called to speak, yet I listen to insult and calumny. You tell me, Hypatia of Alexandria, that because you possess an organ that even a dog possesses I am nothing in the eyes of your god?"

Came a voice from behind, a child's voice. "Woman, be still!"

I turned, slowly. Years before, the eunuch Eutropius lost his head by order of Eudoxia, Pulcheria's mother. As sole master over the slow mind of Arcadius, Pulcheria's father and Emperor of the East, Eutropius had outwitted and thus ruled the court, yet made the fatal blunder of voicing his contempt for Eudoxia, Empress of the East, a woman far from slow. "I who brought you here," he was said to have said to her, "can throw you out." And there went his head. I risked mine with the spawn of Arcadius and Eudoxia. "Dare not silence me, child, for in silencing me, you silence learning. You silence questioning. You silence even divinity, for all are divine, and all partake of what you call god. You have not one idea of the Christ you so love, for if you did, it would be you and your bishop who would fall silent on the instant."

Their bishop had decided to placate this foreign guest. "I forgive you, daughter. Ten times ten I would forgive you as our savior would have me do."

"That is generous of both of you. And I forgive you."

"Forgive me!"

"For so maligning my sex. If I were to say such things of men, and all women believed and applauded me, would you be pained?"

"But I, but you...what foolishness. How could I be pained by what is not true?"

"Is it not? And how do you know?"

"Because all men know."

"And how do they know?"

"Is it not obvious? A man is stronger in every way."

"Are you stronger than me?"

Greatly amused, Atticus glanced at Pulcheria, but answered me. "As I am a man and not a woman, of course."

"If you can prove this to me in body and mind, my soul is yours."

His look proclaimed me mad. Yet I did no more than Socrates would have done. Ask a man enough questions, and his belief in his understanding fades before him as does a dream upon waking—unless it is a true understanding. "Read the book, daughter. That is proof."

"I have read books all my life. I have read your book. Not one has told me the truth because no man knows the truth... and all books are written by the hand of man."

He sucked in his gut with horror. "God wrote this book."

"And how was that accomplished?"

"He dictated it to certain prophets."

"Who said so?"

"Why, they did."

"I see. And were these prophets gods?"

"Dear me, no. They were men."

"Ah. Would you say then your belief in the word of your god is based on the claims of other men?"

Then and there, though I was breathless with insult as well as quickened with catastrophe, I stopped. Atticus was not Theophilus. His faith was no game he played. It was not a mantle to put on or be taken off as the need arose. The stories he took so literally he held dearer than his own life and he could not doubt them. Doubt would have destroyed him. I had no desire to destroy a foolish old man who suffered a fatal ignorance.

Long before this, those who had listened were gasping or coughing or fleeing their seats. But not Gundisalv, who fondled his sword. Or Orestes, observing all with interest.

Flavius Anthemius alone walked forward and I trembled, afraid to live, afraid to die. "Live in the palace, Hypatia. Whatever you want, whatever you need, I will provide you it."

"Thank you, but my cat would go home now."

Sixty-three days at sea, each wintry and cold, I no longer pretend I cannot see the white in the red of Desher's muzzle or note the falter in her balance. Below decks, we sleep, her head cradled in my lap, as Nildjat Miw curls in the curve of Desher's lovely red neck.

This night Desher softly nickered, breathed one last time in my mouth, and "fell asleep." My beloved mare leaves this place, still warm, still sweet with the smell of the truest friend, other than Miw, who is left me.

Epona! Goddess! Accept the soul of this one. Let her race on the cold sands of her cold desert. Let her eat sweet spring grass and nibble white winter snow. Let her remember me as I shall ever remember her.

Cats are far wiser than we; their language is silence.

Holding Miw, I lean over the gunwale.

A mile or more from Pharos, and here is Synesius of Cyrene, his small boat alongside mine of size, following us into the reef and shoal littered Eunostos, the Port of Good Return. How does he know when I come?

I am irritated. He will assail me with tales of woe. I am thrilled. To smell the Egyptian sun on Egyptian limestone, to hear the music of bells in windows, to see again one who loves me, who has ever loved me. All the news I know of Alexandria, I learn most fully from faithful Synesius—all but news of Minkah. I have not asked and he has not sent a single word.

"Blessed lady!" Synesius must shout, and if he must, he will. "I cannot express my joy! I choke with it!"

Men are running to and fro as the Blue Raven readies to anchor. I must shout back. "But are you not yet a bishop!"

His shudder is obvious. "All too soon!"

"For my sanity's sake, tell your brother no! Tell Theophilus you are not worthy of such an honor."

Down goes the mouth of Synesius. "My life is over, teacher! All that is left me is intrigue and the bickering of bishops!"

"Your life can begin again at a word. Speak out before it's too late."

"I can't! All shall deride me."

"In that case, think! Bishops become invariably rich."

"I am already rich. It is worse than this."

"How so?"

"I am afraid."

"Of what?"

"Of my brother Euoptius. But even more, of hell!"

"What hell?"

"That which awaits the sinner."

I stare down at him. "As a Companion, how *have* you come to believe this?"

"You were not here to protect me. Four years, teacher! I was alone!"

Synesius provides litters, one for me and Miw, one for him. On these we would quickly leave the harbor for home, a home I am beside myself to see—but we cannot. A great noisy crowd gathers at the entry to the docks, one that pushes forward on either side. I am astonished. Is the whole of Alexandria here? Faces I do not know, faces I do know, are held back by the soldiers of Rome. There is shouting. Some weep. Some laugh. It is as if Cleopatra had returned to them, this time triumphant in the Battle of Actium. But it is only Hypatia.

"Synesius! What is this?"

"You are beloved, Hypatia. These are those who love you."

I stare about at those who "love me." By the smiles and

the proffering of fresh papyrus stalks, by the flowers thrown: chrysanthemum and chamomile and poppies, by the crying out of my name, Synesius is right. I am loved—or am at least a thing to do on a day normally devoted to toil. But he is also wrong. There are those here who love me not. Here and there, as soot on clean linen, gather the black monks.

Nothing has changed. Yet I remain consumed with surprise. That Father could see this, that Lais could see it...somewhere among all these, does Jone see it? Does Minkah?

I enter my house trimmed in garlands of welcome in a city on the brink of the hell Synesius fears. One step, two, and we fall. Alexandria will be no more than brutalized Rome, no more than Sparta, each man's life bound with the rope of rigid belief.

How fast Christians have turned persecution of themselves into persecution of others. The orthodox, led by their bishop, kill thousands of their own, calling them heretic...many more than Diocletian could claim. And then to hear, that on penalty of death, no one is to read a book not written by a Christian! I pace my house. How far will this go? And how long before they turn, again, on the Jews and the pagans—how long before the fires are relit?

I hide in my books and my Companions. Most are scattered, become important in some important city, but for those who remain, I am as ever the Divine Guide, and each has someone he would have join. None are poor and none are women.

Synesius' *Dion* was right. I am well painted, and made troubled by it.

As well as private, I return to public teaching for my house grows no less expensive with the passing of time. And as I leave for each lecture, Nildjat Miw does as she has ever done, leaps into my chariot to attend, sleeping throughout at my feet. Thankfully, paying students arrive in great numbers and of them, full half are foreign and full half are new, as new as my lecture hall in the Agora. The Agora has many such, each as large as the other with stepped benches in semicircles. Through the Jew Meletus, I find my trusted Rinat again. To help her, I hire stenographers and scribes. Though I were to become old as Didymus, I mean to place copies of my new work when complete in as many libraries as now hold Plato.

φ

Synesius is this day consecrated Bishop of Ptolemais in the once Caesarium.

Before he finally fell into "grace," to his credit, he forced the church to allow him his wife, to allow him dissent, and on certain questions: the soul's creation: a literal resurrection, the final destruction of the world...he is allowed his say.

The ceremony is hours long, the heat intense, the air choked with incense, the benches hard. Three have fainted and been taken away. Closest to Synesius, sits his union of four friends, those Companions who pattern themselves after the *tetractys* of Pythagoras: Herculianus, Hesychius, and a Syrian of great wealth named Olympius. I myself sit in a place of high honor; the place next to mine is occupied by the sister of Theophilus, Theophania. She has not looked at me once. I have looked at her. She is angular and shocking in a bright red wig and thin linen dyed the thick red of her dyed red lips. Cyril, her son, is now fat as a bladder and sweats as a wine skin. This one sits on my left so that *his* place threatens to spill into *my* place. Beside him slumps a man as narrow as a needle. This is Hierax, spoken of by Synesius. Synesius claims that by words alone Hierax could make hot seem cold, wet seem dry, wrong seem right. It is hard to imagine.

As Synesius is declared by Theophilus a thing he would not be in an endless exhausting display, Cyril leans towards me to breathe, "Does this not move you, Hypatia? Do you not admire its splendor?"

I am about to answer, about to say, yes, it *is* truly a thing of great expense and great ceremony and even great seriousness, when I see that behind him, hidden by his bulk, sits Jone. I would jump up and open my arms, I would pull her close, but though Panya sees me, she makes no sign. I do not jump up. I do not open my arms. "Yes, Cyril. This moves me."

As reward, he offers a crooked smile full of brown and yellow teeth.

Synesius is now Bishop of Ptolemais. Later, privately, I will hold his hand as he weeps. But for now I am confronted by Theophilus, Bishop of Alexandria. "Hypatia! All were diminished by your absence."

"I am more than pleased to be home."

"I see you continue as before."

I answer as he hopes I will. "If it pleases you."

In truth, I would teach with or without the consent of Theophilus, and therefore his protection, but it is good to have the latter. Pulcheria, sister of the Emperor of the East, poor God-ridden child, now writes him misspelled letters—they arrive as quickly as runners can carry them—each one condemning that "heretic woman."

Where Lais once slept, I now sleep. Nildjat Miw sleeps where Paniwi once slept. But long into the night, night after night, I am found at my mother's green table. Parmenides claims "nothing *is*." Heraclitus states "all is change." Through Seth, the Magdalene speaks of the ultimate singularity of "All That Is." There is a thread running through I weave as carefully as a weaver weaves cloth. There is a secret here, hidden in words. I will see it. I swear, if not by the intellect, then in some other way, I will learn it.

I am home. It is better than not being home.

Autumn, 410

Minkah the Egyptian

When my darling came back, I posed in a window four stories above the mouth of the Draco. Every moment stays with me: the delirious crowd come to meet her, Synesius and his litters, the monks in black gnashing their rotted teeth, the constant cup in my hand and the wine in the cup. On that day I lost both my latest bed and my latest "friend." How to blame her? Shâshafi was only one of many, and none were Hypatia.

Not invited, yet I saw her again at the consecration of my once Companion Synesius. Shoved to the back with the rest of the public drunks, as drunk as they, I held up my cup. "A toast to the craven!" I piss on his feet for showing the back of his neck. I saw too Cyril. And Jone...broken by Theon, gone mad with faith, as foolish as a chicken. As for Cyril, he acts the fanatic, but is not. He is as cunning as a rat. Assuming himself unheard by any but Hierax, he once hissed: "Religious men are a homo-erotic cult." He is right, but to *say* so?

And me? I drink in taverns, alone, not alone, what does it

matter?

If I pound on her door, will she open it? I regret nothing for what does regret change? The path offered by Peter the Reader seemed a wise one. That it would close doors as well as open them did not occur to me.

Over a house of wine on a decaying street in Rhakotis, sunk in a hole that is mine alone, I remember John of Chrysostom. Dragged to exile in Pityus on the shores of the Black Sea, yet he hoped to return to Constantinople as bishop. John died in the rain and the mud. Shall I die in mud?

What else should I be but still *Parabalanoi*? I am a drunken thug digging out the enemies of Theophilus. Only men, yet they seem to breed, hidden in caves as spiders in holes. The more we catch, the more there are, clinging to the idea of Origen, if not his teaching. Origen is become a symbol, his teaching untaught.

I go about this work as a jackal goes about feeding. All seems pointless. Numb, I am more feared than ever.

Though I cannot go to her, I can make her a gift. A counting board, an *abakos*. Hers, when last seen, was a clumsy thing compared to the one I will make. Mine will be grooved so that the balls, though they move easily back and forth, cannot fall out, or get stuck. The wood will be finest cedar, the counting balls purest silver.

I will not ask to see her, but will leave my gift in the hands of Ife, in spite of herself, fond of fallen Minkah. Hypatia will know who has made it.

THE FIRST AND THE LAST

Early Spring, 411

Hypatia of Alexandria

At my mother's table, Miw and I read letters.

Gone to the city of Ptolemais, Synesius composes his missives as he has ever done: daily. He laments his new home; it has no harbor, no theater, no library. He is bishop of nothing. Orestes and Flavius Anthemius both write from Constantinople, months of hard travel away. Anthemius begs that I return, but if I would not, he begs I instruct him through letters. Through his, I am instructed. The Empire of the West reels from calamity to calamity. Britain is left to fend for itself. The Visigoth Alaric besieges Rome yet again. Honorius, Emperor and chicken lover, panicking, kills his best advisors on the advice of his worst. The letters of Orestes make me laugh. Augustine, now bishop of Hippo, travels rarely, but writes as often as Synesius. Knowing that Hippo will not be converted, still he labors mightily. Something dark has begun to color his letters. More and more he pleads for my soul. In return, I reason with his pleading. I leave the best for last. Galla Placidia sends colorful tales full of love and life. She lives openly with Athaulf the Visigoth. Nildjat Miw is envious.

Yet no matter how many write me, I feel myself alone...and filled with thoughts of Minkah. He is alive in Alexandria. He thinks of me. All other counting boards are set aside, even that one once belonging to Ctesibius, inventor of the "water thief" by which all the world keeps time. I see him in the Serapeum as first I saw him. I smell the stench of his burning hair. I hear his voice as he tells me he owes me his life. I remember the devices we made together, his wit and his laughter. And the books! It was Minkah who hid the books. Which remain hidden. If they were not, all Alexandria, pagan and Christian, would have been forced to witness their burning.

Memory upon memory crowds my mind. He haunts me.

The day before I took flight, I took up the map he left on my mother's green table. This I placed in the tomb of Lais so that she might keep it safe, and with it Father's "new" will. I saw also the letter, thick with writing, and knew it for what it was: Minkah's "Confession." But I, fleeing fast and fleeing far, did not read it. And now, I have been in a panic to find it again. It is not in my nature to destroy paper, and never paper on which a word of import or beauty might be written. Ife, who maintains my house, cannot recall where she put it. Where is it? Where *is* it?

We spend weeks of frantic searching: in boxes and baskets, between the pages of books, under beds and in storage rooms. And then, as casually as misplacing a sum, a Greek scribe, only lately hired, finds it among scraps of computations.

I rip it open and read it, over and over. I read it aloud to Nildjat Miw who listens most carefully. If *I* had listened most carefully, Minkah would not be gone from this place, and I should not have traveled, stirring up passions for and against me.

I know every word of Augustine's confessions. The confessions of Minkah are nothing like as long, but they are many times sadder. Augustine took pleasure where he found it, found himself mistaken in the teachings of Mani who thought the flesh as evil as he thought the world. Augustine loved and was loved. But Minkah lived no life at all. Motherless, homeless, betrayed and brutalized, to be tempted into the brotherhood by a creature called Peter the Reader was a choice any would make. And I would not listen. After years of love and of trust, I would *not* listen.

Minkah brought a gift to my door but did not bring himself. More than any desire left me, I would give Minkah the gift of my repentance. Nildjat Miw tells me I must not commit yet another sin of pride by requesting he come to me. I must go to him.

But where is he?

Recommended as he who could find one grain of salt in a

bucket of sand, I've used the services of a certain Wati, a man of Kush. As black as Bia, the furious new filly I name after the goddess of force and compulsion, Wati is not as beautiful or as willful or as wild, but he is at least as clever. Even so, the whole of two weeks pass before he has news of my "brother."

On this, the evening of the fourteenth day, Wati leads me on foot to a door on the cobbled Street of the Herbalists, takes the purse I offer him, and disappears from this dusty canyon of a hundred sneezes. I would faint from the crush of my fellows. The whole of the city seems gathered here.

Covered from head to foot in a rough blue cloak borrowed from a stable lad, I press back against a mass of monk's hood, dried root and dried leaf, ignored by those who shove past me. Between sneezes, I stare at a faded red door to what is surely a house of beer. Or of wine. I honestly don't know. Those who enter begin more or less erect and steady on their feet. Those who exit often crawl. Three stories above is the home of my "brother." The walls either side of the tavern's red door are splashed with urine, daubed with crude graffiti. I have seen worse. I have seen better. But I have never seen inside such a place.

Heart racing, I push my way across the street to enter a world clamorous with heat and stench and noise, and so much darker than the night. How do they see what they drink and with whom? There is only a lamp on a hook near the door, a second by a staircase seeming unattached to its wall, a guttering candle on the one stone counter behind which moves what I think a woman. Humpbacked under the great jug balanced on a muscled arm, slopping drink into cups, "she" is as dark as the room, as twisted as its staircase. Staring, I am pushed aside by a naked boy whose lips are bright red. Where did I read that lips painted red advertize fellatio? Is it true? An image rises of Theophania, sister to Theophilus. Turning, I would ask the *lupa*, but my feet, for once shod, slip on the wet uneven floor and I seek balance against a fellow whose nose is as a falcon's beak and whose eye is single. I stare into his one eye. The other is a socket, brown and puckered. His one eye stares into mine. Our gaze unlocks at a bray come from the deepest reach of this cave of drink. Shadowed against a shadowed wall leans a man of enormous girth. If bear became man, it would look as this man. In his paw of a hand, he holds a drinking cup, dwarfed by his grip. In a place where all shout, he is clearly heard. "Alexander was a drunk! I am a drunk! Does this make me great?"

Another voice is raised, its owner obscured by the man like a bear. "None greater, Felix Zoilus!"

I know the voice I hear. Even slurred, I know the voice. And from some recess in my mind, I know the name Felix Zoilus.

Minkah is as drunk as Alexander the Great. I have never seen him drunk. But drunk or sober, calm or angry, it is my Egyptian and, trembling with both fear and eagerness, I will speak to him. Though first I must get to, and then around, Felix Zoilus the Great Drunk. To do so, I must push and shove. Not known to any, I am elbowed. I am called *cunnus*. Stumbled against, *muni* is hissed in my face. My breasts gripped, and my ass, I am called *kenes*. A blue-eyed man who reeks of fresh shit grabs at my crotch while he offers a cup for a *nek*. No need to rent a crib, he says, no need for even an alley. He would have me on the slime of the floor. What? No? Then two cups! I decline, sweetly I think. My answer earns me a cup of wine dumped down my back.

My Alexandria is a place of privilege. There, I live as a creature of the air lives, sipping thought for sustenance. But in Rome and in Athens and Antioch and Constantinople, I have walked the streets, picking my way through offal and slop, swatting away flies. In Constantinople I reclined on silk in the inner chambers of a palace as the fetor of corruption overpowered my senses. I sailed for months in huge ships with crews of all nations and stations. After such places, this place is no more than is found anywhere. If these are those who would inherit the earth, then should the books that are "lost" be found, who would read them? Who would Lais be to any of these? And who am I? The answer comes so quickly I cannot silence it. Here, I am no one and I am alone and I stand after so many years before Minkah, clutching my borrowed cloak, my hair dripping with the poorest wine. And yet, when I speak I speak as if I sat above all in a *tribon* white as a wall in the sun. "Companion! Would you hear me?"

The bear on its back legs looks down from a great height. I *do* know this one. Once, long ago, stopped by the drawbridge between the two harbors, he would kill Augustine and then he would kill me. I understand much now. He did not kill us because my Egyptian asked him not to. Beside him sags Minkah, one arm propping up his head, the other around the slim waist of a girl whose lips are red. She too is naked and she too is drunk. Her body is soiled with sweat and with grease and with the bites of fleas, yet remains enticing. "Who is this?" she says, "I am not paid yet. Tell the slut to fuck off."

Returning stare for stare, I will not fuck off. "I ask only a moment."

Minkah has raised his face from his cup, and his eyes to mine. Certainly I am not one, but two, even three...but his voice is steady enough. "A moment? How long is a moment? Felix! Fetch a cup. For a moment, I would drink with my sister."

As would a bear, Felix Zoilus shakes his huge shaggy head. "Sister? You have no sister."

"A cup, Felix. We shall both drink with my sister. Excuse me, but who are you?" This is said to the girl whose waist he still holds.

"Money."

"Fair enough. Felix. I need a cup and a coin. As for you..." This is said to me. "Tell him, Sage! Tell my friend who you are."

I look up at his friend, a giant, a man whose brain would not threaten a cow, yet whose hairy arms and hairy legs and hairier back could lift a bullock and its wagon. I do not say, but shout, "I am the sister of Minkah the Egyptian."

Holding up his cup, the giant shouts back. "Well then! Here's to the ship-owners. To own a ship is to plunder the world!"

Two hours later, I am as drunk as the drunkest man here. I have never been drunk before and I may never be drunk again, but for now I revel in its loose-limbed loose-lipped freedom. Felix is delightful. The man who smells of shit is delightful. All those with red lips are delightful. Even I am delightful. But most delightful of all is Minkah, my brother, who forgives me. I sink into his forgiveness as I would sink into the sea, down and down and down...and I tell him so. I admit my faults, my errors, my sins. I am cleansed in a hole as fetid as sewage.

The whole world, and all that lives in it or on it or over it, is—delightful.

By Isis and Osiris, what pain is this? In my head beats a hundred broken hearts. My eyes. I cannot open my eyes. If I open my eyes they will burst into flame. And my tongue. What has become of my tongue? It seems a lizard in my mouth, dry and cracked and swollen with rot. I stink. I have made my bedding stink.

Help. Did I say that aloud? I say it again. *Help.*

"Here, drink this."

A cup is placed in my hand, but too unsteady, I cannot raise it. The cup and my hand are raised for me, placed against my lips, tipped. Water spills over my lizard of a tongue, dribbles down my chin. *More.* I am given more.

"Keep drinking."

"Minkah?"

"Yes?"

"Where am I?"

"Home."

"My home?"

"Yes."

"Then you are home too."

I sleep the rest of the night and half the following day. Miw sleeps with me. Now and again I awake so I might vomit. No matter the time, Minkah is there with a bowl. The ache in my head is monstrous. But I am content. Unless I die, all this will pass.

Minkah is home.

And when I am well and when I am ready, I go to him. And he takes me as others have done, but not as others have done. I know now I love Minkah as I have never loved any. Through the flesh of my Egyptian I am made to feel pure, for the flesh is innocent when touched with love. And we touch in this way. In the dark I whisper the words of Medea's love for Jason into his ear: "*...a dark mist came over her eyes, and a hot blush covered her cheeks...so they stood face to face without a sound, like oaks or lofty pines, which stand quietly side by side on the mountains when the wind is still...and murmur ceaselessly, destined to tell out their tale, stirred by the breath of Love.*"

Before Minkah, I have had no lovers. I have been as a virgin. But now I am what I have thought I might never be, a woman, whole. I will have no other lover.

As for Ia'eh, yet young in her huge black eye, in the arch of her white neck, in the lift of her white foot, she has pressed her forehead against Minkah's chest, and spoken in her own tongue. I knew what she said to him. *Master, you have come back. I, Ia'eh, never doubted you.*

Wherever Minkah is, I am. If sailing the *Irisi* or at table with Miw in her own place listening, or in the midst of an alchemical interlude, or on the backs of Ia'eh and Bia, we talk. Or I do, my thoughts tumbling forth as springs in the desert, sharing what I have shared with no one else: the thoughts I now think, the books I no longer need read but know by heart, the book I myself write. I neglect the practice of mathematics. I have no time to disprove Ptolemy's earth-centered system.

Listening, he has said this, "Your Magdalene sounds as

Lais, knowing because she knew. She sounds also as you."

"Me?"

"An asker of questions."

"But not cruel? Not arrogant?"

His answer, quick and ready, shocks me. "Hypatia is cruel and her cruelty is vast."

"Minkah! How so?"

"She frightens those who cannot understand her."

"I am frightened by some I understand."

Minkah laughs. To make Minkah laugh is as honey to me. But to hear I am cruel is like reading a poem by Enheduanna, Sumerian priestess, daughter of the Akkadian Sargon of Kish. Two and a half thousand years ago, she spoke of the Goddess Inanna: "*...Woman, most driven, clothed in frightening radiance.*"

Minkah does not choose Father's old room, but instead takes that which was mine so Father's is again what it was when he lived, a gathering place for all those who come. If a man of stature arrives from some other city, I am first he pays court to. If a meeting is planned by Alexandrian powers, it is my house that hosts it. If students would debate, they do so in the House of Hypatia. If poetry is read, or a new work of philosophy or mathematics is introduced, it is done in the House of Hypatia. When Augustine allows himself a reprieve from Hippo, he comes here.

But if not one were ever to visit again, I should not care. I have my work. I have Minkah.

But to say all who visit benign would be false. Minkah is still *Parabalanoi*. We find marks on our walls. I do not understand them. But I see Minkah does.

Each night when I enter his bed, he holds me. He bids me not to worry. His strength is mine.

Minkah the Egyptian

I swear off drink. I walk away from the *Parabalanoi*, followed by the threats of Theophilus. Let him pound his table and stamp his foot. Let him rant of the wrath of his god. Who gives a pig's bollocks for wrath of god or man when I am free and my darling is mine!

In darkness I trace the form of her sleeping arm, cup her breast, lick the salt from her belly. She is like iron and my phallus like lodestone. It stirs at the sound of her voice a room away, hardens at her smell, would find release at only the sight of her. But to touch her! To give her pleasure! To bury myself to the root in my own true home, ah! This I would not trade for life everlasting. If I should die tomorrow, let it be with the taste of her salt on my lips.

One year later, 412

Hypatia of Alexandria

How changed is Augustine. But then, how changed am I, no longer a girl but a woman whose years number one and forty. Forty-one years! What would Father, who so loved numbers, have said of this? Four is the Tetrad. Three points define a flat surface, but when a fourth is added, depth is born. I think I once said that numbers were sly. In Father's perfect world, age brings experience and experience is rewarded with wisdom. I will never be perfect.

Aelia Galla Placidia is not changed at all, save to glow all the rosier now she is "captive of Athaulf," new King of the Visigoths with the death of Alaric. Athaulf trusts her to accompany his envoy to Alexandria requesting grain. He is not wrong in his trust. She is besotted. She is also my guest and no happier guest has ever disturbed our neighbors with her laughter.

Minkah, Augustine, Galla and I visit the Eleusis Plain near the rising walls of Theophilus. Both Augustine and Galla have seen at a glance how it is with Minkah and me. By expressing nothing, Augustine expresses his acceptance. Galla grips my hand when no one sees. "You see, my friend! Love knows nothing but love." I see.

Minkah sweats. Augustine sweats. In the last of this year's summer, without motion, heat lies across the city like a body lies on a slab. Galla's fine skin has a sheen. I do not sweat. Why my own body keeps its moisture, why I might eat beyond hunger and yet not thicken in waist or thigh, I do not know. Of my body I know only what I have learned entangled in the body of another. Of my mind I know a great deal. Of my heart, I only now begin to learn.

Theophilus uses slaves to construct his city walls. But we four have not come to see hungry men beaten. Augustine makes no comment on the methods of his fellow bishop...wise but disappointing. With the last and deadliest siege of Rome and the violent deaths of her guardians, Galla has seen too much to find more astonishing. We have come to visit the Hypogea, an ancient underground temple to the Iron Queen, white-armed Persephone, for some reason untouched by Theophilus. As yet. Her gifts are long since stolen but the Queen of the Underworld remains. What does she see as she herself slowly fades from sight?

Minkah stands close to the pink marble goddess as Augustine circles her and Galla seeks other sights. He has read Augustine's "Confessions." "Confess it, old fellow, you were never as vile as you write of yourself."

"I was worse."

Minkah laughs. "I do not believe you."

"And what would you, an innocent, know of such things?"

My love knows such evil as Augustine has only shuddered at. He catches my eye as he answers. "No one can claim sole possession of what is vile. In each heart lives a wolf. We might feed it or we might let it go hungry. The choice is ours."

Augustine turns to me, smiling. "Only with Hypatia could I find such discourse as this. Here the wolf in my heart starves."

Is it because his heart starves that I confess to Augustine that I have books his church would destroy, that it thinks it *has* destroyed? I tell him that in these books I have learned a great deal about his Christ.

Augustine's brilliance gives him wings, but his fear tethers him, as a leash bound to his jesses tethers a hawk. His eyes do not move from mine. He will listen, but he listens as carefully as I speak.

"Augustine, as I love you, I believe the faith you profess lost its way so long ago, few if any remember or even know where once lay its wisdom. I believe you have made a god of a man who would have made gods of us all. By which I do not mean gods as Romans mean gods, or as symbols of natural forces or human abilities, or even as your god, called Infinite Love yet feared as a Being of infinite demands. Christ knew true divinity—the Force driving All—and he died desiring that all would know what he knew. I believe you have denied the one he called 'Beloved,' Mariamne Magdal-eder, she who tempered and taught him. Tell me, dearest friend, as a once lover of women, what possesses men that they should so hate and fear she who bears you, nurtures you, loves you when all others revile you? I am a woman. I would understand your mind."

My love has closed his eyes. But a small smile sweetens his lips.

We have talked like this before, Augustine and I, but never before have I been armed with such proof of his faith's demise. He touches the cold lips of still-living Persephone. "I have not read these books you mention. Like others, I thought them destroyed. But there is truth in what you say and I grieve this is so. You do not, but I *do* believe our Christ is God on earth and in Heaven, but that does not mean I do not know what man has made of God or of Heaven—or that I am blind to what he has made of woman. I would say this only to you, and I would not have it repeated of me, but man has come to fear woman's sexual power before which he is helpless, so turns it back on her, making her the one who is helpless. Being stronger in body, and more capable of violence, he tramples what is so deeply desired beneath his feet. I watch this happen and I weep for my mother, for my lovers. My love for women does not grow less but my love of God grows greater. I cannot have both."

To tell him that he might have both would fall on the alabaster tiles beneath our feet and grow cold.

Even so, as once with Didymus, through Augustine I am allowed a taste of Christian beauty.

Minkah the Egyptian

Alexandria's weak Augustal Prefect, Lucius Marius, is replaced by one all know to be strong. The Companions can speak of nothing else. I am not the Minkah of old. I do not spy here but am one of these. And what should Theon say if he knew? He would be proud. He would raise his head an inch from his pillow and call me "son." Without warning, I suddenly miss the old fool.

Our house—I call it *our* house!—is yet again filled with men of importance talking of important things. Endlessly. And though they talk round and round a thing, and no action is planned, still I am not bored.

In the fifth consulate of the Christian reign of the Emperor Theodosius II, the city of Alexandria is sent Orestes of Constantinople. Flavius Anthemius not only wrote to discuss his decision with Hypatia, she has suggested the choice.

I discover now what it is Egypt's prefect actually does. As the most important imperial official in the Empire of the East, he rules on taxes, estates, civic obligations, the propriety of secular activity, the confiscation of all that is gained by subversive or criminal activity, protects the imperial mint, and pronounces on religious opinions.

By Hermes, god of thieves—a larcenist's dream! No wonder so many seek public office.

But most important of all his duties is the collection and distribution of Egyptian wheat. Egypt feeds both Empires. If I were Prefect, in no time I should be rich as Croesus.

Hypatia tells us that upon his appointment, Orestes was baptized by Constantinople's bishop, the dimly devoted Atticus. Such pretense was the only sensible position to take, one that men—and women—have taken from time beyond remembering.

Alexandria crowded the docks to watch the arrival of the Imperial fleet: its pennants flying, horns sounding, men of all stations scurrying to be first to greet the new Prefect and his new Military Commander, the exceedingly tall and well named Abundantius. What it saw was that the moment Orestes arrived, he directed his goods be unloaded and delivered to his home, wherever that might be. It saw him greet with all due reverence Bishop Theophilus and one or two others, then turn away to demand a litter take him directly to the House of Hypatia. That neither he nor his bearers knew the city mattered in the least. The first man he asked knew where Hypatia lived. My darling *is* Alexandria.

We hear the displeasure of Theophilus shook the walls of his stolen Greek house.

My new position suits me well. No longer considered Theon's "man," I am now the first friend of Hypatia. Funny this should come when I no longer care for status or power or money. Here I will speak a truth I have longed to speak aloud for years, and now *do* say: all that truly concerns me is Hypatia herself.

And here is a thing that comes with loving and being loved by Hypatia of Alexandria. I speak my mind. I laugh when I wish to. I come and go as I please. I kiss no man's ass. I kiss Hypatia wherever I like. Delicious.

Jone, youngest daughter of Theon of Alexandria

As handmaid, I bring Cyril his letters and take away those he writes so they might be distributed to messengers. So many fly between Cyril and Pulcheria in Constantinople, and I try not to peek, but once in awhile—I fall into temptation. One more sin to pay penance for. But I cannot resist. Pulcheria sounds as one I would know. So young and yet so devout. If hero I have, it is Pulcheria, Empress of the East.

Cyril, now as fat and as glossy as a river horse, took great pleasure in his uncle's displeasure that the new prefect goes first to my sister and not to the Bishop of Alexandria. I take pleasure in Cyril's pleasure. Pleasure must come from somewhere and other than in love of God, I have found it hard to find.

As I wait for today's letters, keeping the proper distance between Cyril and I (there is a mark on the floor, this is what I am told to stand behind), Theophania, his mother, thin as an ibis, has slunk up to her son, saying, "If all goes well, you will be bishop." She must think me a slave, why else would she be indiscreet before me? What does "all goes well" mean? But I know what she does not say. What she does not say is how much better for her to have power held in the hands of a compliant and loving son, than held by an arrogant brother who barely tolerates her.

This too I know. Cyril understands his mother as I understand her, but he thinks of Hypatia. I know this because he mutters. When I wait for a letter or do some other thing he wishes me too, it seems often he forgets I am there. I remain as quietly as I can so he does not remember too soon. His muttering shows me his mind. That he does not understand Hypatia disturbs him. He asks himself what attracts men to her and not to his uncle or even to Cyril himself? Are they not wise and powerful and do they not speak for Christ? Certainly Cyril does. He is as sure of this as I am. He also asks himself: how to manipulate that which is not understood?

Three days later, I follow when he goes out. Cyril so seldom leaves his home now that his back and legs have begun to ache, I must know what could compel him. Cyril, in the company of his favorite Heirax, seeks out one of my sister's lectures! They sit on a bench far up in the highest tier of her hall. Below them sits row after row of bent heads and scribbling hands, one of which is mine, my head and face covered in cloth, though what I scribble is nonsense. All are listening to Hypatia with all their faculties. I peek up at Cyril now and again who does not sit, but reclines on cold stone. Seated by him, Hierax is using the opportunity to read *The Quest of the Golden Fleece* by Apollonius of Rhodes. I wonder if he's come to the good part about the Harpies? I know Hierax. Other than her beauty, which is too far away to be leered at, my sister holds no interest for him.

Cyril is seven years younger than Hypatia, and though I revere him for his piety, his mind is no match for hers. She is now saying that though geometry had its origin in the physical world, weights and measures and such, it transcends the world by deriving not *things* but *ideas* from the physical. Mathematics turned the mind away from material and towards the abstract. Through mathematics, she says, one could reach the divine.

At this I quickly turn to catch Cyril's reaction to such blasphemy. He is as struck with as much horror as I am. Or so it seems to me.

But if he not?

Impossible.

JONE

Jone, youngest daughter of Theon of Alexandria

I pace my cell. I fall to my knees to kneel as long as I can. The pain makes me bite my lip. I bite it until I bleed.

Only Jesus is perfect. Only Jesus is perfect. Only Jesus is perfect! Only Jesus is the Perfected Man. And only through Him do we reach God.

Lais is in my head. I have tried and I have tried, but cannot remove her. All thought Lais was perfect. Hypatia is in my head. I have slammed my skull against the wall over and over, but still she remains. How many once called Lais "perfect"? Blasphemy and evil. Only Jesus, at one and the same time both man and God, was perfect. I rise only to pace some more.

The small space allotted me is long since contained within the house of Cyril, which in truth is the house of the godless Theophania provided her by her brother Bishop Theophilus, but neither Cyril nor I think it the house of Theophania. He knows it to be his house. I think it "our" house, but would never say this, never. What should he say if I were to claim as mine any part of it? I should endure penance. I have endured a great deal from Cyril, all of it deserved. It is exceedingly hard to be good enough for Cyril and for God—and as for Theophania, impossible! I should not hate, but I do. *Only Jesus is perfect.*

Seven years I have devoted to Cyril, and where does he go so soon as my sister returns? Even now, though I follow faithfully, he thinks no one knows, that no one sees him or judges him. But I do all of these things. God has never spoken to me. I do not deserve it. But if He did, I know in my heart He would want me to protect his favored Cyril. I have no other way than to make myself his guardian, a keeper of his every word and deed. As for his thoughts, even with his muttering, these I can only surmise...although it helps to read his letters, both sent and received. I admit I am often shocked. I think I shall never understand how God chooses who He would favor. In any case, each time Cyril returns from hearing Hypatia, I return with him, all unseen and unthought of. He is easy to follow. Those who bear his litter labor to bear his weight. He interrupts traffic.

Once home, I see that under the sweat he mops from his face, his skin glows. His eyes are as the eyes of a black monk. They are eyes that seem to see more than my eyes. Does he see Hypatia is as all thought Lais to be: perfect? Has Satan taken root in my favorite's soul? Only God knows what is perfect and what is not perfect for only God is perfect. And His Son Jesus Christ. Every other soul that has ever been born or will be born is imperfect. Each merits Hell unless it is saved by Jesus.

I pace and I fall to my knees and I stand and I pace and I fall to my knees. What does God want of me, for even Jone is of use to God.

Of a sudden I know! Knowing is as if night turned to day or day to night. It is as if the walls of my cell opened out into the stars and the largest of them grew larger, became so bright I was blind.

Lais is gone. There is none she can hurt as once she did. Father is gone. Forgotten before his death, his work reaches fewer and fewer. If Hypatia were gone, who then could she tempt with her evil?

The solution is simple. Theophania is as expert with poisons as was Livia, the deadly wife of Caesar Augustus. How often have I been ordered to shop or to mix or to bottle for her? I will remove Hypatia. Surely God wishes this, for why else would the art of Theophania become mine? And it can be done as easily as feeding fruit to Cyril. Of all that grows in his garden, Cyril loves best his pomegranate tree. He will not miss one, or even two, not if taken from high in the branches.

Minkah the Egyptian

On a day of fire and blood, I was saved by an Angel of angels come down from the stars, clothed only in soot and skin. On that day was Minkah the Egyptian truly born.

And now I am reborn. To love and be loved by Hypatia, I ask no more than this. And if it should suddenly be taken away, even this I accept with a ravished heart. To have little of what is beyond wondrous far transcends an eternity of mere pleasure.

More than ever an Egyptian is reviled in Egypt. For me, thrown at birth into a pit of filth, Alexandria was a city of bitter betrayal and helpless fear. But Hypatia's Alexandria was as a city in the clouds: fabulous, unreachable, unimaginable. As a Greek, her young life was spent in a place awake in spirit and free in speech just as mine was spent dead to spirit and alive to horror.

Our worlds come together now. Mine will live on and on, for a few men, battling for great power, ever do great harm to all other men. But hers is dying. I rejoice that I live to see it even as it disappears before our eyes. It has done so for years, but now it fades so fast we must reach out to grasp what will be gone tomorrow. Once more, Christians walk the streets so they might do unto others as was done unto them, even though their Christ said: *thou shalt not kill.* These kill with a vengeance only the ignorant can feel. The bodies of their "enemies" fill a new section in the City of the Dead. My old friend, Theophilus, passes edicts daily. One week it is death to profess belief in the pre-existence of the soul. The next it is death to confess even ownership of a book penned by Origen. The following week one might die for the simple act of reading at all. This week it is for not believing Jesus entirely "God."

What face to wear? What skin? When will it be death to be Jewish or Egyptian?

As once *Parabalanoi*, each new edict would have shriveled my sack, for as *Parabalanoi*, it is I who might well have been the weapon used. Now, I would not be surprised to find myself subject of an edict. Oddly, this pleases.

But tonight I am wary unto deep suspicion. Jone visits. Jone who loves neither her sister nor me has come to our door after many long years living mere streets away, yet for all we see of her she might as well dwell in Gaul.

She arrives without notice. No letter was written beforehand. We knew nothing until there came a knock on a door that has never been locked against the youngest daughter of Theon and Damara. My darling is disarmed. She displays her heart openly, a heart which has never been closed to this sister. And Jone? Grown thin, as ever short, and stinking with incense, she covers her head. In the heavy robe the women of Jesus wear, each calling themselves his "bride," she is wed to her savior. Chaste, severe and humorless, sincere and horrifying—if her "husband" lived, I would pity him.

"Panya!"

I know what I see. Have I not been *Parabalanoi* long enough to smell rank deception? It takes an effort of will for Jone to remain where she is, looking down at the ground, yet it takes no effort at all to bring forth from one of her long wide sleeves a wooden bowl.

Hypatia claps her hands. "Oh, Jone. Pomegranates!"

"From the garden of Cyril. He loves them."

"And you brought them to me!" Hypatia is stepping back, making room for her sister to enter the house in which she was born. Her face is flushed with surprise and with pleasure, her eyes alight with hope. Jone's eyes do not raise themselves from the tile of the courtyard. My love calls for wine. Jone will not have wine. She calls for water. Jone will not have water. She calls for a chair, a bench, pillows. Jone will not sit. She will not even cross the threshold of our house... *her* house.

"I come to welcome you home, sister," says she, and no one mentions that Hypatia has been home for two years and more. "I cannot stay. Cyril depends on me." Here she thrusts forward the wooden bowl containing fruit grown in the garden of Cyril. "Take them. But I must bring back the bowl. No one knows I have it."

"You will come again?" Hypatia's joy has fled her face, her sorrow has curved her back. In her left hand she holds a pomegranate, and in her right.

Jone is quickly backing away. "I will come if I can." She then turns and is gone into night. Not once did she raise her eyes.

Only Nildjat Miw expresses herself. Her strange ringed tail twitches in irritation.

Hypatia of Alexandria

In the season of pomegranates, my sister has brought me the fruit of Persephone: Queen of the Underworld, the Iron Queen, unfathered maiden, mothered by Demeter, stolen away by Hades...and with her loss came the dying of the Earth. Hermes, sent to steal her back so that the world would not die, succeeded, but not before Hades tricked the daughter of the fruitful Demeter into eating seven seeds of the pomegranate. For this, Persephone would forever return to the land of the dead for four barren months of every twelve.

Jone knows this story as well as I, just as she knows other tales of Persephone, for Jone was once a voracious reader of more than Christian theology. Persephone is the tale of Inanna retold. Inanna of Sumer came first, her story so old no one can say it has a beginning, just as no one knows if the world itself begins or ends. Inanna was not stolen away into the Dark World, but walked forward in full knowledge of what she risked, nor was she tricked into staying, but came forth brighter than before—for there she found Glory.

Pomegranates, one in each hand. How heavy they are, as heavy as my heart as it mourns what I learn. Jone will not come in nor will she come back. As I did not know what Minkah thought of my father, I *do* know what he thinks of Jone—but Jone is blood of my blood. Surely these are not insults or warnings, but gifts? Jone is as Jone has ever been. She knows no other way of offering peace. As for love, how could she offer what has never been offered her? Save by me, but who am I?

I place my red gifts in a blue ceramic bowl on my mother's green table. In a day or two, they will ripen. Nildjat Miw sniffs them once, twice, but it seems they bore her.

I, who attend so many dinners, am having a dinner! Mine is to welcome Orestes. What shall I serve? Who shall I invite? Romans choose guests numerically and so shall I. *No fewer than the three Fates, nor more than the nine muses.* In Constantinople, Orestes was a perfect host. I must return in kind. Who would he wish to meet? As Prefect, his life will be full of schemers. I invite those who do not scheme but think. Or laugh.

Minkah and I plan the guest list, Ife, the menu.

There will be eleven at table. Aside from Orestes and myself and Minkah...Augustine, Bishop of Hippo, Synesius, Bishop of Ptolemais, and his wife Catherine. Olinda of Clarus. As a physician Olinda possesses little in social or political standing, but she is witty and wise. Pappas the astronomer, old of body, soft of heart, and acerbic of tongue. Meletus the Jew who is sure to add a level head. And of course, my houseguest Aelia Galla Placidia. The old will be leavened by the young. What the young will think is for Galla to feel. As the daughter of the dead Emperor Theodosius, she is surely used to tedium. But should laughter be wanted, Galla laughs as Didymus once laughed. And last I invite Felix Zoilus.

"You do what!" says Minkah.

"Invite your friend." I see he cannot believe what I am saying. "I am serious, beloved."

"Zoilus is a lump. All we will add to our dinner will be bulk and a huge wine and beer bill."

"But would it not please him?"

"To meet old men and the young daughter of a despot?"

"Exactly."

"Be it on your head."

My household turned upside down, I hide away to prepare a class in optics. But in truth I turn instead to an alchemical process, a copy of the *Divine Pymander* open before me, an alembic at my elbow, and a crucible of heated silver under my nose. I am so immersed in what must be manifest not only in the physical world, but a hundred times more in the spiritual, that I would miss my own dinner party if not for a servant sent to fetch me. Unwashed, unpainted, uncoiffed, undressed, there are moments I annoy myself. Offering my home and my hospitality, and then to utterly forget about it—shades of Father.

I do what I need do at top speed, helped by the kitchen maid. Out the door I would now go, but my eye strays back to my work with corrosive sublimate, red oxide of mercury, and nitrate of silver, and I struggle with the urge to stay and the urge to go, and there, by Hades, are my pomegranates.

Shoving the blue bowl into the hands of my helper, I say, "Get cook to find a way to make these feed eleven." And off I rush to greet my guests.

How surprising. My dinner party goes well, twice as well as those I attend. Orestes is as ingenious at table as he is on parchment. Synesius does not sulk nor does he complain of his lot. Olinda fascinates with her talk of digestion. Catherine tells us a tale of Synesius as a child that makes Minkah weep with laughter. It makes Catherine weep with laughter. Augustine, Pappas and Meletus engage in a historical topic that engrosses us all. Felix Zoilus is subdued before royalty and prefect and the learned, though becomes less and less so as wine flows. Any minute I expect he will shout out some interesting word. I keep an eye on him. So far all he has done is pinch Olinda who slaps him, but discreetly. And Galla, lovely in her youth and her character, enthralls us entirely with her tales of the Visigoth king, Alaric, who died of fever attempting to cross the Great Green Sea. So loved was he by his men that they landed in some secret place, and there turned aside a river so they might bury him in its bed, then let loose the river again.

Even I am acceptable, never once lost in speaking aloud some obscure concept only to look up and find all glazed over with ennui.

Cook has made a splendid table...and such an assortment of dishes. In our house, only Nildjat Miw feasts, but now my small silver spike hovers over fish from the river, fish from the sea, fish from the lake, cold water oysters, eggs, fava beans, snails, nuts, cheese, a huge bowl of pungent *garum*, and wine, a great deal of the finest Egyptian wine. I know what it is to drink with Great Drunks, Minkah and Felix Zoilus; I know what it is to suffer. So I drink, but sparingly. More accurately, I drink less than everyone else save Galla. How enjoyable, this. How light my heart. A thought visits. Why not form a salon as did Aspasia of Miletus! As a woman, forbidden to learn, her father Axiochus, like my father Theon, taught her all he knew, which was a great deal indeed. In search of more, Aspasia traveled to the seat of all knowledge, shining Athens—only to find that as an educated unmarried woman, she was immediately assumed *hetairai*, a "paid companion to men." Wise to the ways of the male, Apasia accepted their assumptions, then turned all on its head by coupling with Pericles, the most powerful man in Athens. She not only taught, but gave succor to other young women seeking knowledge. Anaxagoras who understood the moon shone by reflected light, understood this because of Aspasia. Socrates took instruction from her and was well pleased.

Looking about at the faces of my guests, I am decided. Under my roof the Companions may continue as pleases them. I shall be pleased to remain as Hypatia. But there will be a new Hypatia, born in the drowning sea, born from reading

Valentinus and Seth of Damascus, born as she wandered as Io, born from seeing herself in Synesius' *Dion*...a new Aspasia who holds in her home a salon open to all: rich, poor, men and *women.* As I hope these things become eventually mine, I will ask only for sincerity, intelligence and grace.

Orestes tells us he finds his position in Alexandria much easier than expected. "Politics is lucrative. An amazing amount of civil servants do the actual work, yet I am the one well paid. Though it is tedious, and when not tedious, dangerous. For instance, in Constantinople, Atticus poses as a learned bishop but is as a prattling child. Our emperor *is* a prattling child—oh, fire and rancid fat, excuse me, Aelia Galla Placidia."

Helping herself to more oysters, Galla laughs, "But my brother's son *is* a prattling child."

Relieved, Orestes speaks on. "Neither bishop nor boy rules the East. Flavius Anthemius rules. If he did not, the empire would sink as fast as a block of cement in a cesspool."

My love, on his couch, is half drunk and half sober. That part of him half-sober, asks what I would ask if he were not faster. "And the danger?"

"In a word—Pulcheria. Only thirteen, yet already an oddity exceeding any. The royal court is as quiet as a tomb, as pious as the word heresy, and as dim as the mind of Atticus. There, the eyes weep with incense, the throat chokes with it, the senses dull. The sister of Theodosius II swears eternal chastity, forcing her younger sisters to swear also...and neither knows the meaning of the word! If Pulcheria is not praying, she is praying, for all that she does is a kind of prayer. The idiocy of Atticus has driven her mad, or madness is her birthright, oh Cocytus!" Galla, who has been making faces at Felix who has been making faces at her, waves this away. "But mad she is, and the madder she grows, the madder grows the empire. Or would, if not for Anthemius."

Synesius raises his cup. "A long life to Anthemius!"

We all raise our cups, even Galla whose nephew is emperor and whose niece is "mad." "Long life to Anthemius!"

"As for Alexandria's bishop," continues Orestes, silencing all on the spot, "the man is a politician through and through. One knows where one stands. So long as Theophilus is bishop, good sense and self interest will reign."

"Long life to Theophilus!"

We have finished the savories. We have finished the cheese and the olives. Nildjat Miw and Galla have finished the oysters. A servant enters bearing a bowl of steaming something or other.

"Ah," says Pappas, ever a slave to his belly. "What is this? What have you prepared for us, Hypatia? The smell intoxicates."

I have no idea what I have prepared, save this: it must contain the juice or the seed or both of my sister's pomegranates. I glance at the servant as she sets the bowl in the middle of the table. One glance is enough for her to feel free to speak. "Mistress, cook made a pudding dressed with pomegranate sauce. There is a sweetness that comes from an Indian cane."

All at my table say, "Ah!" as each holds forth a small glass bowl for a share of this exotic sweet, but Minkah is more eager than any, so eager his small bowl is first there, tapping the larger bowl which sends it sliding across the table and into the lap of Felix Zoilus. Felix is up on the instant, hopping in place, his crotch a mass of pudding and hot pomegranate sauce, and we are treated to a string of fabulous expressions, most I have never heard in my life—so inventive!

As one, all stare at Minkah. He acts the drunk. He acts out a drunk's contrition—and suddenly I know he is not contrite. He is not drunk. What he has done, he has done deliberately. No one will taste of Jone's gift.

I laugh. I clap my hands. I call for Cook to devise some other treat. All laugh with me. All think it great fun, even Felix who must change into a tunic of a long dead servant. None other would fit him and this one barely.

As we wait for a second sweet, I catch the eye of my lover. Neither fools the other. We know, he and I...Jone is not to be trusted.

My evening is ruined. As is, yet again, my heart.

And yet, later with Minkah, how intense the pleasure! A touch with hand or mouth, a look in the eye or the scent of a secret part of the body—intoxicates.

My body arcs with pleasure. That Jone is as she is, for this moment, does not matter. All that matters is the cup of his fingers lying spent beside mine, the slick of sweat on his belly, his sated member slowly curling in sleep as sweet as a newborn.

Jone, youngest daughter of Theon of Alexandria

I listen and I listen for word, but none comes. I call out to the Virgin, even to God Himself, but no one hears Jone.

Two weeks pass and Hypatia lives on, not even fallen ill. Yet our Holy Bishop, who only this morning was as he ever is: demanding, fearsome, busy with a dozen schemes at once, and not yet old, has gone to bed complaining of pain in his gut.

I do not live in the House of Theophilus, nor does Cyril or his mother Theophania. But Theophania had pestered her brother for days. She would eat at his table. Cyril, who would eat anywhere, rolled his eyes at his mother's impertinence, but finally Theophilus had said: if you must, come! and off they went. No more than an hour later, just as I had settled in to read Didymus the Blind, came a reader, the lowest of the low in clerical office, looking for me. "Me?" I asked him. For answer, he pushed me and pulled me into the House of the Bishop of Alexandria right past the outer room where Theophania paced and Cyril sat, taking up the whole of a couch. Why are they not at table, dining?

I called out to mother and son, "Why me?" Both looked at me in much the same way I looked at them—we were all three astonished. And then I was shoved into the presence of the Patriarch.

For three hours now, Theophilus has twisted his face full of pox and his body grown gaunt and his limbs grown thin into every conceivable shape. I have held a bowl over and over as he vomited. I have held a second bowl to catch the content of his bowels. How much does he contain? What is wrong with him? Does he die? If he is dying, where is the archdeacon? I call for slaves to empty bowls. I call for incense so I do not lose my own dinner. Why are Cyril and Theophania outside? Do they not heed his cries?

He moans as he clutches his belly, tears of torment leaking down his face, his beard soaked with sweat. I know this torment of the bowels, it plagues me, though his seems so much the greater. And then he grows quiet. Holding my breath in order to avoid his, I lean over him. Has it passed, whatever torments him? His eyes are closed. Will the poor thing rest? Quietly I turn away. If I am quiet enough, I might leave. His chamber reeks of vomit and feces. I reek of his vomit and feces. The robe I wear will need to be soaked for a day or more to clean it.

My hand is reaching for his door handle, when he calls out to me. Our Mother in Heaven, if I did not know, I would never guess this the voice of the powerful Patriarch of Alexandria.

"Jone."

"Yes, Holy Father?"

"Come back here." I sigh, but take care he does not see me sigh, returning to seat myself on the stool I have used throughout. "I am dying, Jone." I would deny it, but he denies me the effort of denial. "I was not dying this morning, but I am dying now. A whole life lived, and it comes to this?" I shake my head. Though I have thought of death often, it has never been *my* death. I cannot imagine such a thing as my own death. As for his, what *has* he come to? "Not once did I dream I would die in this way. Where is God? Where are his angels? Where my solace and my reward—and where is my church? I've chosen the site. I've drawn the plans. This year I would lay the first stones. Will it be built? Will I be honored as I should be? Do I care? I find I do not care. Shall I tell you, poor thing that you are, what has gone through my mind?" If he will tell me, he will, though I wish he would not. I sit quietly. "Hypatia." I am now as still as he will be when he dies...which for the first time this night I hope will be soon. "Your sister troubles my dying as she has troubled my life. Why else forbid Isidore her and her Isidore? Why else did I banish my favorite? All think it because of Origen. Pah! His heart was full of Hypatia and would not empty itself of her! Only one thing is left me. That I could *know* Hypatia."

My God, my God, my God. Is there no end to this! I have thought I could feel no more. I have thought my hatred had limits. I find it does not. Long ago, Isidore who I loved, loved Hypatia. I pined for Minkah, but Minkah loves Hypatia. For weeks Cyril has waddled into her lectures and when he comes home there is a look about him I have seen before. Am I nothing? Do they think I feel *nothing*? Did Father cast me aside and assume I *felt* nothing! I feel *everything*! And all that I feel is as bile to me.

Theophilus, dying, desires Hypatia? I will tell him of his precious Hypatia. He would take her with him to the hell that awaits him? Then he shall take also the one thing that might prove worse than hell.

I lean close. I do not gag at his stench. I do not take my eyes from the vomit that coats his wrinkled lips or fills the marks of his pox like mud fills potholes. I say this to him. "The books exist, Theophilus."

His eyes, dim, yet wet with a foolish desire that does not die as he dies, grow suddenly bright. "What do you mean?"

"I mean that all the books you thought burned are not burned. They were taken away, book by book, out into the desert, and there they are now, in jars, protected and safe. Hypatia did this. My sister Hypatia has saved the books. They live, Theophilus."

He stares at me. If I know hate, so too does he. "You knew this? You knew—"

"I knew."

"And you never told me?"

If he knows love, I too once knew love. "I would protect Minkah the Egyptian."

"By the sack of Satan! You name *Minkah*!"

The news is too shocking. The books exist. He cannot accept it. He cannot reject it. He reaches for me, the fat gold rings on his long thin fingers slipping down his knuckles, the jewels on each slimy with the sweat of his dying, and in that moment I know why I am called here this night. I am called because I am as close as he will ever come to Hypatia. And now he would kill her, as I would kill her, but as he cannot, he would kill me.

But before his will can be done, Theophilus, Bishop of Alexandria has one last terrible spasm, and is dead. It is ugly, his dying. It has been painful and loud and satisfying. And it is just in time.

I do not shut his eyes or his mouth or cover his face. I do not straighten the great gold medallion stuck through with rubies and emeralds that lies on his sunken chest in a puddle of vomit. I walk from his room as a cat would walk from a room: indifferent, indolent, in search of its own pleasures. I leave him as all leave me.

Cyril is asleep on the couch, his fat red mouth puckered and his snore like mallets on stone. Bald as an Egyptian, Theophania is also asleep, slumped on a chair, her legs splayed out as if she gives birth, her head bent at an awkward angle. Her braided black and orange wig lies on the floor. I would kick it into a corner, but I am no longer a child. I pass the open door to a great dining room. Theophilus has served his pest of a sister and his uncomfortable nephew a goodly meal.

Beside each plate is a pomegranate. All three have been sliced in half. Only one has been eaten. God listens to some.

THE SIXTH GATE

Late Fall, 412

Minkah the Egyptian

Theophilus is dead. From the Moon to the Sun Gate, from the sweet lake to the salted sea, Alexandria is in shock. Nothing ailed him. He had no accident.

He would not be at all surprised to note the many who offer up thanks at his passing. He might be surprised to find that I, Minkah, was not among them. Theophilus stood between Hypatia and his Christians. But would it surprise him to know Hypatia mourns? Would it please him? My beloved attends his funeral in all sincerity. I go only to protect her. All know a handmaid of Cyril's attended him on the night he died. All know her name: Jone. Not all, but many know her as daughter of Theon and as sister to Hypatia. These are suspicious.

But this is as nothing beside the horror of Cyril, son of Theophania, now Bishop of Alexandria.

Cyril is unwanted, unloved, and feared. Christians, at least those who believe in the right of succession by high office, expected as Bishop Archdeacon Timothy. Cyril would have Cyril as bishop. The city only now calms after three brutal days of terror. Cyril's black mantles threatened Timothy and the supporters of Timothy. Fires were set, women raped then gutted, men knifed, the heads of children were smashed against walls. Even as Prefect, Orestes could do little as Abundantius, his Military Chief Commander, commands only a single detachment. Abundantius could not be everywhere, arrest everyone, save more than a few.

On the 18th of October, accompanied by riots all over the city, Archdeacon Timothy lost an election his by popular right and Cyril "won" what he had no right to win.

Bewigged and bejeweled, his mother, now thinner than an eel, sleeker and more slippery, immediately clapped the robes of office around her son's great bulk, crammed the pharaohnic hat on his enormous head, handed him the golden scepter of office to seize in one fat hand, the golden staff to grip in the other, and there he sits now, stuffed into the throne of Saint Mark.

The son of Theophania is thirty five years old. He may live for years. For too many, they will be years of pain and tears and loss.

But while Alexandria is terrified, a small group of men are made jubilant. Of these, most are my good friends, the ever pestilent *Parabalanoi*, or Isidore's associates, the increasingly malignant monks of the Nitrian Mountains. With Theophilus dead, the *Parabalanoi* reforms itself around Cyril. These renew their vows. Those who would not, do not. I do not, nor does my friend, Felix Zoilus. Does Isidore? Long since, he left the thugs of Theophilus to join the thugs of Nitria who love Cyril. Under Cyril, will Isidore become again Archdeacon? Better to ask: how much will any man pay for position? In my experience, he will pay his very soul.

None wait long for fear to coalesce into terror. Any who had ever ignored Cyril, or laughed at him, or did not agree with him, or who had opposed his reign as bishop...all who he did not agree with, or felt contempt for, or threatened by, or believed inferior to his Christian "truths," were either killed or banished. Of those killed, no trail led back to Cyril. Those who were banished were banished openly.

Cyril turns first on his fellow Christians, primarily the Novatians. As my darling does not call herself pagan, these do not call themselves Novatians, but rather the Pure, the *Katharoi*. Believing their faith corrupted when those, under threat, denied the Christ and sacrificed to idols, they resist Cyril who welcomes apostates back into the church. Say the Pure: what insult to those who willingly died appalling deaths rather than deny their faith! The *Katharoi* are mathematicians, philosophers, men of letters. They supported Timothy against Cyril. They attend the lectures of Hypatia of Alexandria. They now pay dearly for each of these crimes. Cyril closes their churches, robs their treasuries, drives their bishop and his flock from the city.

I hear Cyril will soon turn his thoughts to the Jews.

And I, Minkah, prepare for the day he looks farther afield.

The life of man turns and turns again, wheeling like the stars from sign and to sign, and every sign known in advance. If times are good for some, they are bad for others. But whether good or bad, they will reverse themselves as inexorably as the moon in its course. For Cyril, times become very good, and for those who pant out his praises. For all others, times become very bad indeed.

No longer under the protection of Theophilus, nothing but death could force me from Hypatia's side.

Summer, 413

Hypatia of Alexandria

Though it causes the Companions no end of silent complaint, my salon is a great success. And if its luster pales when compared to that of Aspasia of Athens, it seems a success to me and I am content.

Because women attend, men do not. This turns out a blessing. Aside from Lais, in all my life I have spent little time with my own sex. To do so now is a revelation. With these, I am merely a guide. I am taught as I teach. The talk of women is not the talk of men. It is freer, less contentious, more eager to speak, a great deal more eager to listen. It holds within it touches and tastes of Lais.

Beginning only with Catherine and Olinda and Galla—until Aelia Galla is called back to her willing captivity, for all see she is anxious to return to King Ataulf, her Visigoth abductor—we grow quickly in number. First come the wives and daughters of Companions, then those of rich men, and then come women I scarce knew existed. Women free of men, women who have traveled from place to place, women who live by their wits. These last amaze and humble me. My world was ready made for me; I am cocooned by it. These have made the world their own. And they have sought me out. One heard me in Athens, one in Ephesus, several in Antioch, one in Constantinople. I question them closely, find homes for those in need, offer stipends.

No matter that Alexandria trembles before Cyril—surviving so much, surely she will survive the ambition of one fat man—I am happier now than I have ever been.

As we talk, as we sip wine, as I read to them from Seth, from Valentinus, from my own unfinished pages, as I am asked this and asked that, and as I ask of them, Nildjat Miw prowls among us, as large as a caracal. On the tip of each ear grows a curved tuft of dark hair and her color is as shaded sand. If I thought it possible, I should imagine she *is* a caracal. She grows no less vocal.

We discuss the words of Mary Magdalene, beloved companion and teacher of the Christ, she who once lived and studied in Alexandria under Philo Judaeus, then taught her beloved what she herself had learned as they walked to his death. We discuss the words of *The Gospel of Philip.* "God created man and man created God. So is it in the world. Men make gods and they worship their creations. It would be fitting for the gods to worship men." I wait for intake of breath, but it does not come as it would from one or more of the Companions. "Most who heard such words would dismiss them. Others would misunderstand them. Philip is not saying God is no more than a fabrication of man. He is saying, as did Parmenides of Elea, that out of our own Thoughts, through our own Minds, we brought forth the World...and with the World came the idea of God. He is saying that out of his own Thoughts and through his own Mind, God brought forth Man. But how can this be? God made man and man made God? Is it not one or the other? The answer is simple. Man and God are the same. There is no separation."

I tell them further, as a faith named for Christ drives our gods from the world and makes the source of "evil" a woman, they are made rapt to discover that the Christ is not a history but a spiritual myth, that the word "Christ" is not a name or a title but a state of being: Christ Consciousness, which in Greek is called *gnosis* or divine knowing, and in the language of those I have met from the land of the Gupta it is *Moksha.*

As we talk my women and I become runners of the sun, those who would *know.*

"By their own laws, Christians are forbidden taverns, brothels, and public assemblies. They are forbidden the theater." Bishop Synesius tells us this. After a moment of thought, he adds, "Few obey."

Meletus, who stands in the Agora's center courtyard as I do as does Minkah and Orestes, nods. "Jews, no different, attend theater even on the Sabbath. They become unruly, for the Law that binds the Jews has loosened and many have escaped." He says this in all seriousness and I see he does not mean to be amusing.

Synesius sighs. "The true faithful of any religion are not many." At this my old friend and student looks at me knowing I know he does not count himself among the true faithful.

Orestes, as Prefect, laments: "If they do not stop, Jewish theater must stop." This he also says, "And yet no Jew threatens Imperial authority. Only Cyril does. As I labor to return order to the law courts and to public gatherings, his people, forbidden by their church to attend either, create hell on earth. Now they attack Jews for attending their own theater on their own Sabbath, as if it was any of their accursed business...yet as Prefect, I am required to maintain public order."

"Orestes," say I, "when you do this, might I come along?"

Minkah grows alert beside me. "Why would you go?"

"All I have known of Jews is Meletus. I would know more."

"There are better ways than maintaining order with Orestes."

"Are there?"

Since the death of Theophilus, I well understand Minkah protects me. Even Felix Zoilus protects me. Do they assume a bloodbath? But knowing Meletus, stranger to a smile, we are all eager to see a Jew revel. Orestes agrees. How could there be danger? Wherever goes the Prefect of Alexandria, so too goes any number of imperial guards.

We go on a night when the moon is full. From the theater, built into the side of a limestone ridge on the Street of Theaters, one can look down at the Great Harbor and across its waters to the island of Pharos...but once inside—by Queen Vashti, hero to all wives—what a sight! Jews stand on benches. Jews throw dates, olives, bread. They shout, they stamp their feet, they pull their beards. As for those on stage, dancing and miming, who sees them? Jews are here not for the stage, but for freedom.

Keeping well back, I revel in the revelry, until beside me Orestes sighs, "As myself, I would not, but as Prefect it is time to pour cold water on heads." And with this, he and his men push their way to the stage. Orestes leaves a handful to look after us, making Minkah bristle and Felix growl. How long Orestes must shout before he is noticed, I could not say, but man by man, the Jews grow quiet.

"Friends," he calls out to them, "In my person I am required to keep the peace. It does not matter who breaks it: young or old, man or woman, Christian or Jew, if the people of Alexandria cannot or will not govern themselves, then it is I who must govern for them. Complaints have been made against you."

'What complaints?" shouts one, his face still red from blowing the horn he holds.

"You ignore your Sabbath."

"These complaints...do they come from our rabbis?"

"They come from certain—"

"Christians! And do we Jews complain when a Christian is found in a whorehouse? Or a gutter?"

"Never," shouts someone I cannot see, "Instead, we laugh!" At which point all laugh: mimes, dancers, Jews, and Felix.

I remember what Orestes has said: Jews are not the problem, Cyril's Christians are. He would treat these laughing men well, but before he can, a scuffle breaks out nearby. We cannot see who hits whom, or why, but our guards and half those gathered around Orestes, push and shout their way through the crowd, and there set about whacking heads with the flat of their swords.

"Well," says Minkah, "We get our money's worth tonight."

Felix says this, "I am minded of home—which is why I seldom go there."

Four Jews are dragged to the stage where stands Orestes. Five others, not Jews, are forcibly made to kneel.

"Look!" Minkah pokes Felix. "Peter the Reader." The smile of Felix fades from his bearded face.

Peter the Reader! I look and I see that all five who kneel are those Synesius named in his book "Black Mantles," and that one has a face as white as bone. I have seen this face before, long ago when the Serapeum burned. He called me Satan's child. So this is Minkah's nemesis!

Orestes poses before the fires that light the stage. If he were not a fine politician, he would make a fine actor. He is angry, yet appears calm. "Choose that one," he asks of the four Jews, "who is most able in speech and least able at lying. I will know what happens here."

"That one" chooses himself. "As you have come, agents of

Cyril have also come, so that you might witness our 'supposed' violence. But it was they who began it this night."

"Is that so? And who are these agents?" Dozens of fingers point at Peter the Reader. "You!" he shouts at this Peter, "is the truth spoken here?"

Not Peter, but another lifts his arm, both arm and man so thin I would feed him on the instant. Actually, I would not—but Lais would. I know him. He sat beside Cyril at the consecration of Synesius and now sits beside Cyril who pretends he does not attend my lectures. "My name is Hierax and I am a Christian."

"Do you deny you cause trouble?"

"One of those," and now it is this Hierax who points, "looked at me oddly."

"I see. And as a Christian are you in the habit of attending a theater when you know it to be full of Jews? As a Christian are you in the habit of attending *any* theater?"

"No. Well, yes. I mean yes. Tonight we, by which I mean my friends and I, thought we might..."

"Cause grief to the Jews?"

Orestes shows favor. He has taken sides. If all thought Cyril troublesome before, it will be nothing to what comes now.

Minkah's eyes glitter with interest. This is the world he understands, the world he and Felix were born into. I have stepped out of my world for only this moment; I know I shall quickly step back.

Hierax may be thin as a marsh reed and his voice as high as a child's, but he does not lack courage. Quickly rising, pushing away from the guard, he strides towards the stage. "I am Hierax the Christian and favored of Cyril, who I favor. These are the Jews who killed our Christ. Do you speak out for them?"

Before Hierax disappears under a mass of furious Jews, Orestes' own anger flashes forth. "Flog this man where he stands!"

Hypatia of Alexandria, rescuer of books and guest of Rome under siege, has seen much, but she has never seen this. Cyril's spy is stripped on the instant. A man I thought thin, I now think emaciated. A man I thought brave, shrinks away from the lash. But then, so should I.

Hierax is nothing but blood and the theater nothing but hoots and howls and the stamping of feet by the time Minkah covers my head and Felix carries me out into the street.

I dream of caves again. I have no candle, no lamp, no lantern, but feel my way by trailing a hand along the cold rough stone of the walls. I cannot see, but I can hear. A murmuring, a sighing, the slight skitter of something small near my unshod feet. And though I do not move, all else moves about me. Unmoving, I listen. Through air, scented with bat dung, I hear the papery beat of papery wings. I am touched by the tips of bony claws. And all the while I grow colder...and when I fold my arms around myself, I know I stand naked against what I cannot see.

In my dreaming caves, I search for what I cannot find.

I come awake to screams.

My house is awake. My horses are awake. They kick out at their stalls, tossing their heads. Nildjat Miw running before me, I quickly pass frightened servants, each peering out into the night as Alexandria is shaken by the tumult of men. Have Galla's adopted Goths crossed the sea and we are attacked? Has a burning star shaped as a spear fallen through the roof of the Agora? Does a Leviathan, its great mouth wide and ringed with a thousand fearsome teeth, rise from the lake?

Minkah, whom I have sought before all else, stands by the window that once was mine.

"Why do they scream, beloved? What do they say?"

"There is a fire."

"Where? I see no flames. I smell no smoke."

"They say the Church of Alexander burns."

"But the Church of Alexander is Christian."

"Indeed."

Enheduanna, poet of Ur, wrote of Lugalanne who so hated her father, she destroyed the great temple Eanna. The Romans razed the temple of the Jews. Greek temples were desecrated by Jews. Christians burned the Serapeum. Now Jews burn the churches of Christians.

"Oh Minkah, is man ever this foolish?"

"Yes."

"Will he ever grow less foolish?"

"No."

Minkah the Egyptian

Christians found not flames but Jews. Emboldened by the public favor of the Prefect Orestes, maddened by the outrages of Cyril and his monks, they had run through the streets shouting, "Fire! The Church of Alexander burns! Fire! Fire!" Christians, hearing this, fell from their beds and rushed from their doors, desperate to stop a fire that would take their church as they themselves had taken temple after temple by fire. What a night of slaughter followed! Before the *Parabalanoi* could act, Jews killed at least a hundred Christian souls, then vanished back into the night...this time without a sound.

As a "heretic" and ex-*Parabalanoi*, I am not allowed into the House of Theophilus so cannot see Cyril, as fat as Nero was fat, nor can I see Theophania, thin as the flogged half-dead Hierax. But all Alexandria sees them in the streets. At daybreak, he bouncing on a laboring litter, she prim and poised on hers, and followed by a great crowd who love them—or, if not them, then carnage and plunder—they rushed to the nearest and largest synagogue. Within an hour, nothing remained. Cyril took the tiles from the floor and the brass from the doors. What he did not take, he smashed, the rest he burned. And then he and his mother went home. But monk and *Parabalanoi* cut through the Jews as a scythe through grain, exacting a revenge so terrible the wiser, faster, richer Jews ran before they came, fleeing the city of their birth and their father's birth and their father's before them. Their homes and their shops now plundered, Cyril closes their synagogues, destroying or stealing what he finds inside, then—as his uncle before him of temples—makes churches of them.

We will sink under the weight of churches.

Cyril will rue this action. He would lose the Jews, down to the last babe in its cradle, but he would not lose their business. With them go riches few Christians possess. Even Felix Zoilus, whose brain would not incommode a fly, understands the sense of this.

The rage of Orestes is the equal of Cyril's. Seated on the edge of Hypatia's pool, she watches as the man strides up and down her atrium, trampling Theon's stars. "Cyril goes too far! He would hold both reins, religious and secular! All that he does, he does to this end. But I am the Prefect and he is a pig! A dog! The shit of a pig or a dog! How dare he call himself a man of God? He knows only one god and its name is Cyril!"

In her innocence, Hypatia speaks. "You have troops. Can they not protect the Jews?"

"Cyril's mobs outnumber my troops by hundreds. But that will change."

So saying, he writes immediately to Anthemius, taking care to address himself to Theodosius II, Emperor of the East, who has attained the advanced age of twelve. He is as his father Arcadius was: useless. Not so his sister Pulcheria. All thank the stars in the heavens for Anthemius.

Who doubts a second letter rushes towards Constantinople, this one written by Cyril.

No matter who or what weighs down the Throne of Mark, Hypatia's lectures at the Agora fill to the point of bursting. Her salon lifts her heart. We sail the *Irisi.* We ride Ia'eh and Bia. I will not allow Hypatia to sail alone, ride alone, teach alone. She does nothing without me.

Tonight the Companions meet. Tomorrow she holds her salon. Before this, she will lock herself away with her work, and I will be invited to join her. These are the moments I treasure above all else in the world. Not only do I speak with Hypatia whose mind knows no equal, I sit with her, breathe the air she breathes, touch her hand as I make a point. She listens to me! If Glory there is, this is Glory to me.

Hypatia safe at home, Ia'ah and I move slowly along the Street of Gardens, and I am filled with pride that I sit a creature more beautiful by far than anything made by the hand of man, even by Minkah the Egyptian.

Unknown to Hypatia, Orestes awaits me. Seated in his *praetorium* within a building of shining white marble, his notary beside and surrounded by guards, day in and day out, the poor man listens to pleas and supplications. If I were he, which even if asked I would never be, half those whining and waving papers I would bang on the head with their own staffs and half I would kick out the door with my boot.

Some time back, Orestes had asked help from Aurelian, old friend to Synesius, and Constantinople's Prefect. How Aurelian answered caused the words of Orestes to sound as the hiss of water on hot coals: "I am counseled to care for my own city as he cares for his." But a second letter has come, this from Cyril. If our new Patriarch has any more support in the East than Orestes, he would never have written such a unique and curious document. Orestes read it to us, meaning Hypatia and I, more than once, savoring every word. As boastful as it is cringing, as demanding as it is giving, Cyril has backed down. Hypatia called it a triumph of irony.

Orestes also wishes private words with Felix Zoilus. Felix is exceedingly pleased. What could Orestes want with Felix but a crusher of bones and a buster of heads...which means money. As I do not rejoin the brotherhood, Felix does not rejoin the brotherhood. As I do all I can to protect Hypatia, so too does he. Hypatia finds a valuable friend in Felix Zoilus. Felix decided this the night she drank herself stupid so that they could talk as equals.

There stands Felix, a good head taller than all around him, and a good foot wider; even his beard is twice as wide and twice as wild as all others. All skirt the place where he leans on his sun-warmed wall. And there is Orestes, striding along surrounded on all sides by imperial guards. This man stands between Hypatia and all who would harm her. As do I. But I do not command a troop of imperial guard.

I ride Ia'eh. Felix is on foot. Orestes steps into his chariot. "By Pluto, Minkah! Listen to this! Cyril waddled into my private chambers, not alone, of course, not alone. With him came a man with a face so white I thought him embalmed..." Felix looks up. Again, Peter the Reader. "And a monk of some beauty, even dignity." Felix winks at me. I know what he means by it. Isidore walks openly with Cyril. "He held out a book of Gospels, saying 'Take it! Accept its truths. Honor your God, and then we shall be friends and equals as is wished for by God.' But I knew if I took his Bible, I would not be showing obeisance to God, but to Cyril, and those who had come as witness would tell all I had done this." Orestes taps his horses. "Come. We will have Cyril show obeisance to me, or Anthemius will know the reason why."

Orestes is off, Felix and the guard trotting as fast as they can, but Ia'eh dances beside the chariot of Orestes. He knows his business; the handling of the reins is finely done. Rounding a corner, the matched bays would run, but there is no going faster, there is no going anywhere at all. Before us, blocking the whole of the street, stand a silent mass of black robed monks. As soon as Felix and the guards of Orestes are caught up with us, behind them appear a second group of silent monks. And here we are, trapped between a hundred men before us and a hundred men behind. Our number, counting Orestes, is no more than a dozen.

Separating himself out from his fellows, as alike as one black snake to another, steps Peter the Reader. "Minkah, brother! Why do you ride with this killer of Christians?"

Ia'eh is made skittish by so many so close. She would rear up under me, but I lean over so that I might whisper in her uneasy ear. My whisper is for all to hear. "Why does Peter the Reader, who honors Christ who preached love for all, show nothing for all but hatred?"

He calls me thief and spy and a bugger of men, and is through with me, turning instead to shout out to all who stand before us and behind us, "This Prefect came to us claiming to be Christian."

Orestes, no coward, is also no fool. We are vastly outnumbered here, his men no match for so many whose knives are no longer hidden, or who bend low for loose stones in the street. "Atticus," he cries so that all may hear him, "Bishop of Constantinople, baptized me Christian before the Emperor Theodosius II and before the blessed Pulcheria. I have killed no Christians."

"You kill Christians by allowing Jews to kill Christians!" Peter struts about once he has said this, pleased at the sound of it, as are those who have heard it. As one, they shout, "Hah!"

Growling, Felix leaps into the chariot of Orestes, placing his great bulk between Peter and the Prefect. Ia'eh paws the ground as those behind us now move forward, and as they do, Orestes' guards move back. Numbering only ten, most are unseasoned. The eyes in their heads dart here and there, hoping, if it comes to it, to save their own skin. I understand. For little in return, much is demanded.

From out of the mass one has stood forth, as young as I when first I was seduced by Peter, to say the following with perfect assurance: "The Prefect refused to clasp the book of Gospels. I am Ammonius who needs no more proof than this. He lies!" In his hand, the youth holds a stone the size of his fist. "Admit not Christ, but the devil lives within you!"

Orestes, no Cyril, hiding behind fat and mother and monks, stands all the taller. "I am no pagan, boy, and you are no Christian, for no follower of the true Christ would do as you do."

Before another word is spoken, Ammonius throws his stone. The crack of rock meeting skull stuns all. A spray of bright blood covers half the face of the astonished Orestes and half that of the outraged Felix, as Orestes falls senseless, if not lifeless, to his knees. Roaring as a bear roars, Felix leaps from the chariot, plowing his way through suddenly frightened monks, running straight for Ammonius, no matter a hundred more stand near him. Confused, they do not advance, they do not retreat...and none dare Felix. As for me, drawing my short Roman sword, I wheel Ia'eh to face those hundred behind us, and in so doing I see Peter the Reader who sees me. As a cur, he bares his long yellow teeth and our guard disappears through doors along the street. By this, only Felix and I stand against all.

And here we will die, Orestes the Prefect of Alexandria and Minkah the Egyptian and Felix Zoilus the Great. Even my beloved Ia'eh will die.

We do not die.

All the while, though we could not see them through the mass of monks behind and in front, the people of Alexandria have been gathering, until they number many more than Peter's monks. As most do not, these do not love Cyril. Wielding whatever they find: shovels, stakes, sticks, the canes of the old, they drive all away but Ammonius who cannot escape the headlock of Felix. The youth's robes drip with blood, for Felix has bitten off his ear.

Many who save us are Christians.

Orestes lives through this day and he lives through the night. But Ammonius lives only long enough to endure a torment even I, once *Parabalanoi*, shudder to watch. The dunce of a boy dared attack a Roman Prefect. As Ammonius hangs in chains, Orestes might live or he might die, but whichever, the Empire's retribution is most delicately done. Does not this boy's faith say: thou shalt not kill? In the Egyptian *Book of Coming Forth by Day* it is written that to enter the afterlife one must be able to swear: "I have not murdered or given such an order."

I, Minkah, who have murdered and ordered others to murder, will never pass into the afterlife—unless Hypatia is right. All live forever, all are divine. All only dream they live in body. But I say, living forever does not appeal. One short life is hard enough.

The thing that was Ammonius is dumped on Cyril's doorstep from the back of a donkey cart. Cyril cries aloud and thumps his chest, ordering others to gather up the mess and to lay it out on a prominent slab in Alexandria's largest church, a piteous martyr to his holy faith. Moments later, Christians are already filing past the gruesome display, weeping. Candles are already lit, chanting already heard. Cyril then writes not one, but a dozen letters to Constantinople.

One morning soon after, what was once an ardent youth, is gone from its slab. Who saw it go? No one I know.

The response could not be favorable. But what can Cyril expect? In the form of the Prefect, the Emperor himself is attacked.

As for the name of Ammonius the monk, it has vanished from Cyril's lips.

THE DYING OF THE LIGHT

Summer, 414

Hypatia of Alexandria

I was mistaken. The work I thought would take the rest of my life is done. All I believe to be worthy I have written down and all that I honor I place beside it. I have the women to thank for this. My salon has forced me to think in ways I have never thought before. Sharing with women the books of the Labyrinth, I am made to see them differently and it is this difference that changes me. All my life I have depended on logic, I have been entirely Greek. In my salon, I have become an Egyptian, a Sumerian, an Indian. To be all these at once is to use all that I am at once.

In the Book of Seth of Damascus, he writes that the Magdalene called what Lais knew "Glory." Other names live on other tongues, but all mean what she meant: a direct experience of the Divine. How came she and Jesus to *know* Glory was long in the seeking and fire in the learning. It changed everything; it changed nothing. The woman was content to *know*. But Jesus was driven to succor the poor and solace the suffering, giving his life to teach that to awaken to Glory was the birthright of *all*.

I would be as Lais and the Magdalene: content merely to *know*. I would stand in a dark fire, burning with pain, to know Glory as Lais knew it, as the Magdalene knew it, as Jesus knew it.

I am only Hypatia. I have finished my book, that one that contains all I am. I preserve the papers found in the Labyrinth. Though my work is of no lasting importance, it was mine to do.

Once again, a library forms in Alexandria, housed in the Agora. It is Cyril's library, the books within chosen by him. In it, no copies of my new work will ever be found. None will go to the libraries of the once great cities of Antioch or Ephesus or Athens.

Cyril speaks out against me. His black mantles call me witch as do certain highborn women. Yet Cyril, day after day, hides away on the highest benches in my lecture hall. Seth, who taught the Magdalene, said: "All men and all women are angels of light clothed in the cloth of self—but do not know it. Not knowing it is the Dark in the Center of the Soul." Cyril does not know it—and I cannot show him.

All that is left in me, besides my love for Minkah, is the desire is to be as Lais, as the Magdalene. As did they, I would know I am free. As did they, I would *know*. I do not miss the irony. I live through times when freedom as well as gnosis is fading as fast as the last light from a winter's day.

Ia'eh nibbles my arm. Neither lame nor broken in spirit by age, she would have her date and she would have it now. Bia dozes in Desher's stall. Nuri and Nomti, the greys that pull my chariot, stretch out their heads from the stalls across the aisle. Where are their dates? Alone with creatures whose beauty almost transcends this world of illusion, leaning my head against the flank of Ia'eh, I myself feel transcendent. Here, with these, whatever others think of my work, it is enough to have done it. What are the works of man compared to these? Outside my stables there is only confusion and a blind seeking for safety.

All are angels of light—but do not know it.

Minkah has appeared beside me. "Pulcheria is proclaimed Augusta." He rubs first the nose of Nomti, then of Nuri.

"We knew it would happen."

"At fifteen, she is now effectively regent of the East. All know her brother Theodosius a fool."

"This too we knew."

"Did we know that Pulcheria favors Cyril?"

Both Minkah and I talk as if we chat of nothing when in truth we speak of that which means everything. He has crossed to Bia and Ia'eh so he might rub their noses. "It is no surprise."

"Pulcheria is now Empress of the East but as long as

Anthemius lives..."

"We live?"

"Perhaps."

And then we are quiet, my beloved and I, breathing in the breath of our horses. What Minkah says next is as a sudden flight of frightened doves. "Synesius is dead."

My hand closes over the last date, pressing it into my flesh. "Of course he isn't! Only this morning I read a letter..."

"Last night. He died suddenly."

I bury my head in the mane of Ia'eh to hide my shame. How long now has Synesius written and I not written back? How long has he complained that though he will ever love me, I have already forgotten him? But I have not forgotten. *My* work. *My* lectures. *My* salon. Sailing and riding and loving Minkah. Other letters to those with needs more pressing. Or—the truth!—less sniveling, more interesting. For all these reasons, and more, I have put off writing to my faithful Synesius, even when this morning's letter, so full of longing and love, begged that I answer.

"How did he die?"

"A fall from his horse. His brother Euoptius will be made bishop in his place."

Synesius! Companion. Forgive me! And yet, this I also think: ah, but now, freed from the mystery of life, my Companion knows more than I.

Autumn, 414

Jone, youngest daughter of Theon of Alexandria

As he has no one to talk to but Daniel of Gaza and me, though I am merely here to hold a bowl, Cyril addresses himself to his physician and his handmaid.

"You would think," he is saying, "that the Archbishop of Alexandria would deserve God's intimate attention. I myself think more of God than do all others; it seems only fair that God should think more of me."

I assume he is making light of what he endures. I would smile to please him, but just in case he is serious, I remain serious. Seated in an enormous chair, one designed for him, his leg is stuck out so that his huge right foot is supported by a stack of pillows. His foot is bare. It is the big toe on this foot that Daniel of Gaza, the best physician in Alexandria, is inspecting. But not touching. If he were to touch the swollen red toe of Cyril, Cyril would scream. Apparently what ails Cyril is a thing called gout and causes excruciating pain. Daniel has long since discovered what happens when Cyril screams. If a poultice of honey and wine and barley flour is needed, it is Jone who will administer it. And Cyril will scream.

But I am used to hearing Cyril scream and he is used to screaming. Cyril, in pain, has often been known to return pain for pain, so I am as well used to smearing on the poultice as fast as fast, and then jumping back before I am slapped.

There seems no cure for Cyril's gout; one day a thing of the past, the next day it is his entire present.

His mother knows no scruples at all. Sweeping into the room, Theophania glances at his toe, simpers at Daniel who is as usual deeply impressed, and sits herself down by the side of her son. "The Prefect of Alexandria has stopped attending church. And do you know why?"

Cyril sighs. "Of course Orestes does not show himself in a church. I know of two reasons and both are self-evident. First, he might be killed. I guide, but do not entirely control, my interesting followers. Second, if Jesus himself had baptized Orestes, he is still no Christian. He favors Jews. He did not grasp the Gospels. He killed a man of God. Really, mother. How obvious."

Theophania adjusts the sheer orange linen of her dress so becomingly Daniel begins to sweat and I to seethe. "It's because of that woman."

"By woman, mother, you mean Hypatia the daughter of Theon?"

"I do. I tell everyone. Everyone tells me. By now, who does not know?" Theophania flings up an arm which displays the fine line of her painted and powdered shoulder. "The woman weaves magical spells that confuse and confound the poor man. That toe, I could have it cured in an instant. A certain sorceress I..."

"Mother! Must I call guards to throw you out of my room?"

"Oh, Cyril, my darling boy. You wouldn't dare!"

"Daniel! Call my guards."

Laughing, Theophania flees on golden shoes. Daniel of Gaza did not so much leave, as escape. Which leaves me and

Cyril and his swollen toe.

"Jone, cover my foot."

"Yes, Holy Father."

"Then help me to my chest."

"Yes, Holy Father."

I know what we do now. Now Cyril will play with pure gold *solidus*, hundreds and hundreds of gleaming coin. How much does it weigh? More than he can lift. How much is it worth? More than he can spend. All this gold was gathered by Theophilus. But for now, to distinguish himself from his profligate uncle, Cyril cannot use it.

"I find solace in gold, Jone. God created it, then secreted it away in the earth for men to find. And once we found it, surely he meant its beauty to soothe us and to prove his love?"

"Yes, Holy Father."

"But more than gold provides me solace. I think of the monks of the Nitria. Hundred and hundreds of them, and all to be relied upon—trust Peter the Reader for that. Trust even Isidore. Educated by no less than your sister, yet there he is, coated in the dust of the desert, huddled in hot black wool, for company the snarls of ignorant men, and for his belly, roasted vermin. A man who would go to such lengths for his faith—eleven years of vile discomfort to both body and mind!—will go to such lengths for his bishop. Add to this, the *Parabalanoi*, ever the hidden might of our church."

"Yes, Holy Father."

"God's position is strong here. With these to back me, it will grow stronger still. What is gout? A small punishment for some small transgression? If so, I shall learn from it, and by learning, the pain shall leave me."

"Yes, Holy Father."

I have helped him dress and then helped him into his bed, a huge thing of many pillows. And as he lies there, thinking his holy thoughts, a thought comes to me. It is time. Somehow I know it is time.

"I have something to tell you."

"Yes."

"I have told no one else."

"Yes?"

"I have kept it a secret."

"Would you mind telling *me*?"

"My sister has papers."

No matter the pain in his toe, Cyril sits up. I see he would hear of Hypatia. I am as used to this as his screaming.

"There remains in my sister's house one whose ear I have. This one tells me Hypatia has finished a book long in the making."

"Hypatia is forever writing books few can make heads or tails of. A sane man would have no interest."

I allow myself a quick uplift of eye and a quicker unholy thought. If Cyril had used the word "slow" rather than "sane," I would agree. I am only a cuckoo in the nest, yet that nest contained birds as far above the common man as an eagle above a sparrow. "This is not on mathematics or geology or astronomy or..."

"Enough of what it is not. What is it?"

"Philosophy, as well as what she terms history, based on the work of forbidden books, especially one that is claimed to be composed by one called Mary Magdalene."

"She *has* such a book?"

"She has."

"And she has written her own book concerning what is said in an obviously counterfeit book of this woman?"

"Yes, Holy Father."

"I need these books." With tremendous drama, Cyril points a finger fat as a cattail. "And you will get them for me. Immediately."

I have long since decided Cyril need never know of the unlost library—with his bulk, the news could kill him—but once I'd decided to tell him of Hypatia's work, I'd formulated a plan. "Of course, Holy Father."

Hypatia of Alexandria

Alexandria dies before our eyes. It breaks our hearts and threatens our freedom, such as there is left of freedom.

Minkah calls my house the House of Hypatia. Here gather bankers and businessmen, members of consortiums who own land for miles around, ship owners, wine and grain merchants, lawyers, orators, the *archontes:* holders of public office, certain of my students who are one or more of these things, come to stand or to sit or to pace, all the while talking of Cyril. Some are Jews, some "pagans," full half are Christian even so far as priests. One is Timothy himself, cheated of his bishopric by

Cyril. All are resigned. Long accepted as one more belief in our city of many beliefs, we come finally to accept Christianity taking precedence over all others by imperial decree. But to accept its demand that it enter our minds and there dictate our thoughts under penalty of banishment, even death! None, not even those of us Christian, find this tolerable. And to have it, through such as Cyril, govern not only a people's search for meaning, but the way a man conducts every aspect of his life—impossible! Timothy, honored in my house, seems older each time he visits. "If Alexandria sickens and dies, so too my Church sickens and dies. Cyril is as a plague."

From my place by our pool, I watch those who pace and speak. Nildjat Miw watches fish. If not for Miw, some would offer their sleek wet noses for stroking.

I have asked: why not meet in the house of Orestes or Timothy whose business this truly is? They reply: Cyril's spies are everywhere. If so many are seen so often at the home of Timothy or Orestes? I have replied: if the spies of Cyril are everywhere, then they are also here. All smile and shake their heads. Hypatia of Alexandria is beyond reproach. Those who come could be attending lectures. They could be students. They could be anything. I concede. They could be anything. But I do not rejoice. And I do not miss the look on the face of Minkah. If I am witch, this can be borne. If I am traitor, this threatens our house.

Hours ago, my "guests" left in a great clatter of voice and horses. I lie awake, covered up to my chin for the night grows chill, Nildjat Miw curled round my head. She growls in her sleep. I neither growl nor sleep. I think of my work. Do I have it copied and sent to those I trust? Augustine, Flavius Anthemius, Olinda, Catherine the widow of Synesius, Galla, who has wed her barbarian king and now lives in Barcelona, old Companions who hold important posts at the courts of Theodosius II and Honorius, if court the latter still has—but could my gift endanger them? Do I keep hidden the one copy written by my own hand, having not yet decided what I do? If I hide my work and all that Isidore found in the labyrinth, where do I hide it? I think of my house. There are earthquakes. There are great waves. There are fires. Nothing is hidden from these. And can any escape from Cyril's legion of spies?

I do not toss and I do not turn, but lie still as death in my bed. Miw no longer growls low in her throat. As still as my cat in the night, do I mistake a slight movement along the hall, one that passes my door? If so, who else but Minkah come to see that I breathe as I would know he breathes—and I think to call out, to assure him I live, to ask that he enter my bed, when my voice dies in my throat. It could not be Minkah for my beloved would not make such sounds. These are slight, quick, furtive.

Does a thief pad by my half-open door? Or one who has come to ensure I shall never awaken again? As if this were not enough, scarcely breathing, I remember my work. Of all nights, on this night I neglected returning the codices to their wooden chest. I did not lock my *armaria.*

Nildjat Miw does not lie still as I lie still nor does she wait. Up and streaking for the door before I can even think to stop her—by the eye of Bast, if she is hurt, if she is killed! Year after year, Father lay abed, hiding from a world grown dark. I am not my father. Before Miw is out my door, I am up and after Miw. And as I go, I take up the knife kept under my pillow.

A murderer takes only my life, a thief only my goods, but an agent of Cyril might take my life's work!

Barefoot, my hair wild from the restless tossing of my head, I make no noise as I move swiftly down cold steps of black obsidian, following Miw who follows the faint light from below. If *Parabalanoi,* then he has come for Minkah. But Miw does not pause at Minkah's door and the light is nowhere near. It shines out from my workroom where my work lies loose on my mother's green table.

Knife in hand, muscles tensed for whatever comes, I slip through the arched door, guarded by Thoth and by Seshat, only to stop as if I have walked into a wall. There stands my thief. An open satchel in one hand, in the other a scroll—one of the Magdalene's, transcribed by her greatest friend, Seth of Damascus—and next to, shading the flame of a small candle, Ife the African, grown old in the service of the family of Theon.

My thoughts burn to ash.

Minkah is suddenly behind me, his own knife drawn, Nildjat Miw stands on the table, her tail violently twitching, but no matter that she faces us all, no matter that she is most horribly surprised and most shamefully caught, Jone leaps for me, crying out: "I do God's work! Why does He stop me!"

Should she mean me mortal harm or merely mortal sorrow, I drop my knife, hear it clatter on the stone of the floor, remain still as my sister beats at me until both she and I are exhausted, for I will not turn my body from her blows or from her hatred. And all the while Minkah holds ready his knife until Jone, without satchel or papers, but a face grown gaunt with torment, turns and runs from a house that is ever and always hers.

No more would I punish Ife than I would Jone, for Ife has ever pitied my sister and given what she could give. But when I look she too is gone.

Minkah and I sit in the window Lais once sat in, our faces lit by the stars and then by the rising of the sun. By the time it stands full above the rim of the earth, as round and as red as a pomegranate, it is decided between us. My work must rest with the Great Library. It must live in the caves, forever if that is its fate. Only now do I know its name: *The Book of Impossible Truth*.

I have decided a further thing, a thing I must do alone.

My world dies. Before it is gone forever, I must learn to Live.

Cyril, Bishop of Alexandria

As Bishop of Alexandria, its true Holy Father, first among many, I call for the bearers of my golden litter to halt, causing the bronze litter beside me also to halt, and the enameled litter behind the bronze. I sit up with the help of a slave, and stare at the house before me.

Staring, the voice of my mother comes to my ear as the shriek of a chariot wheel, shrill with irritation. "Cyril! I could have fallen!"

The play we've just seen was not Roman but Greek. Greek plays are nothing but talk. Roman plays are all action: limbs lost, women raped, men buggered, buttocks bared, cocks waggled, and blood everywhere, squirting like milk from teats. I should have told her it was Greek. That way, she would not have come.

I ignore her. Two years firmly clamped to the Throne of Mark, sending out decrees and edicts to all of Egypt and to Libya, I now ignore Theophania, sister to the deceased Theophilus and mother to myself. If *she* is irritated, *I* am nearing exasperation. Could I send her away, a house in Canopus, order that she never return? But her voice would still reach me: letters, messengers, the gossip of others. Could something more permanent be arranged? Interesting question.

Time enough for that. I turn to my friend, the skeletal Hierax, dwarfed in the litter beside me. I know I am huge. But is this not as God made me? "That house, the one lit like a palace. The courtyard seethes with noise and upset. I recognize faces. There and there! And there! See them? Christians of influence! Who lives in this house to have so many guests of import?"

Hierax is surprised I do not know, but I cannot know everything. If I trust anyone, and I do not, I trust Hierax who bears scars from Orestes that will never fade. Answering, he keeps his high voice flat. Bothersome thing to know one is feared by all. But also exhilarating. "That is the House of Hypatia, Cyril. She is doted on and worshipped."

I show no surprise at Hierax' answer, though I am surprised, and not only because I did not know the house. It is how the house affects me. Unless ordered to, none comes to the House of Cyril—lately the House of Theophilus, and before that the home of rich nameless Greeks. None come happily. No horses clatter in my courtyard. No litters are strewn about awaiting their occupants. No voices are raised in greeting. My halls are not filled with guests, my atrium not filled with discussion and praise, the room in which I dine each night is empty of all save myself. In short, I am not doted on nor am I loved.

My heart shrinks in my chest until it feels the size of a pebble, some small thing rolling at the edge of the sea, back and forth, going nowhere, meaning nothing, a stone among stones. I think of Jone, whey-faced and cringing as she told me she'd failed to acquire her sister's papers, but swore she would not fail twice. Physical violence is a crudity left to others, yet at the whispered news I'd flung out my arm and slapped her. The sound of the slap was meaty. Jone is no more than meat. And yet, could it be I am no more than Jone? Hypatia is loved. Jone is not loved. I glance at Theophania, bitch mother and witch. To think of myself as I think of Jone brings me to the point of madness. Staring at the brilliant house of the brilliant Hypatia, I feel myself a homeless cur in the streets. As a dog, I would howl.

And there and then, as suddenly as if God were speaking directly into my ear, I know my enemy. Not Orestes. Not Timothy. Not Flavius Anthemius. These are mere mortals. It is Hypatia, goddess, pagan, loved beyond reason, a woman. Only a demon has the power to stand between God's earthly emissary, Cyril of Alexandria, and the love of the people of Alexandria. Only a demon could have tempted me to listen to her, day after day. Only a demon could have entered my thoughts, night after night. If I am the emissary of God, and I *am*, Hypatia of Alexandria is the emissary of what is not God, in other words, Satan.

"Walk on!"

Startled, my bearers lurch forward, coming close to tipping my enormous bulk into the street. I see my mother think to laugh, but Theophania is not entirely insensitive. Laughter would be a mistake.

φ

Hypatia of Alexandria

Because Orestes visits the City of the Dead on the very day Minkah and I inspect the work on my family's tomb—Father's artisans do what they ever do; take twice as long and cost twice as much—we find ourselves visiting with him, trailed by his guard, tripled now after the adventure of Ammonius the monk and his well-thrown rock. Behind these, follows a host of those paying court. Away we all go, leaving the riot of living as we pass under the Moon Gate. Guests from Canopus, from Carthage, from Memphis, lift their robes in vain hope of avoiding the dust. It is no easy thing to step around great openings in the earth that descend five or six levels down, no easy thing to breathe the incense, thick as smoke.

Kastor, once neighbor to Orestes, and fresh from Constantinople, trips along speaking to us of Aelia Pulcheria.

"No matter the hour," he says, at the same time yipping in surprise as the gaunt head of a gravedigger appears at the top of a spindly ladder, "the Imperial Palace of Constantinople is nothing but fasting and praying. Men and woman are kept apart, even those married. Children are not allowed to be seen for fear of levity before God. Those who can flee, do flee. My family and I are one of the lucky ones. We had money. But those who do not, fast and pray to keep their heads."

"If not for Anthemius," asks a nervous magistrate from Clysma, a city near the Red Sea, neither of which I have ever seen, "how far would she go?"

Not Kastor but Orestes answers: "Pulcheria rules the Emperor Theodosius II completely. Only Flavius Anthemius stands between the pious madness of a ruthless Pulcheria and the impious ambition of a ruthless Cyril."

A pall has fallen over what is already somber. Minkah's voice, meant to lighten, causes only further gloom. "Fanatics are not to be trusted, not even to act in their own best interests." But before he is finished speaking, a messenger finds us, handing a note to Orestes.

Whatever is written causes the face of our Augustal Prefect to turn white and his lips to thin. I place my hand over his. It is cold and still. "Orestes, what is it?"

In answer, he thrusts the note into my hand. I quickly read: *To Orestes, Prefect and Governor of Egypt. This day we learn that Flavius Anthemius is put to death by order of Pulcheria Augusta, for reasons of high treason.* It is signed by a name I do not know, but is surely one of Orestes' spies, for all men of power have spies. I read it twice more, and then I read it aloud.

There is nothing but more silence in the City of Silence and Death.

Now I take Minkah's hand and hold it. I glance round at the graves. How great the darkness.

THE SEVENTH GATE

The first month, 415

Minkah the Egyptian

I, Minkah the Egyptian fool, was born as most men and will die as most men, never seeing more of the world than I have already seen. I will never read all its books or drink all its wines or be father to those taking the place of myself. I have asked no woman to give over her life to me, not even my darling, though I have known the bodies of many women. I have done my share of killing. I have made certain those I love were not killed. Those I would kill from pique, I have not killed. All these things and more are part of the story of Minkah, but I am ready to leave this place. The dark world I knew is darker now. Man himself is darker, a thing I did not think possible. I grow sick of it all.

But there is one thing I have which no other has. I have the love of Hypatia of Alexandria.

Even so, I, who have never gone in fear, go now in fear—not for myself, but for her. With the death of Flavius Anthemius, the raging bladder that has squeezed itself through the door of the House of Theophilus and stuffed itself into his glittering robes of high office, is now free to act. The ambition of Cyril soars higher than hawks as he has ever had the ear of Pulcheria. Not only is the usurper mad but mad too is the sister of a feeble minded boy—and both are bad. Pulcheria is much the madder, and by virtue of her station, much the more dangerous.

Men who have swallowed the moon creep and crawl

through our deserts as scorpions creep and crawl. But where some cause only themselves to suffer, Pulcheria, once merely a wraith in rain, is now the rain itself...pouring down on all. By her unholy god's unholy wrath, that I could get my hands on that brainless priest-ridden girl—the life she so hates would be over with one red slash. She would be with her god and he, poor *sōpiō*, with her.

But to send Pulcheria to her "heaven," I must leave Hypatia, and that I cannot do. There have been mumblings and grumblings. Felix Zoilus tells me she is called witch by those not fit to look even once on her face. They say she is devoted to magic and astrolabes and musical instruments. Like her father, does she not believe in the sorcery of stars and the witchery of dreams? Shouting at the top of his voice, a man stood in a crowded square near the Port of the Lake: "Blame the pagan woman! She stands between Cyril and Orestes! If not for her, there would be peace in our streets and our hearts!" Felix cut out his tongue. But that is Felix. What can be done?

What fools, men—their foolishness drives them towards evil as fish are driven towards nets. Of all who dwell in this city, none is as dark as Cyril, and none so light as Hypatia. Who among those who shout and those who listen fathom even one portion of the beauty that is her mind or her spirit? Yet, by the wiles of Cyril, they would turn on her, a treasure rarer than rubies.

Hypatia, in her way, is also a fool. Living in mind, she knows nothing of greed or of lust or of envy or the rage of ignorance aligned with the fever of ambition. Before these things, she is helpless. What she does not recognize she has no defense against. In all my life I have known only one who was not a fool. The first daughter of Theon knew what Hypatia does not know. The defense of Lais was to understand and by understanding, to forgive. Hypatia is not as Lais. Nor am I.

Raising a mob is as easy as pissing. A few choice words, a few grievances blamed on some other, a mention of satanic rites. The *demos* fear everything now...omens they are forbidden to believe in, but believe in as strongly as ever: crows, weeping statues, eclipses of the sun. No one will sneeze to the left. All that is needed is a finger pointed, a call to the gods for "justice," and away all gallop, baying for fresh hot blood.

Year after year, Theophilus kept his dogs off Hypatia knowing she was more loved than he. Cyril is not Theophilus. Those called "great" are capable of great evil in pursuit of what they believe great good...by which they mean good for them. I suspect Cyril of great evil, done not by him, but for him. My beloved is not unaware of her danger, but she is innocent of the unthinking fools urged to consider her not with boundless civic pride, but as "the pagan woman."

The second month, 415

Hypatia of Alexandria

Her belly full of stars, black Nut arches over the earth. Fifteen years have come and gone since I last saw the dark ridge where Minkah has hidden the library and the words of Lais sleep.

Bia is easy and quiet as I gaze up at the stars of Nut, worlds as our world, each lost in a dark as sleek as ink, and Mind throughout all.

Beside me, my beloved sits astride Ia'eh. Between us stands Nuri, dim white by starlight, carrying on his back baskets filled with the books I have come to leave with all else waiting deep in the earth.

What I do now I must do alone. Minkah and I have argued long and hard. He would leave Alexandria. To go where, I ask? Dark wings unfurl over all. And to be born again, I must hurry...for what comes now, comes fast. Minkah is stricken, but does as he has ever done: understands.

For twelve years, I have read and reread the words of those who *know*. I have learned it is not something I can learn. No one can teach me it. If I *knew*, I could not teach it myself. How to give to others a direct, immediate, *personal* experience of Divine Consciousness? It cannot be done. It is not meant to be done. Such a thing is a gift given to the self by the self.

Some find it in illness or in grief or through exalted joy. Some suddenly rise through the juice of the poppy. Some spend a lifetime of disciplined seeking. But none have found it through intellect. And did Lais not tell me this...and was I not deaf to her?

A wind has risen so suddenly it causes the sands to circle and dance. The horses snort and toss their heads, dancing with the wind and the sand.

"A storm!" shouts Minkah, "and before it a whirlwind!" The

stars wink out, one by one by one, and in their place come fast moving clouds, clouds like ships of black pitch sailing over a sea of tossing sand. "Hypatia, turn away! We must beat the wind."

My beloved is right. I must beat the wind. I need not ask her: Bia runs as she has never run, though we seem miles from the ridge of dark stone and the caves in the ridge and the books in the caves, and the rain comes like the lashing of loose linen sails, rain enough to fill the gullies and depressions in an instant, rain enough to drown us for there is now more water than air. Nuri, attached by a short lead shank to my saddle, follows—if he screams in the wind or the rain, I cannot hear him, nor, glancing back, can I see him, though I know he is there by the tension on the lead. But of Minkah, I see and hear nothing.

If he does as I ask of him, he does not follow.

Leaning close over the neck of Bia, my face in her mane, I sit high on her back, riding with one hand wrapped in the black of her rain-wet mane, and one hand gripping Nuri's slick lead.

What was rain turns to ice and the ice falls as white stones and the cold white stones are as big as pomegranate seeds and then as large as a nail on the thumb of Felix Zoilus, and Bia leaps forward with such abrupt and sudden power my grip is torn from both her mane and from the lead of Nuri and I would fall from her back but, somehow, I do not. And then, as suddenly as insight, the wind stops and the falling stones cease and I find Bia has entered a vast and echoing cave. Behind us, Nuri's welcome complaint sounds. Bats too have streamed home in tremendous numbers, seeking as we sought, relief from the raging tumult. Blessed be Bia who has run faster than the rain and the stones could fall for all remains well in Nuri's baskets. I build a fire by the opening of Bia's cave.

For strength, I eat a thick paste of olives and dates, feed my horses from the sack Nuri has also carried, watch the great star of the evening fade as the sky lightens in the east.

Lais lies in a cave facing west...as does this cave. All that I do I do with trust. All that occurs is meant to occur. Bia has chosen this cave, therefore it is the right cave. The thing I do will be done though I die in the doing. But I do not come unprepared. For three days I fasted and while fasting made of silver the transcendent *aqua spiritus*. On the third day I drank my Spiritual Water as the full-faced moon shone down upon my head, and I called out to Inanna: *Let me be as you. Lead me out of darkness into silver and Light.*

Bia and Nuri I leave near a seeping spring. Nuri's basket on my back, two lanterns and a sealed jar of water fastened to its strapping, the weight is far from light, but I can walk and I can carry, for days if I must. Looping the curl of rope over my shoulder, covering my hair with a scarf, I wear a youth's rough tunic, thick riding boots, and a girdle round my waist. In this, I keep all else I will need.

For one moment I am Isidore: afraid to stay, afraid to go. Bia shakes her head, snorts down her nose. Chided, I slowly walk east as the sand becomes gravel becomes rough stone becomes dung. It grows darker and darker still, and even with care, I must occasionally slip on the droppings of bats, or snap the bodies of beetles. I am alone and I hesitate to be alone, but I do not stop. I arrive at a place where I must pass beyond the little light that dares come this far. One last look at Bia and Nuri, nose to tail, asleep and I enter a tunneled darkness of twisted stone.

By lantern-light, I come on a rock that seems as a broken-backed slave on a block. Then a raven of a rock, turning its black head full round on its black neck. Father would rejoice at sight of a raven: ravens lead towards revelation.

It is a revelation that my world has come to the hiding of books. It is a revelation that I, Hypatia, lover of Mind, seek revelation.

The path of the raven is no path at all. It is a series of ledges, some that rise, some that fall. I come upon rocks that appear to move or to breathe or to change in some subtle way. I stumble in darkness, fall into what I cannot see, grasp blindly for handholds. But I hear. Sighs as if crowds attend who regret my choice, the rip of cloth as I tear my tunic against a jut of stone, the rapid chee-chee-chee of I cannot imagine what, the sound as if something large has rolled over, disturbed in its sleep. My lantern shows me nothing but what is directly before me, and only so much of that.

Then an outcrop of rock, sharp and deeply ridged, set at the edge of an abrupt drop into deeper darkness. There is a ledge I must reach by squeezing between rocks.

Though not the rock Minkah used, it is one like. As he did, I loop my rope round it, then about my waist, gripping the rope with one hand above me and the other below. Slowly I ease myself down, slightly loosening my grip so that the rope slips through my hands a little at a time. I know my knots... yet suddenly the rope loses its hold—and I fall into an abyss, but only far enough to break my jar of water and to send a jolt of hideous pain up my arm.

Though no one sees and no one hears, I hide my pain and the unease fed by darkness. I will *not* grow confused by anxious imaginings nor will I wander sightless. This is the world blind Didymus knew. He would not be afraid. I must be as Didymus who saw without sight.

Though my water jar fell on stone, my basket and lantern fell on sand. By lantern light, I see there are no jars here as tall as a man, no gentle niches packed with smaller jars, no paintings on walls. There is nothing but rock and more rock as dark as Ket's dark water.

This is not the cave I seek. The storm and Bia have led me to another. And I cannot climb back. I must believe this cave goes on, no matter its twists and turns, and somewhere there will be a place for my books. As for me, I will find my way back to the sun or I will not. Closing my eyes in the quiet and the dark lit by only one lantern, I cradle my arm and I breathe. In the dark behind my eyes, I imagine that Lais is with me. If Lais is with me, all is well.

My eyes open to a way through rock as if the rock was once one and, by some tremendous agency, became two. This is the way I take, and as I do the crevice becomes narrow, until finally I come on a place so narrow, I must push my basket of books before me, only to follow on when they are safely through.

Another crevice yawns open beyond the first. But the way is forked. Which shall I take? There seems the slightest sense of movement, a flow of air leading to the right and down. I go right. And down.

Yet again I stand at the edge of a precipice. My lantern, its oil growing low, shows me I need no rope to make my way down, for this wall does not drop but slopes, is not black or grey, but the color of amber. It glows in my lantern light. Foothold by handhold by foothold, I make my down and down, until I am abruptly stopped by my girdle snagged in a slice of amber rock and no matter that I move this way or that, it will not loosen. I cut it away—a feat which comes so suddenly I fall a second time, dropping my knife. This time a part of me I would not hear whispers: you are lost, daughter of Damara, and you will not be found...and with this, I lose my slim grasp on certainty and with it my grip—and fall again.

I land hard on my hands and my knees...and my arm, which before hurt as a tooth, hurts now as the thrust of a knife. In agony I curl where I fall. Rising on blooded legs to stand on blooded feet, my tunic no more now than a rag, I find this new place faintly glows as if a half moon brooded behind gated clouds. Where is my knife? I search in the silvery half light, but do not find it.

One by one, I have in some way or another been stripped of everything vital. What I was I am no longer. It seems that the farther I go the less I become. This is a world never found in my books, a place no myth has told me of, no poem. Nothing that my eyes see or my ears hear or my mouth tastes touches on the world above. I stand amid tortured columns of color, some rising from the floor of this cave beneath caves, some dropping down from the roof, some that both rise and fall and all are the color of roses, of the sea over white sand, of sulfur, of lemons, of oil on water, of the uncurling frond of a fern.

I am hurt. My water and food are gone. I have lost all save for the books I bring here, for it is here I see I will leave my paper ships, where the work of Valentinus, of Seth and his Magdalene, of unnamed poets, of my own, will rest, just as I will rest...for I know no way to ascend from this place which is more beautiful and more terrible than the abode of the dead. Formed between a column of faintest smoke and a column of a shell's pink heart, there is a small cavern the color of the eye of Nildjat Miw. It is just the size to contain all that my baskets hold. Kneeling on surprising sand as white as milk, I read the words of the Magdalene one last time. On aged paper, brittle and dry, the voice is yet fresh as linen. *I wonder,* she writes, *could not the visible world be God speaking to itself?*

Having hidden what I have come to hide, I might choose now to die or to walk away as if I knew where I might go. If I have accomplished this, if I am in a place I can never leave, a place where my bones will keep company with my words, and if I am never to know what I have come here to know, this is as it must be. Lais would accept what must be. In this, at least, I can be as Lais. But I will not simply lie down. I will live until I die.

I walk. My arm aches as it first ached. The cuts to my feet are like hungry mouths. I carry only my rope for rope is all that is left me. I make my way up and up, climbing if I cannot walk, crawling if I can do nothing else. I do not become used to the dark; there is no gradual sightedness. I do not sleep but I dream and the dream I dream is of caves.

In dark perfection, my mind spins endlessly on. Not as blind Didymus, trusting in a faith "other than himself." Not as Augustine, afraid yet suffused with love of his god. I am plagued by imagining. Goddesses rise and fall before me. Miw threads through my legs. Desher runs ahead. Numbers appear on my skin, burning. Shapes trip me up. Paper folds and unfolds. My hands shake. I cannot remember when last I carried my rope. Food means nothing; it is thirst that torments. I stumble often now. When I stumble I fall more than I do not fall. To rise becomes harder. I find less and less reason to go on. And in great weariness, great despair, great pain, I begin to know myself. The world above calls me wondrous. The world above is illusion. This is the true world for here nothing *is*. Nothing distracts. I am nothing but fear and doubt. If I survive, what do I survive *for*? The world I have known fails. All that I have valued fades. All that I love is dying. By my life, what has my life meant? What did it serve? I have left nothing behind to mark my place. I have given comfort and solace to no one. Synesius died calling out to me. I did not answer. Minkah loved me. I sent him out into the cold. I thought Isidore unworthy of me and forced his leaving. My father gave me all he could give. In return, I grew ashamed of him. Jone was as a leper. Did I gather her in and offer healing? I killed Lais who I called my own heart. All I have done is learn only to learn this one last true thing. I know nothing. All Valentinus taught, all the Magdalene once said, all I believed of Lais, is no more than a hope born of need that the world has meaning. Here, in this last place, I am become numb to meaning. My heart is broken by truth. Yet, I am fully awake. I am fully aware. Even as I feel the gathering dark, there is a shine to the dark as ebony shines. And it beckons as the dazzling darkness.

Once again, I fall and I will not rise for this is as the Void of Hermes Trismegistus. Here I will be found by death, small and meek and helpless. I am not supple in my understanding nor am I subtle in my dying. There will be no escape. No transformation. I do not become silver. I will not be rescued.

My mind, my prideful mind, plagues me to the last. I see without light that I am as a carcass hung on a hook, a corpse left to rot in a hole hastily dug. And my mind rages, it *rages*. I cover my head with my arms. I am unbound and undone and I cry aloud for how sad my plight, how lonely my end. I can fall no farther. There is no pain greater, no sorrow deeper. I am lost to myself, lost to all those I have loved.

I am not Lais. Let me therefore be what I am. I am nothing, Inanna! Let me go! And with this great crying out, I understand as my life falls away that there is left only a giving over, a shedding, an emptying out. I let go the hold on that which I knew as purpose and desire and the force that drives a life. I let go the *me* of me. I do not think to do this, but rather surrender, and it is done. I am snatched away from me and suddenly I fall out of myself, and then I fall into myself—completely.

I do not imagine Nildjat Miw. And yet she is here, every hair, every claw, every drawing in and letting out of breath. Miw sits before me as a sphinx sits, perfectly still, perfectly attentive.

"Cat!" I say, surprised into imbecility.

Miw opens her mouth, yawning so great a yawn her rasped tongue curls and her white teeth gleam. And when she is done with this, she speaks...and have I not always understood her speech by tone or by gesture for her words are her own and I do not share them. Not so now. Her language is my language. "Over the years," I hear my cat say, "you have passed through six gates." The heat of Miw, the scent of her strong breath, passes over me. "This is the seventh gate. The seventh gate is the last gate. Welcome, Mistress, to the Great Below."

And then she is twice her size, three times her size, she is as a lion, and in each of her eyes there is the silver crescent of a moon, as molten as the silver in my crucible and their silver flows into mine. In this moment, I am not in body, yet remain entirely myself as my body remains entirely itself...which is what I have made of it. Just as the world and all it contains is what I have made of it, and I am not dead, and I am not let go. In this endless instant of grace, I find I contain All, that I am All, that I AM.

From deepest despair, I am raised to heights unimaginable by intellect.

Everywhere I am embraced by warmth and by light and from the light comes a snaking out of numbers and of stars and of souls that go on forever and forever and forever and in the exact middle of the wheeling snake of light, Hypatia who is not lost but found, and is not tormented by demons for demons there are none, and of torment there is none, and of levels of hell there are none. There is only an infinity of light and the Light is perfect safety and perfect love.

In this same endless moment, I imagine I raise my arms in revelation and my left hand is suddenly gripped and pulled upward. I know this hand as I once knew my own. It is Lais whose laughter sounds in the Light, causing the numbers to scatter and the stars to spin and the souls to sing...and I laugh with Lais. Mathematician, philosopher, woman, human, Hypatia is free of mind. If nothing *is*, then nothing matters, and if nothing matters, where is fear? There is only bliss.

In bliss, I "think" to look along the length of my left arm, and there is the hand of my beloved pulling me up and up and out of Nildjat Miw's Great Below.

Only when Minkah hands me a cloak, do I notice I am once again naked before him.

ETHER

The sixth day of Lent, 415

Cyril, Bishop of Alexandria

It has to be done. I will rid myself of Theophania. And if where I send her isn't far enough, my second choice is somewhere so remote no man need hear her voice again. She is like the mother of Nero, Julia Agrippina, who had sown the seeds that grew into her son's imperial power, then tried to dig them up. But the time is not yet. For now, Mother is useful. Her tongue wags on and on, driving those who listen—and so many listen for who can resist the allure of cleverly detailed slander?—closer and closer to the will of Cyril, the Bishop of Alexandria, which is, of course, God's will.

And if, as Mother claims, the woman is truly a witch, her witchery would rival that of Simon Magus.

Sipping an eastern tea from a tiny eastern cup, I listen to the comforting sounds of Jone moving about, tidying my sleeping chamber, setting out my robes for the day. How in heaven is she sister to Hypatia as well as the remarkable Lais? And yet, though small and slightly sloped from her constantly hanging head and constantly lowered eyes, Jone's mouth is plump enough. The eye, when seen directly, is bright enough, the shape of the chin pleasing, the color high. As for her body—who knows? Devout beyond need, she wears cloth enough to shelter an elephant. Beneath, she could be a sylph. Or an elephant.

Speaking of cloth. Complex business, all this drapery, awkward and heavy. Jewels are damnably heavy. As is cloth of gold. Not to mention hot. And as for the hat! It makes my neck ache just holding it up. It makes my scalp itch. I'm losing my hair. But once so arrayed, I am no longer a jiggling mass of sweating blue-veined fat, my unseen member hidden in folds of flesh, my tits larger than the dugs of Artemis—I am the Emperor of Egypt. Mine is the voice of God in all Africa. As I knew it would be. Uncle knew it too. And tried to stop it, which is why I was never made priest. But Mother took care of that. Even I would not expose my back to Theophania.

On the day God made clear my one true enemy, I set to work. No more humble letters to Orestes. No more petitions to Pulcheria who will grant them, giving me more and more power and more and more choice in how I use my power.

I am not a cruel man, nor am I greedy...unlike Theophilus. Unlike Mother, I am not viciously insane. What I am is essentially practical. I suppose I might also be, like Bishop Athanasius before me, ruthless. But as any good bishop knows, when it comes to the Church, what has to be done, will be done. If a path was cleared on my way to the Throne of Mark due to Mother's skill with pomegranates, what of it? If my winning the election against Archdeacon Timothy, the more popular man, was achieved by Peter the Reader's *Parabalanoi* thumbing knives near voters, what of it? If driving away heretics and Jews causes them hardship and pain, I understand, even sympathize. But such things should have been thought of before becoming Jews or heretics. If I, as bishop, must provide an example by banishing my own mother to some barren isle, so be it. Not that I mind her loss in the least. I've dreamed of it for years. Even so, the principle remains. And now, if another needs removing from my city, then by Mary the Holy Virgin and the Sacred Mother of God, she needs removing. The question of how I might accomplish this was answered only the night before in a meeting with Peter the Reader. Strange fellow. Not my favorite monk. In any case, she will be carried away and left in a place from which she can never return. It seems fair. And practical. If any complain, it will be explained that the woman is "traveling." She has traveled before, she can travel again.

"Jone!" I loathe the sight of the sister of Hypatia, but in certain ways none is more useful than she. "Any further news of the books I asked you for."

Jone hangs her head. "No, Holy Father."

"No matter. Without the woman, there will be as well no books."

I see Jone allows herself to raise her eyes to my face, certain that I do not notice. She is mistaken. I notice. There is that look in her eye again. She is asking: what does he mean "without the woman"? She may not know it, but poor Jone, the least of her father's daughters, still holds some feeling for her sister. It's why she failed at collecting the books. Never mind. When the woman is gone, her books will be gone. I might even allow her to keep some of them. And when she dies, some time from now for she is yet in her prime, her work will be destroyed. But as I said, I am not a cruel man. I would not tell her that.

"Indeed, Holy Father. If Hypatia were not there to guard them, any could enter her house and take them away. But there is Minkah."

"Pah! Minkah. He is one man and I am many men. Neither Minkah nor any friend of Minkah's will cause us trouble. That is already certain. Just think, tomorrow your house is returned to you...and what better use to make of it other than to give it over to the Church!"

"Tomorrow, Father?"

"Tomorrow. Help me into bed. I seem to be having difficulty lifting my right leg. Look, Jone! A star of good omen falls."

Jone, youngest daughter of Theon of Alexandria

Looking as Cyril commands, I am sure I do not see what he sees. I see a small silver dagger that hisses as it falls. I am the daughter of a once famous astronomer who knew when a falling star was either good- or ill-omened. I know nothing of this. Yet this I do know: my feelings towards Hypatia are my own, and I nurse them as a babe is nursed. To hate one's own is one thing—but for another to hate or threaten?

Tonight, when I return to my cell, I will do as I often do: read one letter at random of all those Hypatia has sent me over the years.

Hypatia of Alexandria

"Nildjat Miw, see! A star falls."

My body feels as it has ever felt: bruised knees and cut feet, an aching arm, a small pain that comes and goes in one eye, the familiar gnaw of hunger. Numbers are still an exquisite delight. They are *Summum*, the sum of all creation. Knowledge still absorbs, alchemy still beckons. Life is still an unfolding, the farther we travel the more truth we can comprehend, and to understand the things that are at our door is the best preparation for understanding those that lie beyond. Yet all this is as nothing. I might, at will, know bliss.

Miw heavy in my arms, we pace the atrium. The night is chill with the Christian's Lent, but I am wrapped in warm white wool and Miw is wrapped in striped fur, her eyes limed in black as a cheetah's eyes. We watch a star fall as water falls, flowing down like silver. Passing under the feet of Osiris, it washes over Isis, brightest star in the sky, lost for this moment in silver spray.

I am ravished by sky and star and cat and wool and cold and pain. I *know* what Lais knew. Nildjat Miw struggles in my arms.

"What is it, Miw? Would you catch a star?"

And with this last thing I say to her, who says nothing to me, Nildjat Miw leaps from a window as Paniwi once leapt from a window, and though I look down to the street below, I do not see her.

Miw does nothing but that which suits her. When it suits her, she will return.

The star has left a smear of silver, as a snail on obsidian. I am as slender as the trail of silver light that has come and is gone across the open mouth of the sky.

Tomorrow morning I give a public lecture on Archimedes. Tomorrow afternoon, I will continue discussing geometric optics with my Companions. All know mathematics a divine discipline. Into this discipline I have introduced light. Light, of which visible light is only an aspect, is the formative principle of the universe, both material and spiritual. Somehow, I shall prove it to them. But if I do not, it is of small matter. All do what they set themselves to do.

Tomorrow night I dine with Orestes. This night I lie with Minkah. As all now ravishes me, my beloved ravishes me most.

Where has Nildjat Miw got herself to? She should be back by now.

The seventh day of Lent

Minkah the Egyptian

Felix Zoilus and I meet where Canopic Street passes under Mount Copron on top of which still stands the Temple to Pan—Theophilus had intended to do as he usually did: gut it, steal all worth stealing, then rename it. The Temple to Pan would become the Church of Theophilus.

Cyril the Cunning has other plans. My interest in Cyril's ambitions is as keen as my interest in food once it's eaten. My interest in Cyril's plans to achieve his ambitions interest me more than wine for word reaches me that his plans include Hypatia and those like Hypatia. What that plan might be, I have yet to learn, but I shall.

I wait with Felix, as we do every morning she lectures, in sight of the door that opens onto her stables. As she speaks this morning, Hypatia will soon pass this way, and I, fresh from our honeyed bed, will follow with Felix, keeping watch as she speaks. Felix Zoilus surprises me. He not only watches, he listens. He too has resigned from the brotherhood. Not I, but Felix, as strong and as skilled as ten combined, is a great loss to them.

These days, Hypatia does not speak as she once did. She does not look as she once did. The sound of her voice: gentle and low, reaches to the top of the circling seats. Light streams from her body when I know there is no light. As for her words, I have never heard the like. Those come to hear her talk of numbers or of philosophers, scratch their heads—but not all. Some forget to breathe. And more come, and more, even as Felix warns that the grumblings of the ignorant who do not hear her, grow louder. Because of Hypatia, they say, Alexandria is plagued by demons.

As if he reads my mind, Felix opens his mouth. "Last night, did you see it?"

"See what?"

"The star, like a spear thrown by Osiris!"

I turn to ask him to describe it further as such things portend events, good and bad. But I say nothing for walking towards us is Isidore and behind Isidore, twenty or more *Parabalanoi*. This much is immediately clear. They do not come to wish us well.

"Felix," I hiss. "Prepare!"

Though Felix is huge, his brain is not. Yet this day it works wonderfully well. Before I have done so, he slips his sword from his scabbard, his knife from its sheath, and is waiting beside me, steady and true.

"Isidore," say I, "I thought we should never meet again."

Once the favorite of Theophilus, once almost a bishop, he looks as he ever did, as calculating as one of Hypatia's counting boards, yet now there is an arrow of madness there, buried to its shaft in his eye. Where once this man could be spoken to, such a gift has left him; he listens only to a voice of rage, the one he mistakes for a god. "This, I assure you, Egyptian, will be the last we meet."

And I am suddenly suffused with fear. Not for myself. What do I fear from death? But these, come to kill me, to kill Felix Zoilus, what can it mean? Our deaths mean nothing, but one thing—Hypatia will be alone.

I, who have never run, would run now. I would have Felix run. But before I can move or cause Felix to move, before another useless word is exchanged, Felix Zoilus has cut off Isidore's head. Even marred by surprise, his is a handsome face. But there are many more behind him and I am not entirely sure we can behead them all.

Hypatia of Alexandria

As is done week after week, year after year, a stable lad prepares my chariot. Nuri is eased first behind the wooden yoke at the end of the center pole, to be secured by a leather band around his great chest and through which the leather reins pass over his muscled shoulders. Then Nomti is placed on the far side of the same pole. All is ready.

From the house of Hypatia on the Street of Gardens to the Agora, there is a grid of small busy streets to traverse. Today they are empty of those who usually walk them or work them—and where is Minkah, where Felix, who think I am unaware of them; where is Nildjat Miw who comes each day for years? All this I ask until my chariot turns into the Street of the Pot Makers.

I know immediately who the men are who face me. None are Imperial soldiers who dragged Zenobia through the streets of Rome clad only in chains of purest gold. None are the Emperor Aurelian who freed the warrior queen, though by her actions she had caused him to raze the splendid Bruchion of Alexandria, destroying even the translucent tomb of Alexander. These are Cyril's private army, the monks from the Mountains of Nitria, each hidden in his robe of black. But here they show their faces: ignorant, brutal, half mad faces made hideous with noxious belief, thwarted ambition, repressed sexuality. How ironic these call themselves Christian, that they name themselves after one who would not recognize them. If the man they love stood here speaking of what truly was and truly *is*, they would no more hear him now than any who listened then. They would not hear the companion he loved whose worth is forgotten: Mariamne Magdal-eder, the Magdalene.

And there is the one who swore I would one day meet the maker he claims for me. And I do, in the form of Peter the Reader.

I have no illusions. There will be no golden chains. There will be no emperor to bestow upon me a villa where I might live out my days in peace and beauty. Peter and his men have come to do me great harm. Synesius is gone, as is Bishop Theophilus, as is Flavius Anthemius. There is only Minkah. And Felix Zoilus. But they are not here. Someone has prevented their being here.

Waiting, I find even now though I have died so that I might Live, thoughts rule my mind. To possess understanding—how glamorous this is. How threatening. Men who do not know me, adore me for it. They fear me for it. The love and the fear is in them all, students and strangers, for there are few who do not know of the woman, Hypatia. Letters reach me addressed by no more than the words: *To the Philosopher, Alexandria* or *To the Muse, Alexandria.* Even more than the love, the fear in them isolates me—for none know what they fear.

Those who love me, do not understand what they love. Because they cannot understand, the love they feel does not touch me. I am alone. Even Father could not reach me. I have only Minkah who is not here and will not come in time.

Those who hate, understand even less. They cannot touch me.

Yet here they are now, the haters: the ignorant, the fanatic, those without questions, those who follow, those who believe the answers given by others. In these, a true thought is as alien as the stars. With pity, I watch them come, each trapped in the darkness of a shadowed mind. There is no way out for any, no way home. Even now, I could try to reach them, I *have* tried, but they hide in their secondhand faith, and they do not know they could *know*, do not *hear* their Christ who tried as I to reach them. In this, they are untouchable. Yet I see they mean to touch me. In this time and in this place, they mean to bring me down, to reduce what I am to what they are. Or so they believe. And as they do this thing, they will be filled for a long red moment with the fierce joy of understanding something. They will understand they are penetrating me. It will arouse them. It will heat their loins far beyond their secret longings in the deep of the night. It will make them show their teeth and they will howl like wolves under the moon. And they will know what lies beneath my skin, how my sinews glisten in the sunlight, how my heart beats in its red cave as any heart beats, how my blood flows like the Nile. I shudder, as human as they. There will be blood enough they might swim in it like fish.

And when I am penetrated, laid open like the carcass of a sacrificed lamb, they will look inside and they will ask each of each: where is the soul this one spoke of? Where is the Glory? There is no glory here. Then, running through all like lightning forks in the sky, there will come sudden shame. They will look away from each other. They will grow pale, dropping the bloody shards of the pots they have used on me, dropping the lids of their eyes like someone caught stealing food. They will try to hide that they wipe my red life from their hands. And then, under cover of night, they will burn what they will think they have made of me. And when I am nothing but charred bone and ash, they might forget this day. But I doubt it.

In my chariot, I stand motionless, wearing the white *tribon* of a philosopher, calming my heated horses by a steady hand on their reins, and I wait for them. I could, even now, attempt flight, but there is no room to go other than forward. My horses would suffer their fury. I could seize my skilled knife, leap among them as I leapt among the bandits of Galatia, taking with me at least Peter with his twisted mouth and twisted heart, and probably more. Is Isidore among them? Is Euoptius the brother of Synesius? He is, though he hides himself behind others.

Even in bliss, I know fear. I am afraid I will die screaming.

I am afraid I might betray myself with a piteous word.

I have always understood my world. Almost alone of my kind, I understood it. But my body will betray me. My body is sorely afraid. It twists and it turns, seeking a way to escape what will happen here. And there is regret. I look down at my feet, innocent of sandals. Nildjat Miw is not here. Miw knew as Paniwi knew when her mistress was dead. I marvel at that.

And all the while I know peace and I know beauty and I know love. I know I cannot be destroyed, that I am as much a part of this as they are part of this. This is our great act and we share it as all do who eat and are eaten. If these men could hear me, if they could hear their Christ, the Light that lived within Lais, and that now lives in Hypatia, would light their way out of the cave they call faith.

But they cannot hear me.

Cyril's demons see me now and when they do, they growl and their hands tremble. They are also afraid. But their fear is nothing. Not compared to the excitement that runs like poison through their veins.

Yes, with this death, I might scream. But it is my body that screams, not my spirit.

I step down out of my chariot, quietly tell Nuri and Nomti to turn back for home. And then I will wait, as I have so often done to speak with those who would ask me questions, or wish to honor me with small gifts. As Nuri obeys, I lean over to whisper this last true thing in her anxious ear. "Do not tell Minkah what you see here. He could not bear it."

Cyril, Bishop of Alexandria

God's will be done.

Come to witness this needful act, I, Cyril, Bishop of Alexandria, protector of the Church, hide in a curtained litter hidden behind a stall that sells pots. How hard my heart beats at first sight of the chariot of Hypatia, at her horses. How splendid they are. When the time comes, I will claim these beasts. And then I raise my eyes to the face of Hypatia...could there be a thing more beautiful? How sad that all has come to this. It need never have happened. If she had visited me instead of Orestes!

As arranged, Peter the Reader walks ahead of the monks of the Nitrian Mountains. As arranged, they will seize her. By week's end she will live in the distant cave we have prepared for her. For all the years she lives, she will be under guard by day and by night. There will be no more lectures, no more secret teaching, no more error with an Egyptian.

And yet she will have books and ink and paper. She will be allowed out on certain nights to study the stars. But she will never return to Alexandria.

God and I have decreed it so.

If any are looking, they might see my eye peeping out from my curtain. They might see it widen in alarm. If any could hear my thoughts, this is what they would hear: why does Peter smash a pot on the stones of the street? Why does he then stoop down to seize, as do others of his kind, the sharpest shards?

There is a long cold moment of disbelief. It stops the questions I would ask, no, would shout. I cry out before Hypatia does. "No! This is *not* what we planned!" Who hears me? I would rush forward, would stop what is now become so feverish, so vicious, so perverse, so dreadful I can no longer lift my eyes to see, but I am too fat, too short of breath. I mean to leap from my litter, but fall instead, helpless and sprawled on stones, my tremendous body shaken with sobs, my face melting with tears that creep into the creases of multiple chins.

Minkah the Egyptian

Felix Zoilus is dead. If not for Felix, I, Minkah, would also be dead. In truth, if I do not find Olinda the physician, I shall bleed out here in the streets of Alexandria. But I have no time for myself.

Where is Hypatia?

The life of Felix was taken in order to take hers. As was mine.

Where is Hypatia!

Running, stumbling, leaving a thick trail of red any jackal could follow, I am horribly answered. That a god allows it banishes forever all gods from my heart.

Those who will destroy beauty, who would trample on

wisdom, hold the shards of pots in their hands and on their faces such lust as I have never seen, not even in the worst of my miserable times. My beloved has walked towards them, has reached them, and it is my fate to watch as Peter slashes at her, a deep and fearful cut across her breast, and then more and more take courage from his blind and twisted fervor, so they too might have their share of this sickness.

My own madness makes a Felix Zoilus of me. Screaming, I cut my way through those who push forward so they too might join in this shame, this outrage, this ungodly thing. I kill five, ten, a dozen...and none can stop me. But I alone am not enough. Dozens more face me, as behind them their fellows drag what they have done into a church so they might finish in private what they have begun in public. I sink to my knees to weep at my loss, at my failure—and I find that I stare at Cyril, sprawled as well on the stones of the street, his face as bloodless as mine.

I have not saved my beloved. She did not save herself. But I am Minkah, feared even by *Parabalanoi*, and I can cut down her killer. Cyril sees in my eyes what I saw in the eyes of Peter the Reader, and is thrashing to be away as his bearers heave him into his litter before I can lift myself from the street.

No matter. It is fitting I die here, my blood mixed with her blood. In the morning they will wash us away. We shall flow together through the gutters of Alexandria until we reach the sea. And from there? Who knows? Perhaps a greater adventure than this.

Hypatia of Alexandria

Poor Cyril. His horror breaks my heart. I hear the words that pass through his head, words he himself heard when they came from the mouth of Theophilus: *Who would kill such as you? You are a gift from God.*

Later, his black mantles will burn my shard-scraped bones in a place called Cynaron. Later still, Orestes will flee this city that descends into madness. And when word reaches Augustine, he too will know madness. Demons will appear to him. Jone will wander away to become crazed under the sun. There will come a day she will cry out to die. I cannot see farther, but may her god grant her wish. As for Cyril—who weeps now for the hell he believes awaits him—he will find a way to distance himself from all that has happened here by his doing, and when he does, he will remove my books from libraries everywhere and burn them all. But before the burning of books, he will burn Peter the Reader.

Though he does not yet see me, I stand beside my Egyptian, and I wait.

As I knew she would, Lais is come for us, and we three turn, and we go.

In Grateful Acknowledgement

Without the sweet patience and constant dedication of my publisher and partner Shane Roberts, without the wise guidance and encouragement of my agent Susan Lee Cohen, without the insight of my Random House editor Allison McCabe, without the savvy suggestions of my daughter Sydney Longfellow and my lifelong friends Nancy Scott Mandl and Worth and Nancy Howe, and... without being curled up on his couch as Ray Lynch spoke of mathematics all through the night, this book would be so much less than it is. That it is anything at all, I owe to these and to gnosis.

Selected Bibliography & Source Material

Adair, Ginny, *Biographies of Women Philosophers*, http://www.agnesscott.edu/lriddle/women/hypatia.htm

Alic, Margaret, *Hypatia's Heritage: a history of women in science from antiquity to the late nineteenth century*, The Woman's Press Ltd., London, 1986

Amore, Khan, *Issues Taken with Maria Dzielska's De-Glamorization and Trivialization of Hypatia*, http://www.hypatia-lovers.com/page21.html

Ancient Navigation & Sailing, http://nabataea.net/sailing.html

Barton, Anthony, *On the methods of famous teachers: Lao Tzu, Gautama, Zeno, Socrates, Jesus, Hypatia, Muhammad, Hildegard, Clare, Nightengale, Galileo, and Ghandi*, Ginn Press, 1991

Booth, Mark, *The Secret History of the World*, The Overlook Press, NY, 2008

Boyer, Carl B., *A History of Mathematics*, John Wiley & Sons, NY, 1991

Brook, Jacqueline, *The Rock Who Art in Heaven, Hallowed Be Thy Name,* Sinclair Press, Vermont, 1999

Brown, Dolciani, Sorgenfrey & Cole, *Algebra, Structure and Method*, McDougal Littell, 2000

Busch, Heather & Silver, Burton, *Why Cats Paint, a theory of feline aesthetics,* Ten Speed Press, Berkeley, 1994

Cajori, Florian, *A History of Mathematical Notations*, Dover Publications, 1993

Cameron, A. & Long, J. *Barbarians and Politics at the Court of Arcadius*, University of California Press, 1993

Canfora, Luciano, *The Vanished Library,* trans. Martin Ryle, University of California Press, Berkeley, 1989

Charles, R.H., The *Chronicle of John (c.690 AD), Coptic Bishop of Nikiu*, Amsterdam: APA-Philo, n.d. [1981?]: reprint of a 1916 original.

Catholic Encyclopedia (see wiki source, Hypatia connection.)

Churton, Tobias, *Gnostic Philosophy: from Ancient Persia to Modern Times*, Inner Traditions, 2005

Clawson, Calvin C., *Mathematical Mysteries, the Beauty and Magic of Numbers*, Plenum Press, New York, 1996

Chuvin, Pierre, (B. A. Archer, translator). *A Chronicle of the Last Pagans*, Harvard University Press, 1990

Dantzig, Tobias, *Number, the Language of Science*, Pi Press, 2005 (1930)

Davis & Hersh, *The Mathematical Experience*, Mariner Books, 1999

Deakin, Michael A.B., *Hypatia of Alexandria: Mathematician and Martyr*, Prometheus Books; illustrated edition, 2007

—*A Talk on Hypatia of Alexandria*, http://www.abc.net.au/rn/science/ockham/or030897.htm

—*Hypatia and Her Mathematics*, The American Mathematical Monthly, 101, No. 3 (March 1994), 234-243. (Available at the MAA web site http://www.maa.org/pubs/calc_articles.html)

De Santillana, Giorgio & Von Dechend, Hertha, *Hamlet's Mill, An Essay Investigating the Origins of Human Knowledge and its Transmission Through Myth*, David R. Godine, 1992

Duckett, Eleanor Shipley, *Medieval Portraits from East and West*, University of Michigan Press, Ann Arbor, 1972

Dzielska, Maria, *Hypatia of Alexandria*, Harvard University Press, Cambridge, Mass. 1995

Ehrman, Bart D., *Lost Christianities: The Battles for Scripture and the Faiths We Never Knew*, Oxford University Press, 2005

Empereur, Jean-Yves, *Alexandria Rediscovered*, British Museum Press, 1998

Evola, Julius, *The Hermetic Tradition, Symbols & Teachings of the Royal Art,* Inner Tradition International, Vermont, 1971

FitzGerald, Augustine, *The Letters of Synesius of Cyrene*, London: Oxford University Press, 1926

Frost, W. Deakin, M.A.B. Deakin, & Wilkinson, M, *The Suda Article on Hypatia*, Monash University History of Mathematics Pamphlet No. 61, May 1995

Gibbon, E., *The Decline and Fall of the Roman Empire*, London, 1898

Green, Peter, *Alexander to Actium, the Historical Evolution of the Hellenistic Age*, University of California Press, 1990

Hass, Christopher, *Alexandria in Late Antiquity: Topography and Social Conflict,* The American Historical Review (online: http://books.google.com/books?id=c2NdJo7uLZoC&pg=PA303&lpg=PA303&dq=Cyril+Hierax&source=web&ots=yXSgnBES0e&sig=ELxyIndewOAlxUDQCUmNobKZHPE&hl=en&sa=X&oi=book_result&resnum=1&ct=result#PPA304,M1)

Hecht, Jennifer Michael, *Doubt, a History: The Great Doubters and Their Legacy of Innovation from Socrates and Jesus to Thomas Jefferson and Emily Dickinson*, HarperCollins, 2004

Hersh, Reuben, *What is Mathematics Really*? Oxford University Press, USA, 1999

Johnson, E. D., *History of Libraries in the Western World,* Scarecrow Press, Metuchen, 1970
Hoyt, E.P, *A Short History of Science, Vol. I, Ancient Science,* John Day Co., NY, 1965
Humphreys, Kenneth, *Murder of Hypatia: End of Classic Scholarship in Egypt,* www.jesusneverexisted.com/hypatia.html
James, Peter & Thorpe, Nick, *Ancient Inventions*, Ballentine Books, NY, 1994
Katz, Victor, *A History of Mathematics*, Addison Wesley; 3rd edition, 2008
Kirsch, Jonathan, *God Against the Gods*, Viking Compass Books, 2004
Koestler, Arthur, *The Sleepwalkers*, Penguin, 1990
Lakoff & Núñez, *Where Mathematics Comes From, How the Embodied Mind Brings Mathematics into Being*, Basic Books, 2000
Lerner, Eric J., *The Big Bang Never Happened: A Startling Refutation of the Dominant Theory of the Origin of the Universe,* Vintage Books, 1992
Longfellow, Ki, *The Secret Magdalene*, Crown Publishing, New York, 2007
Lynch, Raymond, *How do you get two when there is only One*?, Eio Books, Vermont (ms form)
Vermont (In ms form)
MacMullen, Ramsay, *Christianizing the Roman Empire A.D. 100-400*, Yale University Press. 1984
Massey, Gerald, *Ancient Egypt - the Light of the World: A Work of Reclamation and Restitution in Twelve Books*, NuVision Publications, 2004
Mead, G.R.S., *Fragments of a Faith Forgotten*, Theosophical Publishing Society, 1900
Montagu, Ashley, *The Natural Superiority of Women*, revised ed., MacMillan, NY, 1974
Moore, Bob, *Women in the Early Christian Church,* http://www.angelmessage.org/women_in_the_early_christian_church.htm
Morrow, Charlene, *Notable Women in Mathematics, a Biographical Dictionary*, Greenwood Press,1998
Mueller, I., *Women of Mathematics*, Greenwood Press, 1987
National Council of Teachers and Mathematics, *Celebrating Women in Mathematics and Science*, ed. H.P. Cooney, Reston, VA, 1996
Osen, Lynn M., *Women in Mathematics*, Massachusetts Institute of Technology Press, Cambridge, Mass, 1974
Perl, Teri, *Math Equals: Biographies of Women Mathematicians,*

Addison-Wesley, 1978
Plotinus, *the Complete Enneads*, http://oaks.nvg.org/sa1ra6.html
Plutarch, *The Life of Alexander the Great*, Modern Library, 2004
Pollard, Justin & Reid, Howard, *The Rise and Fall of Alexandria,* Penguin Group, New York, 2006
Reedy, Jeremiah, *The Life of Hypatia from The Suda, Alexandria,* Grand Rapids, Michigan, Phanes Press, 1993
Rubenstein, Richard E., *When Jesus Became God: The Epic Fight Over Christ's Divinity in the Last Days of Rome*, Harvest Books, 2000
Russell, Bertrand, *History of Western Philosophy*, Routledge, 2004
Russell, Norman, *Cyril of Alexandria, the Early Church Fathers*, Routledge, 2000
Seabrook, John, *Fragmentary Knowledge, Was the Antikythera Mechanism the world's first computer?*, New Yorker magazine, May 14, 2007
Sri Nisargadatta Maharaj, *I AM THAT, Talks with Sri Nisargadatta Maharaj*, The Acorn Press, New York, 1996
St John of the Cross, *Dark Night of the Soul*, translated and edited by E. Allison Peers, electronic edition (v 0.9) 1994 (from an uncopyrighted 1959 Image Books third edition)
Suda Online: Byzantine Lexicography, http://www.stoa.org/sol/
The Princeton Encyclopedia of Classical Sites, Ed. Richard Stillwell, Princeton University Press, 1975
Treadgold, Warren, *Byzantium and Its Army, 284-1081*, Stanford University Press, 1995
Vasistha's Yoga, New York University Press, 1993
Vernam, Glenn R., *Man on Horseback, the Story of the Mounted Man from the Scythians to the American Cowboy*, Harper & Row, NY, 1964
Voltaire, Francois, *Philosophical Dictionary*, Penguin Classics, 1984
Walteri, Mika, *The Egyptian*, G.B.Putnam, NY, 1949
Zenos, A. C., *The Ecclesiastical Histories of Sozomen and Socrates Scholasticus (Volume* 2 *of A Select Library of Nicene and Post-Nicene Fathers of the Christian Church, 2nd Series*), Oxford: Parker, 1891

LaVergne, TN USA
15 June 2010
186095LV00001B/2/P